SIRENS AND LEVIATHANS

C.D. BRITT

PHOENYX PUBLISHING

PHOENYX PUBLISHING

www.authorcdbritt.com

Cover Artwork and Map by GermanCreative

Editing by Rain Brennan

Published by Phoenyx Publishing

ISBN (eBook): 978-1-7372652-3-8

ISBN (paperback): 978-1-7372652-5-2

CONTENTS

To my father, who instilled a love of water in me from a very young age.
I love and I miss you every day.

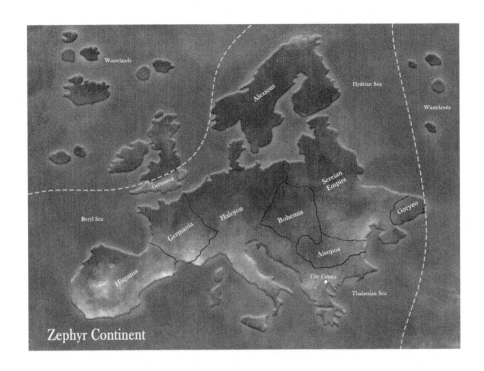

Wastelands

Alexious

Hydrian Sea

Wastelands

Germania

Sereian
Empire

Goryeo

Beryl Sea

Germania

Halcyon

Bohemia

Aisopos

Hispania

City Center

Thalassian Sea

Zephyr Continent

Amphitrite stepped off the gangplank and steadied herself against the sway of the ship as waves met the hull. She looked around the deck, where her ladies were well into the process of commandeering the large vessel.

She took a deep, fortifying breath of crisp ocean air. The salty breeze revitalized her in a way nothing else could. They were still far from shore, a fact belied by the lack of birds calling out to her. She'd have enough time to handle her business here and move on before the human ships found her.

The pirates, having been rounded up by her crew, were on their knees with their wrists tied behind their backs.

Good. This was going to be easier than she thought.

The captives' dark eyes watched them with a combination of anger and shock. Another perk of a ship full of female pirates. Men never knew what to do when faced with her crew. Did they fight the lady as they did a man? That moment of hesitation was all she and her girls needed.

Her first mate moved to stand beside her and, without prompting, gave her the lay of the land.

"A dozen men here. Twenty men, including the captain, are being held below decks." Her first mate paused and ground her teeth. "And thirty-two in cargo."

Amphitrite almost choked.

"Thirty-two?" She tried not to let her voice rise, but she was having difficulty. Thirty-two women sat in the ship's hull, terrified, not knowing that their future meant being sold into a slave trade where the price was innocence and flesh.

"Yes," she confirmed. "They are in a horrendous state. This lot," she motioned to the men bound in front of them, "is lucky I didn't separate their heads from their necks when I found them."

The cadence of her first mate's normally calm voice broke, telling Amphitrite all she needed to know about how to handle this.

"Take me to the captain," she ordered. "Hold the men here. We will let our friends of the sea handle them soon enough and I don't want to miss that." She let a devious smirk cross her face as the men tied in ropes visibly paled at her reference to 'friends of the sea'.

Oh, they knew. All the better.

Her first mate led her across the deck. As she turned toward the ship's living quarters, she heard the tell-tale grunts of her crew taking their anger out on the newly captured men. She did not begrudge them, not if what she was walking into was anything close to what she imagined.

They stopped in front of an ornately carved door, the rich wood mismatched from the rest of the battered ship, and she knew immediately a pretentious bastard waited behind it. Her hand twitched toward her cutlass, but perhaps it was better to let him think her weaker, less able to handle herself in his presence.

Amphitrite was good at misleading people. That was what made her the best spymaster on the high seas. She was unremarkable when compared to her sisters; Persephone and Hera. She could fall back into the shadows, and she knew how to stay there. Even her sisters were ignorant of the network she'd amassed over the years and her role at its head. When her spies went to Hera with information, Amphitrite often wondered if she even questioned who'd accumulated those jewels of intelligence for her. How would that thunderous sister of hers react if she knew the truth? That she spent her days as a pirate, hunting for a treasure much greater than gold: secrets.

She stepped through the ridiculous door, her first mate following behind her, and stood before a fat, bearded man. He was strapped to his seat in the center of the small chamber. A sneer pinched his bloated face when she entered.

Amphitrite knew what he saw. A petite woman in scandalous trousers and a leather corset tied over her undersleeves. A dark blue coat large enough to suit a man twice her size. A tricorn hat with a bold feather. A gleaming cutlass. Wild red hair barely constrained in a wind-swept braid.

A menace.

A pirate queen.

The bane of his existence.

"Sea witch," he growled, straining against his bonds.

Amphitrite shrugged. "Sea witch. Water witch. It matters not what you call me."

The captain glowered.

"You searched him?" she questioned her first mate.

"Sadly, yes. The disgusting things I do for you..." she muttered.

Amphitrite gave her a wink and assessed the briny captain coolly.

Oh, how the tables have turned.

"And whom may I presume you are?" She smiled, but it was all teeth.

He spat on the floor near her feet. Neither she nor her first mate flinched.

"Ah!" Amphitrite held up a hand. "My apologies! I haven't properly introduced you to my first mate! A thorough search without a name. Where are my manners?"

The woman stepped forward and Amphitrite watched the man's weariness grow at the sight of the honey eyes and skin, the dark hair braided with colorful beads from around the world. She could have been a siren had she not been born mortal.

"Captain," she said with flourish. "This is Medusa."

The man jerked against the rope holding him to the chair, his eyes bulging with fear.

Amphitrite smirked at her friend. "Your reputation precedes you!"

Medusa's beautiful face held no smile. "As it should." Her flinty gaze was trained on the captain, who trembled violently.

"Honestly, I did not receive that same reaction." Amphitrite pouted.

"You hide the nightmares in you. I let mine free." Medusa leaned over the desk, her face mere inches from the man's own. "Do you know my story, Captain?"

He swallowed audibly and shook his head. A sheen of sweat appeared on his flushed, dirty face.

Amphitrite grinned at the sight and pulled herself up to sit on the man's messy desk, yanking the dagger from her boot to carve 'Sea Witch' into the obscenely expensive oak.

"I was a priestess of Athena." Amphitrite snorted at this every time, and Medusa shot her a look. The woman had spent her adolescent years worshipping a false Goddess, and it was a sore spot. Medusa looked back to the captain. "I was taken from my temple by men like you, used on their ships as a plaything. Before they got the chance to sell me to some more hideous souls, my captain saved me and gave me my 'gift'."

Medusa crouched, lowering herself to eye level with the man. A moment of silence passed as he continued to sweat profusely. She blinked and her eyes turned reptilian. "The girls you torture and rape in the brig, they do not have my gift. But I am here, so now they do not need it."

Amphitrite stabbed her dagger into the wood and jumped off the desk to stand beside Medusa, the man flinching at the sudden movement.

"You stole this vessel from a merchant friend of mine and used it in the flesh trade," Medusa murmured, unsheathing the dagger at her thigh as Amphitrite unholstered her pistol from inside her jacket. "Now, we are going to have a little chat about who you work for and who you sell to."

When she stepped back onto the deck, the sunlight beamed down on her past the triangular brim of her hat, giving her more freckles across her cheeks. Amphitrite looked down over the cluster of captured men. The screams of their captain had rattled them, but the silence after Medusa turned him into a living statue most likely made them wet their trousers.

Yet, it hadn't cowed them all into holding their tongues. At the sight of her, they grumbled and jeered.

"Bad luck!" one yelled.

"Water witch!" another one.

"Oy, either way, it's the gallows for ye or a right burning, ya witch!"

Yes, the same as it always was.

"Perhaps, maybe," she finally responded, calling out over their heckling. They quieted at the sound of her, at the cutting edge in her voice. "I doubt many would find it easy to kill me. You see, I am not quite a witch. I am something much more... powerful."

She walked closer to the pirates and carefully stowed away her pirate persona. Around the ship, the sea grew more and more agitated with each step she took nearer to the captives.

The women of her crew watched her and traded knowing looks.

She revealed her Goddess form on an exhale. Her power flooded the deck, sending the waves beyond it into chaos as they beat against the hull, jolting the ship. The wild swaying sent the men tumbling over their bound limbs, while her pirates rode the undulations with preternatural ease.

The slavers' stunned faces almost made up for the stench of urine now permeating the air.

Her crew shifted restlessly. She could feel their hunger growing. Amphitrite glanced to the nearest woman and nodded her assent. At her signal, they moved forward in unison, tightening their circle around the men. Their teeth sharpened and their skin shone with pearlescent scales. Gills opened along their necks, flashing into view as the wind whipped their shirts.

Amphitrite smiled grimly when the music started.

The beautiful voices of the sea filled the salty air, and she watched as one by one, her sirens latched onto the men with their dangerous song and led them to the ship's edge. At the railing, they struck, taking them in their arms as they propelled themselves off the side and into the water with deadly grace.

Her crew would feast well this night.

She sensed a presence behind her and glanced over her shoulder at Medusa.

"Once they are done, let's get this merchant ship home." She turned away from the now-empty deck and started for the captain's cabin while Medusa headed to the brig to care for the human women.

Amphitrite now had to push a heavy statue out of her new sleeping quarters.

Why couldn't Medusa ever turn them to stone somewhere convenient?

2137 A.D., City of Halcyon

Amphitrite felt like she had given up her freedom as she stood before the new Maritime Administrative building. Her days of working the seas for secrets were over, thanks to the Great War and pandemic that had decimated most of the world. The unchecked human conflict left most of the ocean inky and uninhabitable. Only the water closest to Zephyr's coasts resembled the seas she'd navigated her entire immortal life.

All those years ago, when she and her sisters took control of the government to avoid more conflict, she'd decided to sacrifice her seafaring days to protect what remained. She'd searched for ways to replenish the sea, but found it was too far gone. In the decades since, her only true hope was to keep the waters near Zephyr, the last holdout of humanity once called Europe, safe for passage, people, and sea creatures.

And she'd been doing it alone, too. *For the most part.*

But that time was over; Hera had decided that for her.

Which is why she had built Amphitrite an actual headquarters. She'd also hired a full staff of people, who Amphitrite now needed to tread lightly around to keep her own secrets.

So, here they were.

Medusa joined Amphitrite's side and crossed her arms.

"You are legitimate now. A real stand-up gal," Medusa snickered as they took in the government building from the water's edge. They stood on the docks still undergoing construction, their backs to the ocean. "At least you can stay by the sea to work the transportation routes. Imagine poor Persephone having to leave the Underworld to work in that hoity-toity skyscraper, doing numbers all day."

Her friend was right; she didn't envy Persephone's commute.

"I am sure Hera is not the least bit upset with her lot," Amphitrite murmured. Her sister had resumed her public role as the Archon, the highest appointed official of their government, after years of ruling behind various personas.

"True, but she has to find new senators to work with now that her old ones are aging out," Medusa retorted with a smirk. One that Amphitrite reciprocated. They both knew how much Hera hated to find new senators.

Medusa placed her hand on Amphitrite's shoulder. "We will still be stealing secrets, don't you worry. Just think of it as being an inside man now, one that can reach higher levels of government officials."

"That should get me through the long nights of paperwork," she groaned. Suddenly, a tingling sensation darted along her spine and branched out through her limbs. She turned to Medusa, her eyes narrowing. "Do you feel that?"

Medusa shook her head. But Amphitrite was already turning around and walking toward the platform's edge, where the water lapped against the industrial support beams.

As she neared the water, the sensation intensified. She recognized the feeling, but it had been eons since she'd last felt it.

She knelt on one knee and reached her hand out over the waves palm up. Droplets eagerly lifted to her and at the first splash of contact, Amphitrite gasped. Raw, natural power coursed through her and rattled the Goddess form lying dormant beneath her skin.

The sea was calling out in greeting to a new Guardian.

And yet, there could only be two.

The only possible way there would be a third Guardian was if the person she had been allied with for centuries had lied.

Not waiting on Medusa, she light jumped to Oceanus' home, landing in the landscaped front yard. The large stately structure always struck her as pompous, irritating in its vanity. Right now, it downright enraged her. The mansion reminded her that Oceanus thought he was above everyone, which perhaps he could claim as a Titan. But she would not let him think he was better than her.

"Oceanus!" She light jumped from the front yard to the foyer. The tail-end of her cry echoed in the tiled entry. "Oceanus, show yourself!" She strode deeper into the house, toward the ostentatious fountain modeled after the Titan's true form.

Her blood roiled with anger as she searched for the Titan. She cast out her power to find his and was drawn to an aura upstairs. As she moved toward it, the figure of a maid appeared down the hall and screamed for her to stop, but Amphitrite ignored her and light jumped through the house. She appeared in Oceanus' bedroom where a flushed and sweaty Theta lay nursing a small babe.

Oceanus immediately rushed to Amphitrite, placing himself in front of the bed to block her view of his wife and child.

"Please..." he begged, his eyes wet with tears.

"When you informed us of the pregnancy of your wife, you stated it was a human child. You told us Theta was human. If that is the truth, why does the sea recognize the latent power of the child?"

Oceanus stood before her at a loss for words.

"We allowed you to walk the mortal plane instead of banishment since you were neutral in the fight against our father, but that does not give you permission to play with the power structure we now have in place! How is this even possible?"

Pushing his hands into his light brown hair, he growled in frustration.

Finally, he sighed. "Theta was in a car wreck... she was going to die. I had to save her. When I tried to pull her back from death, I found she had nymph blood, so I used that power to bind our lifelines. I did not know she was pregnant with our child at the time and had hoped the child would be born human if conceived human. At most, I thought him a demi-god. I did not realize... I did not realize he would be... like me."

"A Titan? You didn't think the babe would be powerful when he was born of nymph and Titan blood?" she ground out through clenched teeth.

Oceanus paled and rubbed his temples. The usually polished Titan was unkempt, obviously having been up all night while his wife labored away.

Amphitrite pushed past him to face Theta, who watched her with her soulful, dark brown eyes.

"Please, Amphitrite, he is just a babe. Have mercy," she pleaded. Oceanus moved to her bedside and gently ran his hand over the baby's soft, dark brown hair. He gave the infant a thoughtful, fond look before glancing back up at her with steely resolve. She knew what Oceanus was about to say.

"Let's make a deal, Amphitrite."

"We already have a deal, Oceanus," she reminded.

"I can bind his powers, keep him from ascending until you choose. As a baby who has not yet wielded them, it should be easy enough."

"No," she stated, and Oceanus and Theta's expressions flashed with pain. "I will bind him."

The parents blinked, the misery on their faces transforming to anticipation.

"And, when he is a mature age, let's say... twenty-one, I will unbind him and train him myself," she continued.

"You'd let him live?" Theta asked, her words and face full of hope.

Amphitrite took in the family. She knew deep down that she would give in and choose the path of mercy.

She would not be her father, killing an innocent in a bid to retain her power.

No, she would just control the outcome.

"I will not kill him, but he must be bound well enough that any other deities think he's human. We can let no one sense his power. I will keep my distance from him until it is time for the unbinding so his power does not respond to mine." She looked at Oceanus. "You will have no influence over this bond, Oceanus. You claim bringing a Guardian into this world was an accident, but that is yet to be proven." Her warning was scornful, but part of her felt the loss of trust in the Titan keenly.

To her shock, Oceanus jumped up from the bed and took Amphitrite into a hug, one she resisted at first before finally allowing.

She stepped back from his embrace but held onto his wrist as she called her powers to initiate the oath.

"You, Oceanus, will allow me to bind this child myself, in a way he cannot be unbound by you or anyone else, until the age of twenty-one. At that time, I will unbind and train him to be a Guardian of the sea. To attempt to unbind him before then will negate this agreement and you will be subject to the punishment of myself and my sisters."

"I agree," he stated, and both of their eyes lit up. She felt the slight sting of the oath in her head, and the air in the room thrummed with power. The quaking energy woke the babe, who released a small squeal from his mother's arms.

Amphitrite dropped the Titan's arm and stepped up to the bed. She placed her hand over the head of the tiny, dark-haired infant.

"You are going to cause me a lot of grief, aren't you, little one?" Her power wound around the child, binding him, keeping him safe until she called upon him again.

1

Amphitrite watched the man before her, his dark chestnut hair blowing in the wind as he looked at her over his shoulder. His wide-eyed expression was almost comical, or would have been at least if he wasn't standing less than twenty yards from a tsunami that would have utterly decimated the city of Halcyon.

If not for him.

In a quick move, she threw her hands out in front of her. Her power flowed from her veins, lighting up her ring, as she pushed the water back. She pressed forward, stepping toward the wall of water. She did not want to even think about the sea life, and human lives, lost due to this unnatural occurrence.

With each step she took, the water retreated. It churned behind its self-contained wall, and she frowned at the trace of power she felt there. She neared the man and got a closer look at his profile.

Shock and recognition bowled through her.

"How...?"

"I have no fucking idea," he replied frantically, his eyes still on the water as it fell back onto the sea floor. She could tell he'd assumed her confusion was solely for the stymied tsunami, which rocked several boats with angry, choppy waves as it moved past the docks.

Oceanus. He had unbound him without her knowledge.

Her rage rose to the surface as she watched the Titan, the one who should have been bound and without the ability to access his power, stand before her. This after he'd held the sea in the palm of his hands. Literally.

Her mind whirled with questions. How had Oceanus broken the oath to unbind his son? And this was his son, she knew. She recognized not only the feeling of his power, but also his features, his face. She had kept her distance, but her spies kept her abreast of his movements.

She knew where he had gone, what he had done.

When she'd learned that the dormant Titan had fled the city upon his twenty-first birthday, she had caved on demanding he be called back to Halcyon. Oceanus hadn't elaborated, but the boy had been traumatized.

Something in her had softened when it should've gone cold.

Millenia ago, she hadn't made it to adulthood as a mortal, instead born into godhood with blood and trauma. And so, she had allowed him more time to experience life. The unbinding could wait, she'd told herself.

Her sentimentality bit her in the ass like Hera always warned it would.

Now, six years later, he stood before her, with raw, unbound power simmering around him. Past the age of ascendancy.

That is what she got for making a deal with a Titan.

However mad she was, she could not go to Oceanus at this moment to demand his explanation. She knew, deep down, her sister was in trouble. The plan had been for her to meet at the gates at the base of the mountain that led to the River Styx, but then she'd watched a wall of lethal water heading toward the city. Even now, she could still feel her sister's pull in the Underworld as the water writhed against her power.

Looking at where the massive wave had lost its ground, revealing washed up detritus on the streets, she sensed a tension churning in the seawater. A sentient force. A power different than her own, or even the Titan's beside her.

She felt her temper rise even higher at the thought that someone stood by, using her water against her. She pushed out more power, stalking around the heir still frozen in shock, and moved to calm the sea.

Pushing power into her ring, the one gifted to her by the cyclops, she felt the water ease. The resistance snapped and the sea submitted to her will. She felt the ocean's relief alongside her own at the give. Whatever was pushing against her had finally relented, and the water slowly crept back into the bay from where the tension

had held it hostage further out along the sea floor after retreating from the city. She looked across the area, taking in the damage until her eyes finally met his. The man stood still, his hands finally lowering as he realized the water was no longer a threat.

Her feet carried her to him before she even thought about it. The danger of the tsunami may have been neutralized, but another problem remained.

"Heir of Oceanus," she called, her voice raised in challenge.

Confusion and exhaustion warred on his face. Her stride stuttered as it occurred to her how little he may know as he watched her with raised eyebrows. Even now, she could still feel the power emanating from him, the same power he'd used to stop the tsunami. *Already so strong.*

"West," he grated out.

Taken aback, she glanced up at his burning gaze, somewhat irritated at just how far she had to *look* up at him.

"What?" She stood in front of him, wishing her mortal form had some height, but she and Hestia had always been the smallest sisters.

"My name is West." He ran shaking hands through his hair, looking wildly between her, the wreckage around them, and the docks. His eyes snagged on the bay, watching it with suspicion, as if he expected the tsunami to make a comeback.

Amphitrite hesitated. These weren't the actions of a fully realized Titan. He was in shock. He didn't seem to recognize her power, either.

He didn't know.

Her confusion deflated her frustration, at least with this particular Titan.

"West," she said lowly and almost started at the sound of her own voice. She'd always known his name, but had she ever said it? "It's over. The wave is gone."

He stumbled back and dropped his hands from his head. He looked down at his open palms with desperation. "What did I do? I was about a millisecond away from pissing myself and then suddenly I am holding a wall of water back..."

She felt all the bravado leave her at his softly spoken words. She knew how he felt, how overwhelming the power could be.

"You saved the city," she told him levelly. Truthfully. "But now you need to go home. Calm yourself. The water will not come back up."

His eyes darted up to meet hers. An edge glinted in those depths.

"How do you know?" His throat bobbed as he swallowed audibly. "Who *are* you?"

"I just know. Go home," she ordered, backing away from him. The tsunami was gone, but the fight was far from over. She hoped she could find the entrance to the Underworld and get to her sister in time.

"Wait! Hold on!" he yelled. Her feet halted as she looked over her shoulder. His expression took on a pleading look, one that stirred something deep in her heart, but she had nothing for him. She broke into a run, escaping his line of sight, and opened a portal to light jump. Her form being whisked away in the fresh breeze of her water and light.

He had pulled at something deep down inside of her.

And that scared her more than the tsunami.

2

Long hours after jailing the traitorous Titans in Tartarus once again, Amphitrite left the Underworld to face another traitorous Titan.

She'd light jumped to Oceanus, finding him in his office. The Titan, known to the world as CEO Zale Murphy, shot to his feet from behind his desk.

"Explain," Amphitrite demanded as she cornered him. She had no patience for more of his lies, but she needed to hear what he had to say.

He braced himself against the desk. "West..."

"Is unbound." She clenched her jaw. "Which should be impossible," she reminded him.

"Trust me, I tried at certain points in the past to unbind him," Oceanus admitted. When she started toward him, he held his hand up to stop her. "Just to see if it was possible in case of an emergency, but nothing. Only you could do that." He lowered his hand slowly and gestured out the window, where the dock harbor could be seen along the horizon. "Something during the tsunami caused the binding to loosen to the point that I could undo the spell holding his powers together. At that point, yes, I was somehow able to finish unbinding him, and did so, rather than let him die."

"He should have been unbound by me, the power released slowly," she seethed. "That was the agreement. It seems you have issues holding to any agreement that doesn't end with you watching the world fall apart outside your window, doing nothing to help."

Oceanus stepped up to her then, his eyes narrowed.

"You don't think I felt that power blast, Amphitrite?" Another step. "You don't think I recognize the stench of Tartarus on you?" He shook his head in frustration. "I did what I had to do to protect my son from you and your sisters' mess. Tartarus was opened, wasn't it?"

She glared at him. "Sorry to miss a family reunion, Oceanus?"

He scoffed. "I'm the first to die if my wayward kin really escape. They'd go after my son next." He sobered and gave her a calculating look. "I understand you are mad and coming down from the adrenaline high of battle, but think clearly, Amphitrite. If I could feel when Tartarus opened, that power must have rippled across the realm."

"You're saying you think Tartarus opening loosened his bindings?"

"Titan power calls to Titan power," he said darkly. A real look of fear flickered over his face. "I couldn't leave my son helpless to defend himself after I felt the rift. Regardless of how the unbinding was initiated," he stood back and straightened his suit, "now, we must deal with it."

The growl that left her throat only caused a twitch of Oceanus' lips in amusement.

Yet, she had to admit; he was right. The power structure among the deities had shifted again, and so soon after Devon's awakening. A newly unbound Titan needed to be dealt with.

Nothing felt the same after Devon ascended and became a God. All of their powers had been thrown off. The three sisters had reigned for a long time before Devon, and the power structure was reshaping itself to accommodate a fourth.

Though... the Moirai *had* told the sisters they were never meant to be just three. What did a new Titan add to the mix? And there had been five sisters, five lines of power, so what did that mean when they found the person who'd inherited Hestia's power? More upheaval?

Dread and frustration boiled inside her. Amphitrite hated chaos, or any change she couldn't influence, for that matter.

"There is no 'we'," she growled. "When you sired a new Titan, I covered for you, Oceanus. *I* bound his powers. *I* took grief from the Moirai for unsettling fate. Listened to an hour of how I had changed the way of mankind. Most of it bullshit, but you know damn well I took that grief for you and your heir. And this is how you thank me. With an unbound Titan ignorant of his nature and a broken oath."

She watched as the realization crossed his face. He hadn't known she had gone to fight for him and his son. Sadly, he wasn't contrite enough to hold his tongue.

"I appreciate that you have championed for my heir," he said, "but you must accept that I did not betray you. I did not unbind him myself. The celestial power plucked the strings just enough for me not to cross the line of the oath."

"You missed your calling as a lawyer, Oceanus," she stated, crossing her arms.

"I still have lifetimes to achieve that. Now, that you understand I am not in violation of my oath-"

"Time will tell if that's completely true or not," she interrupted.

Sitting back on his desk, he crossed his arms to match her stance.

"I cannot wait until you find out the truth then, since you don't seem to believe me," he continued before placing his hands on the desk, leaning back. "We are six years behind on his training."

"I am aware of that, Oceanus," she snapped. She turned to look out the window, feeling unnerved by the Titan's claims and could feel him continue to quietly assess her.

"You allowed him those six years to live on his own as a mortal after his trauma. I thank you for that, Amphitrite. I thank you for the mercy you have shown my family."

Looking back at him, she narrowed her eyes.

"Mercy that was repaid with you finding a loophole," she said caustically and looked away again. The Titan remained quiet. "I will start training him. He will begin his ascension at a rapid pace now. The timeline will be tighter than it would have been had I undone his binding myself."

The tension seemed to leave Oceanus in a sudden rush. He approached her with measured steps.

"Thank you." He bowed low to her when she turned back to him and took her hand in his. "I fear my son will need you and your training more than I can say." He dropped her fingertips and straightened fully, looking at her with eyes slightly aglow. "The war... The sea... it only grows sicker."

Amphitrite nodded, frowning. He was right. She was having a hard enough time holding the borders against the putrid water and had yet to find the cause of the rot, even a century after the Great War. Something beyond the Great War's destruction, something more than weapons and neglect, lurked in the dark water.

"More Titans at work," she whispered.

Standing face to face with a Titan, she felt the enormity of what could happen if she failed in her tasks. If she did not properly train West, if she did not find Hestia's scion, they could lose the war they knew was coming.

"I knew one day they would rise against you and your sisters. Cronus and his brothers were always power hungry."

Closing her eyes, she sighed. She felt like she was losing a war before it began

"At least Cronus is still contained," she said, opening her eyes to see Oceanus staring back at her.

"I will begin working with him as soon as I can," she told him, and turned to walk out of his office.

Halting before she touched the doorknob, she smiled softly to herself. Time to let him stew a little.

"Do not think that means I won't continue to look into what happened with the binding." She looked at him over her shoulder and arched an eyebrow.

He gave her an annoying smirk again, one she could easily imagine plastered across a much younger face and stuck his hands into his pockets.

"I'll await your apology for doubting me."

Rolling her eyes, she continued out the door, secretly hoping he had lied when he said he hadn't broken the oath.

Because the alternative meant something far worse.

3

West watched the coin spinning on the bar top, snatching it up in his palm before it could clatter on the wood.

The young, pretty bartender sauntered over to him.

"Every night this week now, huh?" She gave him a knowing look. Her dazzling smile always greeted him when he walked through the door.

Every night this week, apparently, he thought. He smiled back, but he knew it did not meet his eyes.

He also had been enjoying this particular bartender as much as the bar this week.

An escape, he knew, but that was what he did. He used sex as an escape, and he needed that while he was dealing with everything. He had been frequenting this bar since he had spoken with his father.

Since he had stopped a wall of water from destroying Halcyon.

Groaning at the memory, he put his head into his hands. How did his life manage to turn itself upside down constantly? He would love slow and steady. Maybe he hadn't ever thought of himself wanting such a life, but now, he craved it.

Years ago, he'd witnessed a date's rape and murder, and that night had sent him down a path of vengeance. He'd run away and become a mercenary, hunting down those men to exact justice. He hadn't been happy, but he'd been free. *Fine*.

Until Devon died in the field.

Like the death of the woman he had been dating years earlier, the loss of his best friend had him running. Only, now, he'd gone and done the one thing he swore to never do: return home.

And after weeks of grieving and readjusting to life in Halcyon, he'd run into his dead friend fully alive, and at a damned party, no less. Finding out his best friend hadn't died from a bullet wound, but became a God of Rebirth, would have really topped the list of screwed up revelations if his dad hadn't just dropped his own bomb on him.

Yes! Turns out, West was the son of a Titan whose shoes he was expected to step into now that he was home.

Possibly both pairs, the Titan and the CEO. Just like dear old dad.

He could do without being a liar like his father. That was one title Oceanus could keep to himself.

Something had happened to West after he learned of his father's deceit. Something felt even more broken inside of him, which was truly impressive since West already felt like he was damaged beyond repair.

"Whatever you are thinking about is too heavy for two in the afternoon," the bartender joked as she threw her blonde braid over her shoulder. Her brown eyes held all the flirtation he felt battering him every time he sat at the bar.

Maybe he wasn't getting a reprieve here, but more anxiety playing the part of the flirt.

He spent his days drinking, avoiding his father and all sense of responsibility.

Spent his nights with this bartender in an effort not to think.

He hid like a coward, he was not too ashamed to admit, in order to not deal with anymore lies.

"I've had a lot of heavy shit happen in my life lately," he murmured into his glass of whiskey before downing the entirety of it, loving the burn. A controlled pain. And he needed that right now as he was so tired of the emotional pain.

Emotional pain that he held no control over.

Perhaps it was time to find a new bar? A new bartender? He did not want her growing attached. That was the last thing he needed.

"I get off around nine tonight..." she murmured, giving him a sultry smile as she twisted the end of her braid around her finger.

"Not tonight, sweetheart." He winked, wondering how this had ever felt natural to him. Right now, he felt slimy and ridiculous. "Lots of work to do."

He threw back his drink and gave her his megawatt smile as he pushed away from the bar.

She flicked her eyes hungrily over his shoulders and down his body, and something like dread settled over his chest. Her tongue darted out to wet her lips and she met his gaze.

"Maybe you don't need to wait. I have a break coming up... it won't be enough time for... you know." She leaned over the bar, which stretched her tank top across her cleavage, and whispered, "But maybe I can help you... feel lighter." Her raspy voice trailed off suggestively and she bit her lip.

West glanced away. He wondered what she saw when she looked at him. Was he as much a plaything to her as women had always been to him?

This had been his life once. He used to be the 'Playboy of Halcyon', according to all the gossip magazines. Always out with some socialite or star of some show, dining, partying, and then going back to their place to enjoy the rest of the evening. Sometimes with more than one girl. He'd proven all those headlines right, again and again.

But not anymore.

Now, he just had a few photographers snapping pictures of him as he went about his day, but that group was steadily dwindling. After the initial buzz of his return had faded, he'd proven he was far too boring to keep track of now. Just bar, drink, same woman. The front-page stories about a wild playboy had become small features about a sad, drunk heir. Add a photo of him inebriated, slumped over the bar alone, to the morning paper and it was official: West Murphy was a has-been.

"Thanks for the offer, but this is a hell of a lot more than you can handle," he muttered, standing from the stool. He reached for his wallet and took more than enough cash out to cover his few drinks, throwing it down on the bar.

He was glad he wasn't the boy he'd been before he left and become a man. Now, he just wished he knew who he was at all.

He walked out of the bar without a backwards glance and as soon as he stepped onto the sidewalk, the flash of a camera blinded him.

"Fates! Why the fuck do you need to permanently blind me?" he shouted at the portly man holding the camera.

"Are you taking over Oceanus Industries now that you are back?" a woman asked.

Great, he thought as he rubbed his abused eyes. *A reporter.*

Yeah, he needed to find a new bar. One where he could stew in his depression without a sexy as hell bartender bothering him as he drank away his worries. One the press didn't know about.

Rubbing his face, he silently chided himself for not finding a new spot sooner.

He shoved his irritation back and smiled at the woman until her cheeks flushed.

"Who knows, love? Maybe," he said as he sauntered toward the woman. The photographer was quick to hit the shutter again. "Maybe not." Leaning towards her, he put his lips next to her ear. "Only time will tell, huh, beautiful?"

A soft gasp left her lips, and he winked as he turned to walk away. The smile dropped from his lips as quickly as it came. She was flustered enough that he would get a head start, but that was by seconds if he didn't book it.

Who the hell had he become?

He didn't know who he was anymore after his confrontation with his father. His father, the guiding force of his childhood, his safe place, had betrayed him.

All his life he had thought his father was infallible, that he could do no wrong. The pain of his father's secrets was taking more from him emotionally than he could handle.

Fates, he hadn't even known his own father's real name.

The name 'Oceanus' had knocked down West's entire house of cards. He was lost in a tailspin and the only solace he could find was at the bottom of a glass of whiskey or between the sheets.

Feeling the weight of the world pushing down on him, he let himself fall to the curb, sitting down with his head in his hands.

He hadn't slept the past few nights, not well at least. His stomach and mind were both too torn to rest. He refused to speak to either of his parents, though they called almost hourly. They even tried to catch him when he came home, but he would slip past them and shut the door quietly in their faces. And they were far too stately to push the door back open and demand he speak to them.

It also helped that he was almost always drunk, so they would hardly get anything coherent out of a conversation, should they try.

His parents had nothing to say that he wanted to hear. He just wanted to walk into the office of the so-called Maritime Administration and demand the Sea Goddess tell him everything.

Because he no longer trusted his father to do so.

4

As Amphitrite neared the restaurant, she took in the surrounding street. This part of the city hadn't seen damage from the tsunami as the blocks closest to the docks had. Some buildings around the harbor were completely gone, leaving people without homes and businesses. Wrecked boats littered the docks. This area, in contrast, was closer to the city's center and held only a few hints that a disaster was narrowly avoided.

The city was recovering quickly in the affected areas. Hera had organized necessary rebuilding and clean-up efforts almost immediately after the battle's end. Windows were boarded up and debris cleaned off the road. Construction crews were already hard at work on the torn-down structures near the water. The few families impacted were relocated. Businesses were opening back up.

But the people still whispered about the oddity of such the natural disaster. Throwing around words like "offshore" and "earthquake" was the best she could do. They could not erase the memory of an entire city. She only hoped anything to do with the Titans in the future didn't involve the humans.

She snorted at the ridiculous wish. She hadn't seen her father in millennia, but she remembered his dramatics. There was no way they wouldn't attempt to burn what was left of the world to the ground.

Stopping in front of the restaurant window, she checked her hair. It could become unruly in the humidity.

Although Halcyon always managed to stay at a comfortable temperature, the humidity was never the same. She wondered at times if that was Hera's doing, since it was always humid on her dates.

She ran her hand over the fly aways coming out of her chignon and gave herself a final once-over: her blue dress sparkled like the deepest depths of the ocean; her heels were killer to match; her eyeliner was perfect; and her lips were painted a matte pink. She nodded to her reflection, ready to go.

She planned to enjoy a nice dinner with her boyfriend before she had to deal with a young, untrained Titan tomorrow. If he was as frustrating as his father was, it would not be a pleasant experience.

"As always, you take my breath away," she heard from behind her. Smiling, she turned to her date.

Darren, the mortal man she had been with for almost a year. She took a moment to appreciate him. Tall and well-groomed, he was classically handsome with his blue eyes, tan skin, and perfectly styled blonde hair. He wore a suit, tie and all, since that was his daily work attire. No need to go home to prepare since he always looked dashing.

He grinned back at her and took her hands in his before kissing her cheek. "Shall we?" he asked as he opened the door for her.

"We shall." She smiled wider as she took his arm. When they entered, the hostess greeted them with familiarity and guided them back to their usual table. They frequented the restaurant at least once a week and always sat in the back, next to the window that overlooked the sea.

Darren pulled her dark blue velvet chair out for her, which she thanked with a kiss to his cheek, and pushed her in once she sat before seating himself. They had a routine, one they fell into, and Amphitrite was glad for it. Darren was a gentleman in an age when she thought they were long extinct.

He was consistent and stable. Everything her life was not. And everything she was absolutely certain she needed.

Over their appetizers and wine, they told each other of their day, and as they spoke, she had the fleeting thought of how she wished she could tell him about the Titans. About the battle they'd barely won.

About West.

About the ocean.

About *her*.

Of course, he knew she was the head of the Maritime Administration, but he knew nothing of the Goddesses.

He did not know her as Amphitrite. No mortals did. She was Cordelia to all of them, including her own boyfriend. None of her human lovers had known her true name, and she wondered why that bothered her so much all of a sudden.

"Well, they are looking at moving me up to partner," he stated, and her eyes widened as her concerns fluttered away.

"That is fantastic, Darren!" she exclaimed. She gave him a genuine smile as she was truly proud of him. He had worked long and hard hours to get here, and no one deserved it more. Perhaps that was her bias as his girlfriend talking, but she was sure his boss agreed if he was giving him a promotion.

Taking his hand between hers, she kissed his knuckles.

"We are most definitely celebrating this!" She withdrew a hand and waved the waiter over to order some champagne.

Darren smiled down at their interlocked fingers before he looked up into her eyes.

"You are so amazing, Cordelia. I could not have gotten to where I am without you."

"Yes, Darren, you could have, but I'm glad I'm on this journey with you."

If only as herself.

"You alright?" he asked, squeezing her hand.

"Yeah," she said softly. She shook her head, giving him a smile as she released his hand and moved to take a sip of water. She just needed a minute. She would not ruin his day with fleeting thoughts full of nonsense. She *was* herself with him.

She was.

Darren gave her a concerned smile, but glanced over her shoulder, distracted.

"He looks like he is one drink away from blacking out," Darren said, nodding his head to the bar area.

Turning, she groaned.

West.

Sighing, she threw her napkin on the table and stood.

Darren blinked at her, surprised. "Do you know him?" he asked, glancing between her and West.

She halted. How did she explain to him who West was?

"A new co-worker. West. He's not taking to the job well," she muttered and stepped away from the table just as the server walked up with their glasses of champagne.

"I'd guess not if he gets black out drunk like this," Darren said, eyeing West with concern.

"I'll go check on him and be back soon," she told him as the waiter set the glasses on the table. "Before the champagne goes flat," she added with a wink.

He cast another questioning glance at West, so she gave him a comforting smile as she took another step backward. "I promise we will finish our celebration tonight."

Turning toward West, her smile dropped as she walked to the bar, where West was surrounded by empty shot glasses. Taking the seat next to him, she looked him over. His head was on the bar counter, his shoulders slumped in.

Clearing her throat, he looked up at her with bloodshot eyes.

"Great," he groaned, rolling his eyes and putting his head back down. "Go away, Sea Goddess."

She kicked his leg and he almost fell off his barstool. His eyes went wide, and he gaped at her as he caught himself on the bar's edge.

Waiting until the bartender put his latest glass of poison down and walked to the next customer, she then leaned in close enough that no one but him would hear her before speaking.

"You *do not* refer to me as a Goddess in public," she hissed. "Humans are unaware, and we have to keep it that way."

He only rolled his eyes and downed the shot in front of him. "Charming."

He groaned irritably, deflating even more with the realization that she wasn't leaving.

"So," she started, "are you planning to spend the rest of your days inebriated to the point of looking like a limp rag doll?"

In answer, he waved to the bartender, but her hand shot out and yanked his arm back down. He grimaced and shrugged out of her hold. "Yes. Yes, I am. I plan to be ob—oblit---"

She raised an eyebrow. "Obliterated?"

"Yes, ob... smashed, until I wake up from this fucking nightmare that is my life." His hand shot up before she could catch it, and the bartender returned to take his order as if she had been waiting for the opportunity.

Amphitrite turned to glare at the bartender. The look in the young woman's eyes told her everything she needed to know. She would not be swayed against West and his need for alcohol since the woman had quite obviously fallen down the rabbit hole of infatuation.

She would try, nonetheless.

"Excuse me," she interrupted, leaning onto the bar, "my brother here has had enough. Can you please cut him off?"

The bartender nodded, her eyes still hazy with lust, but Amphitrite caught the flash of a smile. The woman was relieved to hear that she was his sister, at least as far as she knew, anyway. No competition.

"Brother?" West sputtered, "I was just thinking about you naked..."

The bartender narrowed her eyes at him before turning to glare at Amphitrite.

Amphitrite smiled thinly and pushed West out of his seat to stand up. The woman grabbed his drink with a huff and shoved her way past another bartender to the kitchen doors. What kind of effect did this man have on women? She turned to him, eyeing him curiously just as he began to sway on his feet. His hair was in disarray and his black shirt was rumpled as if pulled from a pile and thrown on... inside out.

"What the hell?" he slurred, almost toppling over before she could grab him. Putting his arm over her shoulders, she started the slow walk to the door of the restaurant.

In the corner of her eye, she could see Darren rise from his seat, ready to help her, but she waved him away as she passed by their table.

"I'll help him out and be right back," she told him with an apologetic smile.

West lifted his head from where it hung between his shoulders and looked between her and Darren.

"Oh, great," West muttered incoherently, "a suit."

Darren frowned with concern. "Are you certain?" he asked her. "I can help you get him home, and we can reschedule dinner," he offered.

It was not lost on her that West was judging her boyfriend, assessing him with a cruelly amused look.

He swung that look on her. "Date, huh? I guess I was too much of a draw for you to ignore." He smiled and the smell of alcohol permeated the air as he breathed.

She assured Darren and continued toward the exit, suddenly more than eager to get West out of the upscale restaurant before he made more of a scene.

"Trust me, I'd much rather ignore you and enjoy my evening with my boyfriend. But right now, you're a hazard to yourself and those around you," she hissed.

"I cannot imagine Devon being this obnoxious to deal with," she added under her breath for good measure.

West just snorted in response.

"Cordelia, are you sure you do not need help?" Darren called, coming up behind them.

Of course, he followed her. He would never leave her to deal with a giant, drunk man by herself. He thought she was human, with human strength, and West was far larger than her mortal form.

"Cordelia? I thought your name was... OW!" West howled as Amphitrite stepped on his foot.

"Sorry, didn't mean to step on your foot," she ground out. She gave him a warning look and he scowled back. He pushed away from her and leaned against the wall near the hostess station. His dark brown hair hung over his eyes roguishly and his rich chocolate brown eyes sparkled in the warm light cast from the wall sconces. For a minute, she was unable to look away.

Fates, what is with this man?

An arm wrapped around her waist, bringing her back out of her thoughts, and she caught sight of West shaking his head as if trying to pull himself together.

As if he, too, had been drawn in.

She turned and placed her hand on Darren's chest, ignoring the idiot of a man currently attempting to remain upright.

"I will call someone to come get him. Can you get me another glass of champagne? I am going to need it."

She glanced at West just as a sardonic smile flashed across his face at her words.

"Of course. If you need anything, please come get me." Darren kissed her cheek softly before nodding slightly at West. "Good to meet you, West. Perhaps next time we can be introduced under more pleasant circumstances."

As Darren walked away, West let out a loud laugh, which only served to anger Amphitrite enough to push him out the glass doors leading to the street. She didn't dare look back to see what Darren thought of his little outburst.

"Fates, what the hell is the deal with him? Did he fall out of a romance novel?"

"Shut up, West," she growled as they moved down the steps, her walking and him stumbling. She hardly felt like helping him now and simply watched as he barely caught himself from falling on the pavement as he descended the concrete front steps to the sidewalk. He tripped again at the last step, but managed to find a wall to lean against along the side of the building. Once he was steady enough not to fall face first, he began making swaying motions with his hands as if dancing with an invisible person.

Her eyebrow went up as she watched him.

"A dance milady? Can I get on your"- *hiccup*-, "dance card? May I court you? One kiss on the cheek before marriage?" He laughed at his own jokes as she stood with her arms crossed. "Have you guys even done the horizontal tango yet, or is he waiting to maintain your virtue, *Cordelia*?"

Before she knew what she was doing, she walked up and slapped him across the face.

"None of my personal life is your business. You should be concerned with your own fate and grow the hell up, Weston." She growled and his eyes went wide with shock.

"I love it when I show up for the good stuff. Please don't stop on account of me being here." Said a familiar baritone voice from behind her. She didn't turn to greet him, not daring to take her eyes off West.

"Will you see him home?" She asked as she watched West squint in an attempt to focus his eyes on the man behind her, the alcohol working against him.

"Can I slap him around, too?" the voice said in a laughing tone.

"Yes. As much as you want," she seethed. She turned from West and walked back into the restaurant to salvage her evening.

That man was beyond infuriating. She would need to keep as much distance between them as possible during his training.

For her sanity.

West couldn't believe she'd slapped him and left him at the mercy of a stranger. Or were there two of them? He wobbled as he tried to focus his eyes on the shifting figures. *Great.* Drunken double vision was the worst. He blinked until it cleared.

"I like your shirt," West stated, words slurring even to his own ears. The stranger's shirt had a design like an old postcard, with 'Underworld' scrawled beneath an illustration of a fiery river, and 'Enjoy your stay' above it.

The man's only response was to grab West by the shoulder and pull him into a dark alleyway beside the restaurant.

"Well, this seems very stranger danger," West mumbled, trying to loosen the man's hold. "Super safe, walking into a dark alley with-"

He was suddenly thrown into a vortex of shadow before the man let him drop to his knees.

Landing on all fours, West retched a full stomach of alcohol onto an expensive-looking rug.

"Thanks for bringing him back," said a familiar voice, albeit one he hadn't heard in a while. Devon's voice.

Had he missed something? He hadn't noticed Devon in the alley before. Or had he blacked out on the way to Devon's place? Just how wasted was he?

"Your friends are accosting me," West accused, looking up from the floor to the two men standing in front of him. "I've been hit and... whatever the hell *he* just did to me."

"He hit you?" Devon asked, looking over at the man in question. His face held nothing but mirth at that thought.

Some friend he was.

"No, Amphitrite did," the man smirked as he folded his beefy arms across his chest.

"Huh," was all his supposedly very loyal friend said as he helped West stand up.

"Well, enjoy dealing with the upcoming shit show," the shadow man said. He winked before disappearing in a swirl of darkness.

West blinked. *Huh*. Maybe he was not as drunk as he thought. Or much, much drunker.

Devon lowered him on the nearby black couch. Another expensive-looking piece of furniture. He hoped he'd expelled all he had left in his body onto that rug.

"Nice friend you have there," West grumbled as he slid sideways onto the couch, shoving the pillows off before pressing his face flat on the seat cushion.

"Thanatos is more of a tolerated acquaintance. Here, drink." Devon pulled West up by the arm and put a glass in his hand.

West sniffed it. "Doesn't smell like booze."

"That is the last thing you need right now. It's water, so drink up. I remember how much of a grumpy asshole you are when you have a hangover."

"Noted," West rasped, and he took a drink of water. He could almost hear his liver thank him. "Why was he at the restaurant? How did he bring me here? Is he a stalker who takes unsuspecting drunk men into alleyways normally? Like a hobby? And what the fuck was with the shadows?"

Devon shook his head, a smile on his face.

"I cannot guarantee that it's not something he does for fun, but in this case, he was nearby... working..." Devon trailed off as he watched for a reaction. West waved his arm to continue. He wasn't going to question anything ever again. Questions led to answers he did not want. "And he came across Amphitrite and you."

Devon cut himself off and West felt a laugh bubbling up.

"A Titan for a father. A God for a best friend. Getting smacked by Goddesses and taken into dark alleys by their buddies." What a freak show.

West's words became sluggish as the last of his energy completely evaporated. Having just enough strength to roll onto his back, he stared at the ceiling.

"How did you come to accept all this? This new world... It feels like someone just dumped a truck of bricks on me." And he hadn't even divulged all of it to his friend, even though he was sure he'd understand. There wasn't enough spirit left in him to tell his friend about the tsunami, or about the strange power he'd felt coursing through his body.

Devon sighed and settled on the floor beside him. "I'll let you know when I finally understand and accept it all myself. And I was alone when I first learned about all this stuff. Lucky enough for you, you've got me. It's another fun adventure. Just like old times."

West snorted, thinking they remembered their time as mercenaries very differently, before quickly falling into a numb sleep.

5

The Zephyr Maritime Administration building was not the giant tower that Cerberus Financial and Fates Consulting was. It was a smaller steel and stone structure close to the docks. Oceanus Industries towered over it, but Amphitrite hardly cared for the greed of such a building.

No, her building touched the sea. Almost felt like a part of the sea itself. The windows were always opened to allow the coastal breeze through the halls, where it carried whispers of a thousand waves to her ears. The docks were integrated into the steel arches buttressing the back of the building where it hung over the water. Boats with the Maritime Administration official seal came and went on various missions and errands from beneath the building.

Luckily, they hadn't experienced too much structural damage from the tsunami, and nobody had been in the office. Their losses amounted to some totaled boats and shattered windows, which was to be expected for a building with as much glass as this one. She'd been relieved when she received the damage report, thankful Hera had built the place with such a strong, resilient skeleton.

As she entered the building, she passed by a large sculpture of dolphins in the front courtyard. The stone pod of dolphins were depicted in play, jumping and frolicking in the fountain around them. When she walked into the lobby, she was greeted with smiles and nods.

While she'd initially resisted a full staff for the job she could do just fine on her own, she'd grown to appreciate the well-oiled machine the Maritime Administration had developed into. Dozens of officers and analysts filled the office, but hundreds more filled the sea on a fleet of ships. The Administration regulated shipping and transportation on the water. Any vessel that wanted to cross the sea surrounding Halcyon needed clearance from her. She kept the humans honest, especially the big companies. But she was also responsible for their safety. From human, nonhuman—natural and unnatural—threats alike.

They did not need another Great War; one was enough. They'd lost far too much land and people, leaving only the continent of Zephyr, once Europe, standing. Everything beyond Zephyr was an uninhabitable wasteland. Including the dark waters further out from the continent. The ones she worked hard to keep at bay on a daily basis.

But in recent days the effort seemed more arduous. Most of the time, she maintained the border with the dark waters subconsciously through her power. The liquid border was far enough out into the sea that few humans encountered it; shipping routes were purposefully plotted away from those murky waves and leisure boats weren't permitted that far out into open water. The humans assumed the outer reaches of the ocean were polluted, decimated by their ancestors just like the rest of the world.

Now, the darkness in the sea only seemed to grow stronger. And it did so with each passing day since the battle in the Underworld. When Tartarus opened, it threw out power like an atomic bomb, and if Oceanus was to be believed, that had been enough to unbind West. If that was the case, it seemed to have disturbed the power she maintained in the ocean as well. Weakened it. Blurring the boundary there and turning the healthy water murky.

She stepped into the elevator and selected the lowest level, feeling the strain even now. Keeping up the weakened border was like repairing a broken and tangled net, whereas before it had been like polishing a marble wall.

Beyond the exhaustion, there was also the pain, a distant but constant ache, from sea creatures who'd moved too close to the tainted water. Even though she couldn't sense any life within that darkness, she knew what it could do after she'd witnessed a siren get too close. Her fingers had barely touched the darkness and the water swallowed her whole.

When Amphitrite had tried to pull her back, she had lost consciousness from the close proximity of the dark waters. Thankfully, it had been a quick black-out and she'd roused before she was sucked in, too. Caught behind the barrier, her siren had turned into a primal beast, only driven by rage and the desire to kill. The dark waters had made her mindless.

Who knew what it could do to a Goddess? That was something she never intended to find out.

The elevator doors opened to an uninterrupted view of the ocean. It had been decades since the loss of her siren, and even longer since the dark waters' first appearance, and she still felt its heaviness in her soul.

She shook herself from her morbid thoughts and continued down the hall. There was work to do, arguably too much. She knew what she *should* be doing. She should be going down to the barrier to inspect it in person, not just with her power. Getting too close to the border usually caused dizziness and nausea, and it would be more dangerous now, but she needed to figure out how to repair it.

Now, instead of only handling the dark waters, she was waiting for the next battle with the Titans to begin. What would be their next move? Crius and Atlas's strike was not the last.

She stepped into her office and shut the door behind her. Leaning back on it, she let her skull thump against the wood. She could only hope her spies, hard at work across Zephyr and the sea, gathered some critical intel before the next shoe dropped.

She'd worked for an hour before being disrupted. A record.

A tapping noise from below her feet had drawn her attention to the opening in the wooden floor, a plexiglass window to the sea beneath. Something she refused to budge on when the contractor advised against it.

No, she would not sit in an office all day and not have her domain nearby. She was not made to sit in a stuffy office like her sister, Persephone. She could not be away from the place that gave her power and peace of mind, nor the creatures that depended on her.

Both fish and horse, the giant hippocampus beneath her would terrify any mortal, but this creature was one of her most beloved friends. She'd gifted him with a longer lifetime than a mortal horse and he had been an ally throughout the years.

His front hoof tapped the plexiglass again, his agitation clear at her inattention. Through their link, he sent mental images of them together, at first swimming and then running along the beach in their landside forms.

Right. She had promised him a run tonight.

He circled impatiently with flicks of his strong back fins, his pearlescent coat looking glossy in the morning water.

She sank to the floor and looked into the beautiful equine eyes the color of sea glass. She motioned to her office to indicate she was working, which he knew meant waiting until the sun slipped past the horizon. She sent some images into his mind of her sitting at her desk, filling out paperwork. He blasted a bit of water at the plexiglass, making her snort. She knew him and his mulish nature, so to placate him, she placed her hand against the glass in promise.

Smirking at his insolence, she stood and returned to her desk, jumping when the hippocampus slammed both hoofs into the glass before disappearing deep into the water.

As she settled back into her paperwork, she thought of how she missed the days she spent aboard a ship, when she was surrounded by her water, her crew, and her sea creatures.

What she wouldn't give to be out on the high seas again. When she'd been a pirate, her duties as Goddess were far easier to accomplish, and more enjoyable; capturing and punishing slave traders was thrilling and just, and much less dull than reviewing transportation policy and permit requests.

Daydreams of her pirate life were interrupted by the door opening. Her assistant, Mallory, cautiously poked her head into the room and looked around for the source of the loud bang. Little did she know it was from a giant hippocampus slamming his hooves into the floor. Catching the innocent look in Amphitrite's eyes, she shook her head and entered the room.

Mallory had learned over the years it wasn't worth it to ask, which Amphitrite rewarded with generous bonuses.

"We have a guest," she said. "He says he needs to speak with you urgently."

Amphitrite reached out with her senses and felt the thrum of power nearby, pulsing out from the waiting room.

West had come to her, and from the state she left him in last night, she could only imagine how this little conversation would go.

She sighed and nodded. "Let him in."

Mallory stepped away from the door and, a moment later, he appeared. Amphitrite watched a very bedraggled West move into the room. His hair was unkempt, his jaw was unshaven, and he wore sweats. If the scandalized glances Mallory shot his way were any indication, this rumpled version of him was not in any way normal. The celebrity and his downfall. She was sure all the gossip rags would sell a kidney to see him as she was seeing him now.

Mallory sent them a lingering look before stepping back and closing the door behind her.

They were alone.

West fell into one of the seats across from her desk, watching her with red-rimmed eyes. He flinched and reached back to remove his wallet, throwing it unceremoniously onto her desk as if it wasn't made of the finest leather. Something that probably cost most people's monthly rent.

A flare of irritation lit through her blood. She was done with this childish behavior. She needed to train him, and she would not do that with him constantly acting petty and ridiculous.

Spoiled. That was the only word to describe the man-child before her. Absolutely spoiled.

"I will require you sober. The sea will not take to someone incapable of handling their power. She won't take it easy on you."

"She?" he asked, tipping his head back and closing his eyes as if he were about to take a nap in the middle of the conversation.

Amphitrite bristled.

"Yes," she said tersely. "*She.*"

He huffed a laugh before incoherently muttering something about being good with women and she clenched her fists beneath her desks.

He was so entitled. So full of himself. He may have worked with Devon, but he was nothing like her new brother-in-law. West seemed like the ultimate doted-upon heir, disregarding other people and their time.

"Did you not come here to discuss your new powers?" she asked, trying her best not to scream the words at him just to watch him flinch.

Lifting his head, he blinked at her blearily. She fumed silently as she watched his gaze clear.

Maybe she was a little jealous of him and all the attention he received, the admiration that everyone gave him for just existing. Although she'd benefited from blending into the background throughout her immortal life, it still stung. Even in her own family, she was lost in a sea of sisters. The middle child, the one who played peacekeeper while her own internal fire raged. Persephone was stoic, responsible; Demeter was sweet and nurturing; Hestia was calm and perceptive; and Hera was... Hera.

Hestia had been the sister she connected with in the emotional sense. Hestia saw her, tried to bring Amphitrite to the surface, the real one, not the docile peacekeeper her sisters saw.

You are lost in the sea when you have it in you to conquer it. Let it free, my little fish.

Hestia had been right to give her that advice, and she was still right. She wouldn't bow to West and she would tell him so. Now. Before they trained.

She opened her mouth to say exactly that when he cut her off.

"I actually," West started, his raspy voice cutting into her thoughts, "came to apologize for my behavior last night."

She froze, unsure if she was hearing him correctly.

He's apologizing?

That was something she hadn't known he was capable of. She settled back further in her seat, waiting him out as she realigned her estimation of him with this new information.

They both stared at each other in silence, and she realized now he was waiting for *her* to say something.

Well, maybe her estimation hadn't been too far off.

"Ugh, I thought that was the extent of what I had to say." He groaned, throwing his hands over his face.

"That you intend to apologize?" she asked, trying not to laugh. As annoying as he was, he was entertaining. She'd give him that.

"Yes," he sighed. "Fine. Okay, I was an asshole and said things I should not have said. I realize I have not been at my best lately-"

She did laugh then, and his eyes narrowed on her.

"But," he continued, "I was thrown into all of this. There was no choice on my end. I just suddenly had all this responsibility, and with my dad wanting me to take over Oceanus-"

"Oh, boohoo," she interrupted, and his eyes flashed with shock. "You have to do some actual work for once in your life. You were told of your powers by your father, who loves you and thought he was protecting you."

"He lied to me!" West ground out, his teeth clenched, and Amphitrite felt her temper rise. She never realized how quick she could lose herself to anger until this man. She was prone to tantrums as a child, much like Hera, but while Hera was a flashbang, bright but over fast, she was a steady rise, until she boiled over and melted the world around her. A human volcano.

"Yes, he did, but his mistakes are not an excuse to resign yourself to selfish wallowing and drinking your life away. People rely on you. *The sea relies on you.*"

"Well, they can hang for all I care. I asked for none of this," he stated, leaning back in his chair like a king settling onto his throne.

And that was all it took. Her vision went red, and her veins flooded with adrenaline.

Anger compelled her around her desk to face him before her consciousness curbed her. He sat up straighter and leaned away, perhaps remembering her slap from the night before. Good. He was going to get so much more with that mouth of his.

She grabbed the armrests of his seat and swung him around to face her. In a blink, she let the Goddess rise to the surface. Aquamarine light from her eyes reflected in his as she leaned over him.

Almost nose to nose, she growled, "You petulant child. Do you have any idea how many people would die if we do not get the sea back from the darkness?" Her voice was menacingly lower than normal, banked in the Goddess's power. "Yes, your father lied to you, but my father *killed me.*"

West's eyes went wide, shock and something else flashed within them, but she didn't care. It was out there, and she wasn't done.

"I had to come into my powers without guidance. The horrible man who calls himself my father is still haunting us in his attempts to escape his prison and rule again. You may be new to the world of Gods and Titans, but you need to catch up quick. A war is on the horizon. We have Titans around the world right now plotting against us. Do you have any idea what happens to us, to everyone, if they achieve their goals? We die! Game. Over. So, here I am, ready to help *you* when all I want to do is throw you out the window and let the sharks have at you!"

He just sat still, watching her agape.

"Get out! Now!" she snarled, punctuating her words by poking her finger into his chest. She pushed away from him before she did something she would truly regret. The Goddess inside of her was far less merciful than Amphitrite.

"Amphitrite," he started, his voice low. There was something vulnerable in his tone that she did not want from him. Something caring... something that sounded too close to compassion.

She stomped to the door and flung it open. Not looking at him, she pointed out to the waiting room, indicating for him to leave.

He stood silently for a tense moment and finally stepped toward the door, making it only a few steps before halting in front of her.

"I am sorry. I always say the wrong thing around you. I'll... I can do better," he whispered and left before she had a chance to say anything else to him.

For the best.

Shutting the door behind him, she leaned against it and slid down it to the floor, burying her head in her hands and letting the tears flow. She hated the anger she felt around West and she hated being forced to think of her father. But with Tartarus under attack so recently, some things couldn't be avoided. If she wanted to survive this war, she had to deal with West as much as she had to deal with her father's memory. Her millennia-old wound had opened back up and Amphitrite could do nothing to stop the bleeding. For her or her sisters.

6

Minutes later, still seated at the base of her door, Amphitrite shut her eyes and focused on her sisters. Her mind's eye tracked them as they went about their day at the Zephyr Senate and Cerberus Financial. Honing in on them completely, she put out a call, one that only they would hear.

And maybe Devon. The new God was getting used to Demeter's powers, and she still wasn't sure how much he could tap into their connection, whether as a God himself or through his Soulbond with Persephone.

When Demeter and Hestia were unable to ascend to Godhood after their father killed them, Amphitrite and her surviving sisters had decided to place their powers in mortals with a need for it. A pregnant woman living in famine and close to death was given Demeter's powers of nature and rebirth. A fire priestess in the Slavic region, who was desperate to keep her tribe safe from the cold and predators, was given Hestia's powers of fire and hearth. Centuries later, Devon was fulfilling their lost sister's role as the God of Rebirth, and they were all still adjusting.

And still searching for Hestia's scion.

Sighing, Amphitrite stopped her call. Her sisters were busy going about their workday, but she knew they would come soon. They never neglected to find each other when one called, her sisters being her only source of consistency throughout the long years.

Amphitrite stood and smoothed out her wrinkled clothing. She wiped her eyes, drying the tears of frustration.

A flash of bright white light flared to life in front of her on the right, as its counter, shadows and darkness, filled the left side of the room. The light and shadows faded to the silhouettes of her sisters before they fleshed out into their mortal forms.

Hera crossed her arms and eyed both her and Persephone.

"Good, now I don't have to hunt you down and demand answers about that tsunami during the battle," Hera said as she cut her a look. Amphitrite narrowed her eyes at Hera in return.

"You're still not here to *demand* answers, Hera," she reminded her. "We need to talk." Amphitrite turned to Persephone. "Should we summon Devon?" she asked, feeling slightly awkward to include a fourth.

"Devon will come if we have need of him, but he is currently handling some issues with the Furies," Persephone stated.

Hera let out a boisterous laugh.

"Finally found someone to foist those little beasties of yours off onto?" Hera asked, earning a scowl from Persephone. When Persephone did not deny it, Amphitrite managed a smile.

Poor Devon.

"Yes, well, I may need him in the future, but not right now. It involves his friend West, the mortal-born son of Oceanus," Amphitrite started.

Hera sat in Amphitrite's chair, kicking her feet up, and Persephone leaned back against her desk with her arms folded. Both of them stared at her, waiting for her to explain the situation.

"He is unbound, which-"

Hera interrupted with a curse. "I knew that wave wasn't just a damn roll through of idiot Titan power. Damn them," Hera growled, slamming forward. Persephone looked over her shoulder at her with a raised eyebrow, before turning back to Amphitrite and making a motion to continue with her hand.

"West didn't cause the tsunami," she corrected. "But, yes, I do suspect the large flux of power from the opening of Tartarus, and perhaps Devon's ascension," she shot an apologetic look at Persephone, who merely nodded in agreement, "caused the events of that day. The wave. Oceanus also claims it allowed him to unbind West without breaking his oath. I'm not sure if Oceanus is being completely truthful, but regardless, we now have a new Titan coming into his own. An angry one," she stated.

Persephone pulled a sympathetic face. Devon and West were friends, after all.

"Angry at you for binding him?" Hera asked, her hands clasped on the desk in front of her.

"I am not sure what all Oceanus has told him, but I do know he feels betrayed by his father and cannot seem to stay sober for more than a day."

"He spent last night passed out on our couch," Persephone informed with a slight grimace. "Not that I would have kicked him out if I'd known he was unbound," she hurried to explain, "but I would have had Hecate put some protective wards in place."

Amphitrite winced. "I told him today he needs to stop his heavy drinking." *Among other things.*

"I can certainly have Devon speak with him, if you think that will be of any help at all?" Persephone asked. "They are very close and I know he would hold more insight than we have."

Hera narrowed her eyes at Persephone. "Do you think Devon already knows he was unbound?"

Persephone shook her head. "He would have told me, or at least asked what the binding meant." She huffed a humorless laugh. "He might have appreciated such a procedure for himself in those early days." Persephone sobered and gave Hera a stern look. "And besides, it's not Devon's power we're worried about."

Hera rolled her eyes and muttered something that sounded suspiciously like, "Not *anymore*."

Amphitrite tried to get them back on track. "Persephone, I think Devon speaking with West would be our next step. My concern is him being a Titan. Oceanus has been-"

"He has been neutral. Which," Hera held up a finger, "is why his ass is not rotting away in Tartarus or exiled. West could be an ally," Hera stated firmly. "One we desperately need, so I don't care what you have to do to make him swear allegiance to the Goddesses before any other Titans find out about him but do it. For now, we have the upper hand. Let's use it."

Persephone sighed, looking down at the floor in front of her.

"You disagree?" Hera demanded.

Shaking her head, Persephone looked up at Amphitrite.

"Yes, he would make a valuable ally, but he is a man hurting. Trust me, you need to care more for him than what he can do for us. I know some of his back story and..." she trailed off. "Just be careful how hard you push him, Amphitrite. You don't want to risk pushing him in their direction."

Hera stared at Persephone a moment before turning back to Amphitrite.

"Fine. Cuddle, coddle, fuck him. Whatever. Just get him team Olympus or we are all dead," she ordered. Before Amphitrite could retort, Hera disappeared in a flash of light. *Typical*.

Amphitrite turned to Persephone and found her watching her still. Those eyes that had been cold and swimming with spirits for so long were now filled with warmth and concern. She realized something in Persephone had truly changed with Devon. She had so much more compassion than she could remember her sister having even as a human.

"Tread carefully, sister, and give grace. I'll talk to Devon about a conversation with West," she murmured before she became shadows once again.

Maybe it was the rum, but West was thinking about pirates. He sat at the polished marble island in his top-of-the-line kitchen, about as far away from a pirate ship as he could get and took a swig straight from the bottle. He wondered what it must be like to be a pirate on the high seas, totally free from responsibility. A childhood fantasy of his had been to captain a boat in the open ocean, looking for treasure. Land nowhere to be seen.

What a delusional child he had been. Thinking the life he was living was true, and that people cared about him as a person. That there wasn't anything that could really harm him or shake his belief in his family. Or in the world.

A bullet and a lie.

That was all it took. A bullet to a woman who, while not innocent, certainly did not deserve such a death. A lie from a trusted father to a naïve son.

Staring at the rum, he jolted a bit when the liquid rippled in the bottle but held his concentration. Soon, the liquid was swirling in the container and out into the air, dancing in front of him. The amber stream flew in circles and then a figure eight. Just enough water in the drink to control it.

"Impressive," he heard from behind him. Suddenly losing focus, the rum fell from the air and splashed onto the countertop. West caught the lip of the island before he fell out of his seat and glared at Devon over his shoulder.

"Fuck, you cannot..." West waved his hands, "do that weird teleportation thing!"

Devon smirked and pushed his hands into his jean's pockets.

"Yeah, it's pretty unnerving, huh?" He laughed while West grabbed a kitchen towel and started cleaning up his mess.

After a long moment of silence as he finished wiping up the spilled drink, he looked up to see Devon watching him.

"What? Finding Persephone lacking now that you have time to admire my beauty? That's fine, just know I haven't been with a man before-"

"You have a power trail," Devon muttered. "Ocean blue." He let out a huff. "At first, I thought it was from your dad, maybe. I should have known."

West threw the damp towel in the sink. "The wife told you, huh? That you're not the only new guy with powers."

He tried not to sound too bitter, but his friend's protective instincts still flashed in his eyes.

"Yes," he affirmed. "Though you could have mentioned it last night."

He sighed. Devon was right, but... "I was drunk."

Devon lifted a brow. "You're drunk now."

"No," he clarified with a raised finger. "I'm *almost* drunk." He dropped his hand and held the counter's edge with white knuckles. "Besides," he said, "this power thing is so new. This entire world feels new. All this responsibility feels..."

"Inescapable?" Devon supplied, a compassion in his eyes that made West's hairs stand on end.

"Yes," he simply agreed as he stared at Devon.

"I'm sorry," Devon started, swallowing and looking out the window above the sink. "It sucks when you have no choice in the matter, but you cannot run away from yourself." Devon looked back at him. "I know you've got it in you to make one hell of a deity... Which is why I ask this as your friend," he said, standing taller. "Learn your powers and fight by my side in this war. Just like we have every other battle."

"I just financially backed you, I never really did-"

"You were there, by my side, until the end. You are my brother. Far beyond death, apparently," Devon said with a small, vulnerable smile.

"I'm not ready-" West started, feeling all his anger towards his father rising to the surface again.

"You never will be," Devon interrupted.

Closing his eyes, West turned from his friend. It was true, the man was the closest thing he had to a brother. He let his head fall forward in thought, and perhaps defeat.

"I will work with Amphitrite. That is all I will promise," he whispered.

Devon stepped forward and placed his hand on West's shoulder. "That is all I ask. Thank you, brother," Devon whispered back. His voice blended with the soft sound of a quiet wind and rustling leaves. West knew without lifting his head that his friend was gone, once again leaving him alone in the kitchen.

He would learn his power. Then, once he had it all under control, he would confront his father.

Then, he would become the most powerful Titan.

7

West looked around the shoreline and checked his watch again. He had received a note from his secretary, Darla, that he was scheduled to meet Amphitrite at six. Yet there he stood, alone on the shore in front of his place as the sun set over the horizon. Seven minutes past six.

His hand trembled with anxiety. The urge to turn around and walk into his house for a strong drink was intense, but he remembered her demand. He had to be sober.

And he could do it. He knew he was strong enough to push through, so he would.

He shuffled his feet into the sand, having long removed his shoes and socks before stepping off the porch of his home. Sinking his toes into the grainy silt, he let its warmth lull him back from the precipice of anxiety.

In front of him, a wave rolled onto the shore. Instead of falling back into the ocean, the water rippled further onto the beach, moving closer until it took the shape of a woman.

As the watery figure walked toward him, he could see the wet footprints left in the sand. His eyes tracked the woman's shape until the seawater solidified into flesh and Amphitrite stood before him.

Amazing.

"Neat party trick," he stated with an unimpressed tone and hoped she hadn't noticed the truth in his eyes.

"Yes, I can see how much I've impressed you. I can also tell training you is going to go swimmingly," she said dryly, turning away from him to look out over the sea.

"Was that a pun?" he asked. He kept the bored look on his face, trying to push down the little slivers of excitement he felt at the prospect of changing his form, too.

Looking over her shoulder, she simply waved an arm, indicating for him to follow.

When he stepped beside her, she nodded.

"We will work every day until I feel you have a grasp on your powers," she stated before lifting her hands to the sky, palms up, and an oncoming wave rose up from the sea. The water whirled in the air, twisting and turning in a dance somewhat similar to his little experiment with the rum, though on a much larger scale.

"You are a Titan, West, but you are also a Guardian," she told him gravely. "Your powers are tied to the ocean because you're meant to protect it. You will be able to move the sea, commune with the creatures…" She called the water toward them, weaving the stream of seawater in between them as she spoke. "It is not something you dominate, but seek a partnership with…"

She guided the water until it enclosed them in a large dome. He couldn't help but be amazed by her control as he watched the water move like silk around them. He glanced between the water and her serene, focused expression. He'd never seen anything so beautiful.

The water, that is. The water is beautiful, he thought to himself quickly, not letting his mind go further than that on the thought.

Swinging her arms down, the dome dropped, and the water crashed back into the sea.

Amphitrite then stepped forward until she was ankle-deep in the water. Pausing as the wind ruffled her hair the slightest bit, she again lifted her hands.

He heard splashing to his right, toward the caves, and he watched two watery forms materialize from the darkness.

He focused on them, finally making their shapes out in the twilight. Horses. He watched as they galloped over the waves as if the sea beneath them was solid.

"It is all our responsibility, and yes, it is a lot, but it is so much more than that."

As she spoke, a pod of dolphins crested the surface, dancing in the last rays of the sun. Whales joined them, blowing out streams of water before taking in the air they needed to return to beneath the surface. He gaped at them, feeling the buzz of excitement tingle along his skin at the vision before him.

"You will find a friendship with many creatures, and as your power grows, you will find you can speak to them," she whispered as the horses ran up onto the shore. As soon as their watery hooves touched the sand, they turned to flesh. Where he expected a coarse brown coat, they had pearlescent skin that shimmered purple and blue. Fins covered their necks and tail where hair would have been on a normal horse.

"These are hippocampi, and they are incredibly intelligent creatures. One of the few that can speak back, though not through language, but images."

The silvery blue one with bright blue equine eyes, moved around Amphitrite, coming straight for West.

"That is Zeus," she introduced, and he raised an eyebrow at the name. A small laugh left her lips, one that brought his attention to them before she spoke again. "You'll understand the name in time. This," she patted the neck of the violet hippocampus, "is Ingrid. She is Zeus' mate. Zeus is most likely assessing if you are a threat to her."

West stood still as the large animal walked around him, pushing its nose against his back. He'd never even been this close to a horse, and now he was a scant breath away from its mythical relative.

A relative with large, sharp teeth.

Thankfully, the animal lost interest in him, apparently deeming him not a threat. West felt an overwhelming sense of relief when it returned to its mate and nuzzled at her neck affectionately.

Relief and perhaps jealousy at their mated bond. But he wasn't going to delve too deep into that feeling.

"So, I can throw water around and bond with horse fish?" he asked, stealing her attention back from the creatures. He wasn't sure why he felt the need to be sarcastic with her, but some part of him had to rebel against the vulnerability of the moment.

"Yes, fish and water. What a Titan you shall be," she snapped back. "Honestly, if you are going to be such a-"

"Asshole? Prick?"

"All of the above," she sneered. "Why did you come out to train with me? Why not hide in your home with your rum like a baby with its binky?"

"Nice," he let out a derisive laugh before his face fell. He could feel her temper mounting, like the hum of an impending natural disaster, as the hairs along his arms stood up. Obviously, so did the creatures as they danced in agitation near her on the beach, their eyes wide and nostrils flaring.

"Damn it," he breathed, turning away from her and crossing his arms. He thought of Devon, and his promise to him. He swore he'd train with Amphitrite, and he had a feeling being a jerk to the person trying to help him wasn't part of the deal.

Turning back to her, he held his hands up in a pleading gesture.

"I apologize," he said. She looked like she was on the edge of an eyeroll, and he was reminded of his previous apology. "And this time I will do it right. Thank you for coming to help me. I am being... a child. I just..." He ran his hands through his hair and worked through how to speak with her about something so real. "I want to learn, I do. But it's a steep learning curve with so much to take in at once." He swallowed his discomfort at feeling so exposed. "I hardly know who I am. Who my own *father* is. Much less—" he gestured at the creatures and the ocean she'd so easily manipulated— "this entire new world. Power that, a couple of weeks ago, I would have called magic." He met her gaze. "So, I'm sorry. I'll try."

She stayed silent for far too long after the last word left his lips, and he shifted awkwardly in the quiet as she studied him. Finally, she nodded her head, accepting his apology.

Well, look at that, West, you can redeem yourself. Just usually too much of an asshole to do it right, he thought to himself.

Amphitrite sighed and waved her hand to the hippocampi, releasing them back to the sea. He wasn't sure if such creatures could feel gratitude, but he had the distinct feeling they were more than happy to leave the tension on the shore.

Turning back to him, she zeroed her focus on him. "You're fighting yourself, which is not going to help you use your powers. Unlike Devon, you are not a God within human flesh. You do not have some primordial entity's soul that merged with the heir of a Goddess' line. You are a Titan. One and whole."

"That... makes zero sense. I thought in mythology, the Titans were just the generation before the Gods..."

"It's partly about birth, but it's also about power," she explained. "As Goddesses, or God in Devon's case, our power is a somewhat separate entity. We were born without it. All of us were mortal and then killed. We had to die for the power to come forward from dormancy and bind to our souls. You will have control in a way a God does not. Yes, my parents were both Titans, so had I not been made mortal by my mother and then killed by my father, I would have been like you." She grimaced but trudged on. "As a Titan, you were born with the power already part of you. No need for death and rebirth. It just is. Our power allows us to take a God form, which makes us as powerful as the Titans. You don't have a God form because all the power is in your fingertips at any moment of time. That's why I could only bind your powers while you were an infant. As an adult, you would be far too strong."

"Wait," he interrupted, his mind reeling from all the information, but especially from the last bomb she'd dropped. *"You* were the one who bound me? Not my dad?"

She frowned at him in confusion and nodded.

"Upon an oath between your father and I. How much did your father tell you, West?"

"Apparently not everything."

Surprise, surprise.

8

Amphitrite curled her hands into fists as she watched West drop the orb of water back into the sea. It had been three weeks, and he was still losing focus on the most minuscule things.

"If you would pull your head out of your ass and let go of your daddy issues, you could handle this easily!" she shouted.

West should be controlling this small amount of water easily, and with little thought.

"Well, excuse me for not knowing how to corral water when it should have been something I was doing as a toddler!" he snapped back.

Every day, they met.

Every day, she tried to train him.

Every day, he barely made any progress.

She had long stopped asking him if he had spoken to his father, finding that any mention of Oceanus made him freeze up, his powers barely coming to the surface.

His bitterness was hindering him, and she was unsure of how to bring him out of it. Most of their lessons now ended with her screaming and stomping off. Usually before she physically did something she would regret.

Usually.

"Again," she ordered. They'd gone to train by a tide pool, the cluster of rocks acting as a natural basin of seawater to work with. Over the weeks, she'd varied her lessons, but they all centered on the same principle: discipline. It required discipline over one's thoughts and surrounding elements to harness any control over power. So far, he'd failed at creating figures of water, stilling a wave, and manipulating water into the air.

After another few minutes, West had barely pulled the sea from the tide pool, the water slipping back in because of his complete lack of focus.

"Enough," she called. "This is ridiculous. You should be further along after three weeks of training."

West said nothing as he glared at the water. He rarely spoke to Amphitrite at this point, becoming more silent as he made less and less progress. He just did as she asked, saving his sulky retorts for when he was most frustrated.

At first, she thought his sullen mood was due to a lack of drinking. She had yet to see, or hear, of him drinking since they had begun training. Now, she knew he was just being obstinate.

"Have you worked on light jumping at all?" she asked, trying to tone down her irritation.

'Have grace' Persephone had told her. Amphitrite wasn't sure how she'd done it with Devon, but this was *not* a graceful process.

"Yes," he growled, clenching his jaw. She was sure he had to have ground his teeth down to nubs by now. "I can do it if I know the place well enough... but not always."

"Because you are being stubborn!" she yelled. Her anger breaching its containment wall as they'd been at it for too long. "You fight against me every step-"

"I'm trying!" he shouted back at her. "I do my best and work non-stop to figure out what I am doing wrong."

"Quit. Focusing. On. What. Is. Wrong," she growled, tired of his morose attitude. "I did not take you for such a negative person. Giving up," she spat, her inner sea captain taking over. She had to shake him from this rut. She had to do something to wake him up. "I know you have it in you, West. All those years with Devon, you hunted down the people who did you harm." Amphitrite hadn't planned on revealing just how closely she'd had her spies follow him, but she knew it'd been the right move when his face lit with fury.

Narrowed to slits, his eyes showed more energy and focus than they had the last three weeks.

"Yes," she continued, gratified, "I know what happened six years ago. I know you were in that warehouse because a woman lured you there to ransom you to Oceanus. I know the people she helped to kidnap you raped and murdered her. I know you hunted them to the ends of the Earth with Devon and got your revenge. So, do not stand here like you are unable to lift a finger and take control of the power you were born to have!"

West stepped away from her, slowly putting his hands up between them.

"How do you know all of that?" he rasped. "My dad doesn't even know."

"Well, I do. And I know what you are capable of. So quit pretending you are inept and *do it!*" she yelled, shooting a huge stream of water towards him. He deflected due to his natural instinct much like with the tsunami. Using his hands, he continued to shove away the onslaught of water coming at him.

"Would you stop?" he shouted, but she was done being gentle. Done with him staring angrily out at the sea as if something would rise from the depths and come do everything for him. He had all the power right in the palm of his hands, but he was holding himself back. His anger toward his father, his self-doubt, his resentment of responsibility, his trouble grappling with this new identity— it all held him back from harnessing his power.

Enough was enough.

Summoning her Goddess form, she pulled on her reserves, all the power she held, and let the water take her up while it pulled him down.

West fell into a vortex of water.

Water poured over his head and all around him.

His entire body was in shock from the freezing dark water. Had she thrown him into the ocean? How far out had she cornered him? He tried to swim to the surface, but he couldn't tell what direction it was in.

He moved his arms against the swirling, disorienting currents. And suddenly, she was in front of him, grabbing his hand. If he had thought she had glowed on the surface, it was nothing compared to her Goddess form in its element. In the darkness, she appeared lit from within with raw power. He gripped her hand, still trying to swim. He needed to make it back to the top, to get his breath. He could not drown at the bottom of the ocean.

What an embarrassing way to go for a Titan of the sea.

Panic flared to life in his primal brain as his lungs started to burn. Amphitrite tugged on his hand and opened her mouth repeatedly, as if to show him she could breathe.

His panic had him ripping his arm away from her and shooting toward what he hoped was the surface, swimming faster than he ever had before.

Breaking the surface, he greedily gulped the evening air back into his lungs, as Amphitrite broke through the water next to him.

"Are... you out... of your fucking mind?" he croaked out of his aching throat, his chest heaving.

"West, you can breathe underwater," she calmly admonished as if she hadn't just tried to drown him. "I apologize for doing it the way I did, but you were not working-"

"So, you drown me?" he retorted, scowling. The adrenaline seeped out of his pores and his body felt fatigued from all the shock and anger he had been exposed to during this training session.

"You would not have drowned. You are not getting it, you dense man," she growled. "You are the sea made flesh. You are the Guardian, and the Guardian of the sea will not die by it."

Continuing to tread water, he stared at her.

She was soaking wet, her red hair floating behind her and her aqua eyes glowing. Her expression was completely serious, if a tinge astonished.

He took another deep breath. The idea was completely unnatural, and he certainly hadn't felt like he couldn't die by the sea mere moments ago, but why would she lead him astray in this?

Swallowing, he didn't think; he allowed himself to sink slowly beneath the waves, Amphitrite following him.

Trying not to let doubt invade his mind, he pulled in a breath and immediately felt like he was choking. Panic and adrenaline flooded his already exhausted body, making him rush to the surface in dread.

Amphitrite grabbed his shoulders and held his eyes. Her gaze, usually flinty with rage or disappointment, was reassuring. He took another breath, deeper, and closed his eyes. It took several inhalations, and many moments of choking, to feel the water become like air to him. Something along his neck itched, and when he reached up to feel, his eyes widened. Gills. There were gills on his body.

An electric sensation zipped from the gills throughout him, as if the water flowing through his respiratory system was giving him power.

She was right. He didn't need to change forms to use his full power, but he obviously needed some changes to survive in a whole new environment. Instant adaptation, he supposed.

Amphitrite spun around and swam away from him, and while he thought maybe he should follow, he was still unsure how long he could continue to breathe underwater. She looked back at him with a grimace and motioned him to follow, her movements now sharp and full of agitation.

He should go with her, he determined, figuring it was perhaps best not to push his luck after almost being drowned.

The woman had a hell of a temper.

Yeah, she knew he would be fine, but Holy Fates, talk about throwing someone in the deep end. He was guessing the Goddess had never been a schoolteacher at any time in her immortal life.

With a sigh of seawater, he swam after her.

She approached a nearby reef and resumed his lessons by summoning schools of colorful fish and basking in their happy presence. Her mood seemed lighter underwater, he decided. More playful, less angry.

Still scary. Her wide grin when a shark came up from behind and snapped its jaws near his face told him that the incident hadn't been a coincidence.

He tried to do the same, but only ended up calling an electric eel. When she turned and went wide-eyed at its sudden appearance, he managed a pretty decent laugh.

They swam and explored together, and for once, training was enjoyable.

As they moved around underwater cliffs, he almost bumped into her when she halted. He braced himself on a nearby rock outcropping, unable to still himself as completely as the Goddess.

Trying to see what had made her stop so quickly, he craned his neck around and caught sight of a ship. There was something different about it compared to the other wrecks he'd spotted, and he realized that this one wasn't covered in barnacles, or half-rotted away in its watery grave. A more recent wreck. Glancing between her and the ship, his curiosity got the better of him and he swam toward it.

It was a smaller vessel. Not the behemoths used to transport goods like his father's ships. This one was almost like the residential ones he had seen when he was in Alexious, a country to the north of Halcyon, during a rare enjoyable evening. He thought the vessels stayed along the canals there, and this one certainly wasn't built to withstand the heavy storms that the seas were notorious for doling out to unsuspecting sailors.

Floating above the deck, he spotted the door to the cabin and that it was slightly ajar. Swimming toward it, small yellow fish darted out of his way, his eyes focused on the door and nothing else. Pushing his way in, he found the cabin empty, the items of its occupants long lost to the ocean's currents.

Slowly swimming through the small space, he looked in all the little nooks and crannies of the ship.

Nothing.

There was a door in the back that he figured was for the head, and he swam to it, unsure of why he was so adamant to check everything over. No one would have survived underneath the water like this.

There was barely enough light to see from the open cabin door, but his eyes caught on a large shape in the shadows. As he pushed further in, his heart stopped as the dark shape took the form of a child's bunk. The waterlogged sheets were covered in some cartoonish character and a plastic toy was strapped onto the bedframe by a cord.

He was reaching out to the action figure before he realized what he was doing.

The odds the family managed to get help were low, and the only one who would have a record of any survivors was the woman currently in shock at the sight of the shipwreck.

Something told him that this family never made it out alive. Had they been rescued; he was sure they would have heard of it.

Private vessels were rare, and one sinking? That would have almost certainly made the main news outlets.

Yet... where were they? The wreck looked so recent, and the temperature was far too low down here to allow for normal decomposition. Warm water would hasten the process, but cold water slowed decay. Although, there was a chance the bodies had been found by scavengers or opportunistic predators.

That was one of the few things he learned about as a morbid little youth: what happens to shipwrecked bodies. Thanks for the information, Dad.

A hand grabbed his elbow, making him jolt, rocketing to the ceiling and nailing himself in the head. Rubbing at his new goose egg, he turned to see Amphitrite staring at him like the idiot he most likely was.

With something orange in her hand, she pointed to the surface and swam out of the cabin door.

Turning back to take in the small bunk, he reached out and grabbed something. Unable to see what it was, he turned and left the silent wreck, holding the object tightly.

He just hoped there was a family to return it to.

9

Amphitrite paced along the docks after sunset the following evening, trying to clear her mind.

There was nothing abnormal on the voyage data recorder that she had found on the sunken boat, which made no sense at all. She'd checked through all the logs the dispatch team pulled for her and spoken to the coast guard, too. Nothing indicated any personal vessel of that size going down in the past five years.

The ship they had found was very recent, and there was no explanation as to what had happened. No record of a distress signal, or a rescue. There was also no report of a missing boat that fit the small ship's description.

It was time to reach out through her less legitimate channels.

Her steps halted when she spotted West through a gap between buildings. He was standing in the exact spot that the tsunami had changed his fate more than a month ago.

Yesterday, they had departed shortly after they had returned to shore. He had said an abrupt goodbye and left, actually managing a light jump, which she had hoped he had executed properly.

She had jumped directly to her office to check the recorder and gather information.

Walking toward him now, she saw that his mood had not lightened since they last saw each other.

Darkness surrounded him as if he were a deity of the Underworld. The streetlamps hadn't yet flickered on, and the sun's remaining light was quickly fading. As she approached him, something about the dusk's shadows made West seem desolate.

"Why?" he whispered when she stepped up beside him. He didn't turn to her, instead looking out over the road that had once been underwater. The reconstruction of the demolished buildings was almost complete, leaving the road looking as if the day had never happened.

"Why what?" she asked quietly. She kept her eyes off of him, not wanting to distract him from his thoughts more than she already had.

"Why does anything like that wreck happen if there are Goddesses powerful enough to stop it?" He asked as he faced her, his hair mussed from the wind and his hands stuffed into the pockets of his peacoat. "Why did you not step in and take the weapons of destruction from mankind? Why not end the war before it began?"

His voice was not loud, but his meaning was heavy. She tried to think of how to explain it, but he continued before she could answer, his voice rougher now with far more emotion woven through his words.

"Why was my date that night raped by her own people? Why was she murdered while I was beaten and tied up, forced to watch? I begged someone to stop it. Pleaded. Did you not hear me, or did you not care?"

A tightness spread through her chest. She wished, so often, she had more power than she did. That she could predetermine the thoughts of man and prevent the destruction and death their greed wrought.

But none of that mattered in the end, when a life was taken, and the grieving looked to their Gods for answers.

"We can only involve ourselves in human affairs to a point without impending upon free will. To do so would unbalance the world, and Chaos intervenes. Which would mean the end of us all." She looked back at him, trying to instill her sincerity in her gaze. "My sisters and I do our best. Persephone with the banks, Hera with the government, and me with the Maritime Administration, we all work to prevent the threats that arose before. The black markets and economic extremes. The political corruption. The weapons trafficking."

"So, you basically just sit back until the problem falls into your *jurisdiction?*"

She watched him pensively and felt a pang of regret. He had so much anger and sadness in his russet brown eyes, but it was the lost look in them, beneath all the other emotions, that suddenly tore at her. She couldn't be upset at his frustrations when she had them, too.

"We work together to keep it running in a state of balance. That is all we can do. We are not powerful enough alone, and even together we cannot bend mortals to our will. And if we could, we still wouldn't."

He took a deep breath before slowly letting it out.

"Why are you here?" he asked. They both looked out onto the street again, avoiding each other's gazes.

"Trying to think. The sea calms the noise in my mind. I found the black box of the ship, but it didn't record what happened. I..." She trailed off, trying to think of how to best describe what it felt like to lose a ship. "I did not feel the boat, nor the people, in any distress on the seas. I always know when a ship sinks. Always. I know when souls pass, when Thanatos comes, when... when the ocean takes their dues from sailors."

"You can feel people dying," he summarized, his eyes moving along the street as if looking for someone or something.

"I can feel anything that happens in the ocean," she corrected gently. Death was her sister's domain. "I can sense the life signatures of anything in the water, and so I can feel when they go out."

"Something I will feel when I finally manage my powers."

"In time-"

"A while ago, you told me I needed to catch up," He turned and faced her fully, his gaze burning into hers. "Well, consider me caught up. You've spoken about a war brewing. I'm guessing you almost drowning me yesterday and screaming about powers and control means you want me as a soldier in this war. You want my power." He stepped closer to her, leaning down to whisper in her ear. "I am not fighting in a war that has nothing to do with me. I am not your puppet. I'm a part of Oceanus Industries, and that is the extent of my involvement. You want someone powerful in the ocean? Go find my liar of a father and recruit him. I am done playing the games of the Gods... Goddesses."

He pulled away from her and stepped backward.

"Let me know when something falls into my *jurisdiction*." He walked past her, leaving her in the road with his words hanging in the air between them.

Amphitrite stood frozen in the street as a streetlamp finally flickered on, casting a yellow light over her. She reached for her frustration, anger, and disappointment in the man but could only find an odd feeling of loss.

"Well, I hate to see a gorgeous man mad, but my oh my, does he look better angry."

Amphitrite swung her head toward the voice. A figure shifted in the darkness of a narrow walkway and the person leering at West stepped into the light.

"Calista," Amphitrite greeted, attempting to keep her tone cool and level, as she turned to face the Senator. Hoping her reaction to the words West had left her with, that had singed something deep in the core of her being, were not obvious on her face. "Skulking around in the shadows again?"

"Ha! Returning from an event and caught you in the midst of an argument with that beauty of a man. It's been far too long, darling. I've missed you," she purred. The woman took Amphitrite by the shoulders and kissed her on each cheek. Even in the sallow light of the streetlamp, her honey skin and eyes glistened with perfection. It was difficult for a siren to look poorly. Or half siren as only her mother was one, her father the offspring of a demi-god long descended from the Titan Pontus. Calista's father had been a fellow spy and died in a mission gone wrong. So, Amphitrite had always felt some responsibility for the young siren pup. Now, the woman was a senator and the most lethal of her spies.

"How is your mother?" she asked as Calista released her. Amphitrite took a healthy step back from her, her feelings too erratic and all over the place about West to handle the woman's siren power. Calista could make anyone sexually aware of her just with proximity.

"Oh, you know," Calista said airily with a wave of her hand. "Slowly rotting in the sea since she refuses to surface after father died. A siren who mates is not quite a siren anymore." Calista shrugged. "Anyway, *she* is not why I am here. "

Amphitrite raised her eyebrows at the statement but said nothing. She wouldn't point out that the mated pairing, albeit rare, was the reason Calista existed.

"I've been puttering around, listening to the sea, and darling... I have a treat for you!" Calista exclaimed, clapping her hands together as her face spread in a saucy smile.

"Do tell."

"Oceanus," she started, and Amphitrite immediately stiffened, "has called off a search."

"For?" Who or what could he be searching for now that West was home?

"For Hestia."

10

West took another swig straight from the bottle of wine he had been nursing all morning and light jumped home. Or his best attempt at light jumping.

Unfortunately, he was not the best at light jumping on a good day, and drunk, he was so much worse.

He landed in an awkward spot behind his couch, knocking the air out of his lungs. He then climbed up and flipped over the back of the sofa, falling onto his side along the cushions. The wine bottle hadn't broken, so he counted that as a small victory. But it had spilled all over the hardwood floors. Less of a victory.

Closing his eyes, he brought the bottle against his lips and tipped his head back, letting the last drops of wine slip slowly into his mouth.

And just like the rest of it, the final dregs tasted like ash. Everything had since he had confronted the Goddess only to come home to an unwanted party invitation; a gala thrown by his parents. One he was headlining, no less. His parents' subtle way of forcibly ending his silent treatment.

They were going to announce him as the next CEO of Oceanus Industries.

He hadn't slept, instead staying up all night thinking of all the ways he would fail in this new life he'd found himself in. There were too many responsibilities to juggle, too many people counting on him.

For Fate's sake, he wasn't even trained! He could hardly cause a ripple in the water and Amphitrite wanted him to join the ranks in an upcoming existential war.

His life was no longer his own. He felt like it belonged to everyone else. The Goddesses let people die and now, he too was responsible for millions of lives. He didn't know how he was supposed to be a Guardian when he'd failed to protect people he'd cared about in the past. Both his date and his best friend had been shot and killed in his proximity, and he'd done nothing to stop it.

He'd always known he would be CEO one day, never a Titan. How was he supposed to be both?

There was just the hope that he could put it off for longer that he had clung to.

Opening his eyes, he dropped the wine bottle and turned his head to the window. He watched the sun glint off the crests of waves rolling towards the shore. Sometimes there were dolphins, but not today. Today, it was just the sun slowly inching across the sky, counting down like a doomsday clock to his eventual imprisonment.

Although maybe he'd always been in some kind of prison. Even his condo was a gilded cage. The seaside condo building had been built as a place of residence for all Oceanus employees and their families. He had the largest and fanciest unit, one that looked out over the Thalassian sea with floor-to-ceiling windows. His mother had decorated the place while he'd been gone, hoping he would come home to stay here. Everything showed her touch, her preference for coastal décor.

But he couldn't bring himself to find comfort in his cage.

He didn't care the red wine had spilled all over the precious hardwood floors.

He didn't care that he spent most of the day drunk. Well, he *was* a little ashamed of his bender after having done so well, not drinking for a whole month.

He just didn't care about anything anymore.

He heard the door to his condo open and knew who it was immediately. There was only one person he trusted with a key.

"Hey, Ma!" he slurred, laughing a little. His mind was addled from the alcohol he had been consuming since he rolled out of bed that morning. He could hear her steps falter every time she came to a hurdle. His place was a mess by any standard and would be maddening for someone like his mother who craved order.

Tick. Tock. Slowly losing her mind.

He grunted out a laugh.

"Dylan Weston Murphy," she grumbled, her voice thick with an accent straight from Aisopos, the country to the east of Halcyon. The country where everyone had the dark hair and dark eyes that he had inherited.

Her voice used to calm him, her accent like the cadence of a lullaby. Right now, it was sharp like a knife's edge. She moved a pile of dirty clothes with her shoe and stepped into his field of vision, standing over him with her hands on her hips.

She looks weird upside down, he thought as he tilted his head and almost fell off the couch.

"I spoke with your father, West," she said as he pushed himself back onto the couch with a groan. Both at having to move while the room spun and the fact she had spoken with his father about him.

"Hush," she admonished, her narrowed eyes taking in the whole of his condo. Yeah, he had to admit it was pretty bad. Her roving gaze landed on him, evaluating his disheveled state. "We're both concerned about how you're... *handling* this situation." She grimaced at the puddle of wine on the hardwood floors. "And how it will affect your health and the health of the company. So, we came to an agreement."

Could they be considering postponing the regime change? *Fates bless her*. Now she had West's full attention. He tried to sit up, but the slight movement sent a wave of nausea through him.

"We agreed he would stay on as an advisor at Oceanus Industries to help you transition. Also, you are to see a doctor I've worked with in the hospital. He will help you find your footing as well."

"A doctor?" Dread and disappointment filled him. "A psychologist? Again? You are trying to make me see a shrink *again*?"

His mother folded her arms, her only indication of true anger. She was not one to raise her voice and her frame was too small to instill fear in her much larger son.

"You will see one. I tire of your," she mimicked his deeper voice, "*oh woe is me*, this, *woe is me* that." Her voice returned to her normal alto tone. "No, you and your father are at odds, but I will not see you both sunk because of stubborn pride. Go to the doctor. I'll not allow you to say no. You choose not to go, then you're out of the condo. End of discussion."

"What!" He tried to jump up, but dizziness overtook him. "All because I refuse to let some over-zealous dweeb with a desire to make everyone feel inferior dig around inside my head? You'd honestly punish me for not feeling comfortable with that?"

His mother leaned over him and ran her hands through his hair like she used to do when he was a child. Her knuckles skimmed across his cheek, and he looked up at his mother to see the grief etched into her face. *Damn.* He couldn't handle his mother being sad.

"I see the pain in your eyes, and it causes me pain, my son. Please, for me, speak to someone. Please rid this pain from your soul and be free." Her eyes glistened with tears. She had to know tears would break him. He was never sure if she faked it or not, but she always won her battles with that tactic.

Closing his eyes and taking a deep breath, he nodded.

Opening his eyes back up, he saw his mother smiling fondly down at him. Her youthful appearance had baffled him until now. Her olive skin, dark chocolate eyes, black hair... *She's not entirely human either*, he reminded himself.

The reminder jarred him from the moment, and he tried to roll out of her reach, pushing himself up enough to lean against the arm of the couch.

A look of hurt crossed his mother's face before she could neutralize it, and she straightened, letting her face return to the pensive expression she usually wore when speaking to patients.

"Thank you," she murmured. "Truly, West. Thank you. I want you to be healthy and happy for more than what your destiny calls you for. I want you to be happy for *you*."

Without another word, she turned to leave, and he listened to her footsteps as she exited his condo, the door closing behind her with a soft click.

West did his best to heave himself into a standing position but did not gauge the strength in his legs correctly and ended up on the floor. Again. He was going to hurt tomorrow.

Staring at the ceiling, he sighed.

He was going to do this for his mom. Let some head doctor tear his psyche apart for shits and giggles.

Oh, what a good time that will be!

11

It was early in the day when Amphitrite stalked past her assistant's desk, but it was already full of nothing but ships missing their time to dock and nonsense with employees not completing reports.

"Good morning, Ms. Wells," Mallory greeted. Amphitrite nodded her hello as she walked toward her office door. Just before she reached for the knob, Mallory cut in, "There is a gentleman in your office. He has been waiting for a good thirty minutes, even though I told him you wouldn't be in until ten."

Amphitrite placed her hand on the doorknob, an extended her power to sense the room's inhabitants. She was expecting to feel West, only to find someone else behind the door and her shoulders dropped a little in disappointment. She needed to speak to West after their emotional showdown in the street the other night but had yet to do so.

Today, she promised herself.

"Thank you, Mallory." She opened the door to see the back of a black head of hair. Most certainly not West.

Carefully shutting the door behind her, she walked around to her desk.

"How can I help you?" she greeted the visitor.

The man simply gave her a nod and placed a sheet of the local news on her desk. Her eyes moved from the sheet to the man.

"I am here on behalf of Poseidon," the man stated, his green eyes moving to hers. She nodded, acknowledging the key phrase. This was the spy she had ordered Calista to find and send out for intel on Oceanus' search for Hestia. She needed to know why Oceanus, the man who had been neutral for millennia, was choosing this moment to make a play.

She didn't ask his name. Most of her spies were anonymous, even to her, and everyone had a codename they used if they needed to give enough information to be found by the network. By the look of him, he was a deep agent and would give her nothing he was not tasked to find out.

Settling in behind her desk, she clasped her hands over the paper, not yet reading it.

"What have you obtained for me?" she asked, keeping her eyes trained on the spy.

"I followed him and his core associates, yet there is nothing to indicate Oceanus is looking for Hestia. I've been through every record he owns, both in house and out. His financials show no evidence of obtaining investigators in such a search. At this time, I would say the whole thing is inconclusive and will return should I hear or find anything different."

"Keep a tail on him," she ordered. "I want to know the exact minute he has any information, anything at all, before he has a chance to move on it."

"Already done."

She nodded and he swiftly stood to silently depart the room. There was no small talk between her and her legions of spies.

Small talk led to loose lips, and loose lips killed.

Unfolding the paper, she looked it over, hardly surprised to see that things were progressing quickly at Oceanus Industries.

'Oceanus CEO announces retirement and succession plan.'

She knew Oceanus would turn the company over soon enough. The article reported only complimentary statistics for the Murphy business dynasty, but word was that

Oceanus employees were worried over whether the new CEO would clean house.

Yet, here they were, barely getting off the ground with West's powers and Oceanus was going full tilt in handing the reins over to West.

But not much to be done about that right now. She would speak with West about their last encounter, and then they'd continue to work on his training and hope for a breakthrough.

No, now she needed to know if Oceanus had found her sister.

It was a good thing Amphitrite was attending his party tonight. If he knew anything about Hestia's scion, she would find out about it herself.

Just like the good old days.

The waiting room of his new psychologist made him wonder if the doctor was crazier than him. The paintings decorating the room were macabre depictions of fire and metal. They seemed a tad bizarre for a psychologist, but what did he know?

Maybe all psychologists are weird like this. You probably had to be weird to handle weird, he thought to himself.

He had never seen one before since he usually found a way out of it, canceling the appointments and hiding out until his mother's wrath had waned. The cycle started again the next time the idea popped into her head.

That wouldn't work this time, though, since he was at least ninety percent sure he would actually be out on his ass if he dodged the appointment. He had pushed his parents' goodwill a little too far with his extended silence, and he knew it.

There was not a receptionist when he had walked in, just a room with a dark leather couch facing two black plastic chairs. An old, scuffed coffee table had a few magazines laid out along the surface, but nothing of interest unless he was a middle-aged mother.

Seating himself on the couch, he stared out the lone window, which faced the mountains. The trees were far too thick to see anything, and the fog obscured the mountain even further.

The distance from the sea made him uncomfortable. Ever since he had started training with Amphitrite, his connection to the ocean had strengthened. It was happening every day, the growth of his powers that the Goddess had told him about. In some moments, he swore he could feel the energies of sentient life in the water outside his home. The sensation buzzed somewhere deep in his mind, like an itch he couldn't scratch. He spent his waking hours either drinking to ignore it, practicing with his powers to distract himself, or both.

It was when he did both that he found himself naked on the beach with dolphins screaming in his head and sand in horrible places.

So caught in his musings, he hadn't heard the large oak barn doors sliding open, and he jolted when a throat was cleared loudly. A man stood there waiting for him with his hands in his pockets and a pale eyebrow raised.

"When you're done daydreaming, we can proceed with your appointment," he said. The doctor didn't wait for him before he turned back to his office and sat in a dark leather chair.

West pushed himself from the seat and sauntered in after the doctor, taking in the lowly lit office. The only sources of light were a small fire in a stone fireplace and a softly glowing lamp on his oak desk. He lowered himself into another leather couch across from the doctor.

Sighing, he looked around the office, avoiding the man's watchful gaze. The space was minimal. Simply a desk, chairs, couch, fire, and a steaming mug of coffee. The walls were dark and barely adorned. Unlike the waiting room, the office had only one large painting. In the same style of the others, the framed oil painting depicted a mechanical beast crawling down a hallway of mirrors.

Definitely a weird man.

"It's nice to meet you, West," the doctor started, crossing his legs at the knee.

West raised a brow. "Is it really?"

"Why wouldn't it be?" He returned West's look with one of his own, his blond brow disappearing behind long, sandy hair. What sort of doctor wears his hair so shaggy? "I am Dr. Viktor Alden. You may call me any of those names."

West frowned at the prospect of addressing the shrink with any sort of familiarity.

"Your mother mentioned you were having issues with a previous traumatic event," Dr. Alden started, not looking at him as he spoke, but favoring the notebook he opened across his lap.

West withheld a sigh. Of course, this doctor got right down to the heart of the matter. That meant West would have to play harder to keep the doctor running in circles before he could call it quits on his therapy. He only had to go for a month, his mother said, twice a week. He could do that and play his way through all this. He knew how to bluff.

"Jumping right in, doc? No 'how are you' or 'how's your day'?"

Dr. Alden glanced up sharply from his notebook. Despite the odd lighting in the room, his eyes were an unnervingly bright hazel. West's breath stilled as he was sure the man was staring directly into his soul.

"I can guess you are someone who will try to disrupt a conversation so you can avoid any deep and meaningful issues." Now, the doctor pinned him with a glare, "I am not so easily distracted, West."

Well, shit.

"Awesome," West grumbled, shaking his head. He looked away from the doctor and gestured at the walls. "As a doctor, aren't you obligated to have a ridiculous amount of degrees hanging from the wall in order to make me feel inferior?"

"Would you like me to make you feel inferior?" he asked in a blasé tone.

West snorted.

"I do not like clutter," the doctor replied, watching West for a moment before writing something down.

And so it begins.

West slapped his hands together and smiled. "Let's get to it, shall we? I'd like to go home and drink before dealing with my parents."

"Yes, Theta has been extremely concerned about your impulsive behavior."

West shook his head with a smirk.

Of course, they acted like this was all on him. They never took his behavior as a result of anything they ever did. He loved his parents, but they were clueless.

"Okay, Doctor, did she tell you that my father lied to me about my origins my whole life? Or that he threw me under a bus, and I am now the CEO of the biggest shipping company in the world in oh..." he looked at his watch, "six hours and twenty-three minutes? They are planning a fancy party. Did you not get an invitation?"

Dr. Alden's face did not change. He was so still he could have been made of stone before he looked down and wrote again. He paused and his pen tapped out a cadence on the paper.

Tap, tap, tap.

West watched the doctor tap the pen against the paper after he finished each note.

He finally looked up at West.

"So, you're scared. Do you want to escape? Disappear until the dust settles only to once again reappear?"

"Would that not be most people's impulse when shit hits the fan?"

"Perhaps. Some also rise to the occasion."

"I couldn't find my superhero cape."

"Your sarcasm is a default coping mechanism. Do you feel trapped, West? Trapped by the new responsibility that was hoisted onto your shoulders?"

Tap, tap, tap.

"Wouldn't you? You only ever have to worry about yourself, and then *boom*. One day, you're not the person you thought you were. You are someone different, who has to run a fucking company you spent your entire life ignoring!"

The doctor gave a slight nod.

"Yes, I imagine someone very spoiled would react that way to any type of responsibility."

West's jaw dropped.

"Did I surprise you by agreeing with your assessment of yourself?"

"Well," West murmured, shifting uncomfortably in his seat. "Yeah. I mean, aren't you supposed to-"

"Coddle you? It seems like your mother and father did that and it led to you sitting across from me, complaining about your unearned privileges being taken from you."

The silence in the room was thick as West worked out his next words.

Suddenly, surprising himself and the doctor, West let out a booming laugh. He had expected some meek little doctor he could steamroll as he ran out the clock, doing just the bare minimum to meet the conditions of his mother's deal.

"Good. You are going to do well working with me," Dr. Alden told West, making him wonder what kind of upside-down world he was walking into with this man as his mental health professional.

West calmed, wiping at his eyes after such a hard laugh, before looking back at Dr. Alden.

"You're really going to make me do this. This whole fix myself thing?"

"That's my job, Mr. Murphy. Now, I'd suggest we get on with the session since it seems that, as of tonight, you are going to have a lot less free time to wallow in despair."

West snorted, but sat back, ready to hear the pearls of wisdom only a man such as Dr. Alden could bestow.

12

Amphitrite stepped into the Murphy mansion for the first time since West's birth, her heels clicking on the marble floors as she entered the foyer. Letting the butler take her coat, she took in the splendor West had grown up in. Hardly anything had changed since her last visit except that the luxurious home was now full of dozens of guests in black tie.

Without her coat, she felt a chill despite the crowd. Everything was marble— the floors, walls statues, and fountain. There was no warmth to be found in the hard stone, not the kind one would need after a hard day at work. It was far too formal of a place for a little boy to run around freely the way a youth should.

She found herself feeling a small amount of pity for West. She still hadn't spoken to him after their last explosive encounter.

That's where the sympathy is coming from, she told herself.

The unresolved tension between them, not the mental image of a small, lonely boy with dark brown hair and big, sad eyes.

Amphitrite remembered Persephone's advice to be graceful, to avoid pushing him toward the Titans. She'd already partially failed in that respect, and it was clear her training techniques had pushed him away. Maybe not to the plotting Titans just yet, but certainly away from *her*.

Perhaps she would find herself more empathic with him in the future, if it meant he returned to training.

Her train of thought was derailed as she entered and scanned the ballroom.

Oceanus was speaking to a few businessmen. Medusa was in the corner multi-tasking, soliciting charitable donations for her women's shelter and picking up any secrets from the elite.

Seeing them both together in this room propelled her mind to the past. When it all began and a deal that had been struck long before now. When she and Medusa ran the seas, bringing the ships they commandeered back to Oceanus for his shipping empire.

Oceanus helped them to weed out new potential spies, and she provided him with ships for his growing business.

She could almost hear the waves and seagulls, cutlass crossing cutlass.

A hand skimmed across her back and took her arm as Calista appeared at her side.

"We have five here on the ground, plenty more throughout the city," Calista informed her as she raised her glass of champagne to someone in greeting.

"All positions?" Amphitrite asked, and Calista nodded in response.

"Two working as servers, one of our inside men from Oceanus, and two partygoers."

Her eyes snagged on the spy she'd met in her office earlier. He was most likely the inside man at Oceanus Industries.

She flitted her eyes to Oceanus and caught him looking at her.

Time to interrogate a Titan.

Calista must have felt the shift in her attention since she walked away to converse with someone else, leaving Amphitrite to hold Oceanus' gaze and nod toward his office. The look of dread on his face was almost priceless.

Once both of them were in his office off the hallway, close enough to the ballroom to hear music but not voices, she turned to him.

"I've already told you I did not have a way to unbind his powers before the tsunami-"

"Remember when you first started Oceanus and pirates would commandeer your ships, or a trader would make noise about wanting to take over the greatest shipping company of the old world?"

Oceanus narrowed his eyes at her but nodded.

"You sent me in. We worked in a partnership together for a long time. I went and found both your ships and your secrets."

"I remember. What is your point?"

Amphitrite's hands curled into fists as she stepped closer to the Titan.

"You remember how I told you it was in your best interest to never, *ever* keep a secret from me?"

"You are treading in dangerous water right now, little Goddess," he growled, straightening from his relaxed position, his body now alert.

"If I thought you would jump in and do something, I might be scared," she taunted.

Oceanus narrowed his eyes, a slight glow illuminating his irises.

"Get to your point. Now."

Amphitrite moved even closer as something feral ran through her.

"You've been keeping far too many secrets, and I do not like it. You unbound West without my knowledge." She raised an eyebrow when Oceanus looked like he was about to say something before quieting, his mouth pressing into a thin line. "You also know where Hestia is."

Oceanus laughed. Actually *laughed* at her statement. As if the search for her lost sister's power was a joke. Amphitrite's frown couldn't get any deeper.

"You assume I know anything about that? You give me too much credit."

"Where is she, Oceanus?" she growled. If they found the person holding Hestia's power like Devon held Demeter's, this war could be over. No more surprise attacks from Titans. No more living in fear of how and when they would allow the man who killed her, her own father, free.

Her gut was telling her something was up and the thought that Oceanus was working against her after centuries of collaboration tore at her. So much had changed between them in such a small amount of time.

"You've been looking. Did you think I wouldn't keep an eye on you after what happened with West? I know that you have been searching for Hestia and I want to know exactly what you know. If you called off the search because you found her, then you need to tell me. Now." She could feel the flames of her temper licking along the surface of her skin.

"I don't know where you heard such a thing but check your intel. I have no idea where she is, and I haven't searched for her."

"You're lying," she accused.

"I cannot get into this, Amphitrite. You know that me standing beside you and the Goddesses means my death."

"No!" she snapped, throwing her arms out in frustration. "I don't! I have no idea why you continue to be neutral and powerless when you could swear your loyalty and be whole again! How can you stand it? You alone have the power to destroy them! If you worked with us-"

"Because West will die!" He yelled, getting into her face, neither of them backing down. "Theta will die. My family. I worked against them once before, long before you, and they killed my mortal wife for it! Our mortal children!"

"Who?"

"The fucking Titans!" he hissed. He grabbed the back of his neck and started pacing. "I work with you, and I'm branded a traitor. They will find a way, Amphitrite, to find retribution against me and my family. Again."

"Even more reason to help us defeat them," she argued.

He laughed humorlessly. "Eternity is a long time, Goddess. You may rule now, but I remember both the reign, and the fall, of the Primordial Gods. I chose the opposing side once before." He clasped his hands in front of him. "I cannot risk their wrath if they return to power—now or centuries from now."

"Now, West must fight your battle."

"Yes," he sighed. He slowed his pacing and returned to her. "I didn't know this would happen. As powerful as I am, I cannot see into the future."

"You could pull the Titans out of hiding," she said. "Don't swear sides if you must, but we must know where my father's allies are outside of Tartarus."

Oceanus gave her a withering look.

"At the risk of my wife and child..."

"West is at risk either way and we both know Theta is more capable than she pretends."

"I refuse to lose my family again, Amphitrite."

"You will lose your wife, your son, and your company in this war, Oceanus," she warned. She hated saying the words, hated how much they felt like a prediction passing through her lips.

He looked at her, every year of his age showing on his face. "I trust you to prepare West for the worst."

This is the worst, West thought as he took another sip of champagne. He had already dealt with all the frippery and nonsense he could, and the party had just started. He drank in the corner, watching people mill about in their finery. They came to celebrate him becoming the head honcho at Oceanus, yet none of them noticed his absence.

He used to thrive on the attention of these people, but right then he'd rather be sitting next to Devon in some faraway place, never really saying anything, but letting the comfort of the moment wrap around him. In the old days, those moments had brought him peace. He'd been surrounded by strangers who didn't know his name or the power and prestige behind it. He'd just been a man.

Closing his eyes, his mind fell into a memory.

Sitting on a rooftop in a city far too cold compared to Halcyon even though no snow had touched the ground that year. They had just finished a mission. The last man in the warehouse from that horrible night was gone. Sent to the realm of the dead, wherever that was.

He sat next to Devon, sharing a bottle of liquor, the label long since lost, but it kept him warm, or at least made him think he was anyway. The air was too crisp, his nose was numb, yet they stayed out there, needing to decompress after such a long-time hunting.

The last of the prey, taken down.

All that was left was to return to the motel room where they had set up their base. West wasn't sure what to do now. Devon had offered to let him continue on alongside him, as he had another job in the city unrelated to West's mission, but West wondered if he should return to Halcyon.

"You ever wonder if the Gods have forsaken us?" he asked. His tipsy mind always got philosophical.

Devon took another swig of the unnamed liquor. With his black tactical clothing he blended into the night. West wore a matching outfit, but unlike Devon, he was not armed to the teeth.

"I think..." Devon started, looking out over the city, where lights were starting to flicker out from countless windows as people went to sleep, "We have forsaken the Gods."

Opening his eyes, he pulled himself from the memory and looked around the crowd. Still, nobody glanced his way, so he lifted his drink in mock cheer before he downed it. As he watched partygoers wander around the ballroom with fake smiles, telling all the same stories they've told before, he caught sight of a beautiful woman making her way through; her auburn hair difficult to miss.

Amphitrite.

Suddenly, the ballroom fell away. She wore a lacy topaz gown, all gold and warmth.

His eyes halted on her cleavage for a moment before moving up to her aquamarine eyes. Her long, auburn hair was braided back into an updo, exposing a slender neck his eyes fixated on.

As a living, breathing male, he could admit to having lustful fantasies of her. Unfortunately, due to his inability to be the suave, charming West with her, the most he could hope for was friends. And that was when he wasn't putting his foot in his mouth.

She made her way through a faceless crowd to stand next to a blond man, and he realized it was her date from the other night.

No, not her date. Her boyfriend.

He watched them give each other a quick, affectionate kiss before they turned to speak to another man.

Their easy affection had him imagining what it would be like to stand there, next to a woman he felt at ease with. West had never really been in a relationship, and he wondered what it was like to want the same person, day after day, and be content with that.

None of the women of his past wanted more than a good time from him, which he'd been more than happy to provide.

A throat cleared next to him, and he turned to see one of the staff from Oceanus Industries standing there. West mentally sighed. The man had definitely been watching West stare at Amphitrite for the last few minutes like a creep.

"Your father has requested your appearance in the great hall, sir," the man stated. The formality in his tone made West itch with the urge to run, jump the garden walls, and keep going until he hit the border.

Instead, he handed the empty glass to the man and headed toward the great hall. On his way, he crossed through the ballroom and the garden patio.

The patio was lit up with lanterns and full of people laughing and strolling around his mother's prized blooms. When he came to the great hall's threshold, he paused to overlook more of the party.

As if he could sense him, his father turned to him, a smile lighting the old man's face. His tired eyes focused only on son.

Time to face the noose.

13

Tonight, everything was off.

First, her troubling conversation with Oceanus.

Second, Amphitrite felt like she was being watched, but when she looked around, everyone had their attention elsewhere.

She made her way through the crowd, finally spotting the familiar face she needed to see in that moment.

The perfectly gelled blond hair, the lean body, the beautiful cerulean eyes. She found herself smiling for the first time that evening.

Darren. Her Darren.

His arm went out at the sight of her, and he pulled her into his side as he introduced her to the man he had been speaking with.

"This beautiful lady is my date, Cordelia. Cordelia, this is General Gedeon Olethros." Darren introduced them and her smile faltered. Why did her heart drop every time Darren introduced her by her alias? It had been happening for a year now, and yet she felt the frown cross her face before quickly catching herself and giving the men a thin smile.

"So nice to meet you, Cordelia." The general smiled, holding out his hand for her to shake. When she accepted his grasp, a zap of electricity ran up her arm at the contact. She looked closer at him, at his cropped silver hair and light blue eyes. She could feel faint pulses of power coming from him, like a demi-god, but the power felt... stronger than one and yet weaker than hers.

Who is this man?

"Likewise." She attempted a smile, but it felt forced. He kept his icy blue eyes on her, evaluating her in a manner that made her more than a little uncomfortable.

Darren cleared his throat, breaking the standoff. She was never more thankful that Darren could pick up on her mood than at that moment. Placing his hand at her waist, he excused them.

"That was very... weird," Darren muttered as they began walking to the opposite side of the room from General Olethros.

"Yes," she agreed, but didn't elaborate. He was familiar in some way, yet she couldn't put her finger on how. The odd zapping sensation hadn't felt outright hostile, but it wasn't comfortable either. She caught sight of one of her sirens embedded in the crowd and minutely motioned her towards the general. Without missing a beat, the siren laughed and excused herself, heading in the direction of her new target.

"Have I told you that you look amazing tonight?" Darren whispered against her ear with his hand still at her back. She smiled and turned to give him a peck against his cheek, but as she did so, her eyes caught sight of West over Darren's shoulder. He was watching them. Watching *her*, really. He stood next to his father, who was busy speaking to a small group situated just before a small platform with a podium.

It was the first time she'd seen him in days, and he looked the worse for wear, despite being dressed up in a tux. He held up his glass in mock cheers, his eyes burning with animosity.

He is angry because he is hurting, she reminded herself.

Her eyes moved back to Darren, whose affection for her was evident. She wished he could be a long-term relationship, but he was mortal, and those never lasted long.

She didn't love him. She had never loved a mortal, or anyone really. She felt a genuine affection for him, found him attractive, and he was an adequate lover. She loved the romance of it all, the feeling of giddiness when he surprised her or made an advance. She loved the feeling of being loved, yet she had not felt the same in return.

Sometimes, her guilt kept her up at night, as Darren softly snored beside her in bed. She was wasting his time when he could be looking for someone with whom he could spend his mortal life. A woman who could give him children, who could age and live out their lives together before Thanatos stood upon their doorstep.

But then he would wake up, showering her with kisses, making love to her, and she let him be hers for one more day, promising she would release him the next.

And here they stood together, a year after her first vow to let him move on. She was being selfish, but she hated the loneliness of her position. And she did not want to be with a deity for the sake of having someone with immortality. She saw how that worked out with Persephone and Tristan.

Tristan had ended up bound at the bottom of the sea for his involvement in the coup on the Underworld.

The deities usually were not the type to enjoy the romance of love. Having lived long lives, they didn't know how to live in the now, making the most of every day they had. The mortals did, and she thrived upon how much emotion they put out. She needed that. She needed to feel important and loved, and she had yet to meet an immortal who could give her that.

"Attention!"

Her thoughts were brought back when Oceanus, who now stood on the platform, tapped his golden fork against his champagne glass. As the partygoers quieted down, she caught sight of West staring off into space, his face completely blank.

The moment of truth and it looked like West had mentally checked out.

"I have asked you all here to make a very important announcement. As you all know, my son, Dylan Weston Murphy, has returned to Halcyon City." He waved grandly toward West, and the room clapped politely in expectation. With a broad smile, Oceanus continued his speech. "Tonight, I am announcing him as the new CEO of Oceanus Industries!" Another wave of polite clapping went through the room. Everyone had to have already known about the announcement but cultivated looks of surprise and elation spread through the audience.

Oceanus, with his arms still spread, seemed to enjoy the grandeur of the moment. "I have been honored to be the CEO these past years, but now it is time for me to hand over the reins."

Amphitrite caught West rolling his eyes and worried if anyone else had seen.

Oceanus beckoned West closer, and, in a flash, his trademark smile was back in place as he stepped up next to his father. Flashes went off from cameras she hadn't noticed until now.

"To the new CEO, my son, Weston Murphy," Oceanus called, beaming as he tapped his glass against West's. That was when she saw the despair written plainly across West's handsome features. It wouldn't be obvious to anyone else, anyone who hadn't seen unhappiness on his face every day for a month. His false smile was firmly in place, but she could see the tension in his jaw and the fear in his eyes. Her breath caught in her throat.

She knew that look. It reminded her of pirates on the gallows.

Darren's hand took hers as the applause wound down. She struggled to catch what Oceanus said next, unable to look away from West.

When West's eyes met hers, she felt like the only one in the room with him. Giving him a small smile, she raised her glass up to him.

With a nod, he raised his in return.

She hoped he took that moment for what it was.

Understanding and an offer of peace.

14

W est caught Amphitrite's eyes across the room. Just looking at her had anchored him, bringing him back to the moment, and away from his spiraling thoughts. His entire world no longer felt as if it were crumbling at his feet.

A look of understanding crossed her face, and he realized that, for once, he was not the object of her ire. Instead, a sort of truce ran between them as she lifted her glass, and he returned the gesture.

She broke eye contact when her boyfriend took her hand, leaning in to whisper something in her ear, and the spell between them was broken. A small tendril of longing, of desperately wanting to be seen again, rose in his chest.

He shoved the feeling back down as quickly as it came.

Looking away, he caught a flash of blue as his father's secretary, a woman he hadn't bothered to learn the name of, hastily made her way to where they stood with a tight, severe expression on her face.

His father must have spotted her too, since a sudden tension radiated from him, and West was surprised it wasn't a tangible thing for how clearly he felt it.

Smiling to the partygoers, his father swiftly wrapped up his brief speech.

"Thank you, everyone, for coming and please enjoy the rest of your evening!"

When his father stepped down from the platform, West followed closely. Out of the corner of his eye, he saw

Amphitrite, small but commanding, maneuvering through the bustling crowd toward them.

Her expression was unreadable.

"I felt something-" Amphitrite started, but her lips sealed once her eyes landed on the secretary.

"I apologize for interrupting, sir," the secretary huffed, trying to catch her breath.

"It's fine, Darla. What happened?"

Darla. West needed to remember the secretary's name if he was going to be working with her.

"There was an incident in the Hydrian Sea. We lost communication for a good hour with the Mystic, but when it came back online... We sent the Vesper out to assist..." Her voice broke. "The Mystic sank, sir."

West stiffened. He knew those ships, had seen them in port enough times to remember their names, but he knew nothing of the crew.

Amphitrite swung around to face his father.

"Why were your ships in the Hydrian sea, Zale?" she asked, her tone flinty and her eyes narrowed.

His father only shook his head, his face hard.

"That ship was set for Alexious, but they should not have been in the Hydrian sea. The route for the Mystic was always through the Beryl Sea and docking on the Western side of the country. It's longer, but it keeps them from the..." he trailed off and looked back to his secretary. "Darla, what other ships have responded?"

"In addition to the Vesper, the Neptune should be arriving now. Your boat is preparing for departure."

"Good. Let them know I'm on my way. I should be there in an hour," Oceanus ordered.

She nodded and darted back into the crowd, moving at a clipped pace in the direction she had just come from. As soon as she disappeared, his father turned to Amphitrite.

"The Mystic should not have been near the dark waters," he told her sternly. "I do not allow my ships to go anywhere near its border in the Hydrian sea. I also do not allow my ships anywhere near the Sereian Empire, no matter what the treaty says."

The Sereian Empire. The place from Devon's past, from the many stories he had shared while they moved around the continent. The place where Devon had shot his commanding officer after catching him violating a woman, which in turn led to Devon's life on the run as a mercenary. By most accounts, the Sereian Empire was brutal, led by a mysterious emperor and represented to the rest of Zephyr by Senator Kiran. They were in a truce with the Sereians, but was his father worried about an attack on one of the ships?

Is that what had happened to the Mystic?

"We'll determine what happened, and who's to blame," Amphitrite promised.

"I'll leave now, and you'll meet me—"

"He needs to go with us. He needs to see this as the incoming CEO," Amphitrite interrupted. His father looked like he wanted to argue, but she continued. "He is going to have to take the lead at some point, Zale."

Through the stress, confusion, and worry, West felt a spike of irritation at being talked about like he wasn't right there. "Go where?"

When they did not answer his question right away, the nerves along the surface of his skin tingled. Some kind of battle of wills was happening between the two of them that he could not see.

"To the site of the shipwreck," Amphitrite finally answered and the look of disdain she shot his father confused him. Why was she angry at his father? "I will take you myself, and your father will go with his crew out to the site."

"Why can't we all go together? Seems wasteful to take more than one ship out there."

Amphitrite rolled her eyes and his father edged closer to whisper near West's ear.

"Amphitrite will open a portal to one of the ships already on the water. The Neptune's skeleton crew knows about us. I have to make a public appearance and she can get you there faster."

Somewhat dazed, West nodded. After his weeks of light jumping, it felt like he should have known that, but using power in a crisis was so much different than in training, or even in casual situations. Before he could say anything, his father was gone, striding across the great hall with purpose.

"Once I let Darren know there is an emergency I have to handle, we can head out," Amphitrite told him. She left quickly, walking to a shadowy alcove near the corner. West's gaze lingered on her, trying to puzzle her out. How could she be so steady in an emergency, yet so easily provoked in conversation? Why was she so angry and damned belligerent when she was capable of being level-headed in a tense situation?

Before West could think any more about her contradictions, she returned. West noted a young woman left the shadows where Amphitrite had just been, heading in the direction of Darren.

Amphitrite grabbed his arm, not giving him a chance to brace himself, and pulled him into a room off the main hallway. She shut the door and quickly embraced him. As soon as her arms wrapped around him, briny mist sprayed his skin.

Vertigo overtook him for a moment, like the feel of an ocean wave rolling beneath, and he realized he was no longer in the room, but on a large shipping barge.

Before he could get his bearings, Amphitrite dropped her arms and rushed to the ship's railing.

The evening light was dim, but he could still see the dark waters, and for the first time in his life, he saw the roiling black waves firsthand. He had heard of them throughout his childhood, as every child in Halcyon had, and learned that the sea had been polluted from the Great War.

The visual was far worse than he could have ever imagined.

The normal deep, blue water around the ship met dark, oily black water, like a border almost. And even though the ocean that night was relatively calm, the dark waters were choppier, churned by a current he couldn't see and a wind he couldn't feel.

"How is the water not... mixing?" he asked, his hands tightening on the ship's railing. The crew was nowhere to be seen, leaving him feeling like they were the only two bodies on the ship. In the distance, he could see the Vesper even closer to the dark waters than they were; no other ship could be seen. An eerie sensation that rose the hairs along the back of his neck.

"I keep them from mixing, but the dark waters push in more and more every day. Maybe only an inch or two here and there, but it grows stronger while I grow weaker."

"Weaker?" he balked. "Why weaker? You look perfectly healthy to me..." He felt a sudden jolt of worry she might take that the wrong way, but her eyes stayed on the Vesper.

"No," she whispered.

His eyes darted back out to where the Vesper was moving far too close to the dark waters, the ship parallel to the line separating dark from light. A dark patch of the water looked to be moving closer to the ship as they sent two divers down for search and rescue.

Closing her eyes, Amphitrite extended her arms, palms out, and the dark patch of water closing in on the Vesper retreated to the border. Looking from the water to her, West noticed sweat beading on her forehead.

When she opened her eyes, they were brightly lit; no whites or pupils existed in those aquamarine pools.

"I hold the line of the water day and night," she rasped, her voice ragged, "but when it bleeds through to the clear water, it takes more to push it back..."

He could hear her teeth grinding as she forced the dark water back, and he wished he could use his own powers to help.

Doing anything now would most likely only cause more issues, so he stood silently as she finished restraining the tainted water. Her hands trembled in the air, and he knew she could not call her Goddess form for help with people nearby on the other ship. She was having to do this with the reserves left in a quickly depleting tank.

She swayed, and he grabbed her as her legs gave out from underneath her. Her entire body trembled, so he took the risk of another slap and pulled her back against his chest. Wrapping his arms around her, he tried to help calm her shaking body; the tremors making her difficult to hold on to.

"Amphitrite?" He gently squeezed her. Something about seeing her so prone made his heartbeat falter. "Amphitrite, what can I do to help?"

"We need you, West," she whispered. "Not just your power. *You.*"

He tightened his hold around her middle, bringing her back against his chest, and her breathing calmed as they both watched the Vesper pull up pieces of what had once been the Mystic.

A deep hollow feeling expanded in his gut, and he knew he couldn't turn away from this any longer. To do so would mean the death of more sailors, and eventually, just as his father said, all of Zephyr.

It looked like it was time for him to grow the hell up.

15

Amphitrite and West followed Oceanus to the last house for the day. This one was a quaint bungalow near the northern docks, close to Oceanus Industries. She could tell children lived here from the toys scattered across the brightly colored porch. A wreath on the front door welcomed them, symbolizing a blessing of the Fates.

Though, the Fates held no blessing for this family today, and the thought made her hands clench into fists. To know they brought such devastating news to these families angered her soul. There was no reason for the Mystic to have been so close to the dark waters, and she was determined to find out who caused such a fate for the crew.

Oceanus knocked softly before straightening his dark blue suit. West stood to the right of her behind his father, his black suit pressed to perfection, hair slicked back, jaw freshly shaven, and eyes that held a sadness she was sure could be seen in hers too.

Reaching over, she grabbed his hand and squeezed. His dark chocolate brown eyes flickered to hers in shock before a small smile appeared and his hand squeezed back. They released each other once the door opened, revealing a woman small in stature, but back straight as she assessed them and why they were on her porch. Amphitrite watched as the woman came to a conclusion, her lip trembling slightly.

"Mrs. Snyder?" Oceanus asked. The petite woman, incredibly small at an inch shorter than Amphitrite herself, blinked up at Oceanus and nodded. "I'm—"

"I already know." Her mossy green eyes glistened with tears. "Sailor's wives talk. Robbie won't be coming back."

Oceanus moved closer, bowing his head slightly.

"I am deeply sorry for-"

"No!" she shouted, catching all three of them off guard by the abrupt change in her demeanor.

"No," she repeated. A tear fell down her cheek, tracing the lines of her grimace. "You don't get to be sorry when I have three small children to feed and no money to do so. He was everything. Our provider, my love, their hero, and now the place that asked so much of him took everything else. So, no, Mr. Murphy, I won't accept your apology, or condolences, until you tell me why you sent him on a suicide mission!"

She heard West's deep inhalation, felt her own heart speed up, and watched Oceanus take a step back in shock.

Now she was going to intervene.

Stepping around Oceanus, she carefully approached her. Mrs. Snyder's tiny frame straightened, and Amphitrite had even more respect for the downtrodden woman.

"My name is Cordelia Wells, and I am the government official in charge of maritime activities in Zephyr," she said gently, trying to put as much warmth into such an official and bland statement as she could.

Mrs. Snyder's expression stayed cold and accusatory. "You standing here next to him means you know why he did it," she whispered.

"To my knowledge, the Mystic was transporting goods on an unplanned route, but I would be interested in hearing what you've heard." She nodded toward the door at the woman's back.

"Amph... Cordelia, I am not sure-"

"I will speak with Mrs. Snyder privately, Mr. Murphy," she said, shooting a look at Oceanus. The widow's suspicions of the circumstances surrounding her husband's death, and

Oceanus Industries' potential involvement, meant she was taking over. Now, this visit was more than bringing news; it was part of her investigation into the shipwreck.

The woman nodded, looking over Amphitrite's shoulders one last time before turning to open the door. Amphitrite did not look back as she followed the woman inside but sensed West trailing closely behind her.

Turning abruptly, she was about to demand he step back outside, but he held his hand up to stop her.

"I need to know what is happening. This involves me as well. It is not only about Oceanus Industries," he stated. His expression was serious and heavy with a memory, and she knew he was referring to their moment out on the sea when she told him she needed him.

Nodding, she turned and followed the woman the rest of the way into her home, hoping she wasn't making a mistake by letting West join her.

But there, beneath the worry, was relief that he had taken the initiative to step up and help her.

The bungalow was smaller than any house West had ever been in before. Small, yet comfortable. It was decorated with family photos and children's artwork. Toys were strewn across the floor much like they were on the porch. The light blue couch Mrs. Snyder offered them to sit on looked like it had seen better days, but it was far more comfortable than the couch he owned and knew his mother had spent far too much money on.

When he sat back, he felt something poking him in the side, and he pulled out a small toy figure of a soldier from between the sagging couch cushions. It reminded him of Devon, and he wondered if his friend in the Underworld had seen the Mystic's sailors yet. He was unsure of the process, but he doubted he could give Mrs. Snyder a chance to say goodbye. Having a friend running the Underworld *should* give them that option, but he doubted it.

"Mrs. Snyder, can you please tell me why you think your husband was sent on a suicide mission?" Amphitrite asked the woman as she seated herself next to West on the couch, and across from where Mrs. Snyder sat in a tattered dark blue chair.

West took in the woman's demeanor, her hunched shoulders, lowered brow, all indicating she had given up hope. And when she looked up, he noticed the skin around her eyes was raw and puffy.

His heart hurt for her at that moment. His losses had not been this close, nor this devastating. They hurt, but they were not a void, not like the kind he could see Mrs. Snyder falling into.

After several beats of silence, Amphitrite stood from the couch and kneeled in front of the widow. It felt surreal to him that a Goddess would do such a thing with a mortal. Were the humans not to kneel before the Gods? For some reason, the sight made him recall his conversation with Devon on the rooftop, just before he returned to Halcyon.

Maybe the Gods did not forsake us...

Perhaps she was acting. She used the name Cordelia to hide her identity. So much of her life was not truly real.

But outside, when she took his hand, no... she had not been Cordelia then.

He watched her as she listened to the grieving woman. And, maybe without even noticing, Amphitrite reflexively spun the Triton ring around her right index finger.

His thoughts mimicked that ring, turning around in his head restlessly.

Wiping tears from her eyes, Mrs. Snyder spoke weakly. "The day before Robbie left, him and our neighbor, another sailor on the Mystic, were talking about how odd it was that the Mystic was going to the Eastern shore of Alexious to pick up supplies. Everyone always knew that Mr. Murphy strictly forbade ships in the Hydrian Sea, so they were confused.

"When our neighbor went to Mr. Murphy, he refused to speak with them. They wouldn't even let him pass through the elevator doors into the executive area. It was odd, since in the past he had always made an effort to hear the concerns of his employees." She glanced to West. "I do hope as far as that goes, the heir would be the same." He lowered his head in acquiescence. He would do anything and everything to make sure nothing like this happened again.

"Once the ship was routed, there was nothing my husband could do short of mutiny," she said, voice breaking. Her eyes lifted to his and he saw a steely resolve in them where there had only been sadness moments ago. "But there's something you can do, Mr. Murphy. Fix this and perhaps my Robbie can have peace."

West admired her fortitude in the face of such adversity. Now the soul provider for her children, she would need to go back to work, find care for her kids, all within a small time frame in order to keep the roof over their heads.

West felt a tear fall down his cheek, and he did nothing to stop it. He had to stand up and be what he was destined to be, no matter how he felt, because people looked to him. People like Mrs. Snyder needed him.

Amphitrite, she needed him, too. Her power weakened every time the dark waters pushed further in. He could've helped her on the Neptune, but instead he wallowed like a small child.

He was done with that behavior, his selfishness.

No more people would die because of him.

"Fix this," Mrs. Snyder demanded fiercely.

He could only nod, but the resolve in it allowed the woman to nod back.

A promise made.

16

Amphitrite was not necessarily surprised, but relieved when West reached out to resume their training. She'd hoped the sight of the dark waters and the loss of the Mystic would motivate him, but she'd also worried that the tragedy would only fuel his resentments toward her and her sisters. It had been several days since their argument in the street, but for some reason, his frustration and pain stuck with her, and she didn't want him to give up again.

And on their first session back, she was late from a meeting that ran over.

Figures, she thought.

Rushing to the back of West's condo, an apology ready on her lips, she abruptly halted at the sight before her.

Amphitrite watched as West made the water dance in a way she had never seen. The beauty of it pulled a gasp from her lips and West whirled around at the sound, yet the water did not fall from his loss of concentration.

"I..." She searched for the words that had just been in her mind before she stumbled upon him using his power. Using it in a way she thought perhaps was beyond a possibility at this point.

West let the water gently fall back and, suddenly, a fine mist sprayed across her face as he appeared in front of her. She blinked up at him, stunned. He'd just light jumped the short distance and the energy around him thrummed with power.

"I've been practicing here and there, but today... I... I'm done," he whispered.

Done? We haven't even started today.

"I am done thinking only of myself, or my pain, or my vengeance," he continued. "I will be CEO of Oceanus and keep the waters safe as a Titan, so there are not anymore widows out there. So that the creatures who rely on us have a chance."

He edged closer to her.

"So, you are not fighting this alone. You have my strength behind you now as well."

Her jaw dropped when West got down on his knees before her.

"West, what are you doing? Get up-"

"I swear I will not abandon the fight." He looked up at her, his eyes clear and focused in a way she had never seen. "I will stand by you, and we *will* return the waters to what it once was. This I promise."

She felt the power of the oath run through her mind and down her spine. His eyes flashed a luminous, deep blue as he stood back up.

Something shifted between the two of them, and she wasn't sure what it was. Even though there were not any words forming in her mind to explain it, it felt substantial.

"I am glad you are in this now. I really am," she finally said, breaking the silence. A small smile formed on his face as a stream of water lifted and encircled them.

"Me, too." He agreed before dousing her in the water and making her scream.

"Oh," she sneered, "you do not know what you've just done, Mr. Murphy."

"Oh, I do," he laughed as both of them drew on the water and launched it at each other.

For the first time, she realized, the training session did not end with screaming, but laughing.

And she could breathe again.

The next afternoon, Amphitrite stood looking out of the window in her office as a coast guard ship came in, docking for the day. She watched the men and women disembark for the evening.

"Been a while," Amphitrite heard from behind her.

She turned and calmly took in the sight of her oldest friend. Medusa leaned against the doorframe, her curly hair and gold jewelry gleaming in the setting sun coming through the window.

"We were both at the gala," Amphitrite reminded her.

"Yes, but so much has happened since then," Medusa countered with a smile.

"Too much," Amphitrite agreed as she moved to sit in her chair while Medusa took the one across the desk from her.

"I'll make this quick. Visitors in the area. Not human," Medusa stated. Around her neck, her necklace shifted of its own accord, revealing a golden snake head over her shoulder. Its tongue flicked out to taste the air before it stilled, looking as if it were just another piece of jewelry.

"Titan?" Her heart stuttered at the thought that they already had more of her father's allies infiltrating their domain.

Nodding, Medusa leaned in.

"The power we feel is throwing off my spies. Some of my people in the military have noticed upheaval. The new general you had us follow..."

And that was what Amphitrite was both hoping and dreading to hear. She had known the general felt different and remembered the sickening gut instinct she'd felt in his presence.

"General Olethros. You think he is a Titan?" Speaking the general's name, Amphitrite could see in her mind the cold eyes and imposing figure the man cut.

Medusa nodded.

"I cannot prove anything," she said, "but my gut says he is. He has suppressed his power, but it is finding cracks. If he is-"

"He could be immensely powerful," Amphitrite finished, her eyes focused on her cutlass in thought. Long ago, she wielded it, and now, it sat on the shelf, collecting dust. Would she need to brandish it once again in the war brewing against the Titans?

"Keep at least two of our people on him and see who we have inside the units he commands." She focused back onto Medusa, who simply nodded. Most likely, she had already taken those steps before coming here. "If we get any more actionable information, we need to alert my sisters and preempt any move he may make against us, or Tartarus."

"And if he shows no signs of association with your father?"

"If that's the case, he'll make himself known. To Hera, at least." She sighed. Really, it was odd they hadn't known the stranger was a Titan, that the general hadn't introduced himself to the Goddesses in charge. Olethros continued to unsettle her, but she moved on to the next concern weighing on her.

"Any information on the wreck?"

"Which one?" Medusa asked as she raised an eyebrow in question.

Amphitrite frowned. "The Mystic," she replied darkly.

"Our eyes in Oceanus have found the original route paperwork. The route was as it should have been, completely avoiding the dark waters and nowhere near Sereian territory. There was no evidence of the route being changed. It looks like the ship took an unauthorized detour."

"What?" Amphitrite stared in shock. "A widow reported to me that the ship's normal route had been changed before departure. She said the sailors tried to contest the rerouting."

"There's a chance the route change was never recorded," she considered.

"Did you send some sirens down to see what they found?" she asked, hoping some of them could tell something from the actual wreckage.

Medusa shook her head.

"The dark waters creep too close. They are unsure of diving near them."

With good reason, Amphitrite thought.

The waters could choke and warp a soul. She thought again of watching the siren being pulled in, her body destroyed within seconds. Amphitrite was thankful her border prevented those who'd fallen to the dark waters from passing back into the healthy waters. Once the dark water had them, they stayed there. She shuddered to think that any of the Mystic's sailors had fallen to that fate. And she knew, without a doubt, that if the Mystic had managed to cross the border into the dark waters entirely, there wouldn't even be a wreck left to analyze.

"I'll go," Amphitrite blurted out, earning a surprised look from Medusa. "I have the power to hold it back, at least temporarily."

"You weaken every day," Medusa reminded, both concerned and admonishing. The woman would have made an amazing, yet strict, mother should she have chosen that course in her life. "If you go, I go with you. I will not leave you to handle this on your own."

"I cannot let us lose more to the darkness. I cannot lose *you* to the darkness, Medusa. We have enough to deal with," she sighed. "I have to get a look at the wreckage. There has to be some physical evidence of what exactly triggered the ship to sink so I can make sure this won't happen again."

Medusa let out a huff of frustration. She knew Amphitrite was right. While she could hold off the dark waters, Medusa could not. "There's no chance you'll just chalk it up to the dark waters? You don't think the power it has just pulled on the hull until it capsized the ship?"

While that was the danger Amphitrite feared with vessels getting too close to the border, after having seen the dark waters' pull in living creatures, she was unsure of its scope to do so to a vessel as large as the Mystic.

She shook her head. "I'm not leaving anything to uncertainty. I need eyes on the wreck."

Medusa chewed on her lip, thinking.

"Ask your sister for the ability to speak to the souls should any still be there," Medusa stated. "I don't like this, Amphitrite, but if you have to go to the wreck, you need to get as much information as possible. I'm not convinced a sunken ship alone is enough to warrant the risk, but I will not stand in your way."

Amphitrite sighed. "I'll talk to Persephone."

Medusa nodded begrudgingly.

"I know you'd rather I stay away from the dark waters altogether, but we are low on options." Amphitrite whispered to her friend.

She knew it was killing Medusa not to go down to the depths of the sea beside her and help her.

Suddenly, Medusa stood, walking around the desk and pulling her into a hug. One that Amphitrite was quick to reciprocate.

"Be safe, my friend," Medusa whispered, and something ominous skittered down Amphitrite's spine.

Yeah, this was a horrid idea, and they both knew it.

But it was all they had right now.

Amphitrite light jumped to her sister's office after her conversation with Medusa. The water dissipated in the air and her sister's straight black hair came into focus. Persephone was looking down at paperwork on her desk, her fingers steepled, a picture of authority.

"Yes?" Persephone ground out, not bothering to look up.

"I need a favor."

Still looking down, she flipped a page. "What kind?"

"I need a way to speak to lost souls," Amphitrite asked bluntly. "Temporarily," she tacked on. "And in the water."

Persephone's gaze darted up, an eyebrow raised, and eyes that gave nothing of her thoughts away.

"Why would you have need of such a thing? You understand that something of this nature would mean you could be exposed to a greater danger than just one lost soul? They would be attracted to you, overwhelming you and potentially, if left on this plane long enough, dangerous."

"I am aware of all that could go wrong, sister. I just need to find out what happened on the ship. All the crew passed on and I need a witness to the events leading up to the wreck."

Persephone sat back in her chair and considered her with a closed expression.

Finally, she rubbed the bridge of her nose between her thumb and forefinger, the sapphire wedding ring on her hand catching the light.

"It would only last a day," she conceded.

"That is fine. I don't think I could deal with the dead for longer than that," Amphitrite responded, earning another raised eyebrow from her sister as she met her eyes across the desk.

Amphitrite covered her blunder with a smirk.

Persephone's gaze held hers, and she wished she could read the emotions behind those eyes. How Devon could ever tell what the woman thought was beyond her. They held a special bond, one that she assumed allowed him in on the inner workings of her sister's mind.

But she also noticed that Persephone seemed different with him. She seemed to let him in, in such a way she never did with her sisters.

At that moment, Amphitrite wished she had what her sister had. An equal to spend eternity with; someone who could see *her*, not just the fragments she allowed. The loneliness she'd felt at the party came over her again. Then, she saw a flash of a smiling, sweet Darren and instantly felt guilty. Why was this suddenly an issue? Was it simply that her sister had a soul bond with Devon? No, this had started far more recently, and she loved that her very stoic, withdrawn sister had someone to make her happy. Even if it sometimes caused little tendrils of green jealousy to cloud her mind when she watched them together.

Shaking away her thoughts, she focused on Persephone.

"Is it a yes or a no? I have very little time-"

"On the condition you do not go alone," Persephone interrupted. She stood as she spoke and walked around the desk to where Amphitrite stood. "I will allow it."

"Who would I take?"

Persephone smiled. "You will take West with you."

"Did Devon tell you-"

Persephone cut her off by slapping her hands onto Amphitrite's shoulders, and power surged into her. Everything went white, her knees buckling as Persephone supported her weight and leaned in to whisper in her ear.

"See you soon, dear sister. And be careful."

Amphitrite tried not to lose the contents of her stomach as her eyelids fell shut.

When she opened her eyes, the sun blared down on her and she was no longer in her sister's office. She blinked rapidly as her vision cleared. Sea gulls flew overhead as her fingers clenched into fists and found sand.

Had her sister not just done her a favor, she would gladly light jump back and punch her.

Grumbling, she pushed herself into a sitting position just as a blue light flashed and mist hit her skin.

Her vision slightly blurry, she saw the figure of a man standing next to her. When her eyes were finally able to focus, she recognized West as he gave her a small smile and offered a hand to assist her.

"Word travels fast," she muttered as she took his hand, letting him help her up.

"No, just great minds. I asked Devon if there was a way I could talk to the dead and here I am, waiting for you." He shrugged. "I figured the only people who would know for certain what happened on the Mystic were the ones who went down with the ship."

"Damn Persephone to Tartarus," Amphitrite swore. "She already knew what I was going to ask." She swept sand off of the back of her jeans, her pale pink sweater a loss after landing on the shore.

Stepping behind her, West snorted and swept a hand across her back, helping to remove the sand. "No, just hoping they had an opportunity to send us together and found one. They are far too powerful together and must be stopped."

She let out a loud laugh, and though she was unable to see West, she could almost feel him smiling behind her. The air was lighter than it should be with the task they had waiting for them.

Moving to stand in front of her, they both lost their smiles as they faced each other. The seriousness of the situation pressing between them.

Instead of an easy grin, concern and seriousness etched itself over West's features. She wondered how he would handle all of what they were about to do.

"Are you sure you want to do this?" she asked, unsure herself of how this would all go.

"Am I sure? No. If I could do this any other way, I would. But those families deserve answers. *I need answers*. I need to know what is happening with my own ships."

She put her hand on his elbow and gave him a light squeeze.

"Then let's go get those answers."

17

West took a deep breath as he focused on turning his body to water. Concentrating first on his feet, he worked his way up his body, letting the tingling sensation of his power move over his skin.

He had been working hard on taking this form and had some serious trial and error.

Emphasis on the *error* part.

At one point in his experiments, he'd accomplished liquefying his leg, but couldn't quite manage all of it, so he'd walked around with a flesh foot on a water body. Another time, he'd somehow half-transformed, appearing like a watercolor portrait of himself.

He only hoped he did not embarrass himself in front of Amphitrite. He wanted, *needed*, to prove he was capable of helping her.

Prove he could be the Guardian he was born to be.

When her eyes widened and her lips parted, he knew he had done it.

"You did it," she whispered into the wind with a small, but genuine, smile. One that spoke of relief that he was holding to his oath, his promise, to her.

Attempting a smile, he realized he wasn't sure facial expressions translated to this form. Another awkward moment he was more than happy she hadn't witnessed. He watched as she transformed herself, becoming a liquid silhouette in the blink of an eye, and started for the waves. As her watery form slipped beneath the surface, he followed.

Once submerged, he cut through the water with thought alone. It was like flying. His body moved where he wanted it to with barely a thought as the current changed with his silent demands. He didn't need to move his arms and legs as if to swim; the ocean listened to his intentions and responded.

Fish and sea creatures of all sizes, even a squid, did not dart away as they normally would if they had been aware a human moved among them. Instead, they just swam alongside them, following their currents. If they had not been on their way to an underwater grave, he would have checked out the coral reef, allowing himself the childhood fascination of seeing such creatures up close. Though when a Mako shark appeared, he had to remember to keep his watery form. Thankfully, the shark did not perceive a threat, and though it moved within an inch of him, it continued on its journey unaware of West.

He could feel the intentions of each creature if he focused solely on them; the shark was merely curious, which relieved him enough to forget its intimidating presence.

Moments later, he caught sight of a massive, broken shape on the seafloor. The metal edges of a broken hull glinted in the few rays of sun that reached through the depths of water.

The Mystic.

A heavy sadness ran through him at the sight. The once large, magnificent ship was reduced to a graveyard beneath the unassumingly calm waves of the surface.

An entire ship, all wood and steel, was crumpled up like a piece of paper.

Something inside of him felt another looming darkness. He turned to where the second sensation was coming from and watched as the dark waters rippled less than a mile away from them. Beneath the surface, the dark waters were an endless wall of shadow. Ambiguous shapes floated through the toxic water, some looking eerily like bone. As he stared, he saw a flash of eyes here and there, and he knew without a doubt that nightmares lay beyond that wall of decay and darkness.

Sadness radiated from the ship.

Evil radiated from the dark waters.

Amphitrite tried to focus on keeping the dark waters away, but it continued to inch forward, almost as if called to the wreckage.

Seeing such a large vessel demolished, as if a giant crushed it in their fist, had stolen her focus just long enough that the waters called West's attention. His watery body gravitated toward the border, seemingly without conscious thought. Her power flowed back out to engulf him in a protective shield, hoping to cut off the dark waters' call. His figure stilled and he turned back toward her.

Pushing forward, knowing West would follow, she took an immense amount of oxygen from the sea around her and pushed the water away, creating a pocket of air so that she and West could speak in their mortal forms.

As they moved into the confines of the pocket, she was impressed he was able to summon himself dry as he took his human form, since that was something that took her far too long in the beginning to grasp.

"What was that?" he asked as he waved his arm at the border she was maintaining.

She stepped forward, the waterlogged deck of the Mystic groaning beneath her.

"That was the dark waters' pull," she said. "Something about its power has allure, so be careful once we head back." She frowned in the direction of the dark water. "You don't want to know what happens if you pass through the border I've created."

He shuddered and nodded. "Thanks. For back there."

She blinked, momentarily distracted. "No problem."

West turned in a slow circle, taking in the destroyed ship.

"I'm not sure what I expected," he said. "But this is far worse."

Amphitrite agreed.

"There are support beams here that are completely twisted," she noted grimly as she looked over the mangled ship beneath her feet, her thoughts disrupted by a blueish glow appearing from her left. West's head snapped in the same direction, so she knew she wasn't the only one seeing it.

A soul. One waiting for a guide to the Underworld.

It was unnerving to see someone who had passed, but beautiful, too. The soul was alight with an inner glow, and her heart lurched at how dull his shine was becoming. He was fading fast, but perhaps what he was going to tell them would allow him to move on. She hoped so, anyway.

"Hello," she greeted gently. She could make out that it was a young man barely out of his teen years. "My name is Amphitrite, and this is West. We are the Guardians of the Sea and are here to see what we can do to help."

West stood next to her, his hand grazing hers as he clenched his fist. He had to hold it together. They could not afford to scare the spirit away; they only had a day with the power to speak to him.

"You can help me go with the others?" the young man whispered with so much hope that it became harder for her to swallow. "I wanted to go when the man came. I just... couldn't get to him. I felt stuck, like I was being pulled back."

"So, you are aware you've passed?" she asked, unsure of how much souls knew. This was all new territory for her.

Perhaps she should have asked Devon or Persephone to come with them.

"Yeah, easy enough to figure out when you see your body stuck under a metal bar, eyes open, face blue…" His voice trailed off as the memory came back to him and he crossed his arms over his chest, his frame shaking slightly.

Closing her eyes, she wondered how Thanatos and Persephone did this every single day. When Persephone had gone to Devon, from what her sister had stated, his mortal body had been in horrible condition when he died.

What had West seen of his best friend's final moments? She hadn't thought of what this might do to him with the memory of death so fresh in his mind.

Opening her eyes once again, she saw the soul hadn't moved but bounced from foot to foot as he looked between her and West.

"I cannot transport souls, but I do know the man who took your crew mates. I will do my best to get you to the other side," she promised.

"I'd like that, miss. I worry that the woman wouldn't let me through since she did all this." He waved his hand out as if they could miss the giant wreck of a ship they were currently standing on.

"Woman?" she asked, stepping closer. The young man hesitated at her approach, but relaxed when he saw she meant no harm.

"Yeah. She looked like… just a woman. Me and the men thought we were hallucinating. She was pretty enough, but turned mean, real quick like."

Amphitrite glanced at West as his eyes narrowed on the man, but he said nothing.

Her heart pounded as she looked back to the soul. "What did she look like? Perhaps you could tell me her hair or eye color?" she asked, praying he had enough memory left to tell her. She was aware that souls lost more and more of themselves the longer they stayed earthside.

"That's the thing. When I first woke up here, I could tell you. Now I just remember big things, not any small things. Seems like every minute I am stuck, I lose something," he said apologetically.

"It's alright," she reassured him. Though she was disheartened by his answer, she did not let it show. It wasn't his fault, and he had suffered enough. "Do you remember if the captain changed the route?"

"I'm just a deckhand, but I doubt it. That man was a stickler for following orders. He did get real confused when the woman said something, like he was hypnotized. Then..."

The man furrowed his brow, like he was trying to pull a long-lost memory to the surface. When he finally seemed to have found it, his eyes moved over to her, large and terrified.

"The sea just opened up and pulled us down. Nothing else after that."

Amphitrite's mind raced, but she tried to give him a smile. He could probably tell it was forced, but she was trying, nonetheless.

"Do you have any family you would like me to speak to?"

A wistful smile crossed his face at that moment.

"Now that I can remember... Me and my dad..." His face fell. "Do me a favor, tell my mom, Misha Cornish, that I love her fiercely and to stay tough. Dad did, too, and I am sorry she lost us both at the same time. Tell her to make sure she stays close with Maggie, our neighbor's wife. They are gonna need each other. Misha Cornish, can you remember that?"

"Misha Cornish and Maggie."

"Yeah, Mags is great and tough as nails. Her husband... he left her with the littles, but she will make it. Just, yeah, just tell them. Tell my Ma that. And my neighbor's wife, Maggie Snyder... can you tell her Robbie died loving her? He'd want her to know that."

18

O nce West hit the shore, he couldn't contain it anymore. A surge of power left him in his anger, pushing the water back from the shoreline and leaving fish flopping on the sand in an effort to find the sea again.

"West, what-" Amphitrite tried to talk to him, but he spun on her, his fists tight in anger.

"Their deaths were unnecessary! Families have to carry on in their absence because someone fucking did this to them. And if it was someone at Oceanus..." He growled and clenched his fists so tight his knuckles were white.

"You have to calm down before you create a tsunami! Look!" she shouted, grabbing his shoulders and turning him to face the shore. The water was drawing back, sinking away to build up a massive wave.

Breathing in and out, he calmed himself. He would not be responsible for anyone's death. Halcyon and its citizens were dealing with enough.

With steadiness he did not feel, he turned to Amphitrite.

"I've watched two people die, Amphitrite. Seeing that young man..." He shook his head. "This isn't right. What he said... someone is responsible for the ship sinking. For the route sending them into dangerous waters. For capsizing the ship. And I need to find out who."

"We will, West—"

"No," he said sharply, shaking his head. "You had nothing to do with that ship sinking. It was my company's ship, and therefore, I should be held accountable."

"You're wrong," she said fiercely. "Did you hear what that soul said? A woman hypnotized the captain and brought down the ship. We're dealing with an empowered individual and that's my responsibility, too. Besides, you only just took the job as CEO—"

"So?" he growled. "I should just sit back, then? I'm tired of sitting back and watching."

"We can work *together*, West," she stressed. "Together, we can investigate the rerouting. We can figure out who's behind this."

West prowled towards her, his face a mask of simmering rage she had never seen on him before.

"If we find out who is responsible for the crew's deaths, I promise I will punish them with all the power I have," he seethed, and his eyes lit up, illuminating her face in blue light, as if he had sworn an oath to the universe itself.

Amphitrite took a step back from him, her face paled in response to his words.

He forged on. "If I am such a powerful Titan, I should damn well be able to find out the why and how of this to stop it from happening again. What use is my power if I can't?"

She only stared at him, her irises shining aquamarine. He could see her working through her own thoughts, but he hadn't the slightest idea of what they were.

"Tread carefully, Titan," she said, her voice low with warning. "We may have power, but we are not the Moirai or Chaos where we may tamper with the mortals' timelines."

Tilting his head to the side, he looked at her.

"Fuck the Moirai. Fuck Chaos. I am done waiting for others to come to the rescue. You want me to stand up and work to fix this? Then get out of my way, Sea Goddess, and let me do my damn job."

He disappeared before anything further could leave her lips.

Concern rushed through Amphitrite.

What was West going to do?

Light jumping to her home, she fell onto the couch in her living room as anxiety froze her blood to ice. The outing had spiraled out of control so quickly. As soon as Thanatos had shown up at the wreck to transport the soul, West had taken off and she'd struggled to keep up as she followed him to shore.

Something that any other day would have impressed her.

West's final words before departing were going to keep her up until morning. Logically, she knew he couldn't do anything in the span of a night, yet it tugged on her mind and set her on edge.

Normally, her home calmed her, but she struggled to settle down. Her little house was hidden away in a sea cave, and it had been her sanctuary for centuries. It was built to be one with the environment. The rooms were oriented toward the small beach at the cave's mouth, and part of the floor was open to the water, allowing her beloved creatures to visit.

This evening, the water was clear and glowing with tiny, bioluminescent sea critters. The lapping waves cast beautiful patterns on her white stone walls that she would have enjoyed so much more if she hadn't felt so horribly conflicted.

A neigh from below stirred her from her morose thoughts and she peered over the back of the couch to see one of her beloved hippocampi looking up at her. Ingrid blinked in question, her split eyelids moving separately; horizontal and vertical.

"It's been a day, for sure. Where is Zeus?" Amphitrite asked as she lowered her chin onto her folded arms along the back of the couch.

Ingrid shook her head, shaking the fins along her long horse head that grew there instead of a mane.

She glanced at the clock on the wall and realized her mistake.

Ah, much like his namesake Hera, Zeus went sullen when things did not go his way. That was how he had earned his name, after all. The fact she had missed their weekly run had obviously made him surly. She felt the same and thought perhaps they could sulk together this evening.

"Is it too late?" she asked Ingrid, hoping she could make up for at least this one tiny mistake in the scheme of all of them. She needed to let West decompress and sitting around worrying wouldn't do any good. There was nothing he could do until tomorrow and she would remind herself all night long if need be.

Ingrid answered by diving into the water, her long fishlike tail splashing Amphitrite as she disappeared beneath.

Smiling, Amphitrite stood from the couch and dove into the water after Ingrid, following her through the tunnels of the cave beneath her residence out into the open sea.

Zeus waited at the opening of the cave in his ephemeral form, a barely visible silhouette of water. He always went into this form when he was mad; he did not want anyone to touch him. When he saw her, he stamped his front hooves agitatedly, only managing to disperse the water around him with his tantrum.

Amphitrite laid her hand over her heart in apology as Zeus approached her, morphing into a tangible creature once again and nuzzling his horse-like head into her shoulder.

Forgiven.

She smiled and gave him a peck on the center of his head. Ingrid took off, annoyed at the display.

Maybe I should have named her Persephone, she thought as she took off after the exasperated hippocampus.

Zeus moved quickly alongside her, nudging her with his nose over and over until she relented and allowed him to carry her on his back. Staying in her mortal form, she straddled the hippocampus and leaned forward to hold onto his neck as his speed increased.

Schools of fish darted out of the way as Ingrid and Zeus raced around the sea floor, weaving in and out of currents.

As they played, she noticed they were nearing the shore. The hippocampi broke the surface and climbed onto the sand as mortal horses. Their mercurial coats shone in the moonlight as they ran along the beach, kicking up the sand beneath them.

Amphitrite took a deep breath and closed her eyes, enjoying the evening ride with her beloved creatures. She spread her arms wide, feeling free even though she knew her responsibilities would be waiting for her tomorrow. Her fingers closed on the wind, trying to hold onto that freedom for this one moment before the world came crashing back down around her.

And just like this moment of unrestrained freedom, the wind slipped through her grasp.

Page after page of nothing.

West knew it was futile at this point to find anything in the records indicating why the Mystic had been off course. Why had they been so close to the dark waters in the first place?

Reports were coming in from the Maritime Administration, signed off by Cordelia Wells, which had the statements of both the sailors on the Vesper and Coast Guard.

And no one had a bloody clue as to why the ship sank. No record of a woman on board. Nothing stating any route change. Nothing mentioning why the ship's captain would take them off route.

Over and over again, the pages read the same.

Inconclusive.

Putting his face in his hands, he tried not to scream out his frustration. He had been reading through anything and everything in relation to the ship since three this morning when he'd finally given up on the pretense of sleep.

A knock on the door broke him of his wallowing and Darla appeared, her graying brown hair held up with a pencil, and her soft and kind brown eyes apologetic.

"Sorry to bother you, sir, but you have a ten o'clock meeting with an analyst from the Board of Transportation Safety."

Looking at the clock, he realized he had been at this far longer than he thought. When he nodded to Darla, she opened the door wider to let the analyst in, and West stood, straightening out his suit.

He almost swallowed his tongue when a striking woman in a pencil skirt, wearing it much tighter than many women in his office did, walked in. Her long dark brown hair was pulled back into a low ponytail, and her eyes were a rich brown, much like his own.

"Mr. Murphy," she greeted, walking towards him with her hand extended. "My name is Mira Flint. I am here to speak with you about the incident involving the shipping vessel, the Mystic."

Shaking her hand, he tried to find his words, but the rich depth of her eyes mesmerized him, pulling him from the moment.

Clearing his throat, he broke eye contact, and dropped her hand before gesturing to the chair in front of his desk. "Please have a seat."

Barely restraining an eye roll at his internal fumbling, he seated himself behind his desk. He was West Murphy, for Fate's sake. He'd used charm to get his way for years, and it did not disappear overnight. This was an opportunity to find out something, anything, about the wreck.

And it looked like he would need to use it again to get as much information from her as she obviously planned to get from him.

He really wanted a drink right now. Really, really did.

Folding his hands on his desk, he gave her the trademark Weston Murphy smirk that he had perfected in adolescence.

"How can I help you, Mrs. Flint?"

"Ms. Flint, please. I'm no longer married."

West smiled at her obvious ploy.

"I assume you've spoken with Cordelia Wells?" he asked as he moved into a pose of effortless masculinity that had yet to fail him. Leaning back with his elbow on the edge of his desk, he adjusted his tie before tapping his fingers on the wood.

"I have not spoken with the Maritime Administrator yet, no, but I will be speaking to her soon enough. For now, I would like to discuss the incident with you *personally*, Mr. Murphy."

Hook. Line. Sinker.

"I know that Oceanus Industries has a strict policy in place on the exact routes their vessels take while in the process of transporting goods," she said. "I also know that the Mystic was well beyond the route it was assigned."

"Correct, Ms. Flint," he said with a nod. "I have reviewed all the paperwork related to the Mystic. The shipping plans, the crew lists, any communications to or from the ship, and the orders to respond to the distress signal. And I have yet to find anything that indicates the Mystic was sent into the waters where the ship sank."

Her eyebrows rose delicately. "You mean to say there's no internal record of the ship recharting?"

West paused. "I spoke to a family member of one of the fallen sailors," he told her, trying to hold firm and keep the sadness from leaking through. To not let the internal anger dictate his words, as they had last night with Amphitrite, knowing he had so much at stake in this discussion. "The wife stated they had been informed of a route change prior to the ship leaving the docks."

She let out a dry laugh that caught him off guard. Hackles raised, he narrowed his eyes at her, but she only shrugged.

"You're new to the job, so I'll tell you one thing," she said. "Families in grief look for someone to hold accountable, and they never want to pin it on one of their own. Your internal records didn't indicate a route change, and neither do the government's. The transportation logs show the Mystic diverging from the planned route early in the trip, which means Oceanus is not responsible for the tragic event that took place. No, sadly, we've been seeing some incidents recently that are concerning, but no fault of any one person."

"What do you mean?" he asked. It made absolutely no sense why a ship would go so far off course without intervention of some kind.

"A recent wind pattern is blowing fumes from the polluted water closer to the coast," she explained. "We have reports of crews losing focus, experiencing mental fatigue, and even some mild hallucinations. Who knows what toxic chemicals are in there?"

West leaned forward. "That doesn't make any sense. You are saying that there are chemicals leeching from the water and causing people to wreck their own ships? Have you *seen* the Mystic?" he asked, dumbfounded at her blasé approach to the situation.

"Capsizing a ship is certainly an escalation of the symptoms, yes, but I think it is pretty obvious that the waters are dangerous. Soon, it will be too perilous for navigation. It's a wonder the pollution stayed back as long as it has, and it is only natural that it moves closer, which is how a ship might be caught in it."

A sudden tension ran down his neck and into his back. Something felt off about what she was saying. Everyone knew that the dark waters were there, a byproduct of the Great War that decimated the human population, but did this government official know more?

"The routes will need to be changed if that's the case," he stated, leaning back in his chair.

Ms. Flint gave him a nod of confirmation at his statement.

"Yes, as the pollution changes location, so the routes must change, too. I will be happy to send a team from the Safety Board to assist Oceanus Industries in rerouting ships." She stood, putting her hand out to shake once more.

Standing, he matched her stance and accepted her handshake, eyeing her carefully. "Thank you, Ms. Flint. If you have need of anything else, please let my assistant Darla know. I'll put my dispatchers and upper management in touch with the team you assemble."

Ms. Flint nodded and dropped his hand.

"It was nice to meet you, Mr. Murphy, even under such circumstances," she said. "As we all know, the sea is capable of anything. Remember that." Grabbing her briefcase, she turned to leave. "I will send you my final report on the incident."

He narrowed his eyes.

"That's it? You are sending a team to reroute and its case closed on the Mystic?"

Stopping before the closed door, she turned to look at him over her shoulder.

"On your end? Yes. Now, the Maritime Administration? That battle is far from over."

19

Amphitrite stared at the woman sitting in her office as she walked in, coffee in hand, to start what she thought was a meeting free morning.

"Can I help you?" she asked. Mallory wasn't at her desk yet, busy making coffee and grabbing the reports from dispatch, since there were no early morning appointments to handle. Or so she thought.

The woman swung her dark head of hair, her dark brown eyes holding something close to a challenge in them as she stood, holding out a hand that Amphitrite reluctantly accepted.

"Good morning, Ms. Wells. My name is Mira Flint, and I am here on behalf of the Transportation Safety board."

Damn the Fates.

"And how can I help you, Ms. Flint?" she asked as she released the woman's hand and moved to stand behind her desk. She wanted this over with as quickly as possible. "If this is regarding the Mystic, I sent over all my records concerning the ship, including the ones from dispatch to the coast guard for search and rescue. I am not sure what else I have to add."

"Nothing. I closed the case with Mr. Murphy less than an hour ago."

Amphitrite froze.

"I am sorry, you did what now?"

"You should receive an official statement this week that the case was closed. Mr. Murphy and I agreed that the fumes from ocean pollution compromised the ship's captain. A chemical in the waste is causing psychological effects among those who are at sea."

Amphitrite schooled her expression. She knew very well that the dark waters had a pull on those who neared the border, but she hadn't heard any reports of sailors experiencing such effects. Not to the point of it being a classified phenomenon among humans, and not to the degree that sailors would change the route and sink their own ship.

"And Mr. Murphy agreed to all this?" Amphitrite asked, but she knew the woman was lying. If he had, it was to have the investigation closed so he could do his own. No, she knew he would not settle it here and call it a day. He had been far too worked up last night for that.

"Yes."

"Then, Ms. Flint, why are you in my office without an appointment?" she asked, keeping an eye on the woman.

"Because this is going to be an ongoing problem and the safety board is unsure if you are up to the task of handling it. We need someone in this position who knows what to do should the pollution move closer to the population."

Amphitrite's blood boiled as she planted her hands on the desk and leaned forward.

"You have no idea how competent I am and that I am perfectly capable of handling this moving forward."

"I am sure you think so, Ms. Wells," she returned, giving Amphitrite a condescending smile before she stood from her seat. "But we will be keeping a close eye on the Maritime Administration from now on. Should there be more wrecks, we will petition the Archon to remove you from this position."

Amphitrite smiled with all her teeth.

"Go ahead. I dare you."

Dr. Alden watched West as he tapped out his usual cadence with his pen in thought.

"It's impressive that you managed to put your grief behind you to take on the role at your father's company," he said from his usual seat, the chair across from West.

West stared down at his fingers.

"I had no choice. People needed help and I was the only one who could do anything," he murmured. He looked up as he spoke, but Dr. Alden's face gave nothing away.

"You always have a choice. In any situation."

Shaking his head, West looked out the window to the forest; the trees were starting to bloom again after the semi-winter in Halcyon. He thought of Devon, having gone through his own dark winter and blooming again after.

A laugh escaped his throat and Dr. Alden raised his eyes to West in question.

"Sorry, I was having a poetic moment. Internal sonnets and all that."

Looking around the room instead of elaborating, he noted nothing ever changed. The man had to be an absolute freak about where things went, since everything in his office was simple and uncluttered. It was like he was... static.

After another long, awkward silence, Dr. Alden leaned forward, his elbows on his knees.

"Mr. Murphy, let's cut this down to the heart of it. You are here to work through your trauma. If you would prefer to make progress on your own, fine, I get paid whether or not you talk. So, please do not delude yourself into thinking I will not happily sit here while you stare out the window. However, that is not going to help you, now is it?"

West stayed perfectly still as he met the doctor's gaze head-on, when a wild thought popped into his head and, before he could consider the consequences, he was rolling with it.

Leaning forward, he mirrored the doctor as he put his own elbows on his knees and smirked.

"The stuff I said my father lied to me about? Well, my dad is a Titan, like the ones from your history books, and he controls the seas," West leaned back against the couch again before he continued. "I am taking over, both with the ocean and the company. Not only that, but his company has people dying in freak accidents. People with families. So, as the new CEO, it is my job to find this person and make them pay for the deaths of the sailors. Just as I did-"

He cut himself off and looked back out the window, feeling lost in that moment.

Dr. Alden didn't move, just watched West with a closed expression and in complete stillness.

After a beat of silence, Dr. Alden tapped the pen to the notepad once. Something he did when West gave him some interesting new information.

Looking back at the doctor, West watched him in return. He was such a man in control of himself and the world around him; it made West want to break that all down and burn it.

"Let's go with this as if it is all true," Dr. Alden started, making West snort out a laugh. "You think your father is a man who controls the providence of our world through the water, and now you must step into his shoes. It does seem to be a big adjustment, but is that truly why you walked through that door? Your father is still here to help you move into a job you've known was yours since the cradle." He shook his head. "No, I believe something deeper is at work here. What happened before your father admitted to his dishonesty?"

Well, crap. He hadn't expected the doc to move right on past fantasy land. It figured the man would want to play with the possible delusion a bit longer.

Wetting his suddenly dry lips, he looked out the window once more. The silence was heavy again, and this time, West was completely out of his depth.

"I..." He felt like an idiot, an idiot with his ribcage ripped wide open and his heart vulnerable to anyone nearby.

Tap. The pen hit the pad again.

"I failed... I've..." Why couldn't he speak?

Tap. He needed to get that pen and throw it out the window, but that wouldn't help him with his thoughts right now. His stomach started churning and the hairs along his arms stood up as a charge of anxiety moved through him. He did not want to rehash this, but something in him was pushing it to the surface against his will.

"Fuck!" West roared, shoving his hands into his hair. "Fuck it!"

He threw his head back to glare at the ceiling before looking at Dr. Alden, who continued to sit serenely, his focus solely on West as if he wasn't having a breakdown right in front of him.

"I am tasked with protecting the ocean. *The fucking ocean!* I cannot possibly be the right man for the job when I have only ever failed to protect. I failed to protect a woman from rapists, myself from getting beaten and stabbed, my best friend from dying, and now... I have to protect something so critical to our world? Is this a cosmic joke?" He let out a tired, deranged chuckle.

"Which of your perceived failures happened first?" Dr. Alden asked.

Tap. Tap.

Arg! That damn pen, West thought.

"The woman I was with one night... she led me into a trap. Men were waiting to kidnap me and hold me hostage, all for a ransom. Before she could get her cut, they turned on her. She was raped by the same men she worked with to capture me. I watched while they took her, abused her."

"I assume they held you back?"

"Yeah, they restrained me, beat me bloody while I tried to get to her. She was in on the abduction and... they felt like she was disposable and not worth splitting my reward money with."

"How long ago was this?" he asked, making notes.

West stared at nothing; his eyes unfocused as he let the memory wash over him.

"The day before my twenty-first birthday," he answered, swallowing down bile. "I left right after to hunt them down. I met my friend..." He let the thought trail off.

"The same one who had died?" Dr. Alden leaned forward. It was the first time West had seen a spark of interest in the almost robotic man.

"Yeah, I looked for a mercenary to financially back and team up with, and I found Devon. He was at a pub, drinking but not yet drunk. He didn't seem to be the same soulless killer as the other ones I had run into. I offered him the money upfront, and he hesitated," West let out a small, sad chuckle at the memory. "It was a lot of money, too. I could tell he didn't want to accept, didn't seem suited to it, but he just shrugged. Told me he didn't have any better options.

"He had me help with getaway and surveillance but wouldn't let me kill the marks. Told me my soul was still unstained and I should keep it that way. We became close, and then, after the last man in that warehouse was taken care of... he was killed."

"Devon was?" Dr. Alden quietly asked.

West could only nod as tears flooded his eyes at the memory of his friend lying on the floor, bullets having torn through him, his eyes unfocused and breathing shallow.

As he watched the last of Devon's life drain from him.

As West cried in true pain and loss for the first time in his life.

The room was heavy with silence, the doctor pensive as he sat back in his chair, putting his paper and damnable pen down. Reaching up, Dr. Alden pulled his glasses off his face, cleaning them on his flannel shirt.

"A group of people made the choice to take you captive for financial gain. One of the captors was horribly beaten, abused, and murdered, yet you felt like you should have protected her when she betrayed you..." Dr. Alden put his glasses back on before holding up a hand to stop West from interrupting. "You felt the need to avenge the woman who betrayed you and found the man who would become your best friend. Your best friend passed, which led to you returning home in which you will now take over the mantle of... protecting the ocean. The job you say you were born to do."

West could only nod, surprised the man was playing along with this. It all sounded so crazy to him, and he was the one living it.

"How do you think you could have protected these people from their fates? Do you assume you can control the universe and human will?"

West only stared at Dr. Alden as he put words to the feelings he had taken deep inside of himself for far too long.

"It doesn't sound to me like you failed at anything. You went about your version of justice and found a way. While not legal nor morally correct, I cannot see fault. I think the only true issue here is not your perceived failure, but your lack of understanding of your own capabilities due to a life of never needing to do anything but exist. And that is where we will start."

Frustration poured through her veins as Amphitrite made her way to Darren's place. Her workday had been ruined after Ms. Flint's unpleasant visit that morning and the fact that she had no new information about the Mystic. She should be back at work figuring out a way to gather the needed information, but her calendar indicated she had been neglecting Darren for far too long.

And the worst girlfriend award goes to...

Using her key, she pushed open the door and stopped in her tracks at the calm, meditative music playing. Shutting the door quietly behind her, she silently walked into his living room and took in the cozy space. The room glowed with the light from far too many candles, a fire hazard to be sure, yet she didn't care. The ambience was relaxing and just what she needed after a day like today.

Darren stepped out of his kitchen wearing pajama pants and a college shirt, holding two glasses of wine.

"I know I talked about us going out for dinner, but you have been so busy and stressed, I thought a night in would do you some good," he said with a smile as he placed the two glasses of red on the coffee table. Straightening, he greeted her with his arms wide open, and she was falling into them before she even realized she had moved.

"You can talk to me, Cordelia," he whispered as he held her, one hand rubbing up and down her spine.

Cordelia.

Her heart broke at the false name and shattered the spell of comfort she always fell into around him. He didn't know the real her. He was holding the woman he knew as Cordelia, who was only in her mid-twenties and had no family to speak of.

It was all a lie.

Feeling a tear slip down her cheek, she held onto Darren a little longer until she had control of herself and let the tear dry against his shirt.

Stepping out of his embrace, she smiled at him.

"Shall we have dinner?" she asked, but she didn't wait for him to answer as she walked around the coffee table and sat on the couch, taking a sip of her wine.

He lowered himself next to her, leaning back on the couch with his arm stretched out behind her. For the first time in their relationship, she felt awkward pressing her side against his. The hug was one thing, friendly, but this felt more intimate and somehow wrong.

And she knew then that this was why her sisters never bothered with relationships.

"Yes, I have some chicken in the oven. I thought we could talk. If you have anything you want to-"

"What do you get out of this, Darren?" she blurted out. "Our relationship? I hold things back from you. I have never invited you to my place... I am not the best girlfriend." She spun around to face him and held her finger up, knowing Darren would not let her speak unkindly about herself. "Don't. I am not and I know it. You are perfect and I am barely able to... say..." she found her words failing her.

Sitting up, he took her hands in his.

"Perfect, huh?" He shook his head and laughed. "Well, I know for sure you're not in love with me if you think that way. And that's okay. You were very truthful from the beginning that this was not a long-term thing. I think we just fell into a nice companionship; one I have been enjoying. I may have strong feelings for you, but I don't expect the same from you in return. I've waited for an invitation... but I can tell you hold your cards close to your chest."

"It's been a year, Darren. Not sure how many red flags I can give off before you realize this isn't worth it."

"Well, good thing I didn't propose marriage," he replied with a laugh and his handsome smile pushed her frustration to the surface.

"How? How can you be so even keel about this? And why does thinking you're perfect mean I couldn't love you?"

Still smiling, he shrugged a shoulder.

"I am even keel because I know you're not mine, but you're here and I will enjoy my time with you while it lasts. As for the perfect part, well, it means you don't really see me. I have flaws, Cordelia. A lot of them, but you don't see that because you are only looking at superficial aspects of us. That I say the right words or try to think of romantic things to do. If we lived together, if you were invested deeper, you'd see that I am forgetful. I lose my keys once a week and tear everything apart to get them. I forget to close the bathroom door half the time..."

Amphitrite snorted, before covering her face in embarrassment. He let out a little laugh as he pulled her hands away from her face.

"I am disgusting. An animal really..."

She laughed again as he tucked a piece of hair behind her ear.

"But..." he continued, and she was pulled back to that moment with that one word, "if you cannot see that, cannot be annoyed by it and at the end of the day say, 'That's my person, disgusting animal that he is'... it's not love."

The laughter in her throat turned into a burning sensation. "Oh, Darren..." she whispered.

"Nope, not tonight. Tonight, we eat and watch something terribly crappy from the pre-war era," he said as he stood to check on the chicken, and Amphitrite settled back on the couch.

He was completely right, and she wished with every part of herself that she could feel that deep connection with him. But hours later, when their stomachs were full and the movie was finished, he let her rest her head on his shoulder as they relaxed, and she knew that her feelings for Darren wouldn't change. She imagined the relationship Darren had described. Knowing a person's flaws, annoying and infuriating, and still caring. Seeing flaws that did not detract from the pull she tried her hardest to ignore. Would continue to ignore.

West.

20

The sun had set when West had left Dr. Alden's office, and after an immense session of the doctor blasting apart his psyche and digging into his past, he'd felt like a tiny, tired child. Dr. Alden was not human and had to be some kind of evil mind reader with what West assumed was an origin story befitting the most notorious of villains.

Sitting on his back deck that opened to the Thalassian sea, West took a drink of seltzer water, which tasted like piss, but it was all he had. After speaking to the soul on the wrecked ship, he had a moment of hysteria and dumped all his alcohol.

Which is why he was trying to relax the best he could while sober, as he leaned back in the Adirondack chair on his deck and watched the waves crash in. This ritual used to calm him, but now he was only reminded of the colossal mountain of responsibility weighing down on his shoulders.

Digging into his front pocket, West withdrew a tiny toy. The little metallic object was a sailboat, a historic model. He lifted the toy up close to his face and it glinted in the waning sunlight.

It was the toy he had taken from the first shipwreck, when he'd learned to breathe underwater with Amphitrite. He'd kept it with him since, but he hadn't been able to find the owners. Instead, the little toy had become a talisman for him. He brushed his fingers over it in his pocket when he needed a reminder on why he was going to be the Guardian, the Titan, he needed to be.

A green light flashed in his periphery, announcing his best friend's arrival. He pushed the boat back into his pocket as the leaves and light disappeared, leaving Devon sitting in the chair next to him.

"Why bother with doors, huh?" West asked, not looking at Devon. "I could have been indecent or doing something embarrassing."

"If I was worried about catching you doing something embarrassing, I would never visit. Plus, blackmail is a handy thing to have."

West tilted his glass to Devon in concession.

"Got me there." West took a sip, then looked at Devon. "Out with it, asshole."

Devon raised a brow and said, "I heard the trip to the shipwreck didn't go well."

West frowned, another wave of exhaustion hitting him. "That's an understatement."

"What happened?"

"I, well I, kind of lost it. I just... wanted revenge. I wanted to punish whoever sank the Mystic. Still do," he admitted.

Devon sighed before turning to look out at the ocean. Several yards away, a heron went about its business over the water, the bird a mere shadow in the darkening sky.

"Say it. Shit, I don't remember having to prompt you so much to speak before you died."

Ignoring West's jab, Devon shook his head a little before pushing a hand through his hair and turning slightly to look at West.

"You sound like you did before," he said. "Craving punishment." He pressed forward, making West meet his eyes. "Don't take that on yourself, West."

Devon sounded like Amphitrite now and West threw his hands up in the air. "So, I should just give up, then? What do you people want from me? If I don't take responsibility, it's all about how I have to step up. I do take responsibility, and now I should step back!"

Shaking his head, Devon stopped him. "It's not stepping back," he said. "Focus on figuring out what happened, finding who could be at fault. If there's justice to be had, then pursue it. But revenge and punishment aren't justice for the sailors. It's for you."

West clenched his hands on the arm rests, his knuckles going white. "It's the only thing keeping me going, Devon." He swallowed. "You didn't see the ship or hear the soul's account. Someone rerouted the Mystic into dangerous waters without Oceanus headquarters knowing. And someone brought it down. Someone with powers."

Devon's brows furrowed. "Did the soul give any details?"

"A woman. That's all he could remember," West replied and his friend's frown deepened.

"If it's another move from the Titans, I cannot take the chance of losing Persephone again," Devon whispered with so much vulnerability it actually hurt West. He looked at Devon's arm, right where he knew the serpent soulbond marked him under his green long-sleeve shirt, connecting him to Persephone.

"You won't," he told him. "I'm not letting this mystery woman get away with it. Titan or not." Devon gave him another warning look, but West waved it away. "I want revenge, yes, but that's not it... I'm in this now. A Guardian, a Titan, whatever. I need to take care of this. *With* Amphitrite."

Devon paused thoughtfully. "I understand that."

"I've got your back now, Devon, and with me, the all mighty and powerful West-"

"Dumbass," Devon chuckled, the tension leaving his shoulders.

"All will be well under my watch!" West lifted the glass of seltzer in mock triumph.

They both quieted as a knock on the door sounded through the house.

West stood up from the deck chair. "At least someone knows what a door is for," he muttered.

Shaking his head, Devon stood up and followed.

As they walked to the front, Devon shoulder-checked West, and he felt their camaraderie coming back after the discomfort of the past several months. Something West didn't realize he needed so much until that moment.

Opening the door, West tensed up again at the sight of Amphitrite on his doorstep.

She glanced over his shoulder and offered a small wave. "Hey, Devon." Then settled her attention on West. "Can we talk?"

"I'll just get out of here," Devon said. "Maybe you can help him be less of a crybaby." He stepped back, readying to light jump.

West looked at Amphitrite.

"I don't cry."

"There were tears," Devon stated. Amphitrite stayed quiet, only raising her eyebrows with her lips pressed together in a thin line.

"Okay, maybe I did a little when—"

"A lot."

West shot him a look. "You can leave now."

Winking at Amphitrite, Devon disappeared in a flash of green light.

Standing in silence, West and Amphitrite stared at each other, an obvious tension, and the curiosity of who would break it thickened the air.

"You're sober." She blurted out, making him laugh.

"Yeah, surprising huh?" He held up his seltzer. "Just fancy rich boy water."

"I didn't mean-"

He waved away her apology. "I haven't drank since the Mystic went down. I took all my alcohol and dumped it. I am finding my behavior becomes even more annoying with every drink that crosses my lips, especially in the presence of a certain Goddess." He looked her squarely in the eyes as he finished the statement.

"I've been concerned..." she trailed off as she bit down on her lip, worrying it.

"That I was going to go off on another rage filled march of vengeance across the continent?"

"I was a bit less dramatic in my thinking, but yes. I've been worried."

Shaking his head, he moved aside to let her into his condo. She smiled a little as she stepped in, brushing past him, and he caught a whiff of coconut. Was it her shampoo or just her? He shook himself, knowing those thoughts led to lustful fantasies. Nope. Not the time.

Focus, Murphy.

"Well, I am going to do this the right way this time. Me and you are going to handle this as a team."

She spun around to look at him.

"A team?"

He nodded. "Teamwork makes the dream work, right?"

"What an archaic saying." She laughed.

"Go team." he replied with a devilish smile.

Amphitrite followed West out to the beach with the bottle of seltzer water he had offered her. Stopping at the water's edge, she wished the moon gave off more light so she could see the amber specks she knew were in those dark chocolate eyes. But looking into his eyes was dangerous for what she came to say. The moon must have known she came to air out her sins and she sent a silent thank you to Chaos.

West shuffled in the sand beside her. "So, what brings you here?"

She needed to be honest with him and she looked to the ocean for the strength to speak. Never had she told another all of her secrets, but it was time. He needed to know everything if they were to be equals.

"We haven't spoken since we talked to the sailor," she said, angling toward him. "I understand your anger, and it is justified. I haven't been very understanding of it, mostly because of my past and partly because I am just not that great of a person. You've been handed so much in such a small amount of time and while my story started off one way, it does not invalidate yours. It is just... different." Her eyes moved from the crashing waves to his face. "I promise not to compare and judge any longer... and West?"

His gaze flicked over her face before moving back to her eyes. "Yes?"

She found the courage to hold his stare when she spoke all her truths. He had lost confidence in her as a Goddess because of everything that had gone down recently, and she needed him to know what was happening behind the scenes. To know *her*. She needed to restore his confidence in both of them. Her own confidence, as well. She could no longer act like she was unaffected or not at fault for what happened between her and West.

"I am so sorry about what happened to you and your date in that warehouse so long ago. If I had been... if I had been able, I would've done what I could to stop it. I may control the waters, but as much as I want to, I cannot control the will and evil of mankind."

West looked down at her, his eyes roaming her face once more, and she wondered if he even heard her. She caught something in his eyes, as if a memory surfaced.

"How do you know everything that happened that night?" He turned to face her fully, his eyes narrowed.

A perfect segue for her, yet she still hesitated. Swallowing, she gathered her willpower and pushed on.

"I am more than I seem. I am the spymaster of all of Halcyon and Zephyr. My own sisters... they may know, but I never speak of it with them. I have a network of people who branch into all levels and places of our political climate, our social environment, our day-to-day citizens and activities."

His jaw dropped, his hands going loose at his sides before he pulled himself together and crossed his arms.

"You... are in charge of a legion of spies?" he asked. His voice held no inflection, completely monotone, like she might expect of Persephone.

She swallowed her fear and nodded.

"I have been for a very long time. I do it from an office chair now, but I used to cross the oceans hunting secrets. I was the reason your father was able to start Oceanus Industries. I would commandeer ships of pirates and flesh traders and bring them to him to repurpose into a useful, and legal, trade."

She stopped talking as West put his hand on his face, rubbing along the side and covering his mouth. He turned, walking down the beach several yards before he swung back around and moved to her.

"You knew about me this whole time? Everything that happened from the moment you bound my powers to... what happened and what... followed... when I was with Devon?"

She looked at him, unable to get a good grasp of how he was feeling and what he was thinking. His face held nothing, and his eyes were clear.

"I bound your powers as an infant, but I agreed to keep my distance until you were twenty-one. Since then, I did have spies assigned to you, but only to make sure the binding was intact. So, that's how I knew about the warehouse. The spies continued to keep tabs on you when you left."

"Why did you not pull me back when I was twenty-one?" His voice took on a softer pitch. "Why give me more time?"

Looking down at the water lapping at the shore, she sighed and crossed her arms.

"I wanted you to live. I wanted you to know mortality as an adult. My father killed me when I was a youth and I ascended, losing two of my sisters who were unable to hold their power. I have lived a long time, but I do wish I had known mortality as an adult. To live every day, truly live, thinking I only had a set amount of time... I think I would have made the best of it and been happy as such." She looked back up at him. "I did not want to deny you that. I am sorry you had such an ache in your heart from such a horrible trauma, but I worried making you ascend then would only increase the distress on your psyche."

His lips parted and she could no longer look at him. Turning away, she stared at the moon instead, quickly swiping away a rogue tear.

A slight pressure on her arm pulled her attention to West's hand there, his slender fingers wrapping around her elbow. She looked back up at him as he stepped closer to her and now, she could see his beautiful eyes in the moonlight. The small amounts of illumination making a starry pattern in the dark irises.

"Thank you," he whispered, and a huge wave of relief rolled through her at his words. One she hadn't known she needed. He wasn't mad or upset, and he seemed to have some respite there as well. She smiled and nodded as his hand gave her elbow a light squeeze.

It was then she found she liked his touch a lot more than she should.

She had broken some part of him with her honesty. He knew she had put it all out there for him, even things he technically didn't need to know, and he felt... steadier.

Pulling her arm from his grasp, she grabbed his hand.

"What are you doing?" he asked as she tugged him toward the water. The waves hitting his shins and then knees as she pulled him deeper.

Still holding his hand, she looked back at him and smiled. "One of my favorite things," she said, and his breath caught in his chest. He nearly stumbled, but he played it off as the impact of a wave.

She was so gorgeous in the moonlight. He had never seen such beauty, and a sense of clarity washed over him.

He wanted her.

All this time, he had kept himself from acknowledging how much he desired her. His anger and frustration had blinded him so much.

She dropped his hand as soon as they had waded into the water up to their hips and whistled. A bright flash of light came from his right.

The hippocampi burst onto the surface of the water, looking even more otherworldly than the last time he had seen them. In the night, they glowed with an internal light, brightening the waves around them.

Zeus, alight in blue, blew out a loud huff of air, staring at West as he trotted up to where they stood in the water.

"Still not a fan of me?" he asked. "I have that effect on males— across species, apparently. An alpha in their presence and all that. Emasculating for sure."

"Remember, he can understand you. And I won't keep him from giving your backside a good kick if you decide to challenge him to some alpha male pissing contest."

"I would think one would want to keep my backside in good shape should she come around someday and want to see it. Perhaps worship it." He caught his tongue between his teeth and chastised himself for flirting with her. Apparently, he was going to have to muzzle himself in the future. Drinking was no longer the problem. Now, it was his libido.

She laughed, something that made her even more gorgeous, and he swiftly looked away. Somehow, acknowledging his desire for her made it impossible to even glance her way without being overcome by it.

She has a boyfriend, he reminded himself. The devil on his shoulder told him that it didn't mean she was married. The devil on the other shoulder raised a beer in agreement.

He was going to have to watch himself.

She rolled her eyes. "Well, then." She nodded toward the hippocampi. "Want to go for a ride, lover boy?" she asked. The wink she gave him threw him into a momentary tailspin of hormones.

Zeus stared at him forebodingly. Could the hippocampus sense the attraction toward his goddess?

"On *them*?" He was sure his face took on a bit of green hue.

Amphitrite laughed again and nodded. "Come on. We'll ride Ingrid."

She swam forward and mounted the female hippocampus. He watched her strong legs wrap around the beast's equine torso. She drew his attention back to her face when she called for him. "Come up behind me."

Fates save me.

Shaking his thoughts away, West slowly approached them and tentatively hauled himself up onto Ingrid. It was not a graceful attempt, and it took him an embarrassingly long time to get all the way on but sitting behind Amphitrite made it worth it. With his front to her back, many a sexual thought fluttered through his head at the feel of

her in between his legs.

Stay down, boy. Do not embarrass yourself.

"Ready? You are going to want to hold on really tight," she warned lightly.

West carefully set his hands on her waist. Before he could say anything, Ingrid took off at a far faster speed than a normal horse and West yelled, his hands tightening around Amphitrite's waist.

This was how he was going to die. He was sure of it.

They galloped across the waves, half swimming and half running. The hippocampi's hooves splashed in the water as they forged on, spraying him in the face. He glanced over his shoulder, just barely glimpsing the glowing tail in the frothy, churning water in their wake.

West faced forward and leaned his cheek close behind Amphitrite's neck as her hair whipped around him.

As they rode the hippocampus, West lost sense of time. He was exhilarated, but at his core, he felt peace.

When they finally slowed, he realized they had looped back around to the beach outside his condo. Ingrid strode confidently onto the shore, and while he didn't see it, he felt the strength of four equine legs beneath him instead of the two and a tail they'd had in the water. Amphitrite dismounted and he awkwardly tried to follow her example. His legs were sore, especially the inside of his thighs, from hanging onto the beast at high speed, and so he stumbled slightly once the solid earth was beneath him.

As soon as they were off, Ingrid sped away, followed by Zeus. They disappeared into the gentle waves, their lights dissipating as their distance increased.

Amphitrite huffed out a laugh. "Goodbye to you, too," she said to the empty air. She made a small move and instantly her body was dry as if she hadn't just been plunged into the Thalassian Sea.

West knew she was joking, but he realized their night was coming to an end. Suddenly, he felt desperate to delay their own goodbye.

He faced her. "Amphitrite?"

She looked away from the water and back to him, raising her brows. "West?"

Now, he had to actually think of something. West internally grimaced. He wasn't used to feeling so uncomfortable around women. But she wasn't just a woman, was she?

She was a Goddess.

He said the first thing that came to him.

"What does your God form look like? Not just the glowing eyes here and there or the slight blue light around you. Your full-blown God form?"

She smiled easily and walked to where the water met the beach, drawing in swirls of water around her. Her body began to lift up from the sand, and as she levitated, robes of aqua silk fell down around her, a crown of sea glass materialized upon her head, and an inner light lit her skin. Her Godfire was bright in her eyes, which held no pupil or iris in this form. As the water continued to whirl, her long wavy red hair blew around her and she truly looked like the vision of a Goddess.

His heart stopped.

"Fates," he whispered in awe. His brain was unable to form more words, but his heart was beating so fast, and his stomach was full of butterflies.

He was an idiot.

An idiot who was half in love with her.

Slowly letting her form go, she slipped back to the ground, her body and clothing returning to what they were.

"Holy shitting Fates." He wondered briefly if that could be considered blasphemy before realizing he did not care.

She canted her head. "That scary?"

"That beautiful," he whispered, his voice deeper. All he could see were her lips. All he could think of was that creamy pale skin under his hands, waking up in the morning to the sun catching her freckles. Days and nights with her.

They gravitated closer together. She tilted her head up to meet his eyes, and he suddenly found it difficult to breathe.

"West..." His name came out like a prayer on her lips, one that prompted his animal mind to move to where their bodies were flush with one another. Something in the back of his brain warned him to stop, but he was past caring about small things. There was a bigger picture here, and she was the main part of it.

His face tilted forward, and his lips brushed across hers. He closed his eyes, lost to the sensation, and again, he chastised himself.

How had he not seen what was in front of him this whole time? His anger had made him blind in so many ways.

He trailed his lips along her cheek on the way to her ear. "I want to kiss you so much."

Feeling her jolt in his arms, his brain clicked back on, and he moved back on his heels to give some space between their bodies. She pushed his arms from around her waist and took a full step back.

"I... Darren," she whispered as her fingers touched her lips.

Shit. Shit. Shit!

"I am sorry... I lost myself and—" The flash of aquamarine light cut him off and he closed his eyes against the glare. When he opened them, she was gone in a light jump.

You bloody idiot, West.

21

S tanding in the control room at the Zephyr Maritime Administration, Amphitrite ordered one of the dispatchers to pull up the route map for Oceanus ships for the day the Mystic had sunk to the bottom of the Hydrian Sea. A yellow line plotted the original, approved trading route. A blue line tracked the Mystic's path from their departure at Halcyon to where the ship lay now. Such a huge deviation from the original that it made absolutely no sense.

The dispatcher, Jones, pointed to a spot between the peninsula of Halcyon closest to the northernmost country of Alexious. "They followed the route until about here," he said. The point of divergence was not terribly far from the departure dock. Then, he indicated an area several nautical miles to the west, closer to the border but technically still in safe waters. "It is assumed the ship sent out a distress call from this point," he said, "and another one twenty minutes later, from the same location."

Jones typed something into his computer, and the blue line extended crookedly, turning sharply toward the dark waters. "This is where the boat traveled after the last distress call, when our ships were en route."

She leaned over Jones' shoulder to look more closely at the screen. "How long between the final distress call and our ships finding them in the Hydrian Sea?" She was unnerved by the reality of two distress signals. If the first one had been answered, would they even be in this situation?

It was in her waters, yet she never knew the ship was in trouble until it was too late.

Nothing was adding up.

Jones glanced nervously between her and the computer. "Twenty-three minutes."

Amphitrite reeled backward.

"Twenty-three minutes? That is a six-hour journey, at least. How did our ships get there so fast?" she asked, trying to piece it all together in her mind.

"A patrol was out near Goryeo when they received the second distress signal. They responded to the call and on the way saw something black explode in the distance. They called it in and was told to check it out by one of our dispatchers on shift. I can get you their name."

"Please," she said, and Jones jumped up from his seat to get the information. She sat in the chair he vacated and looked over the map again.

No matter how she reasoned and ran the route discrepancy through her mind, there was not a way this could be done naturally—or humanly. She recalled the sailor's testimony; a woman had influenced the captain. But at what point? At the first point of divergence—earlier? Later? How had the crew not mutinied when they headed so far off course?

The movements of the ship told a story, a riddle she needed to solve.

Minutes later, Jones returned. "Ms. Wells?"

She turned to see a tall woman wearing a dispatcher's uniform standing beside him. "This is Monica Calder. She took the call and dispatched our coast guard ships to the wreck site."

Amphitrite stood and nodded to the dispatcher. "Hello, Ms. Calder—"

"Monica, please."

Nodding again, Amphitrite acquiesced.

"Monica, can you give me any details? Any impressions you gathered from your interactions with the ships that night?"

The woman looked down to the floor for a moment, seeming to gather herself.

"I told the investigative team everything, but some of what I told them was not put in the report. When I asked about it, they told me it was irrelevant to the investigation, which seemed odd..."

Amphitrite's ears perked up at this.

"What was not put in, Monica?"

The woman finally looked up at Amphitrite.

"They, the crew, called in that a strange woman was aboard the Mystic. That they had pulled her from the water and needed a boat to come out and gather her so they could continue on."

Amphitrite looked at Jones, who only shook his head. No, there was no mention of this in the final report.

The sailor they'd spoken to had the right of it.

"And then?" Amphitrite prompted. She could feel Monica working to steel her nerves. Were they worried she would be mad at them for the negligence of the safety board?

"You did nothing wrong. You told them what you knew, and they failed to report it. If you tell me, I promise to look into it further."

Both the dispatchers let their shoulders relax a bit at her words, but not as much as she would have liked. She would find out who treated her team in such a way that they were scared to say anything. She would not have her people in fear of anything, much less her.

"I dispatched our closest coast guard ship near where the original signal had been put out, but when they got there, the Mystic was gone. I ordered them to search the coordinates provided again and called into Oceanus. That was when I received a ping from the wreck site, and I radioed the coast guard ship on patrol near Goryeo. They stated something had appeared on their radar. As I confirmed the coordinates, they saw what looked like an explosion in the water. They had moved closer to investigate and saw the black hull and rudder slowly going beneath the waves."

"Intact?" she asked. It had been a crumbled mess when she had seen the site herself.

Monica nodded.

"A much as the guard could see, it went under that way. No explanation as to what the underwater explosion could have been."

What in the Fates?

Amphitrite leaned back against the desk and folded her arms across her chest.

"At Oceanus, they told me they had it handled, which I thought was strange since I've worked with several of the teams over there on search and rescue missions, but they've never been so... dismissive. It was a new voice, so I thought perhaps it was a trainee and put a call out to an upper manager. I never heard back. By the time I had finished that call, the second distress call came in. I sent the guard there, but they disappeared again. That was when I got a call from the other ship about the explosion in the Hydrian Sea."

"This was all within twenty-three minutes?"

"The last call was at the ninety-eight-minute mark. The one where they explained the ship's state."

That timeline made sense from where the ship had been prior to the call.

"Thank you, Monica. I will look into this further. I appreciate your time."

The woman nodded and Amphitrite did not miss the visible relief in the woman's posture at the end of her questioning.

Someone in Oceanus had known about the Mystic's initial distress signal and had not followed up on the calls from the Maritime Administration. Nothing West had found in the paperwork indicated they had received a call from her people.

So where was the miscommunication happening?

The spirit had stated that the woman had hypnotized the captain. The dispatched just confirmed a woman had been aboard. That was moments before they had taken a deadly detour. Could the woman have manipulated the mind of the captain to turn the ship toward dangerous waters? Did that mean a siren was working against them?

Had a Titan turned one of her own?

Amphitrite light jumped to the deck of West's condo the next morning. He stood at the railing with his back to her, looking out over the beach as the sun went up for the day.

She took a minute to take the man in. The man she had come dangerously close to kissing two days ago and had been avoiding since.

After her conversation with the dispatchers, she had sent a missive to West through one of her trusted spies but hadn't heard back from him. So, she sent a message to

his secretary requesting to meet him the next morning, and she had received one back in feminine handwriting in agreement.

Now he stood before her and her mind was no longer on saboteurs and traitors, but what it would have been like to let him kiss her. To feel his lips on hers.

In the early morning light, his olive skin seemed flawless. Even without seeing his face, she knew his features were sharp and lively and unnervingly handsome. The longer she knew him, the more of him she saw.

And she now knew him in a way she was sure few did. There was more to West than the inebriated party boy. Before her stood a man that cared and would move the world to make it safe for everyone, even those that may not deserve it.

"Admiring my beauty?" he asked, bringing her mind back to the present. Embarrassment crawled over her skin at being caught watching him.

"Idiot," she mumbled, but noticed it no longer held the harsh edge it once had when she spoke with him.

"Guilty as charged." He turned to face her. "I can feel so much out here. I can feel the creatures under the surface, the pull of the tides, even the riptides. It's amazing. I realize now that I could feel a little of this all my life, but just chalked it up to something everyone else could do."

Her heart warmed at the wonder in his voice. If he continued to behave like this, she would—

No. Focus.

She approached the railing beside him. "West—"

"I've been meaning to show you something." Holding his palm flat in front of him, he summoned the water into a hovering orb just a few inches above his hand.

"Not much longer until you will no longer be in need of my guidance," she noted as she watched the ball of water rotate quickly in his palm, increasing in speed.

Not looking at her, he thrust the ball of water back into the ocean. It broke apart on impact, splashing into the waves.

"So, what's the plan for this morning?" he asked, ignoring her comment as he wiped his hand on his jeans. A nervous gesture since he did not actually touch the water.

That was how it was going to be then. She sighed and pulled him into a light jump.

They stumbled a step as they materialized on the deck of a rocking ship. The waves were choppy from the winds of an impending storm. No dolphins to jump and frolic with the ship today and she couldn't blame them. There was a certain level of stress among all the sea creatures recently. They sensed something was wrong in the ocean.

The dark waters were strengthening. There was no way around it.

West gripped the railing as the ship crested another wave.

"Is there a particular reason we are hanging out on the sea when we have one seriously dangerous looking storm on the horizon?"

"If this is a natural storm, we can control it."

"As opposed to an unnatural storm of nature?" he asked, turning around to brace his back against the railing.

"Hera would be the answer to that question," Amphitrite told him dryly. "We need to talk about the Mystic. I spoke with people from dispatch. Did you receive my missive?"

West looked at her, his eyebrows up in question and face serious.

"I have a stack of papers on my desk I need to sort through. Darla just told me she received a request to meet from you. What did you find out?"

"The Safety Board's report is missing significant information."

He frowned. "What information?"

She took a deep breath and steadied herself on the deck. "Someone at Oceanus Industries received the distress call from both the ship and the Maritime Administration."

West only stared at her, his eyes blinking.

"I pored over the records. No call was received."

She shook her head. "My dispatcher stated that assistance was denied. She sent a report to the manager on shift, but she didn't receive anything back. When a second distress signal came, she dispatched a patrol ship anyways."

"Fuck!" he growled, tightening his hands on the railing into fists. "Someone on the inside is covering this up." He slammed a hand on the metal. "Someone in my own damn company!"

"The dispatcher also said a woman came aboard the Mystic," she said over the wind, her voice breaking. "Confirming what the soul told us... I'm worried there's a traitor in my ranks, as well. It sounds like the Titans turned a siren to their cause."

His head jerked up and his brows furrowed. "Titans?"

"I think..." She worked her thoughts into an arrangement of words that she hoped might make sense, her mind far too scattered. "I think the Titans are using the ocean as part of their next move."

"How? What could it have to do with the Mystic?" he fumed. The ship crested another large wave and his muscles strained with effort and frustration.

"I'm not quite sure yet. We don't have the full picture." She shrugged and continued, "According to the coast guard patrol that responded, there was an explosion, and the ship was in one piece when it went down."

"There is no way. That was a crumbled mess down there!" He flung a handout to the water.

"I know. There's a seriously powerful being afoot, stronger than a siren. The Titans have to be up to something again. Their first attempt to get Cronus out of the Underworld failed, so it makes sense they would take another tactic."

Shaking his head, he ran his hands over his face. She knew this was distressing, and she had spent almost all night awake with the prospect of having to fight another Titan so soon. "We need to make sure you are ready. If it is a Titan, we do not have as much time as I thought."

West looked at her through his fingers before dropping his hands and nodding.

"You're right," he stated, and she sighed in relief that he wasn't going to argue with her. So much progress was being made, thank the Fates.

"Good." She smiled, but it felt wobbly. His returning smile lightened the mood, but something in his eyes held a secret, and that secret had more to do with her than she could handle right now.

"Let's start." Time to get into gear and stop with the mooning at each other. She crossed her arms and ordered, "Stop the boat."

"What?" he asked, as his face scrunched up in confusion.

"Stop the boat with nothing else but your power. Use the waves and the sea."

He raised his hands, fingers splayed. Closing his eyes, he took a slow, deep breath. When he exhaled, he called out, "Stop the boat!"

His eyes opened and he lifted a brow at her. "Nothing?"

She rolled her eyes at his attempt to dispel the darkness of their conversation from the air. When they first met, she was frustrated by his sarcasm, but now she appreciated his humor. Somewhat.

"Are you talking to yourself right now? Do you know how ridiculous you sound? Focus, West. You can tap into the water easily."

He put a finger to his lips. "Hush. I am channeling my inner Goddess and you are interrupting." Closing his eyes again, he held his hands in the air.

She shook her head, expecting another joke, but felt the boat stopping. It was slow, but she could feel the speed decrease by small increments until it finally stopped, as if close enough to land to drop anchor.

Incrementally, West's arms lowered, and the boat halted, shifting only from the current.

His eyes opened, a supreme smugness burning within the glowing blue irises.

She stepped up next to West and looked out over the railing. The waves had calmed, lapping against the side of the boat, whereas the waves around them, at least ten feet out, were still agitated.

Looking up, she nodded with a smile. "I am impressed, Mr. Murphy." She nodded out to the ocean. "Earlier, you said you can feel sea creatures. Tell me what life forms you can feel beneath us. Bonus points if you bring one up to say hello."

He rubbed his hands together before putting them out in front of him, as if there was a roaring fire there to warm him. His eyes closed and his brow pinched in concentration. No jokes this time.

She closed herself off to the sea, wanting to be surprised by what he summoned. He was quickly catching on, but he was also an enthusiastic learner now that he wasn't on a nonstop bender.

"Huh," West grunted, his brows pinching together tighter and his hands grabbing the rail. His eyes stayed closed, focused.

"What?" she asked, touching the crook of his arm. Their first real touch since their almost kiss. Something she was *not* letting herself think about. She needed to talk to Darren before things went any further with West.

"It's bigger than I thought..."

Opening up her senses, she mentally probed the creatures beneath them until she found what he was talking about. Her hand squeezed his arm harder, and she opened her eyes with a gasp.

What in the Fates was coming up?

"West, stop," he heard Amphitrite beg, but he couldn't cut the connection with this monstrous thing. He thought it was a whale at first, but the closer it got, the more he realized how wrong he was.

"I... I can't," he groaned as a flash of pain hit behind his eyes and his hands flew to his head. He felt like there was a wall in his mind he had never noticed before and something on the other side was ramming itself against it to get through. "What the fuck is going on in my head?"

"Breathe, West. I have no idea what is happening, so I need you to try to tell me."

He could feel her trying to pull him back from the rail, but something called to him below and he found that he couldn't move back. Something kept pulling him forward.

A loud pop sounded in his ears, and his eyes lost focus, his vision going white for a moment, but the pain lessened as something broke the surface of the water. Suddenly, Amphitrite stopped trying to pull him back. Frozen, both of them watched what came from deep below.

"What in the Underworld is that?" West yelled, stumbling backward as a serpent-like creature rose from the water. Sheets of water fell from its massive scaly body, as it breached the surface, and the displacement of water tilted the ship to the side, sending waves crashing against them, and the entire boat rocked violently. Worried they might capsize, he grabbed Amphitrite's arm. Her skin beneath his hands suddenly glowed as she instantly took on her Goddess form.

She flung her arms forward, quickly— and thankfully— righting the boat and calming the giant waves the monster had created. But the beast was still rising fast, making the boat turn and spin with it as it moved.

He was going to throw up if this did not stop. If he didn't die. He stumbled and caught himself on the railing, clutching his body close to it and stared up at the monster. It had to be over a hundred feet into the air now, towering over them. Its dark scales glinted blue in the sun. Long fins broke over the surface, splashing and sending choppy waves their way. The beast opened its giant maw and exposed long needle-like teeth.

"Leviathan..." Amphitrite murmured in a stunned voice.

"A what?" he yelled over the sound of churning water.

The beast shifted and started for the boat. His stomach dropped as he stared at the reptilian face head-on. But at the last minute, it swerved, nearly knocking the boat over, and curled itself around the ship. The boat groaned as it circled until its head returned to West's side. It blinked its slitted eyes before pulling back and letting out a deafening roar. West nearly fell back from the force of it, and the boat rocked sideways again as giant waves from the sudden cessation of movement slapped the hull.

As terrifying as it was, West noticed it did not make an attempt on the ship. The monster closed its jaw and stretched out its serpentine neck as if waking from a nap.

Amphitrite stayed completely still next to him, her face in a frozen state of shock.

The beast turned its head toward them and blinked at him. Directly at *him*.

A buzz sounded in his ears and his brain zapped. He flinched each time they hit.

"What..." West moaned as the pressure built up in his skull again.

A warbled, distorted voice sounded in his head. So light, almost a whisper. He could barely hear it.

Amphitrite was next to him now, holding his head in her hands, speaking to him, yet he heard no words. He pushed through the pain and looked up at the monster, making eye contact. He pulled himself up the railing to see the monster closer and found himself lost for a moment as the buzzing and pressure abruptly disappeared.

Minoan master, you have need of me?

That was all West heard before he passed out.

Amphitrite was stunned into silence and her entire body frozen in shock at the sight of the Leviathan. She was so enraptured by the giant that she missed West leaning too far forward. Rushing to grab him, she only made it to the edge right as he went over.

It would eat him. The monster would eat him, and she would have to do this alone.

"Fates no, you do not get out of it that easy!" she yelled before diving in after him. As soon as she hit the sea, she transformed into her water form to become invisible to the beast. She focused on the dark shape of West as he sank like a rock and a large splash behind her told her the Leviathan was now following her.

The serpent shot past her, and its descent created a rushing, swirling current. She was caught in the water and whipped around before she reoriented and gained momentum. She raced the Leviathan to reach West before it did. She couldn't pull him closer to her; to do so would bring him closer to the beast, too. If only she had the capability to light jump here, but to do so might mean West's death should she gauge the depth wrong.

Or she could end up in the thing's stomach. She did not know if she would survive that, immortal or not. There were too many risks.

Her heart dropped. The Leviathan nearly had him; its massive body twirled around West's much smaller one and she knew she would have to take on the form she despised most if she wanted to outmaneuver the beast.

Her siren form.

She never took this form unless it was an emergency. She didn't know much about this ancient monster, so this would definitely qualify as an urgent situation.

Her legs fused, binding and lengthening into a powerful tail, and her skin hardened to scales. The fins at the end of her tail propelled her faster than before. Even as she swam desperately, discomfort shuddered through her newly transformed body. She hated to rely on this form, as steeped as it was in false beauty.

She darted down to West, where the Leviathan circled him. Like a constricting snake, the beast's vast body coiled around West until she could barely see him among the dark scales. She would have to use the acuity and speed of this form to lunge for the bit of space between fin-covered coils.

When she charged the beast, thrusting her tail with all her strength, it tightened, almost defensively, around West. His body was completely blocked from view, utterly encased by the Leviathan.

Her heart pounded. There was no prying through the hold of this monster.

But she couldn't give up on him.

Raising her arm, she pointed her ring at the beast and shot a vortex of water, but the current did nothing to it. Did it even feel her power?

Amphitrite screamed her panic and agony, but only bubbles left her mouth.

Perhaps feeling the vibrations in the water, the monster paused and canted its snake head. The watchful beast sent chills down her spine. Suddenly, it unraveled its long, serpentine body, exposing the unconscious Titan in the center. She cried out again at the sight, certain now that this was the end.

She would see West die, and all she felt was... regret. And the vast darkness of impending loss.

I should have kissed him.

But the Leviathan did not chomp down on him, or even swallow him whole.

The giant sea monster looked... concerned, if that was possible, and it pushed its nose against the unresponsive West. When Amphitrite instinctively moved forward, its eyes darted to her, and she stilled. Unsure if she could communicate with it like she did other creatures, she only repeated the same thought in her mind over and over: *Not a threat, not a threat.*

Her tail slowly flicked back and forth as the Leviathan evaluated her before looking down at West again.

Amphitrite watched in agony as the beast's huge head nudged closer to West's prone form. Slowly, the Leviathan unhinged its jaw and took West in its maw.

Before Amphitrite could scream again, she sensed more life forms immediately upon them. Many more. Dozens more.

A pod of dolphins rushed from behind her. She nearly sobbed at the sound of their fierce whistles and squeaks. They must have felt her distress. *Brave creatures.*

The pod dove at the monster, attacking it with bites and violent thrashes of their noses. The serpentine head reeled back, surprised by the ambush, but used its enormous tail to push West away from the tussle. Almost as if protecting him.

She took the opportunity to reach West, but the closer she got, the more the Leviathan swept him away. Panic clawed up her throat as the dolphins attacked perilously close to West.

She called the pod away, knowing that they could easily seal West's fate with one misplaced hit. If the monster was going to eat him, it would have. In fact, it seemed like the monster was saving him from the precise, brutal hits from the dolphins.

The pod promptly fell back but hovered near enough to attack again.

As soon as the attacks stopped, the Leviathan wound back to West. Now, Amphitrite was much closer, and her horror was replaced by confusion. The monster slowly— *carefully?*— placed its head beneath West so he rested across the top of its snout. Then, it darted to the surface, its long tail swishing side to side in powerful strokes. Using her own tail, she shot after it.

As she broke the surface, she watched in awe as the Leviathan lifted out of the water and placed West gently on the deck of the ship. As terrifying a sight as the Leviathan was to behold, she couldn't deny the care it was showing West.

As if checking he was okay, its large snout moved over him, pushing at him a bit before it pulled back and lowered itself into the water, keeping West in its sight the whole time.

She watched, breathless, and willed West to stir. She could feel his life force, his power. He was alive.

Of course he was alive, he was a Titan, but was he breathing? she thought

Moments later, West's body jerked, and she heard a deep, pained groan.

Relief made her go slack in the water and she nearly dipped beneath the surface. She looked to the Leviathan, who still watched the recovering West.

Amphitrite pushed out her power to see if she could connect to the Leviathan's mind, but she found only static. The beast turned and met her gaze with its own slitted one and something clicked in her brain right then.

She knew where this creature had come from, a place even she thought long gone.

Would they never get a break?

22

"Well!" West shoved open the door to his parent's opulent home. Amphitrite followed closely behind, having been holding him when he came to. She had tried to talk to him, but as soon as he was coherent enough to understand words again, he immediately light jumped to his parents' front door.

"West, calm down," she called after him. He heard her steps right behind him as he stormed through the house looking for his parents. When he made it to the dining hall, he saw that the French doors were open and wait staff were moving about.

Good, I have an audience.

"West-" Amphitrite tried once more, grabbing at his arm, but he pulled away and walked into the dining hall full of guests, throwing his hands up into the air as twenty pairs of eyes turned his way.

"More secrets and lies! Why am I not surprised!" he shouted.

His father stood and darted around the table to intercept him as his mother gently placed her white linen napkin down. He noticed it, the white. Why were his parents so obsessed with everything being clean and white all the time? Could they get a little dirty for once? Was it the guilt of all the emotional messes they left in their wake that caused them to have such a need?

His mother discarded the white cloth and followed his father. Always following his lead. "What is this nonsense?" she demanded, her eyes flashing with fury.

"Quit with the dramatics," his father grumbled as soon as he made it to him in the hall's threshold. Grabbing his arm, his father halted immediately at finding West soaking wet, so he settled for shoving him out into the hallway. His mother made soft-spoken apologies, blaming the scene on his drinking, and shut the French doors firmly behind her.

Drinking. Because obviously that was all he was good for. What a perfect scapegoat when shit got weird. That thought made him laugh in derision, which only brought more ire from his father.

His eyes landed on Amphitrite. "Am—"

"I'm not drunk! I summoned a fucking Leviathan," he hissed, gesturing his arm wildly like a snake moving out of the deep. At this, his father shoved him down the hallway in the direction of his office.

Amphitrite was on their heels as they moved into the room, her eyes narrowed on his father. An ally. He knew he was not facing this alone and that gave him some courage to finally stand up and demand the answers he needed.

They wanted him to master his power, yet they kept secrets. Well, it was time to fess up.

"Why are you wet?" his mother asked as she moved into the office and closed the door behind the four of them.

"I passed out and fell into the ocean. Thankfully, the *fucking* Leviathan saved me!"

"Enough," his father shouted with barely controlled anger.

West turned to his parents, his heart beating rapidly and his hands curling into fists.

"More lies, father?" he sneered, earning a growl from the older man. Amphitrite placed her hand on one of his clenched fists and gave it a gentle squeeze.

"What nonsense are you spouting?" his father replied, his eyebrows furrowing.

His confusion was cute, but no way was he going to buy it.

"I was training with my powers, you know, the ones you kept me from knowing about my whole life," West started, and he caught his father's flinch. He felt Amphitrite's other hand go to his shoulder. "Then I summoned a Leviathan. *It spoke to me in my mind!*"

He felt the confusion radiating off of his father and Amphitrite. Looking between them, they both seemed shocked. He hadn't mentioned the telepathic moment to Amphitrite earlier; he had been too busy regaining consciousness.

When he looked at his mother and caught the guilt in her dark brown eyes, he went pale. Anger subsided to another emotion he couldn't quite name right then.

"No..." His voice was little more than a whisper. "Mother, no."

"Theta?" his father asked, watching his wife with a furrowed brow.

She stared at West with pleading eyes, tearful with an apology.

Looking at his father, she wiped her eyes. "I didn't think it would matter," she whispered brokenly. She gestured to her husband. "With the power of you and your lineage, I didn't think it would manifest in our son."

"Explain, Theta," Oceanus ordered lowly.

"The night I died, I would have come back regardless of what you chose to do, my love," she whispered, turning to take his father's face in her hands. "I may have been able to come back, but West wouldn't have if you had not healed my body. If you had not given him some of your power as well since he was not yet born and of the age of ascension to have his own Titan powers."

"What... how?" His father, for the first time West could ever remember, was at a loss for words.

Glancing between his parents, West released his clenched hands and realized he was not the only one who knew nothing of his heritage.

Amphitrite put her hand in his, his fingers entwining with hers, and he felt so grateful she was beside him at that moment. "What do you mean, Theta?" she asked. "How does this impact West's powers?"

"I didn't know who I truly was until I died," his mother stated. "When I entered the Underworld... I was told of my heritage and my past. I..."

She looked down and his father pulled her chin back up.

"Please," she whispered brokenly, "please do not look at me differently. I thought perhaps if West was a Titan, you would never need to know who I was."

"Who are you?" West broke in, his patience growing thin. He felt for his mother, but he also was tired of not knowing who he was.

She turned to him, eyes sad, and took the hand not held by Amphitrite.

"I am descended from King Minos," she whispered, and he heard Amphitrite gasp. "When I died, I met him... King Minos, a demi-god of the line of Pontus. He ruled an island surrounded by the Thalassian sea that was once known as Thira, then Santorini, before it became part of Halcyon. My people were called the Minoans and when I died, I was given memories by King Minos, who was honored as a judge of the dead upon his death. I could see through the eyes of one of his daughters... Phaedra. I can see her life through her own eyes, and I hold her memories. I do not know exactly how I am related to her, but I know she is of my blood."

West leaned down and tried to catch his mother's eyes as she looked at their hands. Finally, she glanced back up, and tears dripped from her eyes.

"I'm sorry for not telling you sooner," she said, "If I thought it would have impacted you... I promise I would have told you. But everything happened so quickly with your unbinding..." Swallowing, she looked over his visage before taking her hand from his and moving it to his face, cupping his jaw.

"Theta..." his father whispered in awe as she held her son's gaze.

"There are virtually no true Minoans left," she continued as if she did not hear him. "The Minoan Island was lost to the sea after an eruption devastated our land, and a tsunami finished it off." He felt Amphitrite flinch again. "Which became a legend of its own. Atlantis."

West took a deep breath, his heart pounding as his mother spoke.

"However, the power in your blood... it must have awakened the long dormant Minoan traits," she said. "You can call to our protector and the one we worshipped, the Leviathan, just as our ancestors did."

"How did I never know... *feel*... this creature of the deep?" his father asked as he looked at Amphitrite, who shook her head in response. Neither of the Guardians of the sea felt this creature until West called to it.

"It must have been in a deep hibernation," his mother said. "West has awakened it somehow."

After a brief pause, West spoke. "Is that it, then?" he seethed through his teeth. "What else do I not know? I cannot do this, be this powerful Titan, if I am not aware of who I am!"

"West, I did not intend to keep any of this from you to hurt you."

"But you did. Do you not realize how much it costs me each time I find out another lie?" he croaked. He swallowed; his throat tight. He was trying to be the man he needed to be, and every time he thought he found his footing, the rug was pulled out from under him.

Closing his eyes, he stepped back from his mother and released Amphitrite's hand, feeling too overwhelmed and overstimulated. He needed to think, but there was too much pressure in the room.

And in his head.

"So, my father is a Titan, my mother is a descendant in the royal line of the lost city of Atlantis," he summarized scoffingly. The words were unbelievable even as they left his lips. He ran his hands over his face and sat back on his father's desk.

Blinking tearfully, his mother replied, "You have the power of two of the most powerful lines running through your veins."

He stood back up, dropping his hands to his sides, and stared at his parents. He wanted to shout at them, to tell them that he was tired of living in a family full of secrets. He wanted to call them cowards and ask why they thought ignorance was a gift. He wanted to tell them that they expected too much of him.

But it was all things he'd said before. And that was what hurt most.

A tear slipped down his cheek and suddenly he was in Amphitrite's arms, the sea breeze of the light jump hitting him before he fell into a heap on his own couch. Sitting up, he put his head between his knees and steadied himself.

"Tell me you didn't know," West pleaded as he clasped his hands and stared at the woven rug under his feet.

"That you could call a Leviathan? No, I did not," she whispered and sat down, running her hand over his back in a gesture of comfort.

"Did you know about the Minoans? Atlantis? Whatever... and my mother?"

Her silence had him looking at her, ready to scream in fury at another person withholding knowledge, but he deflated when he caught the lost look on her face.

"I knew of them. I did not know your mother was any relation to Phaedra, or that she was in any way a descendent of Pontus, a Primordial God of the sea. Your father's power inside of her, from when he healed her, must have made it to where I was unable to detect it."

His eyes ran over her features, and before he could stop himself, he took her hand in his.

"Tell me," He whispered, knowing something was hurting her more than he knew from the conversation with his parents.

Her lashes fluttered, and a tear dripped down her cheek. His other hand came up and swept it away. It seemed they were both lost in this moment and, though he hated this for her, he felt less alone.

"I have a difficult time thinking of your mother's people, since I feel responsible for why most of them died."

Confusion shot through him at her words, but he nodded for her to continue. She squeezed his hand before pulling it free to wipe at her eyes and folding her arms across her chest as if putting on armor. She needed space and he could accept that, so he sat back and gave it to her.

"It was a place that I think was the most progressive of the time, personally, and I enjoyed visiting on occasion. The island itself was called Thira, after the volcano at the center, but it was inhabited by the Minoan people. None of them were human, all sea nymphs with varying types of power. There are so many rumors about how the island thrived, but the truth was simple; King Minos was a true leader, and so the royal line were the Guardians of the island. They had an army, but royal blood held the collective power of the people. They could call monsters of the deep to fight, the ones in which they worshipped, and no army dared take them on."

"How does this have anything to do with you—"

"Killing all of them?" she asked, lifting an eyebrow as she locked onto him with her glassy eyes.

He nodded and she took a deep breath before continuing. "I was dealing with raiders coming from the northlands, ones that pillaged and killed, taking land that wasn't theirs by using my sea. I was so angry one day when I came upon one of the coastal towns, and seeing that the raiders had killed and burned everything and everyone... My fury ignited, and..." He wrapped her in his arms. Her slight flinch warned him she might not have wanted this affection, but she blew out a breath and relaxed into his embrace.

It was his ancestors she was admitting to decimating in her anger, yet he would not let her tell him of something that hurt her so deeply without knowing she was safe with him. It did not matter what happened, and he needed her to know that through his actions, no matter what she did, who she was, he was there for her.

"I created an earthquake, one that if I had been of sound mind would have been under my control, but I let it loose. That was my mistake and one of my greatest failures. I never even knew until I went to check the southern isles that it had caused the Thira volcano to erupt. An eruption that was much worse than any before it.

"The volcano was catastrophic, sinking the island with all the people... and destroying so much of the coastal towns. I had destroyed so much more than the raiders ever did. The tsunami that came after..."

Tears finally escaped her eyes for the lives lost, and West only pulled her tighter, resting his head atop hers.

"I moved quickly. I did the best I could to keep it from doing more damage, but I had just created something so violent I couldn't focus. I did stop it... but... after so many had already died."

Quietly, she looked up at West, her eyes overflowing with tears.

"I froze that day on the docks. Had you not been there to stop the tsunami, I am not sure I would have called my power in time. You were a hero that day, and so new to your powers. But you are more than your powers, more than the sea, and more than the people who sired you. You are amazing, and that is only a small part of who Weston Murphy is."

Closing his eyes, he pulled her back into his arms as his lips pressed against her temple.

A tear trickled down his cheek, falling into her hair.

He was more. So much more.

But so was she.

Amphitrite woke up slightly disoriented, the room around her slowly coming into focus. She had fallen asleep on West's couch and, from the arm around her middle, so had he.

Closing her eyes, she realized she finally had the power to do the one thing she had been putting off for far too long. It had been so obvious, but she was stubborn to a fault, and had so much on her plate. Her personal life had seemed so minor to the actual trials they were facing.

Slipping out of West's arms, she light jumped to the familiar doorway.

She knocked and waited.

It took a few moments before Darren opened the door, his eyes half asleep from it being so early in the morning, but she knew this needed to be done now.

She had been selfish long enough, and it stopped here.

"We need to talk," she whispered, and watched as he realized what she meant.

There was no anger in his eyes. She imagined having this talk with West if they had been dating and could not see him being so calm. She had a hard time visualizing him simply standing back, letting her into his home at those words, but instead demanding to know why. And not calmly sitting on the couch as she told him it was finally over but grabbing her, kissing her, proving to her they were far from done.

That was the difference between the men, and it was clear as day. Both men were wonderful people, but Darren's love was not the kind of love she wanted. His felt more platonic, now even more so as she told him it was over and he calmly accepted it, hugging her and wishing her the best.

There was nothing to indicate she was breaking his heart. No sign that the thought of not having her would tear his soul apart. He would go back to sleep and, maybe with a little sadness, move on.

She knew, deep down somewhere, that if she ended things with West after a year, he would drown the world. He would not meekly give up. He would fight for her. For them.

And that was the love she had long thought lost to her.

"We need to talk." West woke to the deep voice grumbling from above him. Instead of waking up to Amphitrite in his arms, which he had fallen asleep looking forward to, he was looking up at his father.

"Hrng..." he groaned as he threw his arm over his face.

"Are you hungover?" his father asked.

"No, not drunk or hungover. But I should be after last night," he muttered. "Need coffee." He found the energy to push into a sitting position.

His father damn well knew he was not a morning person. Which perhaps explained why, the next instant, his father handed him a steaming cup of coffee.

West held it in his hands like a baby bird. Taking a sip, he blinked up at his father. "What are you doing here?"

"We may be... having a rough spot as a family," he said begrudgingly, "but I'm still your father. And I care," he said with an incredible sincerity that had West freezing with the cup of coffee halfway back to his mouth.

"I am sorry about everything," the elder Titan continued. "I am also very sorry that you have to deal with the shipwreck and dark waters, all while trying to handle your job at Oceanus. I made a mistake there, too, and I am sorry. I am here to help with anything you need."

West's tongue felt too heavy to speak.

Oceanus looked at him, and West felt more like a child than he ever had. Not in a bad way, but in a way that reminded him of when he was small enough for his father to hold with one arm. Comforted. Protected.

"Are you still seeing the therapist?" he asked.

West nodded, slightly chagrined. He doubted his father wanted to know that his therapist likely thought he was completely delusional, hallucinating that he was endowed with mythical powers. "He's... something else."

"Well, if you need to talk to me, or want... to talk to me, I am always here. Always."

His father reached for him and squeezed his shoulder before he disappeared into a flash of ocean blue light.

West fell back onto the couch and groaned. It was too early for reflection, but he had not realized how much he needed that from his father. And his mother... he stopped his train of thought.

Torn in two. That was the feeling he could use to describe how he felt.

They lied, and those lies hurt, but he wanted to forgive them. He wanted to have that relationship with them again because there was already far too much hurt in this world and only so many safe places.

He groaned again and slammed his fists down onto the couch, the springs barely squeaking.

More for his therapist to unravel.

The man better be getting well compensated for all of this.

23

Every single report they had at the Maritime Administration related to the Mystic lay strewn across Amphitrite's desk. She'd already read them countless times, but she'd felt the need to have them on hand as she attempted to piece together the puzzle. As she'd told West, she suspected a Titan had to be involved, and potentially a turncoat siren.

If it was a Titan, then who? Would Oceanus work against his own son?

No. Her gut squashed the idea. The wreck had happened while the company was still under his control. And, despite what West may think, she knew Oceanus loved his son. There was no way he would do anything to truly harm West, much less harm his reputation, especially now that his success depended on West's own success.

The conspiracy against the Mystic went beyond a Titan and a siren. They now knew someone was working inside Oceanus, someone capable of intercepting calls and interfering with the investigation.

Yet... nothing.

She had no clues as to who these traitors could be, or why they would target the ship.

And they were not going to find out through the proper channels. She needed her spies, but the people she would normally call in on this were already working on tailing General Olethros and finding Hestia's scion. If this was a Titan interfering, which she knew it had to be one trying yet again to release Cronus, then they needed their sister's power. Now.

Which meant she would have to do it herself.

Sighing, she leaned forward and placed her face in her hands.

She was stretched thin with worry and exhaustion. There were too many things going on, too many questions, too many problems pulling at her.

West, his power, and his parents.

The damn awakened Leviathan.

The Mystic, the Titans, the traitors.

The dark waters.

Pushing away from her desk, she stood up and light jumped to West's office.

"Oh, crap!" He jumped, knocking over a stack of papers on his desk, and she found herself laughing for the first time in days at his startled expression as she helped him clean up the files. She placed the papers she had gathered back on his desk, and he returned to his chair.

"Is there a reason you are literally popping into my office?" he asked, leaning back in his seat with a grin. "Will this be the status quo? Should I keep an extra pair of trousers here? You know, for when you inevitably scare the piss out of me?"

She grinned, but then her smile faded, and his quickly followed. As his expression shifted to concern, she realized even more of why she had called it off with Darren. It was more than just a growing lust for West. Oh, she could admit from the start of this he was a handsome guy, but he meant something to her now.

She wondered if the other women in his varied past felt the same, but she shook the thought away.

"Sorry," she said, smiling again, though this one was forced, and West did not return it. "I hit a wall and needed a break. I pulled all the files on the Mystic again and didn't find anything to help us figure out who was behind the wreck. Again."

West nodded, but then swiftly searched his desk, grabbing a folder from beneath the now haphazard pile and handing it to her.

When she opened it, she saw Oceanus incident reports. Yet, they were the same as the ones she had looked at in her office. Identical. The exact same verbiage, same signatures— nothing varied. Looking up, she knew before he said the words. The only difference was the company's name on the letterhead.

"Duplicates."

"Why? How?"

"I am not sure, but I cannot find anything signed by Oceanus here. All Maritime employee signatures." He stated, referring to her division. Her people had signed off on all of this? Why was it being used at Oceanus as well?

"What the Fates is going on?" she whispered, thumbing through the papers, seeing only the same information she had on her own desk. When she looked up at West, he had a look of resigned anger on his face and his hands clasped over his stomach. His navy suit tight over his biceps.

"Someone somewhere is handing off information and paperwork. I was hoping you would know, since you have a network of spies ready to do your bidding."

"They are currently looking into other matters. I decided this morning I was going to take the reins on this... go through some of my older and less savory channels."

He raised an eyebrow as he used his legs to sway his executive chair from side to side, taking in her words.

"Is that what you were doing when you left this morning?" he asked, his voice was soft.

She sighed. She had assumed this topic would come up at some point in this conversation.

Putting the papers down, she leaned against the side of his desk and swirled his chair around to face her.

"I went to see Darren," she told him, and his face went expressionless, his eyes cutting to the bookshelf across the room.

"Ah. Yes, the boyfriend," he responded before looking back at her with a fake, closed-lipped smile. How he even thought he could pass that off as real, she did not know.

She knew her intensifying feelings for him were reciprocated. If she ever wondered, his non-reaction to her statement after spending the night in his arms told her everything she needed to know. Maybe it was just lust, less than what she felt for him, but there was something.

"Not anymore." She held his eyes as she straightened, and a new worry wiggled into her brain. Perhaps he didn't care if she was single now, and maybe he wouldn't act on it, but she put that thought away. She'd needed to break up with Darren for some time and it wasn't only because of West. Both she and Darren knew this day was coming.

"Why?" he asked lowly as he sat up straighter in his chair, his full attention on her.

"Because I didn't love him." She could barely push her voice past a whisper. "He is a good man and deserves to be loved the way he tried to love me."

Her nerves got the best of her, so she gave him a false smile, one much like the smile he had just tried to play off moments ago.

"I am heading out tonight to do some digging so I will not be able to meet for training, not that you really even need daily sessions anymore," she told him, throwing him a smirk as she called the sea breeze to portal her away. "I'll catch up with you tomorrow!"

She only let the fake smile drop once she was in her own office again. Leaning back against the door, she took a deep breath and wondered what she had just done.

And if it all was going to be worth it.

"Be back in an hour, Darla," West called, throwing on his jacket as he walked to the elevator. He needed a distraction from the bomb Amphitrite had just laid at his feet.

Seeing her discomfort when she'd mentioned her break up, he had let her go without following— but, oh, how he had wanted to.

Nope, he needed to get his head together before he took any step in that direction, so he didn't screw it up.

When he made it to the sidewalk in front of Oceanus, a true smile crossed his face for the first time in a while.

His opportunity to kiss her had arrived, something he had been trying not to think about since the almost kiss in the water. When she was still with Darren, he had tried to keep himself as professional as possible and found a real friendship, so he'd pushed his feelings deep, deep down.

But now, his feelings flared to the surface, far stronger than they had been when he had originally pushed them down.

At this point, if she and Darren decided to work things out, he was not sure he could sit by and push them away again. Actually, he *knew* he wouldn't be able to.

"West, how are you?" The greeting pulled him from his thoughts.

A blonde woman stood outside of the deli he had planned to grab a gyro from for lunch. He looked around in mild confusion at how he had managed to mindlessly walk all the way there. His thoughts were consumed by two things these days: the Mystic and Amphitrite, and he was finding himself mindless on plenty of occasions because of them.

Amphitrite was today's winner for using all of West's brain cells.

He shook his head and returned his gaze to the blonde woman, grabbing the door to open it for her.

"Good afternoon," he replied in a mumble as she passed him into the deli, and he entered behind her.

He would think about how to ask Amphitrite out later. She'd just broken up with Darren that morning; surely, he had to give her some time? He frowned at the thought as he stood in line.

He attempted to reorient his mind back onto the wreck as he ordered his food and waited for his number to be called. His thoughts were only broken by the man at the deli yelling his number at him. West startled and hurried to the counter. The man must've called his name more than once if the annoyed look was any indication.

Taking the gyro with an apology, he turned and caught sight of the blonde waving him over to where she was seated outside at a little patio table.

Confused, he remembered she had used his name before when he was lost in his thoughts. On his way to her table, he tried to place her face.

"My gosh! It has been so long! How are you? Have a seat, please. Let's catch up," she said brightly, smiling up at him with eyes full of genuine interest.

Feeling like a fool for not remembering her name or who she was, he sat down with her out of guilt, even though he was planning on taking his meal to-go.

"Why are you so stiff?" she asked, unwrapping her sandwich. "The man I remember would sit down like he owned the joint with a wink." She laughed and took a bite of the sub she had ordered.

"Sorry, it's been a while. I was gone... for work and I just have a lot going on."

She sent him a closed-mouth smile as she chewed before swallowing.

"You don't remember me, do you?"

"I," he started, halting. He would have played this off before, making it a joke where she gave up her name in a game of flirting. "No, I don't. I am sorry."

Her eyebrows rose, and she laughed.

"You apologized? Oh, my gosh. What the Fates happened to you? Some kind of brain injury?"

His small smile dropped at that. Something like that was no longer a joke to him after some of the things he'd seen. She didn't notice, though. Or didn't care.

Leaning towards him, she waved him closer with a finger. He angled forward and immediately regretted it as her lips moved against his ear, her hot breath causing him to shiver.

"It was one night, and I don't expect you to remember me, but Fates, you did me good," she purred, and instead of arousal, all he felt was guilt.

He cringed away, and she pulled back, looking into his eyes. Her gaze was still heated, and he realized how superficial this woman was; she was not picking up on his cues at all. Had they all been like this?

Had he surrounded himself with people who didn't care so that he never felt bad about not caring either?

He was really starting to not like who he used to be at all.

"Maybe I can jog your memory," she murmured, leaning in again with a sultry smile. "My friend joined for round two," she whispered, her lips a hair's breadth away from his. Movement caught his eye over her shoulder, and he watched as Amphitrite— instantly familiar— whirled around and dashed across the street.

Fates!

He hadn't thought about the fact that Zephyr Maritime was right across the street. That this was a popular lunch spot for their employees and that she could walk by. Of course, she would see him! He was a Fates damned idiot!

Panic overtook him as he jumped up to follow Amphitrite, feeling his chance with her diminishing at each step she took from him, but the woman grabbed his elbow.

"West, wait!" She used his arm to pull herself up.

Spinning around, he narrowed his eyes.

"Look, I am sorry for who I was then, but that's not me anymore."

"Oh, come on, people do not abruptly change." Her hand moved to his tie. "Surely we can bring him back."

He yanked his tie out of her hand, but the woman countered by grabbing his arm.

"No. He is gone, and I hope it stays that way," he growled, pulling his arm from hers and turning toward the street. His sandwich and the woman were forgotten as he bolted, hoping Amphitrite didn't light jump away.

Today, he earned another title alongside Titan and CEO.

Weston Murphy, professional screw-up.

She was an idiot.

An idiot who thought the man known for sleeping his way through Halcyon might have any interest in being with her. At least, for more than casual sex.

Shutting the door to her office behind her, she used one of the old magics that Hecate taught her and her sisters. She quickly cast a shield around the room to block portals. As the power sealed around her, she felt a flash of gratitude for the ancient spell. When she and her sisters first became Goddesses, they had been scared and lost. They wouldn't leave each other's side when night came, for fear their father would find a way to get them.

While Hecate had shown them ways to feel safer, Thanatos had protected them. He didn't know they knew, but Thanatos would stay outside of the room the sisters shared at night, guarding them until the sun rose again and they felt safe enough to go to their own realms. She remembered that centuries-younger version of herself. She'd felt powerless, but really, she'd been *full* of power.

She wouldn't be that young Goddess again.

A man. She was acting like this because of a man. She let out a laugh before moving to her desk.

I am the Goddess of the Sea, Queen of the Sirens for Fates' sake!

To hell with a man who thought she was so easily cast off. She had a shipwreck to investigate and a Titan to find.

She swiftly opened a drawer, the one with a false bottom. When she pressed on the wooden base, the drawer's bottom slid back to reveal a small compartment. Pulling out a key, she knelt at the desk's side panel, where she unlocked a hidden desk drawer. There, perfectly fit against the drawer's walls, was the most important book in her possession.

If anyone else saw this leather-bound notebook, it only looked to contain hundreds of blank pages. Amphitrite murmured a spell, a verbal key to a magical lock only she held, and the protective magic fell away. Names and handwriting centuries-old crossed the open page, mixed with her more recent ballpoint pen notations.

Her informants, their information, their state of immortality, and where they were now.

As her finger skimmed along the page, she heard Mallory speaking outside of her office. Even through the shield, she could feel the familiar power signature beyond the door. Determined to ignore him, she continued to read, but jumped when something hit her door.

"Damn it, I need to talk to you!" West yelled.

She cursed silently to herself. She knew the man wasn't afraid to make a scene when he demanded someone's attention. Wincing, she recalled him charging into his parents' dinner party the other night and was thankful Mallory was the only one in her part of the office today. No one else needed to see nor hear this.

Her finger found who she was looking for and she quickly read the profile. Smiling, she closed the book and put it back in the drawer with its spell intact.

Taking a deep breath, she took down the ward and approached the door. When she opened it, she saw West standing there with his hair in complete disarray from running, and his eyes wide.

"Can I help you, Mr. Murphy?" she asked pleasantly.

His eyes narrowed. What had he expected? Her to be in pieces?

Perhaps, but he would find none of that here.

"I just..." he trailed off, looking her over.

"I am glad you are here actually," she said, and she waved him in with a comforting smile to Mallory, who seemed piqued by the disruption.

West reluctantly entered the office, watching her warily. She closed the door behind him and strode back to her desk, where she sat on the edge and crossed her legs.

"Why are you acting like this?" he asked as he sat in a chair in front of her.

"What?"

"Like..." He didn't go on. He wouldn't. It would mean him acknowledging feelings for her or asking for hers in return, and she was sure he would not humiliate himself. She had done enough of that for both of them today.

"Anyway," she moved the conversation on, "since you showed me the identical filings, I had Mallory pull the Safety Board's final decision on the wreck. It just repeats all the same crap from the papers we have been finding filed at our companies."

She handed him the file, his eyes not leaving hers as he took it and opened it before finally looking down at it. She gave an internal sigh of relief to have his eyes off of her.

"Someone is messing with all these reports," he murmured, turning a page. "All the reports and records from us and the safety board are missing the same important information, like the testimony your dispatcher gave and records of communication about the distress signal."

Amphitrite straightened, recalling the night of the wreck. "When Darla told us about the Mystic at the party, she said Oceanus Industries had lost the comm link with the ship. All of those missing events would have happened during that time period."

He nodded. "Darla had filed a request of information for me yesterday and this morning it was gone."

"So quickly?" she asked, pushing off the desk.

Looking up, he nodded, his assessing look no longer aimed at her.

"Someone with connections to the Administration, Oceanus Industries, and the Safety Board," she said, thinking of the Maritime Administration employees' signatures on a report with Oceanus Industries' letterhead.

Throwing the file on the desk and sitting back, he sighed. "Or someone is posing as an employee at both of our companies," he said lowly. "No one working that day knows anything, no matter where or who I ask."

A good point, she thought as she leaned back against the desk again, folding her arms across her chest. Biting her bottom lip, she thought over who would have access to all three: the safety board, Oceanus, and the Maritime Administration, but could think of no one. Looking back to West, she caught his eyes on her lips before he flicked his gaze back up to her face. She felt a surge of anger at his audacity to eye her up after he just finished with his lady friend at the deli. Was he not satisfied?

"I am meeting someone tonight at Enigma," she blurted. She anxiously tightened her arms across her chest before she realized the movement pressed her cleavage together, and that certainly was not the impression she wanted to give. She loosened her arms and placed them on the lip of the desk in a casual pose.

He leaned forward with a scowl. "The *club*?"

"Yes," she replied primly, "and I hope they will have the information we need."

"What time?" he asked as he pushed up from his chair and looked at his watch.

"I will be going by *myself* this evening. I will report back to you on what I find out tomorrow," she told him. She walked to her office door and opened it. A clear dismissal, yet he shook his head.

"I can come," he stated, refusing to move from his spot.

"But you won't. Don't interfere, West," she growled, walking to grab his arm and pull him out of her office. The moment he was on the other side of the threshold, he swung around to say something else, but he never got the chance as she closed the door in his face.

Mature?

No.

Did it feel good?

Fates, yes.

24

Amphitrite sat at the bar of Enigma, one of the most well-known nightclubs in Halcyon, infamous for pandering to the social elite. It was less known as a hangout of a certain Titan whose confidences could be bought. She had hoped to find him here, as he was part-owner.

She lingered at the bar, glancing around. She really did not want to go to his 'office' located in the lower level of the club; the underground den of sin known as the Reaver's Paradise. If this didn't work, that would be her next step, and she shivered at the thought.

If she wasn't on a mission for information, she might have enjoyed herself more. It had been a long time since she had been anywhere like this. She dressed up, since a woman in a business suit would hardly fit in with the flashing lights and pounding music. Instead, she wore an emerald velvet two-piece comprised of a cropped halter top that twisted around her waist with just two straps covering her breasts— thankfully holding them in place— and a skirt with a slit that went to the top of her thigh. Something she figured would help her blend in when it seemed to only make her stand out.

Still alone with her drink, she shifted her weight on the stool and winced at the pinching sensation in her feet. She could have done without the matching emerald heels that were incredibly uncomfortable. Actually, her poor feet currently needed ice. It had been a while since she had worn these, and she was regretting it immensely. Thankfully, as a Goddess, she healed quickly, otherwise she would be leaving bloody footprints on the floor later.

Across the bar, Medusa winked at her as she prowled through the dance floor looking for the Titan. This was their usual song and dance when tracking down an informant; Medusa would scan the location and get the individual to an isolated spot, then Amphitrite would slip in behind her for the interrogation.

Places like this were Medusa's hunting grounds.

While Amphitrite watched her old friend disappear once again into the crowd, a man approached the bar beside her. He leaned over like he was going to hail the bartender, but then he turned to her.

"You look bored being in such an upbeat place," he said loudly over the deafening bass of the song playing.

When she looked his way, she was met with piercing green eyes. He was gorgeous, but in a mortal way with flaws, like a scar or the slight crooked bump in his nose. His black hair and olive skin reminded her a little too much of another man, but she would not let him back into her head. Not right now.

She smiled and took a sip of her drink. Good, less attention on her if she wasn't sitting alone. "Not bored anymore," she lied.

He grinned and held out his hand. "Robert."

"Cordelia," she greeted, accepting his hand.

Instead of a shake, he placed his lips on her knuckles in a kiss. "Nice to meet you, Cordelia," he murmured.

If only he weren't mortal, she would be eating this up.

She caught movement over his shoulder spotted Medusa lowering herself at the bar on his other side. They locked eyes over Robert's bent figure, and Medusa shook her head.

Damn it. He wasn't here. He had changed his routine or something else came up. When it came to carnal indulgence, like what Enigma could give, the Titan was set in his ways.

Robert glanced up at her and straightened slightly, only enough to lean in close to her. Still holding her hand, he whispered in her ear over the loud music.

"Would you like to dance?" he asked.

Over his shoulder, Medusa wiggled her eyebrows. "Go," she mouthed.

When she was about to say no, Medusa gave her a look. One that encouraged her to just say yes and enjoy herself, if only for a moment or two.

And Medusa was right. The world was falling down around her feet, and should everything burn, she could find a small bit of fun, just for a moment, before she resumed her post.

Nodding, she let Robert lead her to the dance floor.

The music was sensual, and Robert was quick to learn how to meet her in their dance. Letting the music take over, she gravitated closer to Robert as she felt a tingling warmth at their undulating rhythm. It really had been too long since she let go, having been with the same man for a year, but now she could enjoy herself like she used to. Based on the way Robert danced, she knew he could give her an amazing night. And she was here for that kind of release right now.

The song's low, throbbing beat fed her arousal and her eyelids fell shut. His hands went to her hips, pulling her back against his front as they danced. His lips moved to her neck, and she let him, her head falling back on his shoulder. Losing herself completely, her mind was no longer imagining Robert as the one holding her and kissing along her neck.

West.

She froze for a moment as a wave of intense heat overtook her and the fantasy pounded through her blood. She twisted in Robert's arms to face him, and she let him lean in for a kiss as she wrapped her arms around his neck. Yet her mind imagined West again. West's powerful shoulders. West's lush, expressive mouth. Her fingers tangled in his hair— his thick, dark hair.

Suddenly, she was kissing West in the ocean, his dark brown hair dripping with water, and she knew if he looked at her, his rich dark brown eyes would be full of desire.

He responded to her deepening the kiss and pressed their bodies flush together, his arousal against her stomach.

"Wes—" she murmured, but her eyes flew open before she finished the name. Robert didn't notice, his hands continuing to roam and his lips pushing hers back open, but the moment was gone.

She pulled back from Robert. *Robert, not West*, she reminded herself. She couldn't do this. Couldn't indulge herself in sex when it wasn't with the right man.

"Look, Robert, I just got out of a relationship—"

Surprise flooded her when Robert put his finger to her lips and his forehead to hers. She stilled as he whispered so close to her mouth.

"I just got divorced and I just need a moment with someone else. I am not asking for the world, just a night."

Oh, how she understood those words. She drifted closer, until there was just a hair's breadth between them.

"Get. The. *Fuck.* Away. From. Her," a voice she recognized all too well said from behind her. She spun around and Robert tried to grab her arm, but even over the music she heard the growl from West. A growl that had several people on the dance floor flinch away from him.

"This the ex?" Robert asked as he moved to stand between West and her. She tried to stop him as he unknowingly walked into danger.

"Not the ex. I will never be the ex." His eyes shined with fury. A fury she had never seen before. This was not the same anger he'd shown in his tantrums earlier in their training, or even when he'd faced off against his parents. This anger was animalistic and uncontrolled.

Grabbing her arm, West pulled her behind him, giving her no choice but to follow him. She gave Robert a reassuring smile, but she could tell the man was not having it. Robert scowled as West drew her off the dance floor, and she had to turn her back on him to keep from stumbling.

West's grip was still firmly on her arm, but not too tight as he led her to a room closed off from the dance floor, and slammed the doors shut behind them before Robert could make it to them. Her jaw dropped as she watched West use his power to seal off the area, having had no idea he knew how to do that.

Averting her gaze from him, she took in the red plush couch and curtained walls. Of course, he knew the secret rooms here since he was part of the social elite. He used these rooms for his own fun. The same fun he had just interrupted.

West turned to her, his eyes glowing brightly, and his jaw clenched so tightly she worried about his teeth as he prowled toward her.

"What are you doing here?" she hissed. She was frustrated, in more ways than one. Her brain was angry at the disruption, but her skin tingled with anticipation, even stronger than it had earlier on the dance floor. Something in his demeanor was causing her to short circuit.

"Is this revenge? You lie to me about working tonight and then you're all but fucking some guy on the dance floor? If it bothered you to see me with that girl? You. Talk. To. Me." He thumped his chest as he enunciated the words.

"I *was* working. My informant did not show up," she snapped back at him. Good. She needed anger to help her stay levelheaded facing off with West in this state.

"Well, he might have been here, but you missed him while you were tongue—"

She shoved him before he could finish, but he didn't budge. He only smirked, his fists clenching and unclenching at his sides as he took a step forward, his hair falling into his eyes.

The man looked like a demon. Dark, dangerous, and made for sin.

She swallowed, gathering the nerve to put power behind her voice. "Why do you even care?"

"Oh, cut the bullshit, Amphitrite," he growled.

"What bullshit? I went to a club, my informant didn't show, and I let myself have a moment to enjoy myself before you showed up acting like a lunatic!"

West stalked her as she moved back, his movements calibrated perfectly for scary Titan precision. Had she been mortal, she would have trembled in fear.

"You were coming to see me today, weren't you?" he asked as he put his face in hers.

"I was walking-"

"You and Darren broke up, and you were coming to me."

"So what? Those two things were unrelated. We are in the middle of an investigation." Her words stopped when she hit the wall behind her and West put his hands against the wall, caging her in. His eyes glowed ocean blue.

"Did you not come here for the same reason?" she asked, feeling dangerous. "Is this not the same club you've been photographed in with multiple women on the same night?"

"I came," he started, his voice low, "because I knew you were here. Because if you were here, then I would be here, too. And not because of the investigation." He stepped closer. "If you want fun, I can give you that."

"I don't think I can have fun with you..." The words left her lips before she could hold them back. His eyes narrowed, yet she couldn't stop herself. "You're my friend."

"Is that all you want?" he asked, leaning closer until his lips nearly touched hers. She hardly needed to move to kiss him.

Silence sat heavily between them before the word left her mouth. The one word that would see all the careful and meticulous emotional care she had put into avoiding this moment undone.

"No."

"Then fuck being friends," he growled before grabbing her face and kissing her.

She was immediately lost to his kiss, to the fire that engulfed her. She'd never felt a hunger like this, never been swamped by passion so fiercely. All the burning she'd felt earlier had only been kindling.

Opening to him, she stretched upward and arched against him to wrap her hands in his hair. She was used to being petite, but she felt even smaller against him; she almost had to climb him to reach his sinful mouth.

His hands went to her waist, lifting her as he kissed her deeper, and he shoved his hips between her legs to pin her against the wall.

Breaking the kiss, they both sucked in deep, panting breaths, keeping close enough to kiss again and again.

"I won't be part of a rotation," she rasped. She felt vulnerable saying those words, but they were all she had to protect herself with.

The blue light faded from his eyes and his irises returned to the beautiful dark brown with golden flecks, full of something deeper than lust. But she wouldn't— *couldn't*— name it.

He moved his hands from her waist to hold her face, his hips keeping her pinned as his thumbs grazed the corners of her lips.

"There is no rotation. There is only you," he whispered, placing a light kiss on her lips and she felt an oath push through her.

"West, did you just—"

Crushing his lips against hers again, he pried her mouth open and swiped his tongue against hers. She gasped into his mouth as the wall behind them disappeared. For a split second, they were falling, kiss unbroken, and then her back hit a soft surface. A bed. He landed on top of her and braced his arms at her sides as he continued the kiss.

"I need you. I need to see where this goes. I'll try my best not to screw it up too badly," he whispered against her lips.

A laugh broke free from her chest, which, despite having a man pressed against it, felt incredibly light.

"Good luck with that," she murmured. "You make me madder than anyone ever has, and I lived with Hera."

"Well, I accept that challenge," he whispered before his lips fell on hers again.

She was done thinking. She had watched the world move past her. For centuries, she'd tried to find her place among the mortals, tried to make a life, tried to be normal. She was not normal, and she was done trying. She was also done lying to herself that she did not want Dylan Weston Murphy.

Hooking her legs around his waist, she enjoyed the feel of him against her body. His hands tangled in her hair as he pulled her even closer. She reached up to his shoulders and shoved his jacket down his arms, his hands only leaving her to desperately tear it off and throw the piece of clothing to the side. Once free, he returned his hands to gently hold her face as he looked into her eyes.

"Fates, Amphitrite, I hope you are not teasing me right now. I only have so much restraint left in the tank."

With a twist of her hips, she rolled him onto his back. She basked in his wild, searing look and raked her nails lightly down his chest. He shuddered beneath her, and she slowly unbuttoned his shirt with a teasing smile. He growled at her taunting and ripped the shirt the rest of the way open himself before moving his hands back to her hips and grinding himself against her core.

She gasped, but not just at the feeling of him. Beneath her hands, his bare chest was covered in ink, the tattoo fascinating her and holding her interest a moment before West was once again annoyed with the delay. He sat up from the bed and pulled the scanty halter top over her head. His hands immediately covered her breasts, making her gasp again, and he kissed her neck feverishly.

"So impatient," she purred when he grabbed the top of her skirt.

"I have been thinking about this moment for a while," he whispered against her skin.

"Everything you thought it would be?"

Before she could blink, he flipped them back over and pulled her skirt down her legs in one smooth motion, finding her without any underwear.

"I am going to make it so much better than my fantasies," he told her with a smirk. The dark promise in his eyes took her breath away, and she felt heat pool in her belly at the sight of the shirtless man above her.

He unbuttoned his slacks, the muscles in his abdomen and arms rippling as he moved. The tattoo that had caught her eye earlier extended beyond just his chest. The inked lines started on his arm, ran over his bicep and down across his chest until it disappeared beneath his now exposed boxer briefs. She could see enough of the tattoo now to determine what it was; it was a massive water serpent. A Leviathan.

She was distracted from the tattoo when his hands went to his boxers. He licked his lips and locked eyes with her as he removed the last piece of his clothing. Her eyes moved down, taking him in, and some incredibly needy part of her took over, pushing her conscious mind to the back.

Jerking upright, she flung her arms around his neck and pulled him on top of her, slamming his lips to hers. Without hesitation, his hands moved into her hair, and they flipped again, him on his back. She nearly cried out at the feeling of their bare skin pressed together. Had she ever felt this hot before?

She swept her fingers across his olive skin, exploring him greedily. She traced the clean lines of his tattoo with trembling fingertips and her tongue followed in their wake. A small groan erupted from West, and she shuddered at the carnal sound; it was more than she could handle. She sat back on his thighs and took in the infamous Weston Murphy in all his glory.

The man was beyond beautiful. A work of art. If only he'd been born earlier, the Greeks would have happily chiseled his form from stone. Yet she knew they would never have been able to match the true beauty of this man.

Stone could never capture his heat, his vitality. His hair was tussled from her fingers running through it. His lips were swollen from her kisses. And his dark, half-lidded eyes were full of lust.

He wasn't a Titan of the sea in that moment, but a god of desire and lust. Of sex and pleasure.

Slowly, Amphitrite crawled up his body, running her nails lightly over his hips and up his abdomen, his muscles tensing beneath her as she touched him.

With their eyes now level, she braced her arms beside his head and held herself above him without touching. Her torso hovered above his, and their chests brushed with each breath. He clutched her hips, digging his fingers into her flesh.

"You will be the death of me," he whispered, and a feral glint sharpened in his eyes as he moved a hand down to align their bodies.

Grinning, she lowered, letting her body take him in until their hips were flush, and she had seated herself on him completely.

"But what a way to die," she moaned, her head falling back.

He threw his head back, too, and a growl so deep it sent shivers down her spine left his lips. When she shifted her hips, he groaned lowly and dug his fingers deeper into her skin, his body rising to meet hers.

From the corner of her eye, she caught sight of water dancing around them, but in the moment of lust and pleasure, she didn't care.

She took her time, enjoying having this man at her mercy. But when she released a moan of her own, he finally broke his control and sat up. He rose onto his knees without losing contact, sitting back on his haunches. She gasped at the change of position and the inhalation pressed her even more closely against him, nothing, not even air, between their bodies. Still seated on his lap, she clutched onto his shoulders and swore quietly.

Hands on her hips, he guided her body against his. She went along for the ride, eagerly following his desperate movements, him finding his release mere milliseconds before she did as he growled into her neck. She arched against him with her own climax, feeling as if her body had been struck by the most pleasurable lightning.

For a few moments, they were simply still, their foreheads pressed together. The only movement was the rise and fall of their chests, the only sound was their heavy breathing.

Finally, West took her face in his hands, moving the hair from her eyes. His gaze was no longer burning with an intense passion, but contentedly warm and full of something vulnerable. He kissed her with a gentleness that almost broke her.

"Well," he murmured against her mouth, "I didn't die, but think of if I had... Thanatos and Devon would have shown up to guide my soul..."

Amphitrite huffed a laugh and West pulled back, a huge smile crossing his face.

"You have no idea how much I would rub that in for all eternity," he joked, gently turning to lay her down as he pulled himself from her. His smile softened as he guided her back on the mattress and curled up next to her.

Before she could say anything, his eyes widened, taking in the room around them.

"Shit," he muttered. "The room flooded!"

For the first time since her back hit the bed, she realized they had light jumped into her bedroom. The archway leading to the rest of her house, and the private beach, was smattered with sand. A ribbon of seaweed hung over a wall sconce. Craning her neck, she looked at the floor to see the sand and silt of the shore now there instead of carpet. The water that had been spinning in the air during their lovemaking had splashed onto the floor and flooded the room.

Stunned into silence, she jumped when West started laughing, a true belly laugh. The sound was incredibly contagious, so she joined in.

Leaning over him, she put her hand into the water, now an inch off the floor, and pushed it out through the archway and back into the ocean. Her laugh made her sides and face hurt, and she was laughing far too hard to even push herself back over West.

Suddenly his hands were on her, pulling her up and settling her beside him again.

"The sand's still there," she groaned.

"Might as well leave it. It'll flood again here in a little while," he said, earning a good-natured slap on his chest that had him acting as if she had injured him.

"You're ridiculous," she laughed as he pulled her face to his and captured her lips again.

"I'm yours," he whispered.

Corny. He was corny. And Sexy. And sweet.

And yes, he was hers.

Just as she was his.

Amphitrite woke to the sun streaming in through the skylight, naked and tangled in her sheets. Rolling over, she was both surprised and relieved to see West, laying on his stomach with his arms under the pillow, sound asleep. His dark eyelashes fluttered, and he opened his eyes as she curled on her side to face him.

"Huh," he muttered, rolling onto his back, and rubbing his eyes before reaching for her.

"Huh?" she echoed with a slight laugh as she let him pull her to him. She immediately found her place against his chest, and her hand moved over the Leviathan tattoo.

"Never slept with someone before," he stated, his voice raspy with sleep and her toes curled at the sexy sound.

Lifting herself up onto her elbow, she looked down at him. He looked bashful for a moment before he reached up to tug gently at one of her curls. She was sure her bedhead looked like Medusa's snakes.

"Never? But—"

His finger went to her lips.

"Never stayed, is what I mean. I like this. Waking up with you next to me. It's nice even though your hair has a mind of its own and nearly strangled me in the night," he groused playfully, smirking.

She gave him another light slap on his pec, and he pulled her back down, wrapping her tighter in his arms so that there was no escape.

She wriggled against him comfortably and ended up looking into the flat stare of the inked serpent.

"This tattoo..." she started carefully. She didn't want to break their light moment, but she needed to understand why he had the tattoo of the Leviathan before he even knew he could summon it.

"Yeah," he murmured, one hand moving from her to his mussed hair to push it out of his face. "That was a surprise coincidence. I've dreamed of sea monsters since I was little. It used to scare me, but mom was always saying that it was just my Guardian keeping me safe in my dreams. When I was out with Devon—" he halted, and she knew his mind was going back to dark places. Her hand moved across his stomach to pull him tighter to her as she kissed his tattoo.

Giving her a smile, he continued.

"I was honestly scared. The first time I went with Devon, he just became this machine, like he was completely shut off and... well, he killed a man. I didn't see it, but I could hear it from outside the door. Devon refused to let me through, telling me once I saw it, it would be a part of me. My soul wasn't black, and it needed to stay that way.

"I felt really alone and questioned every choice I made. I didn't know this guy very well, and I had just *paid* him to kill someone."

West went silent, but his heart picked up its rhythm beneath Amphitrite's head.

"I dreamed of the Leviathan that night. That it wrapped around me while I was drowning in the sea. It brought me to the beach and left. That was it. The next day, I sketched it out, which looked like a five-year-old did it, but the tattoo artist did an amazing job of bringing it to life. And that delightful story is how I got this tattoo."

She hummed thoughtfully, running her hands over the beautiful dark scales inked into his skin. "Do you still dream of it? Can you feel it enough to summon it again if you tried?" she asked as she looked up into his rich brown eyes. The sun coming through the window above them illuminated the gold flecks in his irises and cast a warmth to his olive skin.

He sighed and glanced up at the skylight pensively. She could almost feel him thinking.

"I don't know. It is worth a try now that we know it won't kill me," he whispered.

"Then we should try. We can take another boat out today." She kissed the tattoo, and the hand that had been rubbing along her spine sank into her tangled hair.

"Later." He gave her a devilish smile. "I had a plan for this morning, and I will not let you ruin it."

She angled her face toward his and he took her mouth in a way that told her she was wholly claimed.

"What was your plan?" she asked against his lips.

"I am going to worship my Goddess."

25

— • —

Finally pulling herself from bed, she left West passed out under the covers as she used the restroom and went to the kitchen for a glass of water.

The smile hadn't left her face since he had begun his 'worshiping' earlier in the morning. She knew this was what she had needed to continue on. She needed this intimacy with him, which both thrilled and steadied her. It gave her even more to fight for in the coming days.

She had never felt anything similar with other lovers. Yes, there was the lust— *Fates that lust*— but with West there was friendship and banter, playfulness and camaraderie. And, even more, she knew he would be her equal. She wouldn't have to lie like she had with her mortal lovers. She wouldn't have to hide her powers, her immortality. He'd cried out her *real* name last night, not Cordelia or the other aliases she'd collected over the years.

He was it for her and she knew it, but West had admitted to never sticking around for anyone before. Her mind went back to the night before when he told her it was only her. But had he meant it?

It would be up to her to show him he was capable of such a thing, and now that she had him, she was not going to let him go.

The pirate captain in her always got what she wanted.

Taking an empty glass from the cabinet, she moved to the tap to get some fresh water when her eyes caught on a shadowy figure outside her window.

A man stood on the beach—her very private, isolated section of beach. She stilled. The man was standing over something, something that looked like another person laying out on the sand. Her brows furrowed as she tried to look closer. Were they some lost sunbathers? It wouldn't be the first-time humans looking for a secluded spot stumbled upon her little beach sanctuary. She peered at them, but they were far enough away, with the sun at their back, that she couldn't tell if they were people she knew or lost humans.

Taking a sip of water, she considered if she should go out. She was only in her robe and worried about exposing herself, not her nudity, which never bothered her, but her home. No strangers even knew a home was tucked in these caverns.

When one of the shadowy figures suddenly had wings, she dropped her glass of water. The glass broke on the floor, but she barely heard it shatter.

No. This could not be good.

Her feet were moving her body to the door before she realized West was yelling out her name from the bedroom, but she didn't stop. Shoving the door open, she ran through the sand toward the figures, and Thanatos came into view. He turned to her with a solemn expression.

No.

She didn't want to look down, but she did anyway, and a sob escaped her lips.

Lying in the sand, almost looking like he was sleeping, was Darren. His eyes were closed, his hands folded over his chest, and his clothes were soaking wet.

She fell onto her knees beside him. "He drowned?" she asked shakily. Her trembling hand hovered over him as if touching him would confirm everything. As if she somehow had control of this situation.

"It was not a natural death," Thanatos stated, placing a hand on her shoulder.

"How?" she asked. When she heard footsteps pounding in the sand behind her, she didn't look up; she could only stare down at Darren's unmoving chest.

"He did drown, but it was not a natural drowning," Thanatos told her, not unkindly. "His death was quick." His hand squeezed her shoulder again before he let go and another pair of arms went around her. Unable to look at Darren any longer, she curled into West's embrace and savored the thumping of his heart against her cheek.

"Shh, I'm here," he whispered against her hair, and she realized she was silently crying against his bare skin.

Darren. One of the sweetest souls.

No. Not him.

Her mind was flooded with memories of him. They may not have been soulmates, but he was her friend in the end. Always there.

When she pulled away a bit, West hesitated in letting her go, but did once she patted his arm reassuringly. She stood and turned to Thanatos.

"If it wasn't natural, then what happened?" she asked him. West stood next to her and took one of her trembling hands in his.

Thanatos stilled and his eyes went pure white, a hint of his skeletal form showing through his tan skin.

"He was asleep in his bed before he tasted salt water. He cannot see anything, only darkness..."

Amphitrite took a deep inhalation at the words before she turned to West. His eyes narrowed and brows crinkled.

"How does a person drown in bed?" she spoke aloud, more to herself than the men.

"Unless there was flooding in Halcyon that we all managed to sleep through..." Thanatos said dryly but shut down the beginning of his murky humor when Amphitrite looked up at him with censure.

"He was killed and then left on the beach in front of Amphitrite's home?" West asked, and his voice held a dangerous edge she'd never heard before.

"Correct. He did not die here." Thanatos agreed and looked back down at Darren's body.

West tightened his hand on hers and stepped closer, moving to stand against her back. The heat of his body anchored her, protected her from the chilly breeze.

"Then this is a message for her. A warning," he said. He grabbed her arms and turned her to face him. "You are in danger. Whoever did this, they know who Darren was to you, and know where you live."

She had never seen West with such an expression before. His mouth was a tight line and his eyes worried. Immense fear rolled off of him in waves.

Blinking, she tried to streamline her thoughts. Why would someone do this to get to her? What was their message?

"I have to take the soul," Thanatos interrupted. "Do you need me to..."

She knew what he was asking. Did she want him to handle taking Darren's body somewhere he could be found and taken care of? That he would do that for her made her love the Reaper even more. He had always taken care of Persephone, and now he was extending his care to her.

Nodding, she turned away from the process of separating the soul from the body. West pulled her against his chest. He held her tight enough that if she wanted to turn and look, she couldn't.

"We will find out who did it," he whispered to her as he watched Thanatos handle Darren.

"There's only one answer. Only one person who would warn me like this."

"Who?" he asked, tightening his hold, and placing his forehead against hers.

"It is the same woman," she whispered, more to the surrounding wind than to West.

"What do you mean?"

"The woman who killed the sailors... she killed Darren."

"There is no way to know that. Why would she even have a reason to kill Darren?"

"She knows I am searching for her. She knows I— *we*— know about the Mystic."

"Then she *is* after you. That,"— he pointed to the beach where Darren had laid only moments ago, looking so peaceful for such a traumatic death— "was a threat!"

"You assume this is the first time I have received a threat," she responded. How could one live forever without making enemies?

Looking up, she focused on West's dark eyes.

"This is much bigger than we thought," he whispered. "I am not okay with letting you out of my sight anytime soon. If this is the same person who had a hand in sinking the Mystic..." He swallowed down his words and looked out to the water before he proceeded. His eyes flicked back to hers with fear. "Please, please promise me you will be careful. I only just got you..."

She ran her hand along his jaw, and his eyes closed as he turned slightly to kiss her palm.

"I promise. I will be careful."

West leaned forward and gently grazed his lips along her temple.

"They know we're looking for them. Whoever they are."

Someone had just upped the ante.

Amphitrite was not as well versed in death as her sister, so the graveyard was not somewhere she would ever feel comfortable. It was devoid of the life she so loved. Nature was around them, but it was the type of life that Devon thrived upon, not her— green, lush flora.

Standing over the marble headstone, it felt far too small to honor such a beautiful man. His life was pure and cut far too short.

There were not many people in attendance. Darren had some work friends, but he had lost his parents when he was in college, and as an only child, he had no siblings. He never spoke of any other relatives, and she wondered how a man with so much loss in his life had been able to look at the bright side so often.

Since he had no family, Amphitrite stepped in to give him a proper burial. Refusing to let him wander the shore of the Styx, she had made sure he had the full rites so he could rest in peace.

"May Hades, God of the Underworld, guide his soul and protect it for eternity..." the Priestess intoned in a low, doleful voice.

Amphitrite closed her eyes to roll them, wishing Hera was here to liven it up with her whole 'there are no Gods' tirade that Amphitrite had been privy to on several occasions.

"I didn't know him," West whispered from beside her, his words soft as he took her hand in his, "but he seemed like a good man. I can't imagine you being with anyone who wasn't."

Her hand tightened around his, clutching it like a lifeline. She was so incredibly grateful to him at that moment. She could not imagine many men who would take the day off work to go to their lover's side as she mourned an ex-boyfriend.

"He was," she murmured, her voice cracking. West put his arm around her shoulder, and she tucked in closer to his side.

Only a few of Darren's colleagues stood alongside the grave as the Priest and Priestess continued the rites. In the distance, three figures stood beneath an olive tree. Her sisters and Devon stood away from the crowd, but they were there to pay their respects. Beside Persephone, her hand in his, Devon gave Amphitrite a nod.

Hera mouthed 'Hades' with a raised eyebrow.

Her heart beat a little harder at the love she felt from them as they took the time to see to her and honor Darren. A life lost was so small when you lived forever, but for her, they did this.

'Thank you,' she mouthed to them.

Lost in her thoughts, she hadn't realized the Priest and Priestess had finished the service. Gradually, everyone started to walk from the burial site, exiting through the graveyard back to their own lives.

She swallowed against the onslaught of emotions that hit her as the graveyard emptied.

Anger and guilt.

Anger at whoever had done this. Anger at herself for not knowing who they were or what they planned next.

Guilt because although she had spent a year with this man, it took only a few short weeks of knowing West to realize she couldn't feel for Darren as more than a friend. Anyone in her past, really. She should have let him go far earlier and so his death was on her. She would find who was responsible and she would make them pay in the most painful way possible.

"If you're hungry, I can grab some lunch and we can go back to my place," West suggested, taking the initiative to give her the reprieve he knew she needed.

Ever since they'd discovered Darren's body, West had been her Guardian, taking care of her while she healed, and taking care of everything else so that the world didn't crash down around her while she was vulnerable.

Looking up into his eyes, something seared her chest.

There would be no reprieve. She had to deal with this danger so that there would be a future to share with West Murphy.

"Let's go back to mine. It's time I faced this and found the culprit. No more hiding from the reality of what was put in front of me."

She needed to find the Titan causing this and if a siren had betrayed her. If a siren was the woman on the Mystic, then there would be hell to pay. She wouldn't take the chance of losing Halcyon. Her sisters. West.

She'd drown the world before that happened.

26

Amphitrite tried to reconcile the quiet beach she stood upon with the same place that had held a traumatic event so very recently.

Long ago, in the human wars preceding the Great War, she had stood upon a similar beach, one that only months earlier had held the dead of two nations. Human history revered the place like a monument, but it was more like a mausoleum since they sent so many young men to their deaths on that beach.

The least the humans could do was honor the dead they sacrificed, as their ancestors did before them.

Always a sacrifice... something in those words stuck in Amphitrite's brain. She couldn't make sense of why such words should mean anything, but they did. She felt it deep in her bones.

"Come inside," West whispered as his arms went around her middle, his warm chest against her back and his lips near her ear.

"I am tired of this," she sighed, and she felt his arms go slack for a moment.

"Tired of what?" he asked, and she could hear the worry in his voice. Turning to face him, she stepped out of his arms.

"Tired of the endless loop we are stuck in. Every piece of paperwork has been tampered with. My spies are finding *nothing!*" She could feel herself losing control and she went with it. Control was not helping her find answers. "What use am I as a Guardian of the sea if I cannot protect a Fates damned thing?"

West took a step towards her but stopped, holding his hands up.

"You've been through a loss, and yes, I am as frustrated as you are, but this will fix nothing."

"What? What won't fix anything, West?" she snapped.

His eyes flickered with blue for a moment. "Losing control."

Her eyes narrowed. "Like with the Minoans?" she asked, taking a step toward him.

"That is not what I said. Do not put words in my mouth," he shot back, edging forward.

Suddenly, the energy to fight fled her completely. She couldn't face him. Not with everything hanging over them, crushing them.

Calling upon a portal, she light jumped the short distance to the shoreline. Stepping into the waves, she began pulling her clothes off.

"What are you doing?" West yelled from a few dozen yards away, where she had been a moment before.

Tossing her jeans to the side, she looked over her shoulder at him. He was walking toward her with long strides, his eyes burning with determination.

"I am going to use my fucking power to find a murderous traitor," she shouted back. "If I can feel every creature in the sea, then I can damn sure find one woman!" With a growl, she ripped off her underwear and jumped into the water. As soon as she slipped beneath the waves, she let her siren form take over.

Before she could make it past the cliffs and out to the open sea, a watery hand wrapped around her waist and pulled her back to the surface.

West took on his mortal form, his eyes glowing ocean blue.

"You are not going alone to face off against someone murdering people. This person, whoever it is, left that threat for you on the beach and if you think I am letting you attempt that alone, you are more of an idiot than I am. And," he growled, "do you actually have a tail right now?"

Her brows furrowed. "What?"

"Holy shit, you do. Fates, that was a thing for me as a teen," he groaned, and he let himself go under the water a moment before popping back up. "Nope. Cold water is doing nothing."

"Are you actually doing this right now? I am having a nervous breakdown and you are... getting worked up about my siren form?" she seethed.

He blinked at her. "Yes? No, I just... come on... give a man a break. There is a reason sirens are known for drowning men at sea."

"So, instead of dealing with your nonsense right now, I could just drown you?"

A small smile crossed his lips. "Yeah, and I'd go to my death willingly."

He swam closer to her as she let her siren form dissipate, her mortal legs kicking in the water.

"Listen, I'll be serious," he said, treading water so close they brushed chests. "I need you to not run off and try to take on whoever this is on your own. I need you to let me be a part of this." He gently pushed back the wet hair from her face. "You promised, remember?"

He gave her a pained look. This was about more than her breakdown on the shore.

"Talk to me," she pleaded, placing her hands on his jaw.

"I didn't care about the woman in the warehouse. It was more of... just the shock of a life lost in such a way..." His hands went around her waist, and he pulled her to him. "I am not sure how I would react to something happening to you. If I hunted down those men for a woman I didn't know... could you imagine what I would do for one I am in... romantically involved with?"

She closed her eyes and hugged him, tucking her face into the crook of his neck.

"I have fought Vikings and pirates, traveled to the darkest reaches of the sea, and stood on my own in the most dangerous of situations, time after time," she said against his skin. "I will make it through this as well."

He pulled back and pinned her with his stare, silently begging her to understand something she couldn't seem to grasp. Perhaps she did, but thought it was unlikely to be what she thought it was. Perhaps she was reading too much into what was between them.

Licking his lips, he grasped the back of her neck and leaned forward until his forehead touched hers.

"You saw what happened to Devon when Persephone was stabbed," he whispered. "I cannot guarantee I wouldn't take it further."

Her heart pounded in her ears. "West—"

He cut her off with a kiss.

If he truly meant that, they were way deeper than she had thought. She returned his kiss with all the frustration, joy, passion, and fear she felt.

West deepened the kiss as she moved her hands to the button of his slacks beneath the water.

Suddenly, his clothes disappeared, and he whispered, "Found a new party trick."

"Oh, that is going to come in handy," she whispered back, wrapping her legs around his waist. With her next breath, she felt him move into her. They dipped under the water, kissing and making love beneath the waves.

West knew the paparazzi still followed him. Since he'd sobered up and stopped haunting bars, most of the photographers had left him alone. But there were a few who still tracked him since he'd taken up the post of CEO. They kept their distance, but they were always there.

What surprised him was how, since they had spent more and more time together, Amphitrite had managed to evade the photographers always around the corner.

Until today.

West clutched the paper in the elevator as it ascended to the executive offices of Oceanus Industries. He wanted to go to the Halcyon Herald and tear it apart from the framework. He wanted to storm into the editor's office and threaten them until they were intimidated enough to leave Amphitrite alone. But he knew that wasn't possible.

When the elevator doors opened on his floor, he was ready to bite someone's head off. As he strode down the hall, he spotted the Vice President of accounting standing there reading the paper. He recognized the boldly printed headline. When he passed him, he released an inhuman growl, and the man dropped the paper to look around for the predator who could unleash such a noise.

"Mr. Murphy, you have someone in your office," Darla called to him. She waited by her desk, which was just across from his office, a coffee in her hand— and only coffee. No paper this morning.

Smart woman. No wonder his father hired her.

Turning back to the VP, he ripped the paper from his hands.

"Watch what trash you read in my presence," he sneered, throwing the paper in Darla's trash bin, and resuming the walk to his office.

His mind ran through the article's words over and over.

"Coincidence or something more nefarious? Zephyr Maritime Administrator starts relationship with Oceanus Industries CEO immediately after death of her longtime partner, Darren Woodstein.'

When he opened the door, he was face to face with Mira, who held a copy of the offending paper in her hands.

Before he thought it through, he grabbed the paper from her and threw it in the trash bin at his desk. The metal bin tumbled on its side and rolled a foot away.

"What can I help you with, Ms. Flint?" he asked coldly as he turned to her.

"I apologize for the early morning interruption, but I need to know—"

"If I am sleeping with the head of the Maritime Administration?" His voice was cool, but he knew his eyes held fire.

Mara Flint squared her shoulders, stood taller and straightened her suit before she pierced him with her stare.

"It would be a huge conflict of interest and would require someone to look into why the head of our government's ocean authority is in a romantic relationship with the CEO of a privately owned company that is required to abide by the rules set by said administration."

Shit.

Why had he not thought of this? Did he think himself already above human law after only knowing he was a Titan for such a short period of time?

However, West had never cared for rules or professionalism before and he'd been focused on actual threats, not corporate or government red tape.

Fixing his cuffs, which had bunched when he threw away the paper, he stepped up to Mira Flint.

She picked the wrong day to bring this shit to his doorstep.

"If you have nothing more important on your plate at work than opening an investigation into my personal life, then feel free. Go ahead and waste everyone's time only to learn nothing has changed on a professional level within Oceanus since my father was in charge."

"A catastrophic wreck happened since your father left—"

"Not only was my father still technically at the helm during that time, but I was also not involved with the Administrator then. Your point is moot," he said, then turned and walked around to sit in his desk chair. Taking a stack of papers, he straightened them before laying them down and folding his hands on top. His eyes held hers. "As I said, go ahead and waste your time."

Silence engulfed the room and hidden from view beneath the desk, his leg jumped nervously.

"I will. I do not want to cause you an issue... but it is a conflict of interest." She gave him a tight smile, and he nodded in agreement and dismissal. She turned to the door, but her hand halted on the doorknob before she looked over her shoulder at him.

"I met my husband in a similar way," she told him quietly.

He raised an eyebrow at the turn of the conversation but stayed silent. She turned back to the door when she received no response.

"He stood up for what he believed in, which was dangerous in his particular field of work," she explained, her back to him, and her voice cracked slightly. "I wasn't aware of how far he had taken it, not until I lost him. I don't know what truly happened to him, but I have theories. Don't follow my path, Mr. Murphy."

Sitting back, West digested her words.

"I am sorry to hear that. I hope you are able to find out what happened to him and that you find peace."

She opened the door and cast a hesitant smile his way.

"I think I am on the right track to figuring it out, actually."

Amphitrite was having a difficult time understanding what was being reported to her.

In her office, Calista, Medusa, and three sirens stood before her.

"Wait, you are saying there have been actual military uprisings in Goryeo?" Amphitrite asked, referring to the far most country in Zephyr. The one that the Senators, Finley and her brother Kiran, were from, and the one that shared a border with their hesitant ally, the Sereian Empire.

Calista nodded, but Medusa spoke.

"Yes, we have intel that in the last week alone, Goryeo has had multiple incidents of military action against its own citizens. There is now a strict curfew, and some cities are in complete lockdown."

Amphitrite sat back at her desk, her mind reeling.

"Does Hera know?" she asked, knowing that her spies always came to her first, but something like this needed Archon involvement immediately.

The women looked at each other.

"Not that we are aware of. Goryeo has chosen to keep it an internal matter instead of reaching out for help outside of their country," said a siren.

"They worry they will look weak and up for invasion," Calista stated. Having her own seat in the Senate made her privy to such concerns.

"I need to speak to my sister," Amphitrite decided aloud. When she stood up, the sirens stepped back and bowed in deference to her status. Calista nodded, but Medusa just crossed her arms. She had worked alongside Amphitrite for far too long to care about proper etiquette when in the presence of a higher power.

"I will call another Senate meeting in a week's time to discuss these new political issues," Calista told her. "I hope to have more to share with them before then." Calista nodded to Amphitrite and motioned the sirens to follow her out of the room. The women bowed again before filing out after the Senator.

When the door clicked shut, Medusa raised an eyebrow. "It never stops, does it?"

"No," she sighed. "Speaking of, do you have any updates on our General?"

Medusa shook her head. "He's a highly regimented man."

"No power slips?"

"Not in use," Medusa answered. "His aura, however... is very strong with Titan power."

Amphitrite frowned and crossed her arms. "It's so frustrating he has an alibi for the Mystic's sinking," she muttered. General Olethros had been at the party— just like Medusa, Oceanus, West, and herself—when the Mystic went down. "Something's not right."

Medusa gave a slight shrug. "Is it ever?"

Amphitrite thought about the potential of a defected siren, something she'd kept from Medusa and hummed in agreement.

"Never."

27

Amphitrite let the breeze dissipate from her light jump as she stood before the thrones of Olympus, all but one filled.

Hera, Persephone, and Devon sat before her, all waiting for her since she put out the call. She knew Olympus was the safest place to speak as no one but them, and those they were bonded to, could stand upon the mountain without interference from the Goddesses... and God.

Hera sat on the throne taller than the rest, as was her right as the Queen of the Goddesses. She was in full regalia, with her golden laurel crown inlaid with diamonds upon her head and her long white dress, which shimmered with golden flecks under the mountaintop's celestial light.

Next to Hera, Persephone sat in her throne etched with a pomegranate surrounded by narcissus flowers. Her sapphire crown glimmered against the black and silver of her long, flowing gown.

And then there was the newly made God. Devon sat beside Persephone in his forest green shirt and slacks. His throne, a startling addition, was carved with a winged serpent to indicate he was the God of rebirth. Like Hera, he wore a laurel crown, but his was adorned with green leaves instead of Hera's diamonds.

She nodded to her family in greeting, and all but Hera responded in kind. Hera only looked at her expectantly, waiting for an explanation with her eyebrow arched high on her face in question.

Stepping up to the empty throne, the one engraved with a trident; her symbol through the ages, the power in her body responded and she transformed. A long aqua dress materialized on her body, fabric flowing like water. A slight weight levelled on her brow, and she knew her crown of sea glass had appeared.

"Thank you for coming so promptly," she said once seated.

Hera impatiently tapped her fingers against the armrest of her throne. "And what, pray tell, is the reason I left a date to come sit on a stone in the middle of a mountain?" she asked.

Sighing, Amphitrite called up their globe from beneath the mountain and watched as it rose from the dark stone floor, lights indicating where the densely populated cities could be seen. There were very few, all grouped in Zephyr, the rest of the globe pitch black.

She cast a sidelong glance at Devon, who appeared troubled by the stark reminder that the majority of the world was still in ruins despite his efforts. Since he became a God, Devon moved from place to place in an attempt to call back life to the dead lands.

The poor man had one hell of a job ahead of him, but he persevered and for that, she held a large amount of respect for her new brother.

Amphitrite reached toward the globe, squared her fingers, and gradually drew them apart, making the view of the planet closer and closer. When she zoomed in on Goryeo, she heard an intake of breath from Hera. Her sister leaned forward intently; her hands white-knuckled on the armrests.

Red points of light, like thousands of ants, swarmed across Goryeo, where the military was currently in action.

"It is true," Hera whispered, and Persephone and Devon stared at her in question, but her focus was wholly on the globe in the center of the room.

Amphitrite held still, not wanting to break her sister's concentration, but she was ready in case Hera called on her to do something. Should the Queen order it, Amphitrite would be required to execute any plan Hera devised.

Instead of saying anything else, Hera let out a musical whistle.

Above them, a large eagle flew towards the mountain, its size decreasing as it wove in between the columns. The sun caught the gold feathers of the beautiful, familiar raptor.

It had been so long since Amphitrite had seen the golden eagle, named Edie by a young Hera, that she was in awe all over again as the bird of prey landed on Hera's throne, its claws large enough to take down a good size dog should it choose.

Hera peered up at the bird with fond, but serious, eyes. "I need eyes in Goryeo," she stated, and Edie tightened her talons on the marble of the throne before pushing off and disappearing in a flash of brilliant golden light.

"You knew of the uprisings?" Amphitrite asked after a beat of silence.

"Knew they were actually happening in the real world? Not for sure. Dreamt of something of this nature happening? Yes, the other night. I've been having Kiran look into the situation with the local government there in place of Finley while she searches for Hestia. I've yet to hear anything back." Leaning back on the throne, Hera looked so much more tired than Amphitrite had ever seen her. "I had hoped it was only stress from what had happened in the Underworld."

Persephone looked at Amphitrite then, concern on her face as her eyes flickered between her sisters and the globe.

"Dare I ask... but do we believe the Titans have already moved forward on a new plan of action?" Persephone calmly inquired. Devon shifted uncomfortably beside her, his expression holding both uneasiness and a seriousness she had only seen immediately before their last battle.

"I think it is far too much of a coincidence that the dark water grows stronger, wrecks are happening without my knowledge, and Darren was murdered and left on my beach to find. Now, we are seeing political uprisings..."

"It's the damn Titans and we all know it," Hera growled. "They would not give up the first go-round. No, Atlas was working on so many backup plans our heads would spin if we knew the whole of it." She pinned Amphitrite with her stare. "What else do we not know?"

Amphitrite glanced at Devon, wondering if West had confided in him about the Leviathan. His expression was still serious and stiff, but there was no knowing look to his eyes. He either knew and his poker face was immaculate, or he was as much in the dark as her sisters. She determined it would be up to her to tell them.

"West called a Leviathan to the surface while we were out training."

Persephone's eyes went wide. Devon frowned, confused.

Hera growled.

"Just now finding this out, are we?" Hera snapped, her fingers tapping a rhythm Amphitrite had long since learned was the precursor to some serious Hera drama.

In for a penny, in for a pound.

"He was able to awaken the Leviathan because he is the heir to the lost Minoan civilization. His mother is the descendant of Phaedra, daughter of King Minos."

The silence in the room was deafening. While shock was plain across Devon and Persephone's faces, Hera looked like she was planning something as her outraged expression faded into calculation. She leaned forward on her elbow and set her chin in her hand, contemplating as she stared at the globe.

"Minoan?" Devon echoed.

"An ancient civilization believed by some to be the Atlanteans from the stories of Plato," Persephone offered, having been one of the people most interested in hearing Plato drone on and on.

"Atlantis..." Devon whispered in awe as he stared off in thought.

"It was not called Atlantis... but West is running with the name and I'm not going to be the one to correct him," she said with an airy tone she didn't feel. Persephone watched her closely, sympathy in her eyes. Her sisters knew her history with the Minoans, knew how she'd mourned the people lost to her rage.

She glanced at Devon and gave Persephone a small shake of her head. The tragic irony was not lost on her, but she couldn't think of it tonight.

Hera straightened in her throne, all regal posture and determined stare.

"Amphitrite, you have trained with West and helped to shape his powers as a Titan. Tell me, will he fight alongside us?" Hera asked in the authoritative tone as the Queen of Goddesses.

In the corner of her eye, Amphitrite caught sight of Persephone halting a response from Devon with a quelling hand.

"Without a doubt," Amphitrite replied.

Nodding, Hera stood.

"Well, I am going to go do some investigating into those little temper tantrums in Goryeo that are causing us to use our military funds. Keep me informed and call me should anyone in Halcyon so much as sneeze."

With that, Hera was gone in a flash of light.

Amphitrite blinked at the now-empty throne and looked to Persephone, who whispered something in Devon's ear before placing a kiss on his lips. Devon turned to Amphitrite and with a nod of farewell, he light jumped away. Persephone stood and crossed the marble platform with eyes full of love and concern.

Grasping Amphitrite's shoulders, Persephone gave her a kiss on each cheek before pulling back to make eye contact.

"Darren took well to judgement and went on to Elysium," she whispered, and Amphitrite felt a weight lifting from her soul at her sister's words. "He had a human illness and wasn't long for the world anyway, which I am sure made it easier to adapt to death."

Persephone paused, allowing Amphitrite to process her words, then smiled gently.

"Before he drank of the Lethe, he asked of you, Amphitrite. He gave his blessing to your relationship with West, wishing you both only happiness and love."

Before Amphitrite could reply, Persephone disappeared into the shadows.

Closing her eyes, a tear fell down Amphitrite's cheek in both loss and joy. A bright light in such a dark place was what she needed to spur her on in the fight ahead.

"Thank you, Darren," she whispered as she called to her sea to take her home.

28

Amphitrite woke feeling so groggy her eyes were barely able to open to the newborn light of the morning. She rolled onto her back and realized the bed was empty. West had already left for work. His sleep pants were thrown over the side chair where he had left his suit the night before.

A headache had come on over dinner, so she spent the night in West's arms fighting off a migraine instead of doing much more thrilling activities. And it looked like today would be more of the same for her.

She normally only got such headaches when she overexerted herself power-wise, but she could not think of what she had done recently that would cause this episode.

With a sigh, she closed her eyes to rest, but it only brought on more thoughts and worries, which in turn irritated her headache further.

The Mystic swirled in her mind.

The lost sailor.

The dark waters.

The uprisings in Goryeo.

And she heard from one of her spies last night— there was no word on Hestia's scion. Her sister's power was latent in some mortal, and they were picking through the haystack, straw by straw.

The Titans would be well and truly done winning this war by the time they found the person who held their sister's power inside of them.

When she pushed herself up from the bed, her arms felt like they were made of lead, and her entire body was sluggish and worn. In previous migraine bouts, she'd diffused her power through her limbs to help ease the various pains, but it was risky to call on her power while it was still recovering, especially if she had overexerted herself. Now, though, she couldn't recall overusing her powers at all, so she decided to give herself a little restorative boost. When she reached for her power, a bolt of anxiety hit her.

There was a block on her power.

Her blood pumped quickly through her, adrenaline in place of where her power should be.

Why could she not call to the sea for strength?

In a panic, her adrenaline helped her to push away from the bed, only to find herself falling forward. She quickly caught herself on the nightstand, succeeding only in knocking her lamp and clock to the floor.

Barely able to hold her own weight up, she tried to stumble to her front door, a sick feeling in the pit of her stomach. She needed to get to the sea. Her mind was in a frenzy of emotions, and it was fear taking the lead.

At the doorway of her home, her entire body broke out into a sweat. Her arms and legs shook from the effort of pushing herself forward. Her chest felt like it was caving in as sharp pains ran from her neck and through her trembling limbs.

For the first time in millennia, she felt mortal.

Curling her fingers around the stone pillars of the doorframe, she used her body weight to slingshot through the threshold and onto the beach.

Stumbling onto the sand, her eyes went wide as she took in the shore and ocean before her.

"No," she whispered as a hum in her mind turned to a roar. The loud chaos was exploding with the painful cries from her beloved sea creatures as they tried to fight the evil of the waters.

Falling to her hands and knees in the sand, she cried out. She tried to call for help, but she was too weak. Her vision went dark, and she felt like she was dying all over again, a sensation she had forgotten after so long.

Losing consciousness, she did not feel her body hitting the ground.

Her last thought was that the dark waters had finally made it to Halcyon.

"We'd love to work with you. Oceanus Indu—" West stopped mid-sentence, his hand going to his head as a wave of dizziness passed through him.

One of the men he had been meeting with stood up. "Mr. Murphy, are you alright?"

He shook his head to clear it, but the action only seemed to make it worse.

"Um..." He tried to focus on what he needed to do. "I will have my assistant write up the contracts and send them over to sign. I apologize. I have a sudden headache."

He stood, swaying only slightly, and the three other men in the room joined. West shook their hands but could feel the fuzziness in his mind increasing by the minute. With a smile, he left the meeting and tried to speed walk to his office.

"Mr. Murphy," Darla called out to him as he approached, her face full of fear. "The Maritime Administration and Safety Board have made a request that we order all Oceanus Ships to dock. As soon as possible."

Her hand shook as she handed him a piece of paper with the Zephyr Maritime Administration letterhead. It was not solely to Oceanus Industries, but all the shipping conglomerates. Raising his head to look at Darla, his vision slowly blurring at the sides, he tried to focus on her face. He had no idea what the hell was happening, but Amphitrite had such a bad headache last night, and now this.

"The sea, it's..." She shook her head as fresh tears fell from her eyes and the scent of fear permeated the air. "The polluted water..."

Were the dark waters advancing?

Alarm shot through his disoriented body, and he hurried to his office where he could light jump to Amphitrite and get some answers. Darla's voice followed him.

"Dispatch has called in all the ships, but it took longer since Ms. Wells was not in today." West stopped in his tracks and turned to Darla.

Amphitrite never made it to work?

"They are operating without an administrative lead? Who is in her place? Who sent out the notice?" He rapidly fired off his questions at poor Darla, earning only a shrug in return. There had not been anything more than the request to dock the ships on the letterhead. No name or signature to be found.

He needed to get to Amphitrite.

"Thank you, Darla. I will handle it from here," he murmured, slurring a bit, as he shut the office door behind him. He called on his power to light jump and found he only had just enough to make it to the shore in front of Amphitrite's house. His legs buckled a little on the sand before he managed to steady himself.

Further down the shore, Ingrid and Zeus were stomping at the ground in agitation. Sand blew up from their hooves as they danced around something lying in the sand.

Another body?

Dread and fear pushed him forward. He ran, stumbling more than actually running, but he wouldn't stop until he knew who lay there.

When he landed on his knees in the sand, a choked yell tore from his throat at finding Amphitrite unconscious, but alive, on the shore.

The headache pounded in his ears and behind his eyes, intensifying as he pulled Amphitrite into his arms. His vision distorted as if he were looking through a kaleidoscope.

He could feel the dark water choking off the sea like it was his own life force. If his weeks-long connection to the sea caused this much dread, he was terrified for Amphitrite, whose bond with the sea had strengthened over *centuries*.

Closing his eyes, he tried to focus on pushing back the water, but he was far too drained to do much of anything. How had Amphitrite been able to hold the water off on her own for so long?

A mental exhaustion like he had never felt before had his brain feeling sluggish, but he pushed through it as much as he could, trying to gather any amount of reserves he had left.

Nothing.

Looking at the hippocampi, he played the last card he had before he lost himself to the darkness, as Amphitrite had. He just hoped it worked.

"Find her sisters. Bring them here..." he whispered as he lost the fight, unsure if the horses even understood or knew where to find Hera and Persephone.

But they were his only hope. His last chance.

And he sent out a silent prayer as everything around him went black as night.

In the darkness, Amphitrite's consciousness stirred.

"Did it work?" Amphitrite heard whispered near her head. It sounded like Persephone's voice, but what was her sister doing here?

"No idea. I have plenty of other things to do than watch them wake up," Hera's voice came in loud and clear, not the least bit worried if she woke anyone up. "Good luck!"

"Oh, no you do not. You are not leaving me here to explain this," Persephone hissed. Footsteps sounded before a bolt of light lit her eyelids.

Amphitrite opened her eyes, wincing at the gritty feeling as she attempted to focus on the room around her.

Her gaze fell on Persephone, who stood rigidly with her back to her. She clenched her fists before she swung around and caught sight of Amphitrite looking at her.

"Oh, thank Chaos. You're awake!" Persephone gave her a relieved smile as she quickly sat into the chair beside the bed, pulling it closer and grasping Amphitrite's hands.

"Why do I feel like I was trampled in a stampede of horses?" she asked, her throat dry.

"That might have been preferable. At least you were unconscious. We tried different ways to help... but... "

Amphitrite's eyebrows lowered as her eyes narrowed.

"What happened?"

Persephone looked away and mumbled, "Damn you to the Underworld, Hera."

Amphitrite tried to tighten her hand around Persephone's, pleading with her eyes since her throat was so scratchy and dry.

"The dark waters came too close, killing off many of your creatures." She waited a bit for that to settle in Amphitrite's mind. Suddenly, she remembered the futile attempt to make it to the sea, the pain of the creatures calling out for help, and tears flooded her eyes.

"I am so sorry, Amphitrite," Persephone whispered as her other hand pushed a lock of Amphitrite's sweat-slicked hair back from her forehead. "You and West were weakening by the second and we had to do something."

Letting her head fall to the opposite side, she saw West unconscious next to her. Devon stood on the other side of the bed with a sad smile on his face, his piercing green eyes gleaming with an empathy that scared her.

Had West almost died?

"We tried to push our power into you both, even had Devon, Thanatos, and Hecate try. Nothing was working..." Persephone trailed off, her eyes avoiding Amphitrite's expectant look. Her sister looked at Devon beseechingly.

"What did work?" she asked, her heartbeat increasing. "What worked, Persephone?" she asked again when her sister remained silent.

Persephone closed her eyes, took a deep breath, and raised the hand holding Amphitrite's between them.

Oh, Fates.

The men around him were yelling, and so he took his opportunity.

With his face pressed against the cold concrete floor, he tried desperately to loosen the ties around his wrists.

He ignored the pain that days of being bound had caused. His wrists were raw, the flesh freshly scabbed over from his last escape attempt. As he maneuvered his hands behind his back, the wounds reopened and covered his fingers with blood. The warm liquid made his hold slip, and he begged the Gods for help.

"Just fucking do it!"

Everything went quiet for a moment, only the dull hum of the overhead light brave enough to make a sound in the tense silence.

"I'll do it. Grab the brat," one of the men ordered, and West fought harder to get out. The cloth gag in his mouth had long ago dried up his saliva, and his voice was raw from screaming. Even so, he yelled.

The brat was him. That was how they referred to him since the day they took him from her bed.

The woman's screams had stopped, and the subsequent sobs had stopped soon after.

Those animals had raped her. He wanted to throw up, but there was nothing in his stomach.

Rough hands grabbed him under the shoulders and pulled him. All the men stank, as if they hadn't showered in weeks. Their body odor was ungodly, yet he couldn't be appalled by that alone anymore.

He looked at her. Her blonde hair was matted with blood. Her body was covered in blood and bruises instead of the sparkling black dress she had worn the night he met her at the club.

His own white shirt had long turned brown from dried blood and grime.

But her eyes... those vacant eyes. She was lost to this world now, but perhaps that was a good thing. The trauma she'd endured... he wasn't sure a person would come back from that.

"Shut him the fuck up!" one yelled and West realized he had been making noise, attempting to yell through his bruised and raw throat.

"Your daddy is finally paying up, brat. Lucky for you because I was about ready to put a bullet in ya and leave you for the sea to have. Seems poetic being that your spoiled ass makes all its money from it. Not sharing with the lot of the world."

"Shut up, Rik."

Another man, one who had rarely spoken, stepped through the door, the heavy metal slamming shut behind him. "Just get the brat to the spot and be done with this. I am tired."

Tired. Tired of raping a woman? Tired of beating him while he sat strapped to a chair, unable to save himself.

"Must... be... exhausted..." West coughed out around the gag. Stupid, he knew, but he was so tired of being at their mercy. He wished he had the ability to snap each of their necks, to end them and let their eyes go vacant like the woman on the floor.

Rik strode toward him and landed a punch to his stomach.

His already cracked ribs ignited a fire in his body, and he fell forward. He would have hit his knees on the floor if the henchmen weren't holding him awkwardly by the shoulders.

"More trouble than they're worth," the quiet man muttered and stepped over to the woman.

For the first time since he was taken, West said her name in his head.

Veronica.

He said a prayer to Hades that he would accept her crossing. Yes, she had done him wrong, but he knew what was coming and while he might have been beaten, she was betrayed far worse.

"Veronica... take her... to...." He tried to pray out loud but earned a hit to the head for it.

Wouldn't matter. None of his prayers to any of the gods had ever panned out.

"Now Rik, you gotta remember not to leave loose ends." The man took out a handgun, clicked the safety off, and aimed the barrel at Veronica's head.

As punishment, West looked at her, keeping his eyes on the victim. The loud pop of the gun echoed in the room, a sound he would never forget.

He stared. He stared until the blonde hair turned red, not from blood, but the actual color. Her face took the shape of the woman he had gotten to know and fallen for.

That was when he started screaming and fighting. His body bucked off Rik's hold. He struggled and yelled, trying to get to Amphitrite. Yet the hole... the bullet wound in her head.

The sight turned him into a feral animal. He swung on his captures.

"Put him down!" they yelled, and the gun came right up to his face. He welcomed it. He would go with her past the gates.

Forever.

West shot up from his bed in a panic. His body was tensed, ready to fight. When hands pushed down on his shoulders, he flinched and nearly vomited from the dread. The memory of the men holding him back by his shoulders was too fresh from his dream. His nightmare.

"Whoa, hey, lay back down," he heard Devon's voice, and realized it was his friend who held him down. And he didn't hold him down at all, really, as much as he gently grasped the sides of his shoulders.

West's heartbeat gradually returned to normal.

"He's awake!" Devon yelled out to someone. West blinked, clearing his vision, and took in the room around him. He was in Amphitrite's room— why was he in her room?

Did I sleep through my alarm? He wondered for a second longer before the deluge of memories fell upon him like a tidal wave.

Dark water. Amphitrite. Unconscious.

"What the fresh fuck happened?" West asked as he pushed up on his elbows and Devon grabbed a pillow to put under him so he could sit up. West raised his eyebrows at his friend.

"Not the hottest nurse I've had, but you'll do. I'll pass on the sponge bath though," he muttered. Suddenly, a bolt of pain went through his skull, and he moved to grab his head, but his hands stalled when he caught sight of something on his arm.

"Devon?" he asked with a concerned tone.

"Maybe we should wait until—"

"What the fuck happened to my arm?" West demanded as he tried again to stand up. Devon shoved him back down and pinned his shoulders to the bed.

"You are in no shape to get up and walk around yet. It took Amphitrite hours, and she is a professional at this Goddess stuff. Give it a minute, will you?" Devon huffed, withdrawing his hands, and straightening once he saw West wasn't moving from the bed.

"Explain. Now," was all West could say as he looked at the blueish-green scales now marking his skin. They started on his left hand and wrapped up around his arm to his elbow. Rotating his wrist, he could see another tattoo-like mark: a trident woven through with blue and white waves.

"Well, we couldn't push the power into you individually..." Devon's voice trailed off as he pushed his hand through his hair, and West's eyes caught on Devon's serpent mark.

West narrowed his eyes at Devon. He had only the barest concept of what this all meant, but he knew it couldn't be a coincidence that their markings were in the same place.

"It's a soulbond mark," Devon started hesitantly, waiting a beat before proceeding with his explanation, his expression careful.

"Out with it," West demanded.

"It's... like a marriage between Gods, only it is for eternity. Your souls are now intertwined in a way nothing can break. Your power feeds hers, and vice versa. Fates, I am not explaining this right..."

West swallowed thickly. "She is my wife now?" His tongue tripped over the unused word, but he needed terms he could wrap his mind around. He needed it spelled out for him.

Devon nodded. "Hera was able to summon Eros from Olympus... and he was able to bind you both even though you were unconscious," he whispered apologetically.

West laid back on the pillow as his mind circled the fact he was now not only married, but his soul was bound to another person. If he remembered Devon's account of the Underworld fiasco correctly, he had used the bond to transfer his power to Persephone to help her fight. Even just now, Devon had stated that he and Amphitrite would be able to share power. She was tethered to him through his mark.

Unbreakable. Devon's words echoed through his brain. He liked the sound of it.

Whether or not they knew it, West was pretty sure he just found his key to keeping Amphitrite safe. Was it how he had hoped? No. Was it really soon? Yes, very much so—they'd only just entered this ambiguous relationship. Had Amphitrite's safety not been at the forefront of his mind after Darren's death, he was sure he would have been freaking out.

His calm demeanor at finding out he was married seemed to worry Devon.

"Are you okay with this?" Devon asked and West evaluated the situation as much as he could in his current state. His strength was coming back to him, but the fuzziness in his brain created a lag.

West nodded.

"Yes, I am," he whispered, and Devon's eyebrows went up.

He only hoped she truly felt the same way.

Otherwise, it was about to get really awkward.

Something neither of them needed when they were about to go toe to toe with ancient and powerful enemies.

29

West strained to listen to Amphitrite's voice filtering in and out of the television as the signal faltered.

"... At this point in time, all ships have been called back to harbor. We are not allowing any transportation via water until the issue with the pollution has been resolved..."

Amphitrite faced the reporter squarely, but her image was fuzzy. A reason he never watched much television, aside from there being far too little to see, was the constant signal disruption. The fall of the old civilizations after the war also meant the loss of their ancestors' technology; their satellites, which had connected their world, were now just dead machines in the sky.

"What happened that there is so much more pollution? How could it reach the shore like it did?" the reporter asked, and West watched Amphitrite work to hold onto her composure. He knew the lack of answers was destroying her mentally right now, and it was all he could do to help her through the day while holding his own at work.

People were scared and he couldn't blame them.

Leaning forward on his desk, he noted the signs of fatigue in her face. She hadn't been sleeping, and as much as West tried to make her rest, he still felt her get up from the bed every night and walk to the shore. Sometimes he followed her, holding her as the sun's rays broke the horizon, and other times he let her have some time by herself.

"At this point in time, I have nothing to go on. We have scientists looking into it, but we ask that people stay away from the water. Currently, we have enough clean water in the system to support the city so there is no reason to panic. All we ask is to stay away from the shores and give us time to clean it up."

"Thank you," the reporter said, flashing a false smile as she turned to the camera. "You heard it from Cordelia Wells, lead administrator at the Zephyr Mar—"

He shut off the tv as he sat back in his chair and rubbed his hands over his face.

It was an absolute mess. His ships were docked, sailors were not earning pay, Oceanus was losing money, and he was still nowhere near figuring out what was going on.

West was losing his composure.

A timid knock at the door had him straightening himself up and putting his professional facade back into place.

"Yes?" he called out as he moved the sheets of paper around on his desk in a moment of anxiety.

The door opened a crack and Darla stuck her head in.

"Ms. Wells is here to see you," she announced, smiling, and opened the door further before West could say anything. His heart beat quickly, as it did most days now. She was his only bright spot in all the darkness and chaos.

Stepping inside, Amphitrite quickly shut the door behind her. Before she could take another step, West was around the desk and pulling her into his arms. He needed to feel her in order to pull himself back from the edge of a cliff. Her touch anchored him in a way he had *always* needed—his entire life, he realized— and he finally had it.

"I saw the interview," he whispered into her hair as she hugged him back. "We will figure this out. I promise you."

She simply nodded and held him tight against her. They were still not as strong as they had been before the water made it to shore, but the bond was helping to stabilize them.

"Our entire source of power is gone," she whispered against his chest, and he could hear the fear in her voice. "Our water... it's just gone."

Amphitrite had been good about putting on the airs of someone who wasn't worried, but that was for the public. Here in their space, alone with each other, she didn't fear talking to him and opening up. They were a team.

"No," he stated firmly, pulling away enough to grab her chin and lift her head up. "We will just have to battle on land to get our ocean back. We are not out of this fight yet."

He hoped what he said was true, but he feared the worst now, too.

"I need to know if this is a Titan's work, or one of their accomplices," she said, her aquamarine eyes beaming up at him with determination. "I am going to have to find the informant that I was trying to meet at the Enigma club."

"I'll go with you—"

"No," she interrupted, pushing back a little. "I will go alone. He doesn't handle surprises well and my presence will be enough to put him on edge. Also, I need you here as backup, in case something happens. I will be unavailable for several hours due to the heavy wards he uses."

"Then why the hell would I let you go there alone?" he asked, bewildered she would even think it was safe.

"Because,"—she put her hand on his chest— "I have done this millions of times before you were even born. I know this world of espionage and sin better than you do. I need you to stay safe and where you can step in if anything else happens with the ocean."

"When are you leaving?"

"I'll go around midnight."

"Alright," was all he said.

As much as he wanted to promise her he'd obey her orders, he couldn't let her go somewhere with wards that could block their communication, or his access to her. He wouldn't know if she was in trouble.

Kissing her, he hoped she hadn't noticed his absence of a promise.

Pulling her moto jacket on, Amphitrite stepped into the alleyway where the opening to the underground was located. The stink of the place alone most likely kept humans far away from ever stumbling upon the den of literal sin, but if not, the wards made it look like a typical dead end between two nightclubs.

She stuck to the shadows, wearing all black to blend into the darkness. Maybe it was the wards, or the tightness of the alleyway, but the moon found no purchase to shine here. Her black boots were soft and worn enough to barely make a sound on the stone as she walked toward the entrance.

A large satyr stepped out of a shadow and into her path.

"Go home, Goddess," he sneered. Obviously, he was not as forgetful as she had hoped. They had many run-ins during her more active spy days, and she usually had to either bribe him or challenge him to fight for access to the den.

"For old time's sake, let's not make a thing of this, Monty," she cajoled, her smile all teeth.

"It'll cost you," he growled.

"It always does," she muttered and sidestepped around him, giving the giant satyr a wide berth. Not out of fear, but the creature failed to understand the beauty of hygiene.

Knowing he would get his money, that she had people inside with the ability to pay out, he let her go, but not without cursing her name in the process.

The wall in front of her shimmered an iridescent rainbow of colors before the red door appeared. Not wanting to startle the already ridiculously irritable satyr, she waited for him to open it.

"I'll be looking for my payment tonight, betcha arse," he growled.

She nodded. "You know where my people are."

Her contacts would be wholly confused on why Amphitrite was suddenly back, but they would pay.

She stepped through the threshold into a pitch-dark hallway, and the door swiftly slammed shut behind her. Taking a breath, she pushed forward, walking until a red light flickered up ahead.

Reaver's Paradise.

Where every non-mortal went to satisfy their primal urges. When her father reigned, they were allowed to indulge their baser desires on the surface, but she and her sisters drove them underground when they took control.

And plenty of them were still bitter.

Plenty.

Putting her hand out, she walked until she felt the ward. Her fingers pressed against an invisible wall, and she cringed at the feeling. The stickiness of the ward's power was nothing like the veil of the Underworld.

When she pushed through, her senses were flooded with noise and flashing red lights. Her nose was bombarded with the smell of sweat, drugs, and sex. They were in full party mode tonight, so she would need to tread carefully not to end up fighting off an incubus, or worse.

Reaver's Paradise was less like a human nightclub and more like an underground market, only they didn't sell fruit and pastries; they traded in flesh and drugs. She policed it the best she could with her sisters.

There were rules: No mortals and everyone must be willing.

Past that, they had the run of the place.

Walking through the winding street of the underground, Amphitrite kept her eyes on the door barely visible at the end of the path. She knew he was there, the man who embodied trickery and deception. Looking anywhere else but her objective would make her vulnerable to the drugging magic around her, a compromising position she would have to fight her way out of.

As she navigated the mass of tangled bodies, hands reached out to her, running over her jacket and arms, venturing where they shouldn't. A body pressed hard against her side, and someone sniffed her hair.

Focus, she chastised herself. The hormones of the incubi filtered through the air around her. Demons were as real as the Goddesses, and they wouldn't stop because you said please. Behind the den's wards, her power was severely dampened, but the incubi's pheromones were a biological reality, not tied to their power.

As she neared the door, she felt the wards intensify until her power was essentially non-existent. For all their lack of laws, one must have a permit to hold their power here, lest the big man not have full control of his domain.

Halting at the door, she reminded herself who she was—she wasn't just the Goddess, or just the bureaucrat. Even though she hadn't been on the ground with her spies in quite some time, she tried not to focus on that little aspect of her life. She was the Sea Witch, feared by many. She'd had plenty of run-ins with the most unsavory of sorts. She had her weapons and could defend herself.

She was the fucking spymaster of Halcyon.

Shoving the doors open before she lost her nerve, the smoke of his cigar hit her, mingling with the stench of sex and drugs.

She heard the deep baritone of her informant before she saw him. "Ah! Look everyone! My beloved sea witch has come to me at last!"

Tensing, she peered into the shadowy haze as tittering laughter filled the air. As the smoke cleared, she saw him lounging in a bed of pillows with enough women around him to define the word 'harem'. They were all naked, covered in sweat, and she resisted the urge to roll her eyes. *Typical.* Probably gearing up for another round.

"Dolus," she greeted with bravado she didn't truly feel. Something that had once been ingrained in her now felt like playing a part.

Dolus smiled, his dark hair and blindingly white smile detracting from the man's crimson eyes. He was the spirit of trickery, treachery, and deception. She'd always had to play her cards right with him, since he was notorious for inescapable deals. Dolus was one of the worst tricksters of his demon brethren, who ancient Celts had called the 'fae'.

He was also the demon equivalent of a Titan, born to the same Primordial Gods Thanatos hailed from. The difference between Dolus and Titans, and even Thanatos, was his taste for blood. He bled both mortals and deities alike, which turned a God or Titan into something *other*.

Dolus eyed her with a hungry, taunting expression.

"What brings you to my lair? Finally taking me up on a ride?" he asked as he moved his pelvis in a vulgar gesture.

"As always, my answer is a hard no. I am here for information," she stated.

One of his women rose from the pillows, moving far too close to her, and poured something red into a glass that she knew wasn't wine.

"What information? Hm?" he asked, taking the glass the woman offered him. "About your precious sea?" He smirked before taking a sip.

"It is to the shores—"

"Yes, I know. And as you know as well, it is no more natural than I am. Yet, why?" He pretended to think, tapping a finger on his chin, gold rings glinting in the low light. He stood, handing his drink off to one of the nude women, and strode towards her, only halting when Amphitrite took a step back. Her hand darted to her hip where a tactical knife was strapped but Dolus only smiled at her defensiveness. "Perhaps you are having trouble finding your answers because you trust the wrong people."

In a blur, he was behind her, grabbing her hips as he pushed his pelvis against her, his arousal pressing into her back. She tried not to gag, since she had been sure Dolus would do something like this, but it was too disgusting not to.

She angled her head and spotted him in her peripheral. "Who should I trust?" she asked with a sneer. When he swept his hands up her waist, she tried to step away, but he yanked her back against him.

"Not all of your allies are so loyal, sea witch," he whispered near her ear. "Some have every intention of seeing you down on your knees before them... and not in the way I have in mind for you."

She felt wet heat on her neck. He was licking her! She grabbed her knife and whirled, pressing it against his throat as she backed him into the wall. The girls let out a collective gasp before they erupted in moans.

Sick.

"Who?" she demanded, but Dolus grabbed her hand and ran his tongue along the blade of the knife, cutting himself. She winced and shoved him away, but he clutched her hand tighter and moaned as blood filled his mouth. When he closed his eyes in pleasure, she successfully freed herself from his hold.

He opened his eyes, revealing brightened red irises. His power flooded to the surface, almost suffocating her.

Dolus looked at her with a jeering twist of his mouth as he walked around her and back to his harem.

"One you will never see coming..."

West understood now why Amphitrite was against him coming. Not only had it cost him a large sum to enter the Reaver's den, but his power was completely gone.

Following Amphitrite had probably not been his best idea, but the thought of her alone in a place like this made his stomach turn.

Trying to avoid several women gyrating together, he accidentally backed into another. She rubbed her naked body against his back and grabbed his shoulder, wrapping her legs around his waist.

Before he could fling her off, she breathed something into his face, and he could no longer remember why he was fighting her. Her legs loosened, and she slipped from him, turning him around in her arms as she ran her hands down his body until she was cupping him through his jeans.

His mind was static, full of a buzz, but then red hair flashed in his mind, giving him enough conscious thought to push the woman away. Her face showed a small amount of shock before she shrugged and walked away. The farther away she was, the clearer his mind became.

What the hell had he just walked into?

A hand grabbed his arm, spinning him around again, but this time it was a different woman, one that was thankfully clothed. She sniffed at him and shoved him into a darkened room he hadn't seen just a moment ago.

She bared her teeth, sharpened to needle-like points, and he stumbled back.

"What the hell?"

A low hiss escaped from between those sharp teeth. "False heir," she growled as her nails elongated to claws.

Holding his hands up, he stepped back as she stalked towards him, swiping at him faster than he could move. Her claws raked across his chest and lines of blood appeared. He grunted as he thwarted her next slashing arc. His power was gone, and he was unable to heal himself.

"Whoa!" he yelled at her, pain searing in his chest. "I am not sure who this heir is, but it is not me..."

"You're right, boy," she lisped, unable to speak clearly with her dangerous smile. "My people will not follow you. We are descended of the Minoan warriors, and you are nothing of the sort! A weakling."

The woman made to attack him again and he widened his stance, readying for impact.

Suddenly, a knife glinted threateningly at her throat, and she halted.

Amphitrite appeared behind the woman's beastly figure, holding the knife firmly in her small, pale hand. He blinked at the coldly savage look on her face. If the soulmark on her arm wasn't visible, he'd think she had a dangerous twin running around.

"Last words, nymph?" Amphitrite asked lowly, all menace.

The nymph hissed at her and shifted into water, moving through the knife before reforming and striking out at Amphitrite. Ducking, Amphitrite swept the nymph's legs, knocking her onto her back.

Shifting back into water momentarily, the nymph rushed like a wave toward the door and reformed on the opposite side of the room. Before she managed to fully change back into nymph form, Amphitrite struck, hurling her blade at her. The knife landed with a wet sound and stuck out of the mortal flesh of her throat. The shock of the deadly blow lit the nymph's eyes before she became water again, only this time there was not any reforming. The rush of water that was the nymph flooded the dark chamber's floor and Amphitrite's knife clattered on the stone.

Quick as a viper's strike, Amphitrite grabbed the knife with one hand and him with her other. She pulled him out of the room and back into the revelry. The crowd was lit with flashing red lights, which showed far too much skin, even for him.

"Move it," Amphitrite ordered as she pulled him along. His eyes snagged on a man being pleasured by the woman who had gyrated on him before the nymph attacked. He stumbled and Amphitrite cast him a dark look over her shoulder.

His steps momentarily slowed as they moved through the sticky, gel-like wall of air. As soon as he passed through, his ears popped from the sudden change in atmosphere. The dark hallway was silent except for their footsteps as they hurried down the hall and she kicked the main door open. Like a seal had been broken, his power flooded back into him.

At least what was left of it.

The large satyr he had bribed to enter Reaver's Paradise appeared in front of them.

"My money, witch!" he yelled, only to earn a rude gesture from Amphitrite. With her face pinched in anger, she turned and light jumped them out of the alleyway.

When they landed on his couch, the air had been knocked out of him by the sudden light jump. He didn't have a chance to recover before she was on him, straddling his lap and clenching the collar of his black peacoat in her hands.

"What the fuck did I say?" she growled, her eyes going completely aquamarine. "Do not come with me. And what the fuck did you do? You followed me and almost died."

She shoved off of him and began pacing the room.

Coming out of his shocked stupor, he stood, his anger rising to meet hers.

"You were going somewhere dangerous! I wasn't going to stand by and let you—"

"I have been in worse situations!" she yelled, stalking toward him. "Far worse! I have battled the sickest of human beings and deities!"

"I get it! If I had known my power wouldn't work down there—"

"Stop!" she yelled. Her voice broke, then lowered. "Just... stop."

Falling into one of the accent chairs, she put her face in her hands, and her look of defeat threw water on the fire boiling in his blood.

"I felt you... through the bond. You were in trouble, and I was sure I wouldn't make it to you in time. Just like I am unable to make it to anything else in time, it seems."

Taking a deep breath, he got down on to his knees in front of her and lifted her chin so they were face to face.

"That was how I felt with you going into that place. I am sorry I underestimated you."

She gave him a small, sad smile.

"I am used to being underestimated."

"Well," he said lightly, smiling back at her, "I will no longer be doing so. That was so unbelievably hot!" He pretended to fan himself.

"It's the incubi pheromones making you that way. Takes a while for them to wear off." She arched an eyebrow at him.

"No way. Watching you dispatch that evil hell nymph got me all flustered," he told her with a wink.

"Pretty sure you watched Devon do that a million times," she laughed.

"Yeah, he was always weird about me coming onto him after, too," he joked, taking her hands in his. "I do trust you, and I am sorry. Next time, I'll stick to the surface."

"Same here. I think I am too old for that life. I had an erection rubbed into my backside and all I could think was how badly I needed a shower." She made a disgusted face and West shot a dark look at the chair she was sitting in.

"I'll be burning that later," he said.

He stood, pulling her up, too. "Let's take a shower and get that skeevy place off of us."

"Deal," she replied gratefully, and walked ahead of him toward his bathroom, taking her clothes off with each step.

West was quick to follow her.

30

Amphitrite ran her fingers over the soulbond mark on West's wrist, her index finger tracing the wave along the inside. He was asleep behind her, exhausted from lovemaking and surviving one of the deadliest nymphs in the underground. She had decided not to let him know about the latter.

"I don't regret it," he mumbled sleepily.

"I thought you were asleep," she whispered back, staring into the fire lit in his bedroom fireplace to warm the chilly night.

"I was, but I felt you touching the mark."

"Sorry," she murmured and turned her head to look up at him as he moved up to lean on his elbow, his other hand moving over her stomach.

"I mean it, though. I don't regret *it*." He angled his head to the mark on his wrist.

"I assumed not since it worked," she replied with a smile, earning a look of confusion from him. "Two souls can only bond if they are completely willing to be with that person. It goes much deeper than mortal fascination and lust. My mother used to tell us stories of soul bonding, and I thought it was a myth until Persephone and Devon found themselves tied."

"So, if I had any hesitations..."

"It would not have worked. The bond would have been rejected," she said, reaching up to cup his face. She ran her fingers over the slight whiskers at his jaw. "But it wasn't, so that tells you I do not regret it either. I am committed to you in a way I will never be with another."

Turning his head, he kissed her palm.

"So... should I get you a wedding ring?" he asked, only half joking from the crooked, vulnerable smile he wore. He took her hands into his and ran his thumb over her ring finger, then he turned her right hand over to where she wore her trident ring.

"I never asked about this," he murmured, the tip of his thumb nudging the band cautiously.

"Gift from the cyclops. My sister has earrings that can turn her invisible—"

West let out a whistle as she continued.

"Hera has a necklace, a lightning bolt, that she wears. It's actually part of her powers. She was given the ability to summon lightning through the necklace."

"And yours?" he queried, turning the ring with his thumb and forefinger.

"This ring can help me both calm and enrage the seas. I wish I could use it to push back the dark waters, but it's almost as if my ring has died. The power I felt from it every day since the cyclops gifted it to me... it's gone."

She hadn't realized how much she had come to rely on that comfort until it was gone.

He lowered himself to where they were eye to eye.

"We will fix this, I promise you," he whispered as he leaned forward to give her a soft kiss, one that felt so much more powerful than it should have. She now knew what Darren had meant. For all of West's flaws, she loved him. He was her person.

Lifting her hand to his face, she cupped his jaw.

"Everything has been going so wrong that I find myself hesitant to enjoy this. Our bond seems almost unreal," he whispered against her palm.

"I know." And she did. She felt like any happiness she found as the world fell down around them was wrong. "But we need this," she stated as she looked into his dark eyes. "We need to have this so we remember what we are fighting for. So, we are determined to win."

He nodded before his lips met hers in agreement.

"I will fight for you until I take my last breath," he whispered against her lips.

"As will I," she promised, taking him into her arms and loving him once more before the sun rose in the sky.

Standing on the old wooden dock, Amphitrite looked at the murky water beneath her. Her heart felt torn seeing such death so close to her home. The screams of her creatures had stopped, but there was no relief in it, knowing what the silence meant.

Death. Or something worse.

Death was if they were lucky. To survive this water was to become something else, something dangerous and wrong.

For the first time, she felt at a true loss. Who could help her? The Moirai hadn't summoned her. Lachesis, Clothos, and Atropos, once known as the Fates, sat in Fates Consulting looking out over Halcyon without a word.

She assumed they had nothing for her since this was not directly affecting a mortal timeline. Yet. She knew it was a matter of time before the dark water leaked in and began killing humans and deities alike.

That was how she knew she and West were well and truly alone in this.

Long after West had fallen asleep last night, she had stayed awake in his arms, thinking over options. The only one she could commit to was to try to get out onto the sea somehow.

She knew to swim in it would turn her into something evil, but a boat...

"Hey you," a familiar voice said from behind her, joined by nearing footsteps.

"Hey Medusa," she greeted without turning to look at her friend and a beat of silence passed as Medusa stared at the water with her.

"I wish I had the power to help," Medusa whispered softly.

"It would only crush you under its responsibility as it does me," Amphitrite replied, shoving her hands into her leather jacket.

"Yes, but I could at least suffer with you. We have always been through hell together and I do not like the fact I am sitting this one out."

Amphitrite turned to Medusa, giving her a small smile.

"You are out there helping me find the culprit. That is more than any other person is doing as of now."

Medusa nodded, but Amphitrite could tell something else was bothering her.

"What is it?" she asked, her attention now fully on Medusa.

"I cannot find what you need," she growled. "I have been to every corner of this place and have nothing to give you to help. I feel... sometimes I feel like I am no help at all. It keeps me up at night, full of anger at the situation. I have always..."

Amphitrite waited in silence.

"I was taken so young, tortured by men. My entire world was upside down and you,"— she turned to look at Amphitrite fully— "you saved me. Gave me power and purpose through my shelter for people dealing with the same abuse I had to endure. I owe you a great debt."

"No debt is owed between friends," Amphitrite said sternly, but not unkindly.

"I want to fix everything, and I promise I will be strong enough," she said firmly. Medusa looked right at her, her eyes flashing with a reptilian green glow. "I will find a way to fight this war alongside you."

Amphitrite took her friend into her arms, hugging her. It was something Medusa never allowed others, her trauma still fresh for being centuries old, but she allowed Amphitrite this.

"You have always been more than enough. You've been my friend and my sister."

Medusa nodded, but Amphitrite felt the tears on her shoulder.

She continued to hold her until Medusa ran out of tears to shed.

West sat behind his desk at Oceanus Industries, his hands clasped as he stared vacantly at the wall across from him. He had stacks of paperwork on his desk, but his mind was unable to focus on them. He could only think about what the next step was.

When he woke up that morning, he had slipped from bed without stirring Amphitrite from her sleep since he knew she had barely slept with her mind turning all night. Every time he'd turned in his sleep, he'd blearily open his eyes to see she was awake, and that worried him.

In the shower that morning, he had heard her open the bathroom door. When he peeked out of the curtain, he saw her, toothbrush and toothpaste in hand, staring vacantly at her reflection in the mirror. He kept quiet as she finished and left the bathroom, almost as if he wasn't there. His natural inclination was to make some flirtatious comment and lure her into the shower for some morning fun.

But he had left her alone.

Frustrated, he pounded his fists on the desk right as a leaf hit him in the eye.

"Can you do that without all the damn foliage!" he yelled as his best friend manifested in front of him.

"Whoa!" Devon held up his hands at the outburst. "Hello to you, too."

West stared down at a paper on his desk, his eyes unfocused as he tried to pull himself back together.

"Sorry," he mumbled as he ran his hands over his face. "I am just losing my fucking mind while I try to figure out what the hell I am going to do about the ocean. It is... shit."

"Agreed, but..." Devon went quiet, and West looked up to see his friend looking around the room with narrowed eyes.

West sat up straighter in his chair. "What?"

"There is a power trail here that is not yours... not recent. It is fading... so whoever it was had to have been here in the last day or so..."

"Who?" He asked a bit more harshly than he meant to and was quick to give Devon an apologetic look before he cleared his throat. "Do you know who?"

Devon shook his head.

"I have never seen this one before, but there are traces of orange... which tells me they are either a Titan or working with one."

Shit. Amphitrite was right.

"Using the sea now to gear up for war. Makes sense. Why just attack the Underworld? Another front. Coming at the Goddesses on all sides. Damn it!" West yelled as he punched his desk again.

"Sir?" Darla called from outside the other side of the door, checking in.

"I am fine, Darla, sorry. Bad morning," he yelled through the door as he looked back to Devon. "I need you," West told him as an idea took form in his head.

Devon tilted his head but said nothing as he waited to hear what West had to say.

"You can find this person. You have always been able to find people who some said were impossible to track down. Help me. I will pay you—"

"No," Devon interrupted, holding up his hands, and West felt his heart drop. "You will not pay me, but I will look for this person. It affects all of us, and I refuse to let what happened to Persephone happen to Amphitrite... or you."

A warm feeling hit West in the center of his chest, and he couldn't help the smirk that lifted his lips.

"I knew you were in love with me. Persephone will be angry, but we can manage—"

"Shut up, asshole." Devon rolled his eyes, but his small smile made West feel better. "I'll start today while the trail is fresh in my mind. Call out to me if you figure anything out before I do."

Devon light jumped, leaving West's office covered in slowly fading leaves.

Finally, West felt some sense of hope again.

31

"Y ou've missed our last two appointments," Dr. Alden stated firmly as West walked into his office, throwing his jacket down over the back of the couch before taking his seat across from the doctor.

"Life happened and it is going to continue happening."

"Mental health is important in all your endeavors," Dr. Alden scolded West. West simply itched his eyebrow. He was pretty sure that was going to be the quote on the man's headstone since he said it so much.

"Yeah, I get that. I'll have that tattooed on my butt so you can save your breath going forward." West clapped his hands and leaned forward. "Let's get a move on. I've got a date."

"I see. Is this a new one?"

Wow. Had West been gone that long or had everything with Amphitrite happened that fast?

"Same one it has been for a while now. For some odd reason, she is willing to look past my jackass qualities and enjoys me for me."

"I suppose that is a sufficient reason to miss. Love can leave one's head in the clouds. Do you think perhaps your ability to focus on one woman, one relationship, is due to you now having more respect and care for yourself?"

"Huh?"

He should be used to Dr. Alden's frustration since the man was constantly taking his glasses off to pinch his nose in exasperation during their sessions.

Dr. Alden put the glasses aside and looked at him.

"When you came in here, you were incapable of a long-term relationship. You were... at sea, so to speak, just letting the current take you wherever it chose."

"Your water references are lacking," West interrupted, earning another pinch of the nose and sigh from the good doctor.

"Just... try to listen and understand?"

West nodded, but his smirk was giving him away. Thankfully, Dr. Alden was used to his bullshit now. It had barely taken an hour for him to call him out on it in the beginning.

The fun had been nonstop ever since.

"A path through the woods, then. You were wandering the woods, not using any tools at your disposal to find your way out. You were depressed and aimless, although you had the power to change your circumstances all along."

West narrowed his eyes and gave Dr. Alden the 'wrap it up' motion with his hand.

"You try my patience, Mr. Murphy."

"Not the first. Not the last."

"You are using your tools finally and you found a path. You can now see the light through the trees. You have hope, and now, the ability to think of yourself as a person who is deserving of love. Once we love ourselves, we can then let that love reach out to others. There is a whole study of chemical—"

"Okay, that's nice. Wow, when it gets to be about the science, there is not an off button for you, is there?"

Dr. Alden leaned back, annoyance lining his face, but when he spoke, his voice was even.

"Do you understand what I am saying? You are finding forgiveness in yourself. You are growing."

"So... I am able to have a functional relationship?"

"It means, Mr. Murphy, that I do not, in fact, suck at my job."

West laughed, and wasn't sure, but thought he caught a tiny tilt of the man's lips.

Most likely the equivalent of a full out belly laugh in any other person.

"This is a horrible idea," West stated for the fourth time since Amphitrite had left the docks in their small boat.

"Yes, I know. You keep saying so. I am open to any other genius ideas should you be holding back on me," she stated with a raised eyebrow. West only shook his head and looked out over the water. "I cannot swim in this, but I hope that maybe being out here will bring some clue... something..." Her voice trailed off.

This was a huge risk; one she was not unaware of. They were stuck out here, and should this all go wrong, they were doomed. Their power weakened even more out on the toxic water.

Pleading with West to stay ashore had done no good at all. He'd refused to let her do this alone, and his determination just increased her anxiety about this trip. She knew all too well that he would follow her no matter what.

What happened if both the Sea Guardians were killed by the dark waters?

There was no going back now, though. She stood at the helm of the boat, her hands shaking on the cold wooden wheel.

"Now," she called to West, and he grabbed the lines to ease the jib and mainsail, the wind no longer catching.

Her heart pounded in her chest, and she tried to settle herself before she walked to the side of the boat. She looked at West, who joined her at the railing. His eyebrows knotted in concern, and he put his hand out.

Stepping forward, cautious of the boom, she took his hand and he pulled her closer as comfort bled through her soulmark.

"You are not alone," he whispered, squeezing her hand as the wind circled around them, mussing his dark hair. She smiled. He looked like a sexy pirate, all wild hair and dark eyes, and her terror lessened somewhat.

Though, the reminder that she was terrified at all on the water, her home for so very long, sent a wave of depression over her.

Slowly, she dropped West's hand and grasped the rail, looking out over the edge. She tried peering into the waves, but the water was so dark nothing could be seen.

Her eyes burned as West moved behind her, his arms caging her in as his hands laid atop hers on the wooden railing.

"We are going to fight this. This is not forever," he whispered next to her ear.

"There is no way to tell what is happening down there," she responded as a tear slipped from her eye, trailing down her face before dropping into the water below.

They both looked on in shock as the tear sizzled like acid when it hit the dark water; the black water bubbling as if it were boiling.

It only emphasized what would happen to them should they breach the water themselves.

As if they needed the reminder.

A sense of futility weighed her down and staring into the black abyss, she knew it was fruitless. They would have to do something from land, as the water held no secrets to their success.

The boiling stopped, the water calming almost instantly.

Amphitrite had only blinked before chaos ruptured the quiet. Suddenly, there was a hand around her wrist that was not West's, and she was going over the side of the boat. A scream lodged in her throat as she lost her footing on the ground and West wrapped his arms around her waist, pulling her back.

She stared at the foreign hand clutching hers. She tracked it to the water, and then the rest of *it* burst from the waves.

She was looking at something with transparent skin, white eyes, slitted gills, and the sharpest teeth she had ever seen in a humanoid skull. In the shadowy water, she caught sight of fins.

Screaming again, she struggled to free her arm. Using her other hand to punch the creature's gills, it screeched in pain as it released her.

The sudden loss of tension sent her falling back into the boat on top of West, both of them dragging in deep breaths and reeking of adrenaline.

"What... the... *Fates*... was... that?" West asked as he struggled to breathe.

Amphitrite couldn't respond. She stared wide-eyed up at the sky, grappling with what she had seen. What she had narrowly escaped.

The fins, the tail, the half-humanoid form. *Could it be a siren exposed to the dark waters?* As she wondered at the creature she'd just seen, she remembered the siren she'd witnessed transform within the dark waters. Her lost sister had been changed beyond sense, beyond thought; it was not as focused as this creature had been.

She'd seen the sentience in the creature's eyes in just those few seconds and knew it was aware of what it was doing.

Dread pooled in her gut. "I'm not sure," she finally answered. "But we're getting out of here."

With her breathing regained, she rose from the deck and helped West to stand.

"Get the sails," she told him, stumbling back toward the helm. West didn't argue, just moved to set the sails out to catch the wind as she turned them back to the safety of land.

West could have kissed the shore when they were back on land, his heart still hammering away at what had happened on the boat.

"Are you sure you don't know what the hell that thing was?" he asked, offering a hand out to Amphitrite as she stepped off the boat.

She moved into his arms, hugging him so tightly he could barely breathe, but he wouldn't say so. He needed this, too.

"Whatever it was, it was not a mindless creature. That thing... it knew what it was doing."

His hands tightened around her. He knew it. She was in more danger than she would admit.

Stepping away from her, he held her shoulders.

"We need help," he stated, and put a finger to her lips before she could say anything else. "Is there any way..." He worried about asking this of her, but his options were limited. "Could we go to my father? Could he help us if you restored some of his power?"

By the immediate look of annoyance on her face, he knew this would be a battle, but they were out of options.

"I doubt Hera would agree to that, West. I am sorry. I can't," she sighed and turned away from him. "He has lied so much to you about who you were, to me about what happened the day of the tsunami. I... I cannot justify it to my sisters."

"I get it, believe me," he said, his hands out to his sides. She turned back to him, watching him pensively. "I do not fully trust him anymore either after he kept who I truly was from me," he said, moving to stand in front of her. "I know it's a risk, Amphitrite, but what choice do we have?"

Closing her eyes and clenching her jaw, she spun away from him again and let out a loud yell.

"Why?" she screamed out, her fists clenched, before her head fell forward and her shoulders dropped.

She was fighting an internal struggle that he knew he could do nothing to help her through, and to try to comfort her now would only result in angering her further.

So, he stood back and waited, giving her the few minutes she needed to work this out in her own mind.

Sticking his hands in his pockets, West looked out to where Oceanus Industries stood tall and proud along the coastline.

She was right. While he was doing better to forgive his father for withholding the truth, he still didn't trust him. He wasn't sure if that would come with time, or perhaps, he never would again, but what other option did they have? He knew if there was any other way, he would jump on it before asking the Goddesses to give his father any power back.

He barely heard her next words. "We need to get Hera and Persephone on board, and your father needs to be prepared to pick a side," she said softly.

Even though he had asked for this, a chill ran over his skin. As if by moving forward with this plan, they would be meeting another crisis head on.

When she faced him again, he saw the same thoughts on her face.

This was such a huge gamble.

Now, they just had to pray it didn't bite them in the ass.

"No," Hera stated firmly from behind her desk.

Amphitrite could understand her sister's reluctance to allow Oceanus anything when he'd refused to help her in the past. Amphitrite looked to Persephone, who sat next to Devon on the leather sofa.

Persephone glanced between her and West, who stood near a bookcase.

"Look, I know this isn't the greatest idea—" Persephone started, but Hera waved her words away.

"No, it's about as fantastic an idea as dousing ourselves in kerosene before a bonfire. Our own personal funeral pyre. Yes, that sounds like what would happen should we give a *Titan,* one who owes us no allegiance, their power back when we are about to go to war with... wait for it,"— Hera held up her hands and fluttered her fingers— *"Titans!"*

"A tad dramatic," Devon retorted, earning a glare from Hera.

"Did you take a hit to the head and get amnesia? Did that fiasco in the Underworld just go *poof* in your tiny brain?"

Devon only responded with an eye roll.

Persephone leaned forward intently. "Empowering a Titan on the cusp of war with Titans? We've already done that, Hera," she pointed out, angling her head toward West. "Amphitrite has been training West, helping his powers grow, for months."

"*Control* his powers," Hera corrected, looking unhappy to have been countered by her sister. "This is different. Oceanus ruled alongside these Titans for centuries."

"What if we could guarantee his help? What if he promised allegiance to us?" West asked.

Hera stared at him as she weighed his words.

"You could guarantee this? How? It doesn't sound like your father has been trustworthy regarding you in the past."

Low blow, she thought.

"What is to say he makes his little promises and doesn't uphold them? No, I need more than his empty promises before I do something like that. You know I do not care to share power if I don't have to," Hera stated with a pointed look at Devon as she finished.

"The Styx," Persephone interrupted. "He could make an unbreakable oath, one that you provide the words for, so that he cannot wiggle his way out of it."

Hera sat back in her chair again, looking at each of them as she thought.

"Hera," Amphitrite started, stepping forward, "I understand your hesitation to do this, but he could help push back the dark water. At least enough that West and I could get some of our own powers back."

She wasn't above pleading with her sister, but she would prefer to not have an audience. Hera stared her in the eyes, and Amphitrite could feel her digging around in her head, which normally would have made her angry, but she let her. She knew her sister would only find the truth of what she had said.

"Fine," Hera agreed, placing her hands on her desk, "but when this all goes to shit, and it will mind you, I want apologies and presents. Fancy ones that show how truly desperate you are for my love and affection."

Devon sighed in annoyance, but Amphitrite ignored him.

"The finest gold," she said with a smile, and Hera rolled her eyes.

"The things I do for you people. It's ridiculous," she muttered as she stood from her desk chair. She straightened a nonexistent wrinkle in her suit and then clapped her hands together. For a moment, the world blurred, and everyone landed on the shores of the River Styx.

Beside her, West winced and swayed at the sudden change of environment. He blinked and whirled around, then froze. "Dad!"

Oceanus had been transported as well, his eyes wide and confused.

"Oceanus, Titan of the Seas, I am willing—" Hera stopped and jumped back several feet as a soul passed her. "Persephone!"

With a huff of annoyance, Persephone called all the dead away from them. The dead in the Underworld could be seen by all of them, unlike in the mortal realm. Here, the souls had paid their fee and been guided to their afterlife.

"Anyway," Hera sighed, pushing her hair back over her shoulder. She nodded to the elder Titan. "Oceanus, I am willing to call to Olympus to reinstate a small part of your power to assist the Goddess of the Sea and your heir in pushing back the dark waters.

"If you are in agreement, you must make an unbreakable oath here on the Styx swearing allegiance to Olympus; myself, Amphitrite, Persephone, and all the new Gods Chaos keeps saddling us with."

"Hera," Persephone growled, "to the point, please."

Stepping back, Hera called her Goddess to the surface. Her body became pure electricity, sparks flew off her skin and her eyes went gold. In place of her work clothes, a long white Grecian dress covered her frame.

In the distance, Oceanus silently absorbed the scene. His gaze flicked from the gathered deities to the Styx. Then, he approached Hera slowly, almost hesitantly. "You're willing to return my power, Hera?"

Hera grimaced. "A fraction," she told him, voice full of warning. "Only enough to help stabilize the ocean alongside Amphitrite and West."

His dark brows rose. "And if we succeed, what happens then?"

"Your fealty has no expiration, Oceanus," Hera said. "You will stand beside us in the war with the Titans. Are you prepared to finally take a side?"

He swallowed and looked at West. "You will fight with them, son?"

West reached down and took her hand, gripping it hard. "Yes," he said, his voice carrying strongly across the space. Amphitrite's heart skipped a beat. He was making more than one declaration.

Oceanus glanced down, his eyes widening, and Amphitrite knew then that he had seen the soul mark.

"You've bonded?" he asked faintly.

They both nodded as West squeezed her hand subtly between them.

He exhaled slowly and gave a wavering smile before his gaze settled on her. "You're my family now, then," he said. "A daughter." His smile widened at the word.

Amphitrite stiffened and she felt her sisters tense as well. It had been so long since she'd heard that term applied to her. Oceanus had been her partner for so long, through good and bad, and now... they were closer than ever before. Somehow, the "in-law" aspect of her bond with West hadn't occurred to her.

She knew Oceanus had remained neutral for so long in an effort to protect his family from the Titans' retribution. And from the resolve in his glinting eyes, she knew he would protect his family still.

Oceanus turned to Hera and squared his shoulders. "I'll take the oath."

Beside her, West's shoulders dropped in relief. But Amphitrite was not relieved yet.

Hera nodded gracefully, but she could see her sister had been shaken by the daughter comment, too.

"Do you, Oceanus," Hera started, her voice and eyes brimming with power, "swear allegiance to me and my sisters in perpetuity? To fight with us against the Titans in current and future conflicts? To protect the reign of the Goddesses in exchange for the return of your power through Olympus, a fourth of it at first, and then more over time should you prove loyal to us and only us, upon pain of true death?"

West jolted at the final caveat. True death. She hadn't expected it either. To make such an oath would strip a Titan or God of their immortality, just like her mother had been.

She looked to Oceanus, who was staring at West, his eyes full of a love only a parent could hold for his son, before he nodded to Hera.

"I swear my allegiance to you and your sisters, to fight by your sides, and should I choose to fight against you, I will be stripped of my immortality and meet my final death."

Hera reached out to him with sparking hands. She raised her arms above their heads and a metallic smell diffused through the air. Suddenly, her fingers trembled and erupted with lightning. The bolts arced around her and forked into the ether above them.

The atmosphere thickened with power and foreboding. Fate and Chaos. Hera was calling to Olympus, she realized.

As quickly as it came, Hera's lightning vanished. "It is done," she stated, dropping her arms.

Whisps of blue power rose around Oceanus, materializing from seemingly nowhere. His eyes lit up a true sea blue as the power circled him and he clenched his fists, which were now covered in a blue light.

They all watched breathlessly as the glowing swirls of power melted into him, flashing brightly once again before disappearing completely beneath his flesh.

His power was restored.

Or perhaps not his, but power from Olympus.

She hoped this wasn't her biggest mistake yet.

"Looks like it worked," Hera said, breaking the silence. She walked closer to Oceanus and crossed her arms. "Time for you to hold up your part of that bargain."

Clapping her hands, Hera light jumped them all to the front of Oceanus Industries where the murky water hit the shore, leaving debris that looked far too much like oil-slicked bone.

Oceanus looked at her and West, then back out to the water.

This had to work. If it didn't, she had no idea what else they could do.

It would mean they were that much closer to having to admit defeat, and she was not willing to go there. Not yet.

"Then let's do this," Oceanus replied as he moved flush with West and her. She offered her hands, West and Oceanus each taking hold. She could connect to West through the soulbond, but not Oceanus. She would need to touch him to access his power. West and his father grabbed a hold of each other's hands as well, and together, they formed a circle.

All three of them called to their power. Amphitrite was the only one who had to change into her Goddess form; West and Oceanus simply had the glow of the Titan in their eyes.

She could feel the hum of their combined power move along her skin. Goosebumps rose across her arms, and it was like a machine booting up. While she and West were low, running off reserves, Oceanus alone contributed more power than the two of them combined.

Blue light surrounded the three of them as Hera, Devon, and Persephone stepped back.

Good idea, she thought. Who knew how this was going to go?

Gradually, the three of them levitated. Her body lifted off the ground as her power increased and danced with the two Titans at her sides.

West's hand tightened on hers, and she realized he was staring at her in concern. Their power was being pulled into her, but why?

She recalled when she and Persephone had harnessed their power into Hera in order to send their father to Tartarus. Hera had died after the strenuous effort and risen to her Goddess form.

She really hoped this didn't kill her.

Permanently.

Her death wouldn't matter though if the sea continued this way, so she let their power fill her until the blue light of the Titans shone out of her pores. Distantly, she could hear Hera yelling at them to cease, but she refused.

If she sacrificed herself, it would be for her sea.

The men on either side of her dropped her hands. The hand West had held tingled even after he detached from her.

A scream pierced her ears, and she realized it came from behind her.

Their entire world lit up in blue as she fell back onto the sand and West immediately pulled her into his arms. His mouth moved but his words were lost to the buzzing in her ears. Without thinking, she pushed away from him and stumbled to where the dark water had receded.

The water came back to life in front of her.

A palpable relief surged through her as the dark water seemed to dissipate before them.

Amphitrite stepped closer to the water as it lapped against the sandy shore.

Fresh water.

She smiled, her hands going to her mouth as she took in the expanse of healthy water she thought she would never see again.

A sudden darkness moved back in from the horizon, heading to where they stood on the beach.

The dark waters flooded back in.

Amphitrite dropped her hands to her sides.

"No... No!" she yelled, falling to her knees. West grabbed hold of her and sank to the ground next to her.

She had failed. Again.

32

E verything around West spun out of focus, Hera having light jumped them somewhere else.

An abrupt halt made his stomach turn, and he attempted to steady himself and his queasy stomach. A soft set of giggles had him standing to see where they had ended up.

A large, all white room with floor to ceiling windows looking out over Halcyon. Long strings of varying color hung from the walls. Three women sat in front of them: an elderly woman, a middle-aged woman, and a young woman. His mind put it all together.

The Fates. The Moirai, if they were to settle into the form of a singular sister that alternated between ages in a small space of time.

The young woman clapped her hands at the sight of them.

The Goddesses did not return her enthusiasm.

Persephone spoke first. "The sea is not getting better, even with two Titans and its Goddess," she said.

"And for once, make yourself useful with something that actually makes sense. I am not above retiring you from the mortal realm," Hera seethed, stepping in front of the group to face off against the Fates.

West observed carefully from where he stood between his father and Amphitrite, who swayed against him. He moved his arm around her shoulders to hold her firmly against his side. He was drained, but he needed to stay strong for her.

He could tell his father was drained as well by the way he leaned against the wall.

In fact, they all looked worn, even Persephone and Devon, who stood on Amphitrite's other side.

"Your power is great but will not cure the water," the young one sang out.

He was sure he heard someone grinding their teeth.

"Okay, let's make this simple, since that is all you are capable of," Hera growled. "What will cure the water?"

"It's a bandage, but the infection is strong," the middle-aged one told her.

"The rot is here and only when it is cut from the mortal plane will the water heal!" the oldest one yelled, a bit too loud for the room.

"What. Is. The. Rot. You. Old. Hags!" Hera seethed through her teeth. The room was suddenly way hotter than it had been when they first arrived.

All three of the women looked at West.

"Me? How?" he asked as the Goddesses all looked at him as well.

"Not you as you."

"But who you could be."

"Determines if the rot can spread."

"Or if it will die."

His eyebrows rose into his hairline. Who he could be? He suddenly understood why Hera was ready to tear into them as soon as they arrived.

"What does that mean? Who will I be?" he asked, looking at the others helplessly. He was begging for some clue he wasn't the enemy in this story.

"Your story is twisty and cannot be told. There are paths to take that can lead to the demise and ruin of those who walk our plane, or you can bring to life those believed lost."

He clenched his fists, his own temper rising.

"Cut the crap!" he snapped. Amphitrite started at the volume, jostling slightly at his side. He heard a clap of approval, probably from Hera. "Tell me how I can fix the sea, then, if it all lands on me!"

In unison, the women's eyes darted between the arm still around Amphitrite's shoulders and his face.

"Only one path is written on you as of now. Your other path has not made itself known if your other arm is bare."

"What the... *What does that mean?*" he yelled, his frustration at a breaking point.

The women only tilted their heads as they looked at him. Each one smiled at the same time in the creepiest way imaginable.

"Time will tell!"

Before Amphitrite could intervene, West was gone. A light mist hit her face from where he had just been.

She looked at Oceanus, who shook his head and reached out to hold her arm, as much to steady her as himself.

"Give him time. This is a lot to process for him."

"What is there to process? They gave him the whole, 'take the path but make sure it is the right one because we personally have no idea!'" Hera shouted, staring right at The Fates. They only gave a small smile before disappearing in a flash of light.

"Yeah, that's great. Super helpful," Hera droned. She turned to them, "Remind me, why do we still come here? What do they say about doing something over and over and expecting anything more than the same?"

Amphitrite ignored Hera, her mind swirling at the words and what they meant, and if she should ignore Oceanus and go to West.

She jumped when a hand landed on her shoulder. Turning, she came face to face with Devon.

"I can go talk to him if you want," he offered.

She glanced over her shoulder where Persephone stood. Her sister gave her a slight nod, so she looked back at Devon with a small smile.

"Please," she said, thankful she could send a friend to him. She wanted to be the one who comforted him, but perhaps the kind of comfort he needed was not of an intimate nature. Maybe it was an old friend who knew more about him than anyone else. Just as Medusa had been there for her, Devon would be there for West.

Stepping back, Devon gave her a reassuring smile before he light jumped, the green light and leaves dissipating quickly behind him, leaving her sisters and Oceanus.

Hera strode toward Oceanus, shoving herself between Amphitrite and Persephone to face off with him. She raised her hand, palm up, and her electricity crackled, creating a ball of energy in her palm.

"Remember, Oceanus, you are not done here. You still owe your allegiance regardless of the state of the sea," Hera stated. Her voice was a whisper but deafening in its power.

Oceanus nodded gravely. "My oath holds," he said. He glanced sidelong at Amphitrite. "We're family now."

The reminder made Amphitrite's chest clench.

Oceanus bowed to Hera. "I will fight until my last breath for you, my Queen," he pledged before light jumping from the room.

Hera sighed, her shoulders dropping now that it was just the sisters. Amphitrite noticed just how tired her sister looked, how pale and drawn she'd become over the course of the last couple of hours. Hera scrubbed her palm against her face and zeroed her eyes on her.

"Keep an eye on the in-laws," Hera ordered. Before Amphitrite could say anything, Hera disappeared in a portal of light.

Persephone only raised an eyebrow as she called the shadows to herself. "Don't let her frustration get to you, Amphitrite. We'll figure this out. Together."

And then, Amphitrite was alone. The empty room was eerie. Even by herself, she felt watched by The Fates.

Exhaustion overtook her body and she swayed slightly before light jumping home.

West paced his office, unable to sit still with the prophecy rattling around in his head. He was going to be the one who had to take the right path? He was what would either doom the ocean or save it? Not Amphitrite? Not the woman who had been guarding the sea longer than he had been alive.

It was like he had been set up for failure.

His office door flew open, startling him. Devon quickly moved into the room, shutting the door behind him.

"I sent Darla away. Don't ask, that's not important," Devon dismissed, hurrying over to West's desk. He flung open drawers and peered into their contents.

"What is going on?" West asked as he moved to see what Devon was doing.

"This one," Devon said, pointing to an open drawer. "What was in here?"

West sidled next to Devon to take a look and noticed that the paperwork from the Mystic wreck was missing.

"The papers from the Mystic wreck. The reports, the ledgers and dispatch information... all of it," he whispered as he looked at the now empty drawer. He looked up to see the serious look on Devon's face.

"Remember when I noticed the orange power trail in your office?" he asked. West nodded, and he continued. "The same power signature is here." He swallowed audibly. "When was the last time the woman with the safety board, the one all over the news—"

"Mira Flint," West provided.

"Yeah, when had she last been here in this office?"

West stepped back and thought.

"The week Darren died. That was the last time she came into my actual office."

Devon was shaking his head.

"No, she has been here today, in this office, this drawer specifically."

West furrowed his brow.

"What—"

"She is the one with the power trail I caught the last time I was here. Just now, I came in the normal way, not wanting to freak you out after visiting the Moirai and caught sight of her speaking with your mother. It's *her* power trail, and she is the one who has those papers."

Devon swirled West's desk chair in anticipation of West needing to sit.

"My mother was with her?" he asked as he fell into the chair.

"Yes, they were talking outside as I walked in. I thought maybe the power trail was your mothers at first, but looking closer, I saw the two separately. Hers is a lighter color and there is not any trace of orange in hers. Mira looked up at me, and I know she sensed who I was. Thankfully, she doesn't know I can see power trails."

Pushing his hands into his hair, West tried to work through all he remembered from his conversations with Mira. She had blamed the wreck on... what was it? Fumes from the dark waters?

He jumped up, grabbing his jacket off the back of the chair.

"Thank you, Devon. Thank you so much!" he yelled as he let the sea mist take him to his wife.

33

━ ● ━

"Are you ready?" Amphitrite asked as they stood on the walkway in front of his parents' house, her hands brushing imaginary lint from his jacket in an odd show of nervousness.

Was he ready? He wasn't sure. What would he find out from his mother, and could he handle it if his mother knew anything about the dark waters? That his mother knew about Mira and her power? That she had lied when she said she had no more secrets?

"It doesn't matter," he replied as he took her hands in his. "We have to know, and this is the only lead we have."

Her eyes held far too much concern. He knew she was worried for him and had stayed up late after they spoke last night. She would need a week or more to recover from the lack of sleep during all this.

"Let's go," he told her, pecking her lips lightly and pushing open the door before he lost his nerve.

Inside, the house was quiet. No servants could be seen running around doing some chore or odd request.

"Mother?" he yelled out, his voice echoing in the white marble foyer. After a beat of silence, the light tapping of footsteps emerged from the direction of his father's home office. The door opened up to reveal his mother in a light blue wrap dress with her hair down and curling around her shoulders.

"West! Amphitrite! What are you doing here?" she asked as she closed the door softly behind her. "Forgive me for not remembering if you were supposed to visit today. Please, come to the kitchen and I shall make some tea."

"No, just came to visit on a whim," he said. They followed his mother into the spacious, empty kitchen. "Where is Dori?" he asked of the cook who had been as much a part of his childhood as his parents.

His mother waved her hand.

"She and the rest of the staff are on holiday," she replied as they sat at the counter while his mother moved around the million-dollar kitchen to prepare tea.

"All at once?" he asked, unsure of if there had ever been a time when all the staff were let off to vacation at once. Never to his knowledge.

"Yes, with everything going on, we decided to keep it down to us until the dust settles," she replied as she filled the kettle with water before placing it on the stove.

"Well, hopefully this will all be resolved soon," Amphitrite said. His mother grabbed a box of tea and set it in front of them, smiling at Amphitrite.

"I am sure it will. We have all seen the worst and come out the other side just fine." She turned away again, and West watched her carefully. He heard something odd in his mother's tone. He couldn't put his finger on it, but she wasn't giving him a chance to think too much into it before she spoke again.

"What brought you both to my doorstep today?" she asked as she placed two mugs in front of them.

He glanced to Amphitrite, who nodded, before he faced his mother.

"You were speaking with Mira Flint outside of Oceanus yesterday. How do you know her?" he asked, keeping his tone neutral.

"Well," his mother started, clasping her hands together in front of her, "we met when she came to speak to your father about the wreck. She seemed curious about how much would change between your father and you. We spoke and found a lot in common and just kind of... bonded, I suppose. I've had lunch a few times with her, and yesterday ran into her and we chatted a bit."

She narrowed her eyes at them. "Why do you ask?"

"She has been hanging around Oceanus quite a bit for someone on the safety board," Amphitrite replied before he could. "We were just concerned if something else happened we were unaware of, since we've been so busy. Perhaps anything to do with the dark waters?"

His mother shook her head.

"As far as I know, no one truly knows the reason for the water coming to shore and Mira is concerned. Perhaps that is why she was there yesterday. To speak with you about what you know."

Yet, she slunk around his office, went through his desk, and stole his paperwork.

The whistle of the kettle broke the conversation as his mother turned to grab it off the stove.

"I think I will pass on tea," he stood, trying not to flinch when his mother whirled around with a sad look on her face. "I appreciate the thought, mother. Just... be careful, okay?"

His mother looked confused but said nothing as he wrapped Amphitrite up in his arms and light jumped them to his home.

"We have to go to Mira's. She is the key to this somehow and if we find out who or what she is, we can figure out her end game. I know if we speak with her, we will only be lied to. If we could just rummage around her place like she does mine..."

Amphitrite smiled, and he knew she was feeling as hopeful as he was that they finally had a new lead.

"Well, good thing you are married to someone who can get us in to do a little rummaging."

West returned her smile.

"Devon has been watching her, too, since he tracked the power signature to her yesterday," he said. "So, he'll have her address."

Amphitrite held out her hand, and he took it, entwining their fingers.

"It's a date."

It amazed him how Amphitrite and Devon were so quiet, like ghosts.

He wore his black tactical gear from his days working with Devon. Amphitrite wore the female version of his outfit, the pants tighter, and the same black leather jacket she had worn in the Reaver's Paradise.

Devon was more than happy to share the details he had accumulated during his stakeout on Mira, and they were able to jump to Mira's balcony from sight alone. The shades were drawn, so they were unable to light jump inside, not knowing the layout of the place. But Amphitrite was quick to pick the lock with an adeptness that was both arousing and concerning.

The lights were out in the apartment. Devon had confirmed that she was out for the evening.

Amphitrite locked the door behind them. The plan was to light jump out of there so there would be no clue that anyone had broken in.

Her apartment was small and cluttered. Mugs, books, and knick-knacks covered every surface. The couch was leather, worn and tearing. Not quite how he envisioned someone like Mira living.

Amphitrite moved quickly to the back room while he wandered the living area.

The kitchen area right off from the living room was a little too messy, even for a slob like him. A sink full of dishes, some fruit left out on the counter that should have been thrown out days ago. He opened the pantry and cabinet doors, finding more items that needed to be disposed of.

Leaving the kitchen, he caught sight of a little alcove just big enough for a small desk. Stepping forward, he saw his papers, right out on top. She wasn't even remotely concerned about anyone looking into her.

Hopefully, that overly confident attitude would be her downfall.

Nothing but those papers and some overdue bills in the apartment, none of which were in her name, lay strewn across the small, cluttered desk.

"West," Amphitrite called softly from the bedroom. He turned and stopped, suddenly realizing he was looking around a pitch-dark apartment with no lights on... and could see everything.

That was a bit startling, but he tucked that information away for later.

He moved to the bedroom, looking at all the overloaded shelves on his way, scared to move anything should he disrupt the thick layer of dust.

"Nothing but some men's clothing," she told him as her arm gestured to the closet. "I'd almost think Devon was confused if he wasn't so good at what he does."

"Think she is squatting in some strange guy's apartment?" he asked as he used a pencil he'd found to lift some magazines from the top of the dresser.

"A strange man with some serious appetite for dark stuff," he snorted as he looked over at Amphitrite, who stared in disgust at the porn. He dropped the pencil, not wanting to carry around anything that touched the vile magazines.

He was not into torture fetishes.

A pulse of power came from a nightstand next to the bed. It was gentle, feather light across his skin, and beckoning him forward.

"Did you check the nightstand?" he asked as he moved towards it.

"Not yet," she said, walking alongside him.

He reached to open it, but Amphitrite grabbed his hand.

"Wait, fingerprints..."

Shaking his head, he pulled the drawer open.

"I have a strong suspicion whatever is in here is something we are taking with us," he said. He peered into the drawer—empty, save for one small item in the back. He reached into grab a hold of it.

"She is not worried about people breaking in," he told her as he dug in. "She left my papers all over her desk without a care."

His fingers grazed the item, something metal, and a current of electricity tickled his fingers. He looked closer at it; it was a cuff of some kind, tarnished gold. Halting his movement, he took a moment before withdrawing it quickly, taking a chance he could get zapped into oblivion.

They couldn't waste any time.

His grip tightened on the cuff and his world turned white.

Blinking at the sudden light, his vision gradually cleared. He looked around to see he was surrounded by ornate columns. He realized he was no longer standing but sitting and staring out over a small sea of people below him. Hundreds of people, all dressed far differently than anything he had seen in his travels.

The men wore headdresses, each with some form of bull worked into the fabric's design. Instead of pants, the men had on brightly colored loin cloths. So much of their skin was showing, exposing tattoos on their upper arms. The inked patterns looked similar to the one on the cuff he had picked up.

The women wore robe-like dresses with golden corsets. And though their dresses were long and sleeved, they were open at the chest to allow the women's breasts free. All of the women had long, dark hair braided into intricate updos adorned with beads. Small children hid behind their parents, all wearing smocks or loincloths.

The strangely dressed crowd all seemed to be paying attention to something.

He realized they were waiting for him to speak.

Turning to his left, he saw a woman that looked startlingly like his mother; she could be her twin. To his right was a woman that looked similar to Mira, but also...

How had he never realized the similarities between his mother and Mira? They could be related. They most certainly were related to these women. He couldn't see the face of the person who's eyes he was looking through, but the body was male. Looking down, he saw the familiar cuff on the man's upper arm, in the same place the men wore their tattoos.

He was in a vision. A vision of the past. It had to be, or he was in real trouble.

A sudden and violent tremble rocked the earth beneath them.

"Go! Leave the island!" the man who he shared a body with yelled in another language. He understood somehow, yet he could hear the difference audibly. "It is the end of us! Leave and start on the islands!"

"Poseidon save us!" a woman yelled, and West shuddered. Anxiety built in his chest, and he wasn't sure if it was his own from being stuck in this vision or from the adrenaline rush of the man whose eyes he looked through.

"Poseidon is the reason we die with our land!" a man yelled out in return. The man he was inside of slammed his fists on the armrest of his throne.

"No one will die. We leave. We spread out and survive and one day... one day we will be great again. Now go before the Gods smite us with lava!"

Part of a column collapsed, and now the people ran. Women's screams and children's crying filled the hall.

Yet the man stayed seated until the last of the people had left.

Another part of the wall collapsed before he stood and turned to the woman who looked exactly like Mira. Removing the cuff from his arm, he handed it to her.

"Save our people. Avenge us and save us," he told her, shoving the cuff into her hands. She accepted it with a blank expression and empty eyes. She only nodded before she too, fled.

He turned to the woman that looked like his mother. No. She was his *mother. He felt it, the familiar tug of recognition.*

"Phaedra," his host said. West reeled at hearing the woman's name. Theta. Phaedra. Theta. Phaedra. Was Phaedra really Theta? Or Theta really Phaedra? "Your sister will not be able to do this alone. Stay the course. Keep her honest."

Placing a kiss atop her head, he pulled back and West saw the unshed tears in her eyes. Where her sister was cold, she was hurting. She pulled him into a hug, and he felt the embrace throughout him.

"Go, my princess. Go," he ordered as he unhooked her arms and pushed her away. She pleaded, begged him to come with her, but he refused. Ordering guards to take her, he watched as she disappeared, and the whole of the world around him collapsed.

West came out of the vision shaking.

"West! Oh Fates, you scared the hell out of me!" Amphitrite cried. She knelt over him with his face in her hands.

"Let's go. We have what we need."

34

"And that's what I saw," West finished, letting loose a long exhale. He stood in front of Amphitrite and Devon, who sat in front of him on the couch in his living room.

"Well, that's... interesting," Amphitrite said, holding the cuff in her hands. She had looked it over as he told her and Devon what he had seen in the vision.

"So, you are the grandson of Minos. His cuff was given to the woman, to Mira... and your mother... so... they are sisters?" Devon asked, his eyebrows pinched in confusion as he worked through the family tree.

"I don't know how else to explain it, but I *felt* it in the vision that it was her. Not just her ancestor."

Amphitrite frowned down at the cuff. "She told us she's a descendant of Minos... why wouldn't she tell us if she's his daughter? Do you think she knows?"

"If she does, she lied when we went to talk to her," he responded, his eyes moving from Amphitrite to Devon and back again.

They were all taking in the deluge of new information. Putting the pieces in place and trying to see the whole of the puzzle.

Realizing Amphitrite hadn't looked at him once since he started explaining what happened, he moved around the coffee table to kneel in front of her. He carefully cupped his hands beneath hers so he didn't accidentally touch the cuff in case it pulled him into another vision.

"I don't mean to talk about this and upset you further," he whispered.

She looked up at him, and though she smiled, it didn't meet her eyes.

"I just... you watched it happen. You watched them die from my error."

He felt something like a feather against his skin, just like when he felt the power of the cuff. Before he could turn, Devon was up and moving to the front door.

"Who else would come this time of night?" Devon asked as he peeked through the curtains to see outside, his mercenary demeanor coming to the surface.

West and Amphitrite followed in his wake, keeping to the shadows of the entryway in case the visitor was an unwelcome one.

At midnight, it most likely was.

Devon dropped the curtain and turned to look at West.

"There are a ton of people hanging out in the front of your condo," Devon stated as he moved aside to let West look.

A sea of people, just like in his vision, stood in modern clothing outside.

"Minoans..." he whispered as his hand moved to the doorknob. He could feel a connection to them once he saw them. The songs of his ancestors echoed in his mind as he looked out of the window at the people who had gathered before his home.

His bones could feel the thrum of the Minoans' call.

"Wait," Devon ordered, grabbing at West's elbow. "How do we know they're friendlies?"

He didn't have an answer for that. He just felt like they wouldn't hurt him. Something deep inside him was tugging at him to walk out and stand before his people. To lead them and guide them. To protect them. A warm sense of familiarity ran over his skin and an intensifying heat smoldered at the back of his neck the longer he waited to step outside.

Turning to Amphitrite, he thought of whether they might sense her or not. He opened his mouth to speak, but she cut him off.

"I am going, so don't you dare try to stop me," she stated firmly, arms crossed, and chin tilted up.

He nodded and gave Devon a signal to stay alert before he opened the door.

Every head snapped up when the door opened like marionettes on a string.

"This is rivaling the Moirai in the creepy factor right now," Devon whispered to where Amphitrite stood behind him.

The crowd shifted as an elderly woman stepped up to the front.

"We felt the call," she said. "Our ancestors told us stories of the time when our island would rise again from the sea." Her shoulders were hunched and eyes milky, yet she was entirely clear in her words. "You have the King's artifact."

Despite the overwhelming sense of belonging he felt, the confidence he had in these people, a slither of unease prickled his spine. Stepping back, he whispered over his shoulder.

"Amphitrite, hide it in the house. Devon, check on Mira's whereabouts. If they felt the call, then she most likely did, too."

They were silent, but he felt both their presences move inside of his condo before Devon's disappeared altogether.

The small, elderly woman slowly made her way to West and held out her hand.

He hesitated before the burning started again at his neck, only abating once he took the woman's hand.

"My name is Emery. What is yours?" she asked with a grandmotherly smile.

"West," he replied as she squeezed his large hand in her tiny, papery one.

And again, his world transformed.

Suddenly, he stood outside of a collapsing building atop a cliff. The area was empty of people, but it appeared to be the same island he'd seen before. He could feel in his bones this was the same one. Overhead, the volcano spewed lava. Trails of white-hot lava streamed into the vacant village, leaving smoke and fire in its wake.

Another vision and this one had his blood pumping quickly from fear. This time he was not looking through anyone's eyes but was a ghost watching the destruction.

"Stop your son!" he heard from behind him and turned to see Mira and his mother standing at the edge of the cliff overlooking the burning city.

West looked over his shoulder and saw a man braced against a boulder, holding his arms up as the lava poured from the angry volcano. West blinked. He recognized the man, somehow. West tried to place his wide, square jaw and stern features.

He was the one that Amphitrite had been talking to at the party announcing him as CEO.

"Oh, shut up, Phaedra," Mira snapped. Her voice pulled him back to the vision. "Sacrifices must be made for Titans to rule. You know that. My son is the only one strong enough to take this island to the bottom of the sea."

The man clenched his fists in the sky and the giant volcano erupted anew.

"Look at me!" his mother yelled. "You have to stop this. What if Amphitrite finds out? Then what? You think her and the other Goddesses are going to turn a blind eye to this?"

Mira laughed. "I do not care. Sacrificing this island will feed me all the power I need to rule as a Titan and be equal to my husband and son. I am no longer chained to this island. I can rule beyond these shores." She turned to his mother. "And I am sure I made it quite obvious I have no intention of letting anyone stop me."

His mother looked confused before a sudden clarity struck her, understanding rippling across her features. "When have I been a threat to your rule, Ariadne?" she asked.

"You think our brother's disappearance was an accident? That Theseus managed to handle that maze all on his own?"

"What did you do, Ariadne?" his mother whispered as she stepped away from her sister.

"Theseus is a Titan," Mira— Ariadne— laughed as she stepped closer to his mother. "I proved myself worthy and loyal by showing him the way through that ridiculous maze he could have easily obliterated with his power. In return, he has promised me the power I deserve. You may now call me Eurybia, wife of the Titan Crius."

"He was a Titan?" his mother echoed.

Mira laughed.

"Yes! My husband is a Titan! My son is a Titan, and now, so am I. Nothing is out of the realm of possibility." Before she finished her sentence, she had swung her arm in an arc towards his mother, the flash of metal catching the light of the raging volcano.

His mother fell to the ground, and he cried out, but no noise came from his open mouth.

Mira knelt down beside her and leaned in close to place her hand on Theta's slashed throat.

"You will survive this," she murmured, "but you will remember nothing with the water of the River Lethe on my blade."

West came back into his own body, and felt the elderly woman touch his elbow as he looked down at her.

"Stop the dark water so we can rise again."

Amphitrite was in the living room when West came crashing through the front door.

"You hid it?" he asked.

Nodding, she motioned him to follow her to his room where she had created a pocket of power, a veil between spaces, and pulled the cuff out. Handing it to him, she waited for him to explain. It had taken her a minute to get the courage up to handle the cuff again, afraid it would trigger a vision and she would have to relive the pain of what happened to the Minoans, but West needed her to hide it, and so she did.

The relief when it did nothing was huge.

He thanked her and gripped the cuff. "Listen, they are Minoans," he said urgently. "They think I am going to bring back the island... somehow. They spoke of stopping the dark water, but I need to tell you—"

"West?" Theta's voice cut him off. He whirled around and caught sight of her rushing toward them.

"Mom?"

"West!" she cried out when she saw him.

"I felt the cuff! Do you have it?" she asked desperately. Her eyes scanned him, and she froze when she saw he did indeed have the cuff. Tears filled her eyes, shining brightly before they fell. Her fingers moved out as if to touch it, but she pulled her hand back at the last moment.

Amphitrite knew what Theta was seeing. The horns with a bee between them, snakes along the border. It was Minoan in every way, and it held the power of a king.

Theta looked up at West with a pleading look.

"Listen mother, it wasn't Amphitrite," he blurted out, looking between her and his mother. "Amphitrite had nothing to do with Thira going into the sea or the Minoans dying."

"West, of course she did," Theta retorted with angry eyes flashing to Amphitrite.

Anguish and regret barreled through her, and she wondered why West was bringing this up again. She stood tall and stared back at the woman, but her eyes held an apology. She was unaware that Theta felt this strongly, but it made sense, after all.

"No." He handed the cuff to Amphitrite before he took his mother's shoulders in his hands. "The cuff and an older Minoan woman outside gave me visions. It was Mira and her son. Her husband is Crius, and her son..."

Amphitrite let out a shocked breath. Crius had a wife and son?

West looked at her. "The son, you've met him. You spoke to him at the party announcing me as CEO."

Furrowing her brows, she was hit with the sudden realization.

"General Olethros," she gasped. The man had Titan powers, but dubious connections— it all made sense. Except— "Wait, you're saying General Olethros was involved with Thira going under?" Grief, rage, and the smallest tinge of hope clashed in her heart.

Was it possible she wasn't responsible for the loss of the Minoans as she'd thought?

West nodded emphatically, his gaze burning into hers. "Yes, he and Mira are the ones who caused the island's demise, not you, Amphitrite."

"You cannot know that," his mother whispered, but her eyes looked doubtful as they flicked nervously between West and her.

"I do. Mira erased your memories. *Yours*. You were— *are*— Phaedra. The *daughter* of King Minos, not just a descendant. I think your father gave you back your memories in order to stop Mira. He was just unable or unwilling to give you everything."

"No, no... No!" Theta stepped back, ripping her shoulders from his hands. "Then everything I've done was for naught!"

"What did you do?" Amphitrite asked as she edged closer to West.

"I thought it was you!" she cried, pointing a finger at Amphitrite. "I thought... Mira let me believe..."

"Mother," West let out a warning growl. "Were you working with Mira?"

A gust of strong wind blew through his living room as Devon appeared, his eyes wide.

"Mira is coming. She felt the call from that artifact," he stated right before a hazy mist of water swirled around the room, creating a watery vortex. Mira appeared in the foyer with her chin down and eyes, full of challenge and menace, trained on West.

"Give me the cuff," she ordered, holding her hand out.

Amphitrite called her Goddess to the surface. Her aqua dress billowed in the space around her, and her glowing aqua eyes lit the room with her power. West took a broad stance in front of her as Devon took on his God form, his skin and eyes glowing green. His serpent of the same green light came alive from its tattooed form and hovered in the air next to Devon.

Vines shot through the windows and pinned Mira to the wall.

"Your... son... killed our people..." Theta looked to Mira as she spoke, her small hands clenching into fists at her sides.

"Theta, you know it was Amphitrite."

"No, West saw the visions from the cuff."

Mira arched an eyebrow at West.

"You told me that I was given my memories to seek revenge. To bring down the Goddess of the Sea so that we could bring our people back to the old glory," his mother stated softly, and they watched as everything his mother had believed came crashing down around her.

A beat of sickening, dreadful silence passed before Mira tipped her head back with a cackle.

"Oh, Phaedra, you are so easily deceived," Mira laughed, confirming West's visions. "Did you give them all the delicious details of your deceit? No? Still trying to save face?"

"Tell us. Tell us what you did to help Mira," West begged, spinning on his mother as Amphitrite tried to hold her composure. She had suffered for so long, believing she was the reason the Minoans lost their land, culture, and lives. The reason half the island of Thira was drowned by the sea.

It hadn't been her at all.

"Yes, sister, tell them! Tell them how you have been working with me to take down the almighty Goddess of the Sea!" Mira yelled from where the vines tightened along her arms and legs.

"I gave her access to Oceanus using your father's code and badge. She told me that we would bring the island back, and I thought that was all!" Theta paced. "I thought it was Amphitrite who was at fault and that Mira was simply going to weaken her, nothing more. Please," she begged West. "Please believe me, that was all I did."

Amphitrite felt dizzy. Theta had been working against her all along. Against *them*.

"What else?" West demanded, his voice dark in a way Amphitrite had never heard. "Were you directly involved in the shipwreck?"

"No, I did not know about that until your father told me." His mother swallowed audibly and visibly shook.

Amphitrite caught sight of Mira shaking her head with a sinister smile. Knowing that Devon had a handle on Mira for the moment, Amphitrite focused solely on the situation with Theta.

"Mira must have used your father's access that Theta gave her to change the route information," she said to West, keeping her eyes on his mother. "And she used her role at the safety board to cover it all up with false or incomplete information. The missing reports. It was her."

In her periphery, she saw West clench his fists.

Amphitrite light jumped to where Mira was bound by vines and grabbed her by the throat. It did nothing to stop the woman's mad grin.

"Kill me, please. I dare you."

Shoving Mira against the wall, she called what little power she had left in her.

Every sink and shower came on inside of West's house, bursting with water.

Amphitrite pulled the water to her and pushed it into Mira, flooding her lungs, and drowning the woman on dry land.

"I... did..." Mira tried to talk as the water filled her mouth and nose. "The... same.... to Darren..."

Amphitrite raged, hauling her hand back and slamming her fist into Mira's face.

A face that suddenly changed.

A smile crossed it, but it wasn't Mira's.

Right before the woman disappeared into a mist of colors, she saw the creature who had tried to drag her into the dark water that day on the boat.

The transparent skin, needle sharp teeth, and gills.

The woman in the water.

It was Mira.

35

Sitting on the corner of Amphitrite's bed, elbows on his knees and his face in his hands, West tried to stop the onslaught of self-doubt and anger that pulsed underneath his skin like a heartbeat all its own. Although they'd sent the Minoans home, he missed the feeling of confidence, of certainty, when they'd been just outside his door.

Amphitrite had called her sisters after Mira escaped, and Hera had created a warded holding cell for his mother that was currently under twenty-four-hour guard.

His mother was in jail. That was the start and end of it until Hera decided on her punishment.

He could tell she had felt disoriented over learning the truth, and as she prepared to speak with Hera, she had kept her distance. He had no idea what would happen to his mother now, and it was causing strain between him and Amphitrite.

They had slept on opposite sides of the bed last night, him not wanting to be alone with his own thoughts, but not wanting to discuss it with her, unsure of what to even say.

She had been tormented for decades, centuries, and now it was all exposed as a lie. One perpetuated by his people. His own mother was working to strip his wife of her power and had killed so many people, maybe not by her own hand, but by letting Mira have unmitigated access to Oceanus Industries.

Coughing to cover the sob that tried to escape his throat, he rubbed the tears from his eyes as he listened to Amphitrite moving around the kitchen. She had simply kissed him on the cheek this morning, thinking him still asleep and went about her day.

He found himself far too cowardly to face her.

Hearing Amphitrite drop something in the kitchen, he realized why when a sudden pulse of familiar power moved through the house, telling him his father had just arrived.

Starting quickly for the kitchen, he stopped at the threshold as his wife and father squared off on each other.

"What are you doing here?" Amphitrite demanded.

"I know she made an error of judgement," he stated, not expanding on what he meant, but there was no need to. "Amphitrite, I beg of you..."

West hung back near the door, watching nervously.

"I do not have the final say," Amphitrite stated.

"I know, but you can ask Hera for mercy. I know you can. Theta was confused and unsure of what was happening. Even you thought you were responsible for the deaths of the Minoans."

"She was attempting to take my power from me!" she yelled, slamming down the spatula she had been holding. The scent of something burning hit his nose, and he darted from his hiding place to shut off the stove. She didn't react to his movement, her ire completely focused on Oceanus, and neither did his father. West was a ghost in the room.

"She was the reason people died on those ships!" Amphitrite shouted.

Something clicked in West's head as he turned back to his father and wife.

"Wait," he quietly ordered both of them. "Hold on..."

"I need you to listen to me, please," Oceanus begged again without acknowledging West.

West let his mind roll through the visions he'd seen. He'd been so shocked at the revelations, the fact that he'd been sucked into those ancient memories, that he'd forgotten to share the details. As his father continued to plea, he focused on the events of the second vision, when he'd found out Mira was both Ariadne and Eurybia... Eurybia...

As he'd watched her—*his aunt*, he shuddered— *become* Eurybia, Titaness of the Sea.

When he'd been too distracted by Mira-Ariadne-Eurybia cutting down his mother, she'd said something... something about gaining power from the island's destruction... to rule alongside her Titan husband.

She sacrificed the island of her own people for more power to rule outside of Thira.

His mind whirled, speeding through all the events of the last few months.

The shipwrecks... Then the ensuing cover-up.

He felt like he had too many questions crowding his skull. His mother had been seduced to aid Mira's plot because she wanted to weaken Amphitrite. She'd said that herself, but he knew he was missing something—a key as to the *why* that would connect all the puzzle pieces.

It was clear that Mira had intentionally brought down the Mystic—and who knew how many other civilian ships— in a bid to debilitate Amphitrite. But it wasn't the shipwrecks that weakened Amphitrite, but the dark water.

The dark water that had been challenging the border in recent months.

The dark water that had flooded to the shore shortly after the Mystic's wreck.

An image flashed in his mind's eye; the sight of the Mystic warped on the seafloor as the dark water pushed through the border to reach it.

Destruction. Power. Eurybia.

The breath left him.

"She is sacrificing people to feed the water!" he yelled as he slammed his palms down on the counter.

The conversation abruptly halted around him.

"What?" Amphitrite demanded, snapping her head around to focus on him.

Not saying anything right away, he pushed out a small pulse of power, which took far more energy than he had expected, calling Devon to him, and hoping the sisters would follow.

Amphitrite caught on and sent out her power as well to guarantee her sisters came.

As quick as the pulse went out, the room filled with the light and shadows of the sisters and Devon's arrival. As the light faded, they stood in the small kitchen expectantly.

"Tell me you have something," Hera demanded. She briefly eyed Oceanus with thinly veiled suspicion before relegating him to the back burner of the situation.

"I've had two visions..." West started and explained the visions from the cuff and the elderly Minoan woman. When he mentioned that Mira-Ariadne-Eurybia's son was none other than General Olethros, the sisters shared dark, knowing looks.

By the end, the silence was intense, as was Hera's stare.

"More damn Titans. Honestly, we should be playing for money at this point. They are so predictable," Hera muttered as she took a seat in one of the kitchen chairs.

"Mira is feeding the dark waters as a move for more power. In my vision, she sacrificed the Minoans for the power to rule as a Titan. To rule beyond the island alongside Crius. The shipwrecks are sacrifices, too. Her power over the dark water stopped us from learning what she did with the wrecks." He glanced at Amphitrite. "The stronger the dark water, the stronger she is. And the weaker we are."

Amphitrite's eyes widened as she leaned forward, her hands catching the lip of the counter. She stared at the white and blue stone as she processed what he had just told her.

"Fates," Oceanus muttered as he ran his hand through his hair.

Persephone and Devon simply stood, quietly taking in the new information.

Amphitrite looked up at him. "Darren?" she rasped. "He was a sacrifice?"

"I don't know," he said, his heart hurting for her. "We can't be certain. He wasn't killed near the dark waters." He swallowed thickly. "He may have just been a warning, a threat to you, like we thought at first. Or Mira is just completely mad."

Her face crumpled with a deep frown, but she forged through. "So, the people on the first ship we found were the sacrifices that made the water harder to push back, but all the sailors of the Mystic gave her enough power to take complete control of the waters," Amphitrite thought out loud.

"Oh Theta, damn it..." Oceanus voiced softly, the pain resounding in the smallest whisper of the man's voice.

"I need to find Medusa," Amphitrite stated as she pushed away from the counter. "She can help us hunt down Mira... Eurybia... whoever the Fates she is claiming to be now. If we find Mira, we can stop the dark waters."

"Yes, if we find her, we can figure out how to *make* her pull back the dark waters," Oceanus agreed.

"Or kill her. That should fix it," Hera added bluntly and everyone in the room looked at her. She held eye contact unapologetically.

"That may or may not help," Persephone said, breaking the silent stare-off. "You could kill her, but what if there is another force at play and we lost our only chance to cleanse the water?"

Hera threw her hands up. "Fine. Invite her over for tea and we can talk shop."

"We find her and interrogate her," Devon piped in, and West nodded in approval. If anyone could break someone and glean information, it was Devon.

"We have to consider that she is working with the army Atlas had built up before we banished him to Tartarus. It is far too much of a coincidence that this all happened so soon after the breach in the Underworld," Amphitrite stated as she stepped back to stand next to West.

Persephone's eyes glowed bright blue for a minute, smoke rising around her. Devon took her hand and she calmed herself enough to keep the Goddess from surfacing.

"One step at a time. We find Mira and we capture her. We interrogate her, and then we can plan from there on out what we need to do." Oceanus pushed away from the wall as he spoke.

"Who the hell made you Queen of the Goddesses?" Hera stood and faced Oceanus.

Holding up his hands, he shook his head.

"I am not trying to step on toes, Hera, just rationalize a tense situation and find the best outcome."

Hera blinked.

"Fine, we can go with that plan for now." Her eyes held a gleam as she turned to Amphitrite. "Find your snake friend and let's get this ball rolling. West, Oceanus, give Amphitrite twenty minutes to assign Medusa to find Mira. Then, rendezvous on our next move. I will go with the love birds over here to figure out a holding cell for a water deity. Seems they are able to escape quite easily."

Persephone let out a low growl, and Devon quickly put his hand on her elbow.

"I gave Medusa her power, so I can find her quickly. I'll have her meet me at the office," she stated, and West nodded in agreement.

"Wait," Hera called out and crossed the room to Amphitrite. "Meet her at the Senate Building. It's empty since the senate is not in session and secure enough that no one can enter without my authorization. Sorry, but it seems like security is lacking at both your offices."

Amphitrite looked to West, then nodded as she called the power of the water to her for a light jump. The jump took longer than normal, which only reiterated to everyone how weak they were all becoming as the dark waters choked the life out of the sea.

Her aquamarine light permeated the air before dulling and disappearing completely, his wife along with it. Next, Hera,

Persephone, and Devon jumped, vanishing from the room. Devon and Persephone the only ones to offer a goodbye. He didn't want to think about where they were going, or who they were seeing.

Now alone in the kitchen with his father, he turned his attention to him and realized the man was at the end of his tether.

Placing his hand on his father's shoulder, he squeezed to give some comfort, grunting when the older man pulled him into a bone-crushing hug.

"I am so sorry, my son. So very sorry. If I had known... If we'd been more honest with each other as a family... none of this would have happened." His father's words were choked with emotion and West felt something deep inside of him break. His father was in a supremely difficult situation, just as West was, but their hands were tied for now. They both had to rely on fate to be kind to them as they waited to figure out their next move.

"I forgive you," West finally found the strength to say. After so long of thinking he may never trust his father again, he was finding that no matter the reason, his father loved him. He may go about showing his love the wrong way, being a little too overprotective, but the man cared.

A sob choked out of his father, and he held him tighter.

Never in a million years would he have thought they would end up like this—embracing as father and son, even as their family was being torn apart. Their wives were at odds. His father was freshly sworn to the Goddesses, which now meant defending them against the woman he'd been married to for decades. His mother had helped a Titan stage a coup against his soulmate. He wondered if she'd known the attempts to weaken Amphitrite would harm him, too, but he couldn't let himself think about that.

He could only hug his father.

"I love you, Dad," he whispered before Oceanus pulled back to wipe at his eyes.

"I love you too, West," Oceanus said with a smile that was full of relief, joy, and sadness.

West gave his father a pat on the back before he called the power of the sea to him, waiting for the feel of the waves that came on when he did a light jump, keeping Amphitrite in his mind so he would go to her.

It took far too long.

They had to do something.

And soon.

Amphitrite jumped to the senate chamber, surprised to find Medusa already there.

"Hey! You're fast. I just put out that call," Amphitrite greeted as she moved to where Medusa sat on the ornate bench facing the senators' seats.

"Actually, I was following a lead on Hestia nearby. What's up?" Medusa asked as she stood in greeting.

"I have a lead. Finally," Amphitrite sighed in relief.

"Oh, yeah?" Medusa crossed her arms. "What do you need me to do?"

"Find Mira Flint. It turns out she is Ariadne, daughter of King Minos. She sacrificed the Minoans to become a Titaness, Eurybia. She is using the shipwrecks as sacrifices to the dark water for more power."

"She is who?" Medusa asked with her eyebrows raised, shock marring her brow.

"A Titan. She did the same thing for power centuries ago. She's the one who actually sank Thira. West saw it in a vision," she explained. "It wasn't me, Medusa." Amphitrite couldn't keep the relief in her soul from shining through. That had been a hellish burden for far too long.

Medusa's eyes widened. Her friend knew how much the loss of the Minoans had grieved her. She wished she could tell her more about West's visions, about the return of the Minoans, and the General Olethros connection, but time was running perilously short.

"We have to get Mira before she strikes again, especially while West and I are weak."

"So, you need me to track her down?"

"Yes. If we can capture her, then we can figure out a way to cleanse the ocean. We can push back the dark waters once and for all."

Medusa looked away as she bit her lip.

"You alright?" Amphitrite asked as she moved to Medusa, placing her hand on her shoulder.

Shaking her head, Medusa smiled at her. "Yeah, just working through everything you just laid on me. Are you sure it is the same woman who is working on the safety board?"

Amphitrite stepped back to look her friend in the eyes before she responded.

"Yes, actually. She came to West's home and demanded we give her an ancient Minoan artifact. For someone who destroyed a city, she sure seems interested in resurrecting it."

Medusa turned away, pacing a bit as she worked through something in her mind.

"If she is Ariadne, then does she not have some claim to the Minoan throne? If my history is accurate, she is the oldest to survive."

Amphitrite snorted.

"After she killed her other siblings, then her people? I'd hardly say she has a claim on anything other than a seat next to her husband in Tartarus."

A sudden flash of ocean blue light blinded her as a gentle mist hit her skin.

West and Oceanus stood in the chambers on the opposite side from Amphitrite, Medusa between them. Amphitrite did not miss the sudden stiffness in her friend's posture.

"Medusa, what is going on?" She eyed her sudden change in body language. Fear rolled off of Medusa in waves. "Did something happen, or did you find something you are worried about?" Amphitrite asked as she stepped closer to her friend.

Her eyes flashed green when she looked at Amphitrite.

Medusa strode to her and gripped her elbows fervently. "You need to call off any search you have going for Mira," she whispered, and spun Amphitrite between her and the men. West was quick to move to Amphitrite, but he didn't touch her. She could feel an alertness in him that seemed unwarranted.

Looking back over her shoulder, she held a hand up to the men to stay where they were. Medusa had a history of being abused by men and having two grown, large males in the space could trigger her.

Turning back to Medusa, she watched her friend's eyes turn reptilian.

"It's okay. West and Oceanus will not hurt you. If you want them to leave, I can ask them to leave—"

"I am not leaving," she heard West growl, shocking her with the savagery in his tone.

"Just calm down!" she yelled at West. "Calm down," she whispered to Medusa.

Not wanting to cause more panic, she put her hands out for Medusa to take, relief flooding her when Medusa placed her trembling hands in hers.

She was going to have a serious talk with West after this.

"Talk to me," she whispered.

"Just... stop looking. Just for a little while longer," Medusa pleaded. She hated seeing such pain and fear in a woman she considered close enough to be her sister.

"Medusa... why? What am I waiting for?"

"Soon, I can help. I can push back the waters and bring West's people back."

A chill ran down her spine at the conviction in her words.

"Medusa... what did you do?" she whispered, her voice coming out low. She heard Oceanus and West move in closer behind her.

"I am doing what I think is right to *help* you," she whispered.

Amphitrite's heart pounded in her ears.

"Tell me," She ordered. She called on the old magic between them, the kind that allowed her power to flow through Medusa's veins. The covenant forced her to comply. "Tell me what you did."

Medusa's eyes glistened with tears and a feral desperation she had never seen in her friend.

Dread pooled in her gut.

Dolus. What had he said?

An ally would betray her. One she would never see coming.

No. Not Medusa. Never her.

"The Minoan worshipped snake deities. If Mira was in power, I would be a Goddess, too. I could help you keep the sea safe." Medusa gave her a small smile that was lost in the tears streaming down her face.

Amphitrite tried to regulate her breathing, and swallowed, before trying to pull her hands back, but Medusa held firm.

"Tell me you are not working against me?" Amphitrite begged; her eyes downcast, unable to look at Medusa when she spoke her truth.

"Just... Mira needed more power. Power she would give me. This way, I would not have to worry about asking even more from you," she explained, her voice tight with emotion. "I knew how to get her the records and was able to help her navigate the shipping side. But listen, I did it because I am tired of not being able to help you. Always standing back while you do the heavy lifting."

Tears fell down Amphitrite's face in loss and anger.

"You did just as much, if not more, than me," she seethed through her teeth.

"No, I didn't. But soon, I can."

Amphitrite pinched her eyes shut before blinking them open again. This couldn't be real. She couldn't be saying this.

"You helped her kill all those people, Medusa," she rasped. "You helped her kill Darren."

A broken, dry laugh left her mouth. "Don't you remember the old days? We took down crews of men a thousand times over. I'm sorry about Darren, I am, but—"

"Medusa, no," she interrupted. She couldn't hear her excuse Darren's murder, in addition to the murders of innocent men.

Her body trembled with rage, but also regret. Massive regret.

All this time, she'd created a monster.

"Amphitrite, please. I did this for us." Medusa squeezed her fingers, trying to get Amphitrite to look at her. In the corner of her eye, Amphitrite caught the snake moving through Medusa's hair.

"That's enough. Let her go," West growled, and Medusa's head snapped up. In moments, seconds even, her snake shot out towards West, who was now right behind Amphitrite.

A split second, an instinctive reaction, had Amphitrite striking her arm out and catching the snake mid-air. West spun around Amphitrite and pushed her behind him.

"Wait!" Amphitrite screamed as she watched the panic flood Medusa's eyes. She knew what was coming.

Before she could say anything else, Oceanus shoved his way in front of West, and she watched in horror as he slowly turned gray, his body becoming stone.

"No!" she yelled, gaping at the statue that was Oceanus. In her peripheral vision, a flash of lime green light appeared and disappeared.

Medusa was gone.

"Dad?" West's voice broke as he walked around to face his father.

Tense, heartbreaking silence overtook the senate chambers.

Then, West broke. His face crumpled and he fell to his knees, his fist hitting the marble floor. She ran to him, falling beside him, pulling his head to her chest as he lost himself to grief.

"Bring him back," he begged as he grabbed her shirt and looked into her eyes. "Please... please bring him back."

"I can't," she whispered as her tears fell and mixed with his. "I don't... I don't know how. I wish I could."

"Please!" West wept. Either he hadn't heard her, or he was praying to someone else.

Shadows appeared in the corner of the room and Amphitrite squeezed her eyes shut, pulling West away and into her shoulder so he didn't see.

Please be quick and quiet, she silently begged Thanatos as tears ran down her cheeks. Her grip on West tightened as he lost himself to his grief.

She only opened her eyes when a small breeze ruffled her hair, indicating it was over.

The soul of Oceanus, Titan of the Sea, had been taken to the Underworld.

36

A cold chill ran up and down West's spine. Goose bumps rose along his flesh as they walked into a warehouse that looked far too similar to the one from long ago. His mind conjured the smell of the blood in the air, his and the woman's he had failed to save. The sweat of the men... the gun powder...

Only his rage was keeping him from falling completely into the memory.

They'd followed Medusa to the warehouse using Amphitrite's connection to the traitor's power. Now, they only hoped she'd led them to Mira.

He followed Amphitrite's lead as she crept silently between the large shelves containing various shipments, all with the Oceanus logo proudly displayed on the side. One of his own warehouses. Oh, the irony that he may die here.

At least those murderous fuckers from long ago took him to a non-Oceanus owned warehouse for their dirty deeds.

Amphitrite froze, holding up a hand, and he stopped. Voices carried from the loading bay doors, which were opened to the docks, as if they anticipated a shipment to unload. The murky, disgusting water lapped at the frame of the steel doors.

He spotted Mira approach from the shadows and his body tensed with anticipatory fury.

"It's fine. That is one less obstacle in our way," Mira said as she walked closer to the doors.

His heart stopped. Who was she talking to?

"No! It is not. I panicked, and I... turned him to stone. None of this was supposed to happen..."

He heard Medusa's sobs, but he was numb to her pain. It didn't hold a candle to his.

A hand to his chest brought him out of his violent thoughts. He hadn't realized he had walked toward the voices until she stopped him. Amphitrite put a finger to her lips, and he nodded, stepping back behind her.

"Did you honestly think this would go easily? Did you think your Goddess would just kneel down for you?"

"I didn't want her to kneel for me! I wanted to be an equal to her!"

Mira laughed, her footsteps coming closer to where he heard Medusa's frantic pacing.

"Darling, wars are never won without sacrifice. You helped me so much, you will earn the loyalty of my people and become a Goddess in your own right, as I promised. But you should know that means that the Goddesses of Olympus cannot remain. In order for Thira to rise again, for the Minoan people to have their home back, the Goddesses must be banished."

"You failed to tell me that part of your plan," Medusa hissed, and he could hear the reptilian monster begin to take over. He looked to where Amphitrite rubbed her thumb over the trident symbol on her ring.

Looking back at him, Amphitrite gave him a nod before they stepped out of the shadows, Mira and Medusa spinning around at the sound of their footsteps.

"Oh good. I get to kill you myself. What a treat!" Mira laughed.

There was not any fresh water to pull on, but he could feel the water moving through the living bodies in this warehouse. He focused in on that. Enough so he could drain them dry.

"I didn't mean it to be like this," Medusa cried out at the sight of her friend. "I thought if I had power like yours, I could help win the war! I could help you stop whatever Atlas had planned. I didn't know—"

"You killed my father," West cut her off, monotone and without inflection. He was solely focused on the woman who took his father from him.

"I am so sorry—" Medusa cried as she stepped toward them, but she stopped at the feral growl that left his lips.

"Your apology means nothing," he sneered.

Medusa dropped to her knees, her shoulders shaking as she wept, and a memory transposed over her.

Instead of Medusa, it was Veronica wailing on the concrete floor. He stumbled back as suddenly his dark surroundings were overlaid with the ghostly image of the warehouse where he'd been held captive. Walls shifted. Tears shone like blood.

Reaching out, trying not to draw attention to himself, he flooded the soulbond with panic. Amphitrite immediately grabbed his hand and pulled him back to reality.

This was why he avoided warehouses; he knew they would trigger memories of his captivity. He had hoped he was stronger than this, that his anger was enough to keep him focused, but it seemed his anger only left him even more vulnerable.

Amphitrite shielded him from the women with her body. She was so much smaller than him, but still she edged in front of him fiercely, protecting him the way he needed.

Focus, he ordered himself as he tried to push back against the memories pressing in on him. He couldn't fight Mira and Medusa if he was battling an enemy in his mind. Those men were dead. He'd had his revenge.

And soon, he'd have it again.

"Look at what you've done, Mira. Was sacrificing your own people not enough?" Amphitrite spat, and he knew she was giving him time to compose himself.

"Don't be dramatic, little Goddess. Some survived; there's Minoan progeny still. Sorry about letting you take the blame all these years, though. I just didn't want my boy to be seen as a bad guy. You understand?"

"No." Amphitrite adjusted her stance to brace against anything that should come their way. "I do not."

"Perses has a bit of a temper. Something he gets from his father. You know, the one you sent to Tartarus for simply trying to get his own brother out."

West gritted his teeth.

Fates, these people screamed toxic, and he wondered what Dr. Alden would say if he were here. He could focus on that thought, work on breathing in and out. He was capable of pushing through this.

"Cronus was banished. He is not getting out."

"Mira, just stop all this," Medusa broke in. "Nothing else has happened yet. Just forget Thira and let's go our separate ways."

Ignoring Medusa, Mira continued speaking to Amphitrite.

"Yes, that was Plan A, get Cronus out to restore our full power as Titans. Once again, you and your sisters... well, that horse has been well and truly beaten. Now, if I can pull this island back to the surface with my father's cuff, I will have what I truly need. Only two things stand in my way... the Goddess of the Sea... and the only other person who can claim heir to Thira."

Mira looked past Amphitrite to him.

"My mother... is she not an heir?" he asked through clenched teeth.

"The cuff decides the ruler. If none of the Minos line are alive *and* with power... that leaves the cuff with only one option. Your mother lost her power the moment she confessed everything to that false queen." Hera. She was referring to Hera, who pulled his mother's power when she jailed her until her punishment was decided.

"Why do you even want to rule an island you sank for power?" Amphitrite probed. "Nothing about your plan makes sense."

"If I pull that island from the sea, bring my people back, I have more power *and* an army. If I have an army, it will not matter how powerful you and your sisters are. I could walk to Tartarus myself and get them out. Then, all the Titans would be back in power, and even stronger with Cronus out."

"What of General Olethros... Perses?" Amphitrite asked, correcting herself on the man's true name. "Is he not an heir? Would you kill your own son to rule?"

Remembering the other threat in the room, his eyes darted to the side where Medusa stood, her body shaking, and her head down. She made no move forward, but he didn't trust her not to put a dagger in his back.

"I used him to kill my own father. I care not for the brat I sired so much as what he can do for me."

Mira started towards them, and Medusa followed behind her hesitantly, staring at Mira with a dead look in her eyes.

"I hold all the cards here now," Mira said, curling her hands into fists at her side. "I have the power of all the sea, and you have *none*."

"Stop where you are, Mira," Amphitrite ordered with the voice of her Goddess. Mira continued, though, and pulled a knife from behind her back. West recognized it instantly; it was the knife from his vision when Mira had slit his mother's throat with the Lethe-soaked blade. It had the same curved handle that looked like a snake tail, the blade with etchings in it. He couldn't tell what they were, but he did see the horns of a bull. Like the cuff, the blade was a Minoan relic. It also dripped with water, just as it had when she took his mother's memories.

She would erase Amphitrite's memories. It may not kill the Goddess, but she wouldn't know who she was when she came back to life.

A sudden stinging sensation pierced his temples as he looked at the blade. He tried to keep his eyes open, but his vision blurred at the sides.

Calling to the water in Mira's body, she stopped in her tracks, swinging her eyes to him. Throwing her hand out, dark water rose and jetted toward him, slamming him into a wall.

His vision flashed completely black as he fell to a heap on the ground, his ears ringing, and pain radiated at the back of his head. In the distance, he heard Amphitrite fighting with someone. He blinked and his vision blurred. The world was sideways, but it was just him; he was on his side, his cheek pressed against the cold concrete. He scanned the room, fear and agony throbbing through his body.

Mira and Amphitrite were fighting blurs across the warehouse. Medusa had called her snakes, but the snakes did not seem to be attacking Amphitrite. They were going for Mira.

Stumbling as he attempted to stand, he focused on Mira. He braced himself against the wall and pulled on the water inside Mira again. But, this time, she didn't slow down as he sensed only a few droplets, not near enough.

A pulse of power rolled through him from Amphitrite. A call. She had put out a call for help to her sisters. He only hoped it wasn't too late.

Mira slashed, but Amphitrite rolled out of the way. She hadn't come armed, and he watched as she spun around in a crouch and twisted her ring. Thrusting her hand out to the side, a golden glow radiated out from her palm, extending and lengthening until it became solid, and she wrapped her fingers around the golden trident.

Shoving the woman away, Amphitrite swung her trident as if getting used to the heaviness and balance of it again. Mira came back at her and turned just as Amphitrite thrust it towards her midsection, almost impaling her.

Amphitrite was weakening this close to the dark waters, just as he was. Only the gift from the cyclops, the ring she had told him about one night when they lay in bed, was saving her from Mira's full wrath.

She'd said it could soothe or enrage the waters, but she held no sway over the dark water. At least she was now armed.

Medusa quickly moved and grabbed at Mira, trying to restrain her. Mira's scream did nothing to stop the trident coming at her as Medusa held her for Amphitrite.

"You will not hurt my friend!" Medusa yelled, her snakes wrapping around Mira's neck. West pulled on the water in Mira's body again, his only weapon, and watched her as she panicked. The dark water rose behind her, so West pulled even harder. He threw the remainders of his energy, the core of himself, into killing her by taking what her body needed most. Titaness or not.

Before he could blink, Mira escaped the path of Amphitrite's trident; she spun *into* Medusa, rather than away, and the trident speared air. In the shock of the collision, Medusa's snakes loosened, and Mira maneuvered out of her hold. Amphitrite arced her trident again, but it was too late; Mira shoved Medusa into the dark waters. His eyes went wide as he heard Amphitrite scream.

Now. He had to get up *now*. West pushed off the wall and started toward the fight.

Mira whirled on Amphitrite.

"Your turn!" She yelled as she ran at Amphitrite.

West moved faster than he ever had in order to reach Mira before she made it to his wife. His vision swam, and around him, the phantom of another warehouse flickered.

"No, it's yours," he rasped. With the last dregs of his energy, he light jumped to the edge of the dock where Mira charged for Amphitrite. Mira's arms pinwheeled as she tried to stop her forward momentum. She skidded to the edge of the dock as he grabbed Amphitrite and pulled her down to the concrete floor of the warehouse.

Mira turned to him with glowing eyes.

"The dark waters cannot harm me!" she yelled, grinning madly. "I control it! I control everything in it!"

Don't be so sure.

Suddenly, a large serpentine body erupted from the dark waters, scales glistening. Dark water splashed and flooded the deck as the large head of the Leviathan swung back around toward them.

Gaping, Mira stumbled back from the edge of the dock as the beast rose high in the sky.

"Proves who the true heir is, huh?" he asked with all the sarcasm he could muster.

The Leviathan bent to snap at her. Her body disappeared and reappeared through a light jump as the Leviathan arched back to strike again.

"So, you can summon a Guardian," she laughed. "One that cannot truly harm me!"

"Oh no, Mira. I can summon *the* Guardians," he responded as he stood and called to the other creature waiting down below. The one just waiting for a chance to attack the woman who had killed the people these two were sworn by the depths to protect.

A tentacle shot up and darted along the docks, grabbing Mira before she could light jump, its own power keeping her tangible as it ripped her from dry land. The tentacle flung her back and the Leviathan snapped her up in its jaws.

The scream of pain was cut off abruptly as the sharp teeth pierced her. The Leviathan's body undulated as it swallowed the Titaness. West silently thanked them before the creatures moved below the darkened waters.

It was all over in seconds, the night that felt like forever.

"They can survive the dark waters?" Amphitrite asked, her voice belying her exhaustion.

"Apparently. They are not of this world," he whispered, unsure of how he knew that. His mind clicked into gear, and he spun around to grab Amphitrite and check her over.

"I am fine," she smiled, though it was a sad one. "I am."

His hands and eyes still roamed over her, as if needing to confirm what she said. His panic abated only when he found no obvious wounds on her.

"Can we please leave?" he asked, hating how his voice wavered. The heartbreak and stress of the last several hours weighed him down.

Taking his hand, Amphitrite light jumped them away from the dark warehouse and the memories that haunted him.

37

Amphitrite felt the rush of power flow into her as soon as she finished the light jump with West. She wasn't sure how much she had left in her, so she had only moved them to outside of the warehouse.

The power flooded her veins the moment her boots hit the sand. Her knees wobbled and she grabbed West's elbow to keep upright from the onslaught.

"The water," he whispered, and she looked up to see the ocean.

Crystal blue water crested and glinted in the sun.

Now, her knees *did* give out, and she fell to the sand, sobs of relief wracking her body. She desperately gasped for breath, too overwhelmed by both the new stream of power and the euphoria of her sea returning to its healthy and vibrant state once again.

As she looked out into the water, she wondered what happened to Medusa when she fell into the dark waters. What happened to all the sea life turned by the darkness? Did they disappear as the water did?

West fell next to her, pulling her into his lap as he kissed the top of her head. He shook almost as badly as she did.

"We cut out the rot," he whispered as he held her tighter in his arms. Lifting her head, she pressed her lips to his, their tears mixing as he deepened the kiss.

"This is why you called me? To watch you make out?" she heard Hera's voice from behind them. West didn't pull away, finishing the kiss before they broke apart for air. She stood, using West's shoulder to push herself up so she could face Hera.

"Mira," she breathed, and Hera went ramrod straight. "We found her... I called because I wasn't sure we were going to be able to battle her... but West called the Leviathan..."

"And soon she will be sea serpent excrement," Hera finished as Persephone and Devon appeared on the beach next to her.

They rushed forward, striding past Hera. Devon clasped West in his arms as Persephone clutched her shoulders.

Her sister leaned close. "What happened?" she demanded. "We couldn't find you. When Oceanus crossed over—"

"I'm sorry," she interrupted. "I tried to send out a call."

Hera stepped forward, never content to be excluded. "You should have sent out the call as soon as you deemed yourself in danger, not after, when the call was too weak to tell me *exactly* where you were," she chided.

Amphitrite pulled away and reached for West, who'd stepped out of Devon's embrace. Taking his trembling hand in hers, she squeezed. They had been in danger, and she didn't want to think about how close she'd been to losing him tonight. If it weren't for Oceanus and his sacrifice, West would be gone. Lost to her forever.

"Yes, I know," she replied weakly. "We have a story to tell, but not right now. Right now, I need to settle my nerves."

Looking back over at them, she saw concern etched over all of their features.

"We can wait for you at Olympus," Devon offered, and then he and Persephone disappeared in darkness and light.

Hera simply stood with her arms folded, staring at them.

"I can meet you there as well," Amphitrite tried again, giving Hera an exasperated look.

Hera only narrowed her eyes.

Sighing, Amphitrite patted West on the chest and gave him a quick kiss on the cheek.

"Just let me give her something to focus on so we can have a minute," she whispered as she turned to her sister.

"Medusa was the traitor," Amphitrite stated. The words burned her tongue, but she kept going. "She thought she was helping Mira raise Thira so that she could become a Goddess and help me fight the Titans. She fell to the dark waters before Mira was Leviathan food."

Hera looked out over the water.

"And Oceanus?" she asked before looking back at West and then Amphitrite.

Not wanting to say it aloud, she only shook her head.

"Ah," was all Hera said as she stepped back. "Then, I shall see you soon."

Amphitrite closed her eyes as her sister disappeared in a flash of brilliant gold light.

Turning back to West, she caught him right as he pulled her against him again.

"He's dead. There is no coming back, is there?" His voice broke against her ear, and she felt her eyes burn again.

"I'm so sorry," she choked out the apology, but West only held her tighter. "If I could have known all those years ago that giving her that power—"

"No," he cut her off. "You hold no responsibility for her actions."

As he looked down into her eyes, she thanked Chaos that West had made it through. Though not unscathed, he could still come back from this. They would make sure of it.

Lifting onto her toes, she kissed him.

"I need you," she whispered against his lips, her eyes half-lidded. "I need all of you to bring us back from all the wrong that just happened."

His hands moved along her jaw and around her neck as he kissed her deeply, light jumping them to his bedroom.

He slowly pulled her clothing off, his eyes holding hers as she watched him love her with touch and emotion. His kisses were hardly frenzied, but sensual and needy. Removing his own clothes, he tossed them aside before moving to her, holding her against him, both of them bare. Her ear pressed against his chest, and she listened to his heart.

When she pulled back, he kissed her again slowly, and very gently laid her against his bed, as if worried she might break. Pulling away again, he lined his body up with hers, but went no further. As he held himself above her on his elbows, he looked down at her and grazed his thumb along her temple, moving a piece of her wild red hair from her eyes.

"You are everything I could ever need. Promise me that if everything crumbles around us, we will still be standing together in the end," he whispered, his eyes searing with more emotion than she thought a person was capable of.

She took his hand in hers and kissed his palm.

"Always. I will always be next to you, no matter what happens. I love you, West," she told him, her voice thick.

He closed his eyes and pushed himself into her, a tear clinging onto his eyelashes.

"I love you so fucking much," he whispered against her lips, kissing her as he continued to merge their bodies into one.

It wasn't the wild coupling like before, but it was deliberate and full of love and emotion. It was their bodies speaking to their feelings through action.

Together, they forgot all that they lost and focused on what they did have; each other.

They met the height of their lovemaking together, West finding his release seconds after she found hers. Their backs arched toward each other before they collapsed. Looking up at him and pushing his sweaty strands out of his eyes, she felt connected to another soul in a way she never thought possible.

For the first time in her long life, she whispered a thank you to the Fates.

38

West had never been to Olympus. He had heard Devon talk about it but standing there in front of the monstrous columns at the top of a mountain was a bit dizzying.

His mind was zapped from the emotional overload of the day, and he was spacing out more than normal as he took everything in. Or tried to.

Too high up, was all he could think as he looked at the clouds floating along the marble floor.

Around him, there were four marble thrones. He felt a bit odd to be the only one standing, as the Goddesses and Devon all sat in their massive, engraved seats. They were all in their alternate forms, subtly glowing with power, and they seemed stronger here.

Even if he didn't have a God form for himself, he was relieved to see Amphitrite's strong again. Although the dark waters had only sapped their powers for a couple of days, it was still far too long for his wife to be so vulnerable to their enemies.

"Come, Titan, and step onto the platform so we can see if you gain your own throne," Hera ordered.

West shuffled a step below the marble dais, uncertain. Amphitrite, decked out in her aquamarine dress and sea glass crown, smiled encouragingly.

He looked away before his body took control and he made a fool of himself in front of the Goddesses and Devon. He was like a horny teen in his wife's presence, and it was worse when she was in her Goddess form.

West released a breath, steadying himself before he stepped forward. He wasn't sure what the Goddesses expected, and so he braced for the awkward silence when nothing happened.

But as soon as his foot landed on the marble platform, the entire mountain shook. He flinched at the rumbling and hurried forward. His second foot on the platform sent a crack in the stone, which quickly spread toward Amphitrite. The fissure split open in the marble beside Amphitrite's throne, and a swirl of water rose from the fracture. The vortex rose high enough that it was hard to tell what was going on until the water dissipated, revealing a throne next to hers.

As abruptly as the transformation started, the trembling magic ceased completely.

Everyone gaped at the new throne in stunned silence. Except Hera.

"Well, looks like you get one after all. Olympus is just handing them out like party favors."

Ignoring Hera, West walked to his throne where the Leviathan was etched proudly at the top. As soon as his hand touched the marble, his body glowed a bright blue and his clothes suddenly transformed into the same button-up and slacks Devon wore, only in dark blue.

Everyone watched as he took a seat. When he lowered himself into his throne, he felt something heavy on his head. Reaching up, he held a crown of sea glass that was darker than Amphitrite's and more masculine.

He looked over at his wife, who beamed at him with love and pride.

Hera cleared her throat, and he put his crown back on with a wink and a smile. It was forced, but he was trying to find a new normal.

"Back to business," she said, and Amphitrite's radiant expression faded.

"As the ruling power, I ask that Medusa Perrin is brought forth for judgement," Hera ordered, her voice echoing within the columns.

Then, Medusa appeared in the center of the room, her hands shackled as she stood before the Goddesses and Gods.

Most of the creatures of the dark water had returned to themselves after the darkness receded. Those few who had not were given a swift death. Medusa had not been in long enough to fully transform into a creature of the darkness before Hera pulled her out.

"Medusa Perrin, you are accused of treason against the Goddesses of this realm. How do you plead?" Hera's voice wasn't loud but seemed to resonate with power.

Medusa looked at Amphitrite before looking down at her feet.

"Guilty," she whispered, and West heard Amphitrite's intake of air. Sending strength through their soulbond, he felt her tension ease. He may have wanted Medusa to rot in Tartarus, but he wasn't cold enough not to see how this was affecting his wife.

"I ask for mercy," Amphitrite spoke up, and everyone in the room swiveled their heads to look at her. "I understand her choices caused death," she said, glancing at him apologetically.

Swallowing thickly, he nodded at her. He wasn't ready to look at Medusa as anything other than his father's killer, but he would not expect Amphitrite to feel the same about the person with whom she had spent most of her immortal life. He was biased, and so he was not the one to ask for judgement nor mercy. He simply was going to try his best to move on and forget about Medusa.

Turning back to Hera, Amphitrite continued.

"I know Tartarus is the punishment for such a crime, but perhaps a lesser sentence is due for all she did to help prior to this? Her reasoning behind it was to help, though it was done the wrong way... can we base her sentence on both the crime and her history?"

Hera watched Amphitrite for a lengthy spell, her eyes moving over her sister as if taking her measure as opposed to Medusa's.

West was losing his focus as the discussion of her sentencing continued, his mind wandering to the cuff he had felt in his pocket once he sat down on the throne.

"Medusa Perrin, I have decided your sentence. I will give you a moment to say goodbye," Hera announced. She stood, waving her hands for Persephone and Devon to follow her as they left the room.

West stood to follow as well, but stopped and turned to Amphitrite, whose eyes were brimming with tears. He walked over to her, leaned in close and kissed her temple.

"I am near if you need me," he whispered as he straightened. When Amphitrite nodded with assurance, he finally left, not looking back at Medusa as he followed the others down the mountain.

He planned to never lay eyes on her again.

Medusa's gaze gleamed with apology so intensely that Amphitrite found it hard to pull in a deep breath. Standing, she walked to her lifelong friend, remembering moments in time when they had sailed the seas together, fought next to each other, been there for each other. How did they end up where they were now?

"I am so sorry," Medusa whispered, glancing down at the floor. "You were the closest thing I've ever had to a sister, and I let my greed push me to make choices that only hurt you when I meant to help."

Lightly grasping Medusa's chin, she tilted her face up to look at her.

"I loved you as a sister of my own, too. What you did was wrong, but I love you for the fact that you wanted to help me, even if everything you did resulted in a punishment I cannot save you from."

Medusa sniffled.

"I do not deserve to be saved, my Goddess," she whimpered, staring up into Amphitrite's eyes.

"Everyone deserves a chance at redemption if they truly wish to redeem themselves."

Medusa closed her eyes at those words, and a tear leaked down her cheek, catching the light of the sun.

"Maybe one day..." Amphitrite paused, choosing her words carefully. "Maybe one day you can stand beside me again should you choose to accept the consequences of your actions now."

Nodding, Medusa opened her eyes once more.

"I am sorry about Oceanus. I know West will never forgive me."

Sighing, Amphitrite pulled her into a hug.

"Focus on making one thing at a time right. Let that keep you going."

"I owe you so much. I will never forget how you helped me. Not for my entire sentence in Tartarus will I forget," Medusa whispered to her.

Distantly, Amphitrite heard Hera walking back into the room, steps following her.

"Time to go," Hera called.

Amphitrite pulled away and turned toward her sisters, Devon, and West. Her husband kept his gaze glued to her and she gave him a small, sad smile.

Looking back at Medusa, she squeezed her friend's shoulder one last time before walking to West's side, where he immediately pulled her against him as Hera and Persephone stepped up to flank Medusa.

Tears flooded her eyes when the world around them went bright with lights and dark with shadows as her sisters escorted Medusa away for her punishment.

Devon approached them and squeezed her elbow before he light jumped away, too, leaving her and West alone.

As soon as the last of Devon's leaves disappeared, she turned her head into West's chest and let herself fall apart with the one person she trusted to put her back together.

Running his hand through Amphitrite's curls, West watched her sleep. She had wept so hard her body shook as he light jumped them to his bed, where he held her until her cries turned to the soft, even breathing of sleep. The intimacy of holding her and bringing her comfort was something he never thought he'd have with someone, especially not someone as strong as Amphitrite, and he was honored to be her mate in this immortal life.

But he had something else to do. Something he'd promised to do. And he was going to be a Titan of his word, unlike the ones who readied themselves on the horizon, preparing for the battle to come.

A battle he knew was going to be much larger than what they had seen so far. They needed an army, and he was going to create one to stand behind the Goddesses.

Slowly sliding out of the bed so he didn't wake her, he tiptoed to the part of the wall where the cuff was hidden. Using a tiny amount of power to open the pocket of space, he retrieved the cuff. He walked into the living room and light jumped to the nearby cliff.

He ran his finger over the cuff, tracing the designs. This was his heritage and destiny, and he knew deep down in his bones, once this cuff was on, it was not coming off.

Closing his eyes, he let the sea spray hit him as he gathered his nerves for what was to come. He did not know if this would work, but he had to try.

Taking a huge breath and a leap of faith, he placed the cuff on his right bicep where his grandfather had worn it. The moment the gold touched his skin, it opened and closed around his arm, the metal welding itself together to become permanent. It was no longer cold metal, but now something almost organic that moved with his arm.

The power of both Olympus and his heritage hummed through his blood, distinctive of one another but symbiotic somehow.

Suddenly, a thunderous roar hit his ears, and he tensed. It sounded far too close to the tsunami that started all of this and he looked up in panic.

A huge, watery sinkhole appeared off the coast, the water cascading down at an alarming rate. His pulse picked up. What had he done?

His panic turned to awe as an island rose from the sea. The more land that appeared from the water, the more he recognized it.

Thira. Thira with its central volcano, that deadly peak that Mira's son had used to sink the island. Thira with its stony cliffs and broken marble columns. The island reemerged completely with an incredible tectonic shift. The buildings were long ago lost to time, but no less amazing in their glory.

This was his city, and he was its king.

Amphitrite's power gently nudged him, telling him she was here, and he turned to watch her walk toward him.

"I felt the call of the ocean," she whispered as she moved to stand next to him, grabbing and holding his arm against her body. "You did it."

"I did it," he whispered back as he looked down at her. "Thira is outdated. I think I am going to give us a new name for a fresh start."

She raised her eyebrows at his smirk.

"Oh really?" she laughed, and he could tell she knew where he was going with this. "Let's hope your people feel the same way."

The power of the king charged through him, and he released it, sending out the call to every person with Minoan blood in their veins.

A call to return home.

He looked out once more at the island, now a part of the world once again.

"I think they will very much like to be official citizens of Atlantis. The humans should get a kick out of it, anyways."

"I worry you might be more like Hera than I thought," she laughed as she squeezed him tighter. He pulled his arm from her hold so he could wrap her up in his embrace.

"Well, we shall see how this works out, my Atlantean Queen."

39

In the weeks that passed since the battle for the ocean, Amphitrite had worked to bring everything back to a sense of normal. For West, pulling what was unanimously agreed to be called Atlantis from the ocean had him working almost day and night to rebuild the lost city alongside his people.

The ocean was wholly back to its healthy state from long ago. The consensus among the Goddesses was that Mira had used the deaths of the Great War to start the dark waters, and upon her death, they cleared without the Titaness to feed them.

They couldn't, or perhaps did not want to, fathom how many people had lost their lives to keep the power funneling into the parasitic waters.

To the humans, Oceanus Industries and the Zephyr Maritime Administration had teamed up and worked to clean the ocean with new technology that had been in development for years. Since the Archon had declared a state of emergency, they could use this 'new' technology, effectively resolving the issue almost overnight. Incidentally, approval ratings had reached a new high.

As for the island, its revival from the ocean was explained away by scientists as an aftereffect of the earthquake that had caused the tsunami.

So much to explain, yet more questions remained.

Now that Eurybia/Ariadne/Mira was gone, where was her son, the elusive General Olethros/Perses? And did he have anything to do with the uprisings in the Eastern part of the continent that Hera was working on quelling?

And, the question that sat on her mind every single day, where was Hestia's scion?

Shaking away the thoughts, she walked along the path to the graveyard on Olympus, where no actual bodies lay but some older deities did rest. Following the path, she made her way to where Oceanus had been put to rest.

He stood proudly; his stone face was fierce with the resolve to protect his child long after death.

"This is not how I envisioned this going," she said to the stone, as if he could hear. Perhaps he could. She was not sure what happened to the people who were turned to stone. "We were supposed to win and work with West to heal the ocean together."

Her voice trembled a bit. She had known Oceanus for so long, had gone to him in the early days of being a Goddess for advice. He'd guided her through the learning process of being a Guardian to the Ocean. And then, right at the end there, he'd been family. Her father-in-law.

Now, both he and Medusa were gone. Lost to her.

And so, she grieved beside West.

She was thankful to Calista for directing her spies in the interim, until she could get a hold of herself, but she knew she needed to get back to work. She had to grieve and then let go. Halcyon needed her. Her sisters needed her.

West needed her most of all.

"I'm sorry I didn't believe you about West," she said, something she hadn't been able to tell him in life. "I am sorry about how everything came to pass. I cared about you, in my own way, and I wish I had made that more apparent before... well... before we lost you." She pulled in a deep breath to compose herself, placing her hand over his heart. "You proved yourself to be a true ally in the end, and I thank you for that. So, I am here to make a promise to you, old friend."

Looking up at Oceanus, she set her shoulders back and hoped the oath would still work if the person on the other side of it was unable to accept.

"I will take care of West. Protect him. Love him. Carry on your legacy. This I vow as the Goddess of the Sea."

Then, a voice responded to her oath, making her jump.

"And the Queen of Atlantis," West said from behind her. She started to whirl around, but suddenly his hands looped around her waist to pull her back against his front. "Accept your fate there as well," he told her.

"You're done?" she asked in surprise. West had told her just that morning he wanted to finish their new home, move from Halcyon, and live among his people. Their people, if he had any say over it.

She had been hesitant to move from her cove, but West had used his charm and won her to his side. He wanted his wife to live with him among his people and the sea, and how could she truly say no to that?

"Done," he confirmed with a smile. "No escape now." He went quiet as he looked up at his father.

"I miss him," he whispered.

"I know." She turned to him and pulled him against her. "We will not let him be forgotten."

West tightened his arms around her and pressed a kiss to the top of her head. It would take time to acclimate to their new life, but as long as they were together, she knew it would work out.

He let out a little hum before leaning forward to kiss her, breaking away with a smile that had won plenty of women over. Thankfully, she was the only one privy to this part of West now.

"Tonight, we dine in our new home," he told her proudly, smiling down at her.

She couldn't help but return his smile as she wrapped her hands around his neck to pull his mouth back to hers. Planting a quick peck on his lips, she said, "I will come right after I finish my work for today."

"I am holding you to that. Got the food already being prepared, then I am sending the cooks and staff off so I can eat naked and watch you ogle me. I will be the dessert for the evening." He waggled his eyebrows suggestively.

"You are ridiculous, go!" she laughed as she playfully pushed him away.

Chuckling, he grabbed her again and kissed her. It was not the playful kiss she had expected, but one full of passion. It was the kind of kiss that told her exactly how much she meant to him, and so she lived for them.

"I feel weird making out with my girl in front of my dad..."

"Now he knows how much of a pervert his son is."

West let out a loud guffaw.

"He already knew there was no hope for me. He probably is disappointed you haven't redeemed me yet."

"I think we all know there is no redemption for you."

"Ouch!" West feigned a broken heart and stepped back from her embrace, giving her a wink.

With one last glance at his father, he light jumped back to their new home.

She knew to enjoy these little moments of time together before he had to go back to Oceanus for work. He was using his bereavement period to work on Atlantis, but there were moments when he was quiet, and she knew he was thinking of his father. Moments when they lay in bed and a tear would slip from his eye, or he would wake up from a dream about his father. It was the down times when the truth of his father's loss struck him. That, or when the news blasted it across the continent.

The world assumed Oceanus had died of a heart attack, and they would let the world continue to assume so.

Amphitrite gave Oceanus one last smile before pulling herself into a light jump. Memories wrapped around her as she landed in the alleyway next to the domestic abuse shelter Medusa had championed. She had brought so much hope to the city with her charity work and Amphitrite would not see that lost. She would not let all of her friend's work fade away.

She would honor her friend by making sure her mission continued on, and that the shelter fell into the right hands; it needed someone just as passionate as Medusa had been.

Pulling her key from her pocket, she halted when she noticed the door was already unlocked.

"Weird," she murmured as she pushed it open and stepped inside. The familiar lavender aroma hit her squarely in the face. Medusa always had aromatherapy going as a way to make the space feel peaceful and relaxing for the victims looking for help. The front desk was empty of a secretary, but still adorned with all the informational posters and success stories.

Everything was the same as it had been the last time she had been here. Down to the dark green waiting chairs, slightly crooked as if someone had just stood from them.

She felt that the shelter should feel different in Medusa's absence. That everything here should have changed, even though logically she knew that was unreasonable. These people were not even aware anything had happened to Medusa.

Walking around the office, she took in the place that her friend had dedicated her life to. All the people she had helped to get their lives back after leaving situations that might have seen them dead.

Steeling her resolve, she moved to the door that led from the waiting room to the back offices. Pushing it open, she stepped into the hallway where more beige walls showcased even more photographs and posters.

Footsteps from down the hall approached her and she spun around to face whoever it was.

"Hi! Are you here to see Gemma?" a young blonde woman asked, her white button up and black pencil skirt the epitome of business casual. She had never seen this woman in the office before.

"Gemma?" she echoed, her brain short circuiting.

The young woman gave her a confused look before holding her hand up.

"Just one moment, I'll grab her," she said with a smile, and headed back to the office she came from, her heels clicking on the linoleum floor.

Unable to wait, Amphitrite followed quietly behind the woman, surprisingly, to the office Medusa had used since the shelter's beginning. At the doorway, she had a clear view of the woman sitting at her computer, listening intently to the young blonde leaning over and whispering into her ear.

Her heart stopped.

As she watched, the blonde left and the woman at the desk looked up to meet her eyes.

Oh, Hera, she thought. Her heart started again at a rapid pace.

Feeling awkward and overwhelmed, Amphitrite slowly crept into the office, sure she was having a hallucinatory episode from all the trauma of the last several weeks.

"Um, hello?" Amphitrite stuttered the words out, frantically trying to line up the few pieces of information she had against what was in front of her. *How?*

"Hi," she greeted. The woman stood up and put her hand out to shake. *Medusa* put her hand out. "I'm Gemma Havu, the director of operations. Do you have need of assistance?"

Gemma Havu... the names meant 'precious stone' and 'serpent,' respectively. Hera just had to do it, didn't she? But, oh, how thankful she was at that moment.

"Hi Gemma," she greeted, blinking back tears as she shook Medusa's— *Gemma's*— hand. "I'm Cordelia Wells and no, I have no need of assistance. I just... I have heard all about your work and would love to be a benefactor."

Her heart swelled as she watched Medusa's eyes light up.

"Fantastic! Let me get the paperwork and I can give you a tour of our facilities."

Medusa turned away from Amphitrite to open a file cabinet. As her back was turned, Amphitrite lost composure for a moment and a tear slipped free. She wiped it away before Medusa returned with the paperwork for Amphitrite to take. She clutched the papers to her chest as Medusa gave her the tour of a place she knew almost as well as the Zephyr Maritime Administration.

During the tour, Amphitrite asked what she thought would be the appropriate questions at the appropriate times. When she was quiet, she just watched her old friend, the one who didn't know who she was, or herself, the memories long gone. It didn't matter, though. She was here, and now Amphitrite had the chance to befriend her again.

Thank you, Hera.

"That about sums up what we do. If you have any questions, please do not hesitate to call. I have a good feeling about you, Ms. Wells," Medusa said warmly and smiled as she walked Amphitrite to the front door. "I think we are going to get along great."

Amphitrite turned to her friend and offered her hand to shake again, wishing it was a hug. Medusa slipped her hand into Amphitrite's, and they smiled at one another.

"Me, too, Ms. Havu. Me, too."

40

It was well past six and Amphitrite had yet to arrive. West paced the palace halls as he waited for his wife to return for dinner. His thoughts were going to dark places as he worried about what could have happened to Amphitrite since he last saw her.

He was turning into a serious worry wart these days, but he supposed it was with good reason after all they had been through.

The palace was relatively empty, aside from the staff on the upper levels cleaning and decorating the rooms they had just finished building. Throughout the palace, the walls were a tan, smooth stone color. In the main halls, air freely flowed between pillars engraved with bull horns. He'd kept many of the traditional Minoan motifs throughout the rebuild to honor the heritage of his people.

People who were, surprisingly, more than happy to rename their island and start over. There were a few who were not wholly on board with the name Atlantis, but they were not persistent enough, or concerned enough, to put up a fight.

This was their fresh start, and they were taking it.

His people were also on board to follow their new king. One of the first demonstrations of loyalty was to share his true identity. A secret he knew they would keep. To have a Titan who sat upon a throne on Olympus as their king was more than many of them could have dreamed.

And to have a powerful queen was icing on the cake.

He knew his people craved the peace they deserved, so he'd been surprised when he told them of the impending battle, and they had promised to fight alongside him.

If he was honest, it was more than he could have asked for himself.

Already, several people who had trained in the military had taken over and begun enlisting and training. He now had an army full of new recruits he only hoped were ready when the Titans made their next move.

He padded on bare feet to their bedroom, the place he had spent the most time perfecting for him and his bride. The bed was huge, atop a platform, and across from a fireplace to keep the chill out. But the best part of the room was the sea glass embedded into the walls. The thousands of stones sparkled when the light hit them, giving the room the sense of being underwater, somewhere he knew Amphitrite found her peace.

There was no need for glass windows, a benefit of being in control of the sea and its weather, so they had large arches to invite the breeze. Even now, the soft curtains billowed in the gentle wind.

Their bedroom was at the highest point of Atlantis, in the palace tower overlooking the sea, and from here, he could see the coast of Halcyon and its twinkling lights.

It was perfect for them to spend their long nights of immortality curled up together.

"It has a decent view, I'll give you points for that," Hera's voice broke his contemplative silence and he spun to see the sky Goddess perched in one of the window arches. She darted her stormy blue eyes his way with a smirk. "Too much water and far too many people for my taste, though."

He rolled his eyes and she looked back outside to the Atlanteans below. His people were just now starting the celebrations they'd had every night since returning to their family home. Until sunrise, the island would be full of dancing and bonfires.

"Guess it is a good thing you will not be living here," he said. "Which, by the way, makes it super weird that you just magically appeared in my bedroom." He raised his eyebrows at her, earning another smirk in return as she hopped off her perch and stood.

"I am here to tell you of your mother's fate."

With no preamble, Hera sat in one of the accent chairs near the fire, her eyes flicking to the other as if an order to sit. Had this not been a conversation about his mother, he might have balked at her silent command, but right now he wasn't going to defy the one holding all the cards.

Once he was seated, Hera crossed her legs and eyed him. She looked regal, like the queen she was, as she observed him.

"She lives," she stated, and the breath left his lungs.

"Tartarus?"

"No. While I would have happily put her there, do not misunderstand, but my sister vouched for her. Your mother will remain on Atlantis, with no powers, and can work as a healer under strict, *strict* supervision," she said, narrowing her eyes at West. "Should she decide to continue working against us even as a mortal, the punishment will be far worse. Do we have an understanding?"

Leaning forward in his chair intently, he nodded. He tried to draw the breath back into his lungs to speak.

"She will not be a problem," he rasped, and looked into Hera's eyes earnestly. "I promise."

"See that you keep that promise, young king."

When she stood and approached him, he flinched, unsure of what Hera might do, but was shocked when she gently placed her hand on his shoulder.

"Your father died an honorable death and for that, I chose to leave you a parent. I would not wish such a fate on anyone."

With that, she stepped back, energy crackling around her.

Before she could leave, he stood up to face her. "Hera..."

"Not quite the cutthroat bitch everything thinks I am?" She replied with a sardonic smile.

"Thank you, Hera."

The smile dropped from her face.

"Yes, well, I am not quite as horrid as the stories of my male alter ego. Always smiting and fucking everything... well, at least I am not constantly smiting. Anyway, you'll find your bride on a bench in the middle of Halcyon, looking ridiculous with that zoned out zombie look on her face. Do take care of her so that she doesn't embarrass me."

The wind picked up as Hera gave him a wink, and a blast of golden light flashed, making him shield his eyes. When it faded, he lowered his arm and looked at the empty space where Hera had just stood.

He didn't wait another moment. He light jumped through the island until he found his mother working in one of the newer buildings set up for healers. He stood in the doorway as he watched his mother stitching up a worker who had been injured. The worker nodded when he saw him and his mother turned around, her eyes lighting up. She quietly gave orders to the nurse at her side and walked to him.

"West?" she murmured. His mother's voice held such happiness at seeing him.

He strode toward her, his arms itching to hug her small frame. "Mother," he whispered.

She stepped forward but halted before he could wrap her in an embrace.

"I thank you and the Goddesses for allowing me to live, even though I do not deserve it." She stepped back and a serious frown took over her beautiful face. "What I did was horribly wrong, and everyone was punished fairly but me. I am allowed to live out my life, only my power taken as a penance. I never cared about the power, so it was not a true loss for me."

Staying silent, he looked over at his mother and thanked Hera again for giving her back to him.

"I'm," he started, clearing his throat. "I'm sorry about Dad."

"Oh, West," she sighed, smiling sadly as she finally closed the distance between them and pulled him into her arms. "He died saving you. That is all I could ask for. I could not deal with losing you both and I thank him for that, even if I no longer have him."

West wrapped his arms around his mother, and let a tear slip free.

"To live is pain," she whispered as she rocked them. "To love is glory. And I loved him with all of myself. I will see him again."

Stepping back from their embrace, she took him in.

"It suits you." She squeezed his arm where the cuff lay under his shirt. "You will make a fine king for our people."

"Goddess, I hope so," he chuckled lowly, smiling down at his mother.

"Oh, you will. You and Amphitrite will bring true glory to our people, the likes of which we have never seen. I can feel it in my blood. Now, I am sure you have kingly duties to attend to, so I will get out of your way. I am staying in the village, so find me when you have a chance, and I will make you a meal."

He didn't tell her that the kingly duties he had in mind for the evening were to seduce his wife.

He owed the Goddesses— Hera, specifically— for allowing his mother to be free. He knew all too well that his mother was granted way more leniency than she deserved.

Distantly, he wondered if Hera was already planning to collect the debt in the future. He didn't care though. He had his mother, his wife, and his people.

He was content.

Amphitrite sat on a bench near the fountain in central Halcyon, her mind spinning.

Medusa was alive! She didn't remember who she was, but she was alive, and there would be the chance to still see her. She doubted they would be as close as they had once been, but she reveled in the fact that Medusa was not suffering in Tartarus.

And, really, she was no longer suffering at all. With her memory, the trauma of her past had gone, too.

Her heart felt lighter. Her friend was here. Her people and sisters were safe for now. Her husband—

"Oh shit," she muttered. She looked at her watch and realized she had been sitting out there for hours, lost in thought.

Standing, she turned to head back to the alley for her light jump but stopped in her tracks when she noticed a man walking in her direction. He caught her eye and gave her a wave. She looked around to see if there might be anyone else he was looking for, but no, it was just her.

Giving him a small wave back, she frantically tried to place his face. Had she seen him before? If she had, she couldn't remember him.

He was wearing dark cargo pants, a flannel shirt, and work boots. He had messy dark blond hair and glasses, which covered what looked like hazel eyes.

No, she did not know this man, but from the look on his face as he approached, he was looking for her.

"Good evening," the man greeted, and she nodded to him in return. His hand gestured to the bench as if to indicate she should take a seat.

Without thought, she did, her mind too scrambled to politely decline. He took a seat next to her and crossed his ankle over his knee, seeming completely comfortable on the other side of the bench, as if they knew each other and were just sitting for a chat.

"Hello...?" she trailed off, hoping he'd fill in the blank with his name.

He watched her keenly and she shuffled uncomfortably on the bench, getting an itch under her skin at his presence. Something about him, something she still couldn't place, was pushing around the power inside of her. Yet she couldn't feel any power emanating from him.

"My name is Dr. Alden. I am the—"

Instant relief suffused her. West must have shown his therapist a picture of her.

"You work with West. You helped him with... everything." She cut herself off before she told him about what everything actually entailed. From when West told her about the doctor he worked with, albeit in the beginning, West was less than thrilled with talking to the man. Now, she and West could both appreciate his place in helping West heal.

"My name is Cordelia Wells. Nice to finally meet you."

The man didn't smile, but he nodded.

"He hasn't been to see me in a few weeks, so hopefully all is well, and he is healing."

She nodded and gave him a small smile.

"It is. Thank you for all you did to help him. He is taking on the responsibility left to him in his father's absence quite well."

"Well, that is my job, but you are welcome. I am truly sorry to hear he lost his father. Should he need to speak with me, please let him know my door is always open. And it is for you, as well," he offered and moved to stand. The conversation was quick and concise, over as fast as it had started.

The man was obviously not one for too many words. She could imagine his reserve made him a damn good therapist. It was probably why West was so annoyed with him in the beginning. West was a talker, but not one that could just keep going without input. No, he needed interaction, and she was sure this man drove West crazy as he sat there in thought, watching and observing him.

She stood, too, and offered her hand to shake.

Dr. Alden looked down at it for a moment, before slowly placing it in hers.

What an odd man, she thought.

"It was good to meet you, Dr. Alden," she told him, shaking his hand briefly before he snatched it away.

Not much for words or contact. Noted.

"You as well. Take care, little fish," he murmured, and with a final nod, he spun on his heel and walked away from her. His shadow longer now that the sun neared the horizon.

Amphitrite strode toward the alley in the opposite direction, hoping to light jump home, since she was certain West was worried. She was formulating her apology when she suddenly halted on the sidewalk.

Little fish.

Little. Fish.

Her heart pumped loudly, and she whirled around to where she'd last seen Dr. Alden. She needed to talk to him. To pull him back, make him sit down again, and ask why he called her that.

But the man had disappeared.

She looked in every direction, but he was nowhere to be seen. Only the waning light and gurgling fountain gave any proof that the world hadn't stopped entirely with this revelation.

Someone grabbed her shoulders, spinning her around. She found herself face to face with West, and her heartrate settled marginally. She'd been so wrapped up in what had just transpired that she hadn't even heard or felt his approach.

"You alright?" he asked with concern marring his beautiful face. She took a deep breath to calm herself.

She would hunt the doctor down, but right now, she needed to fulfill a promise to her husband. He was excited to show her their new home. She'd learned too many times over to take these small moments and cherish them.

Tomorrow, she would gather the information she needed and confront the doctor.

"Yes, sorry," she said, shaking her head. "Let's go check out our new home and I can tell you all about my crazy as hell day."

"After I've worn you out, we can talk all about it. I have other plans first," he murmured seductively. He grinned as he pulled her to his side and brought her where they could light jump without being seen.

"Should I be worried about what you have planned?" she asked, catching the smirk on his face.

The devilish look on his face gave her chills as the sea breeze spun around them to take them home.

"Always."

EPILOGUE

Rubbing his temples, Dr. Viktor Alden sat back in his chair, sighing with irritation at the career path he had chosen here in Halcyon.

Sometimes, he truly did not have the patience for these people.

His last patient had been a textbook narcissist and was always so difficult to deal with. It took everything in him not to tell the man to take his pompous attitude and sense of self-grandeur to the bottom of the ocean. The fact the man had a wife at home made him feel like he should find a way to save her. He could only imagine what her daily life must be like with such a person.

Turning to the fire, he let the heat lull him into a relaxed state. The warmth always did that for him. He could never stand the cold, preferring the harsh heat of summer to the chilly air of winter. No, he needed heat, and he was lucky to find an office with a fireplace. Most of the newer facilities were without, but this office had once been a house near the city's edge, which may have been off the beaten path, but he did not lack for patients.

His home was right up the road, too. Right on the outskirts of the forest that sat at the base of Mount Olympus.

Taking a deep breath, he wished he had a glass of whiskey to truly enjoy this moment, but that serenity immediately came to a halt when the door to his office opened.

Looking at the old analog clock on his wall, he confirmed that he did not have another patient on the schedule for another hour. He always made sure to schedule a break after this particular patient so he could get his wits about him before he dealt with more trauma. He felt these people's pain far too much, and if he overwhelmed himself, he would find himself lashing out.

Without his break, his control wore thin. He ground his teeth.

Finally turning his chair to the interloper, he watched Cordelia Wells walk into his office with a file in her hand.

And then he knew what was about to happen. Could see it all playing out before him as if it had already transpired, and he was looking back on the event.

He had been waiting for this moment since he had first stepped foot into Halcyon.

In lieu of a greeting, she threw the file down onto his desk and speared him with her predatory gaze.

No, he was not the prey, but he would let her think that for the moment.

"It took a while, but I got all the evidence I need," she said. "How much do you know?"

"Everything," he replied evenly.

"How did you know my sister called me that?" Cordelia took a shaky step forward.

"My mother. She was a priestess gifted with visions."

He calmly sat up and took the file from his desk. Flipping it open, he arched a brow at her.

"Impressive. You managed to find every tiny detail on me in quite a small window of time. I am truly astonished." He smiled as he flipped the pages slowly, taking in everything this woman had managed to dig up on him.

Considering he had just seen her last week; her investigation was truly staggering. She was certainly living up to her reputation.

Closing the file, he looked up and met her aquamarine eyes. He caught so many emotions there; anger, disbelief, relief, and something he couldn't quite put his finger on. Perhaps mirth?

"You must be pretty damn good to have kept to yourself all this time. How long have you been here, Dr. Alden?"

He gave her an assessing look as he took his glasses off, slowly cleaning the lenses with his flannel shirt before placing them back on his face.

"Two years," he replied and watched the shock cross her face before she hid it.

"Impressive, yourself," she said, crossing her arms. "How did you manage to hide yourself all this time?"

He smiled. At least, that was what he thought he did. It was not something he did often enough to have perfected like West.

"I've been around for longer than you think and found that I had to suppress my powers if I wanted to see my next sunrise." He leaned forward. "How many know?" he asked. His curiosity was just as piqued as hers.

"Just me," she snapped back, her temper rising to the surface. "Are you planning to give me anything? An explanation, perhaps?"

"I have plenty to explain. I am just not in the position to do so as of now."

"Cryptic. Nice," she spat, and he knew he was about to feel her wrath, but he didn't capitulate. No, he was not going to make this easy. His father had warned him against it.

No, she had to figure this out herself. He'd already said more than he should have and would pay dearly for leaving that breadcrumb with her.

Grabbing onto the edge of his desk, she leaned forward intently. Her small stature was hardly terrifying, but the look in her eyes would cut through a weaker man.

"Well?" he asked, hoping she understood. Just because she looked up his lineage did not mean she necessarily understood what it meant.

"You are done hiding," she growled. "Welcome home, Dr. Alden. I hope your allegiance is to us in this war."

I have been waiting for this for far too long, he thought and returned her smile.

"My allegiance is to the sister who bestowed the power upon my mother and helped my village thrive. I will, Amphitrite, Goddess of the Sea, fight at your side using the power Hestia blessed me with. Now, the question is..."

He leaned forward to meet her eyes.

"When do we begin?"

Acknowledgments

Again, thank you to my amazing editor, Rain Brennan. You have been with me since the beginning, and I could not have brought Amphitrite and West's story to light without you. Be ready for my next series because you are the only editor I could imagine working with. You're stuck with me now!

To my Beta Readers: Bettina, Samantha, Rain, Shika, Gennifer, and Emily. It was a joy to work with you all and I hope to do so again with Storms and Embers! Thank you for the amazing feedback!

To Kate, thank you for helping me to prepare this book for editing! It is always a pleasure to work with you.

To my ARC team and Street Team, thank you so, so, SO much for helping me ready this book for publication and getting the word out there. You are all so amazing and I love chatting with you!

Alyssa, thanks for putting up through the midnight crying sessions and keeping me from killing off too many characters. Most of them owe you their life now. Take advantage.

GermanCreative, you are such an amazing artist and your talent brought my characters to life. I cannot wait to work with you on my next series!

Mom, you have been my biggest fan through all this, and I cannot ever tell you how thankful I am for you.

To my children, my loves, thank you for understanding mommy was working and only asking every thirty minutes for a snack instead of every ten. I love you more than life itself.

To my husband, thank you for sticking around through the hard times and loving me at my most caffeinated, sleep deprived, "where the hell am I going with this book!", moments. Thank you for always having my back even when I am not aware. I love you. Like alot. Its embarrassing.

As always, thank you dear reader! Please consider leaving a review. It means a lot to us authors!

So... Storms and Embers? Who is ready for some Hera?

ABOUT THE AUTHOR

C.D. Britt began her writing journey when her husband told her she needed to use her excessive imagination to write stories as opposed to creating a daily narrative for him. Ever since she penned her first words, life has been a lot more peaceful for him.

She currently resides in Texas where she has yet to adapt to the heat. Her husband thrives in it, so unfortunately, they will not be relocating to colder climates anytime soon.

Their two young children would honestly complain either way.

When she is not in her writing cave (hiding from the sun), she enjoys ignoring the world as much as her children will allow with a good book, music, and vast amounts of coffee (until it's time for wine).

C.D. Britt is the author of Shadows and Vines, Sirens and Leviathans, and the upcoming book, Storms and Embers. All books are part of the Reign of Goddesses series.

Stay Connected!

www. authorcdbritt.com
Instagram @authorcdbritt
Facebook.com/authorcdbritt
Join C.D. Britt's Street Team on Facebook for new release information and giveaways